Can it, M

4 cpy

HUNTERS AND HIJINKS
BOOK ONE OF SALVAGE TREASURE

Nick Steverson & Melissa Olthoff

Theogony Books
Coinjock, NC

Copyright © 2023 by Nick Steverson & Melissa Olthoff.

All rights reserved. No part of this publication may be reproduced, distributed or transmitted in any form or by any means, including photocopying, recording, or other electronic or mechanical methods, without the prior written permission of the publisher, except in the case of brief quotations embodied in critical reviews and certain other noncommercial uses permitted by copyright law. For permission requests, write to the publisher, addressed "Attention: Permissions Coordinator," at the address below.

Chris Kennedy/Theogony Books
1097 Waterlily Rd.
Coinjock, NC 27923
https://chriskennedypublishing.com/

Publisher's Note: This is a work of fiction. Names, characters, places, and incidents are a product of the author's imagination. Locales and public names are sometimes used for atmospheric purposes. Any resemblance to actual people, living or dead, or to businesses, companies, events, institutions, or locales is completely coincidental.

Cover Design by DW Creations.

Ordering Information:
Quantity sales. Special discounts are available on quantity purchases by corporations, associations, and others. For details, contact the "Special Sales Department" at the address above.

Hunters and Hijinks/Nick Steverson & Melissa Olthoff -- 1st ed.
ISBN: 978-1648557378

To our amazing spouses who had to put up with months of space hyena ridiculousness.

This entire trilogy is dedicated to you both, as we're fully aware of how insufferably silly we were during its creation.

Thank you, Jolie.

Thank you, Dan.

We're not sorry and we regret nothing... but you're both the best for putting up with us.

Chapter One

Reggie rolled his eyes for the hundredth time that day as he listened to the never-ending complaints of the Caldivar on the other end of the call. So many beings refused to understand why he needed remote access to their computer to solve their issues. The most common excuse was they were uncomfortable with a stranger rummaging around in their private information. He'd heard it all before.

In any case, he'd already told the customer three times how to solve the issue, but she stridently insisted she'd done all that, and it didn't work.

"Ma'am," Reggie said patiently, "unfortunately, if you won't allow me access to your terminal, then I'm afraid there isn't much I can do to help you. Will you allow me access?"

"Absolutely not," she said sharply. "I don't even know you or what system you're in. Why would I give you access to all my information? You're just trying to steal my hard-earned credit. How do I know you won't steal my identity and use it to open up new credit cards?"

Exasperated, Reggie braced his elbows on his desk and rubbed his eyes with the pads of his paws. He was tempted to tell her if he really wanted to steal someone's identity, there were much easier ways of doing so. He knew of several.

Instead, he politely said, "I would never do anything of the sort, ma'am. We have a zero-tolerance policy for theft here at Galactic

Solutions. However, since you're unwilling to allow me access, I'm afraid there's nothing I can do to help you any further. Galactic Solutions would like to thank you for calling today. Your business is very important to us. Have I been of assistance and met your needs for the purpose of your call?"

"No, you most certainly have not!"

Reggie's ears flattened at her shrill voice. "Thank you, ma'am. Would you like to take a short survey at the end of the call to rate my performance and that of Galactic Solutions?"

"Yes, I would," she replied in a pompous tone. "You'll be getting the lowest score possible. I'm going to be calling customer service to inform them of just how useless and rude you are, too!"

"Wonderful," Reggie replied, his tone neutral. "Thank you for participating in our survey, Mrs. Karenski. Please consider Galactic Solutions for all your future technical support needs. The survey will begin immediately after our call ends. Have a nice evening."

Reggie ended the call and leaned so far back in his office chair he was staring at the ceiling. Some enterprising being had drawn a dartboard on one of the ceiling tiles, and several slate styluses were stuck in a cluster around the bullseye. His vertebrae popped as he stretched. With a loud sigh, he sat back up and was about to answer the next call when he heard wheels rolling down the hallway.

He leaned out and tried to yell, but it was too late. Ed, the company janitor, entered the cubical farm and jammed his mop bucket into the carpet's threshold. The front wheel caught the corner of the carpet, and it tipped over. Ed, lost in whatever daydream had his attention, tripped over the bucket and landed in the puddle of dirty mop water. He also managed to snap the mop handle in half during the process. Again.

"Seriously, Ed?" Reggie asked, his tone much gentler than his words implied. "That's the third time in two weeks."

"Freaking Ed," an irritated voice said from behind Reggie.

He twisted in his chair to see Maddy, the department's accountant, standing behind him. She shook her head at the fallen janitor and took a sip from her enormous coffee mug. As coffee mugs went, it was... unique. The thing was a pink skull with spikes all over it and a bedazzled handle. It even had bloodshot eyes in the skull's eye sockets. The side of it read, This cup is made from the last moron who touched my coffee.

Maddy—short for Madeline—was a Joongee, like Reggie. She was of the smaller Striped genus, though, and barely topped four feet tall. Her attitude more than made up for her small stature. Maddy was fierce and never backed down from anyone. As a matter of fact, she was normally the aggressor. Their Human coworkers often accused her of having RBF. Reggie wasn't exactly sure what the initials stood for, but he *did* know it meant she had a constant sour look on her face.

Her pure white mane was cut short and worn in spikes, and her ears were pierced no less than five times each. Each piercing was different, too. It was almost like she couldn't decide on a single set, so she'd bought them all. Reggie thought her most striking feature was her purple eyes. They were always bright, like they were on fire.

The majority of their coworkers avoided conflict with the fierce little Joongee female. Since talking with Maddy usually ended in conflict, they'd learned to avoid talking to her altogether. Even most of the other Joongee tiptoed around her. Reggie wasn't positive that had been her original goal, but he was pretty sure she encouraged it now. Her new coffee mug was simply the latest example.

"Give him a break, Maddy."

"He's doing plenty of breaking all on his own," she quipped with a mean little smirk.

"Would it kill you to be nice?" Reggie demanded with a quiet frown.

"Yes," she said shortly before she sauntered back to her desk.

Reggie sighed and turned back to Ed. "You good, buddy? That was a nasty fall."

Ed sat back on his hindquarters, his brown fur soaked in sudsy mop water, and rubbed his ribs where the mop handle had jabbed him. "I think so. The bucket broke my fall."

Edward—Ed for short—was a Brown Joongee, the largest genus of their species. Broad, thickly muscled, and a little over six feet tall, he was rather intimidating at first sight, with his sharp teeth and claws. Nothing could have been farther from the truth. The best way to describe Ed was "gentle giant."

Reggie had, on more than one occasion, caught Ed disarming rodent traps around the office and space station. The infestation had come from a delivery ship that was also carrying used farm equipment for one of the system's planets. Galactic Solutions had declared war on the little rodents as soon as they'd been discovered. Unfortunately for them, breeding had already occurred. Lots of it.

Worried about trouble from corporate, he'd confronted Ed. The larger Joongee had shrugged his massive shoulders as he released a struggling rodent from another trap, unable to tolerate the tiny animal's suffering. He'd said, "They don't hurt anyone, so why should we hurt them?" Reggie hadn't been able to come up with a viable argument at the time. The best he could come up with was that corporate didn't like pests. Ed had been undeterred and lumbered off in search of more traps.

"You gotta be more careful, Ed," Reggie said as he stood and walked over. He reached a hand down, and Ed gratefully accepted it. Reggie, being of the Spotted genus, was firmly in the middle as far as Joongee sizes went. He was an average five and a half feet tall, and he weighed at least eighty pounds less than Ed. Nevertheless, he hauled his friend to his feet with minimal strain.

"Come on," he said. "I'll help you get this mess cleaned up."

Suddenly, a load of towels plopped down at their feet, and a freshly filled mop bucket with a new mop rolled up next to them. Reggie and Ed both looked up to see Maddy walking at a brisk pace back to her cubical. As she went to sit down, she gave them a look over her shoulder that dared them to say anything. Neither male was that stupid. Her lips twitched in what might have been either a smile or a snarl before she grabbed her coffee mug and went back to her numbers.

Reggie and Ed were mopping up the last of the dirty water when their friend Harold rushed up to them. The older Spotted Joongee had a distressed look on his face and was short of breath.

Reggie furrowed his brow in a deep frown. "What's wrong, Harold?"

"Has Supervisor Glorp been up here yet?" Harold asked between gasping breaths as he clutched at his side. Reggie really hoped he wasn't about to have a heart attack. The older male wasn't in the best shape.

Ed shook his head and shrugged. "Haven't seen him, Pops."

Harold wasn't his father—or any kind of relation, for that matter—but Ed had always called him that. Reggie guessed it was because all the gray fur around Harold's muzzle and on his face made him look fatherly to Ed.

"No," Reggie said slowly, fighting to keep the distaste from his expression. "Why?"

"Well, it's…"

"Spit it out already, Harold!"

Reggie and Ed both jumped at the sudden outburst from between them. Neither of them had noticed Maddy slide up and join the conversation. She could be sneaky like that. The harsh interruption only made Harold stammer and lose his train of thought.

Before he could begin speaking again, the lift doors at the far end of the office opened, and Glorp slowly stepped out, as if marching to his own funeral. It was typical behavior for a Torniack. Their race was known for their lack of a sense of humor and dull personalities. They seemed to thrive in corporate environments, though one would never know it from their perpetually gloomy expressions. Their oversized, rounded craniums and protruding foreheads tended to overshadow beady eyes, and their small faces had exceedingly puffy cheeks. It gave the impression they were constantly hoarding food for later.

Supervisor Glorp was easily the most hated being employed by Galactic Solutions, not to mention the worst dressed. Today he wore large, black-framed glasses, black dress pants, and a white, short-sleeved, button-down shirt with a red tie. The shirt even had a pocket on the left breast where he kept his mini-slate and stylus. His polished black shoes blinded anyone who looked directly at them.

With perfectly stiff posture and his hands behind his back, Glorp approached them. The first thing he did was look down at the broken mop handle Reggie and Ed had yet to hide. The supervisor let out a disappointed sigh and shook his head.

"That makes three mops in the last two weeks, Edward," he said. Glorp never rushed to say anything. His words came out slow, his breathing was slow, and he even blinked slowly. It was infuriating and the main reason everyone hated him. The other was his unwavering devotion to company policy. "The cost of this one will come out of your salary. Galactic Solutions will have to look into cleaning bots if you cannot do your job without destroying company property on a weekly basis."

Ed hung his head. "Sorry, Supervisor Glorp. It won't happen again."

"See that it does not," Glorp replied with a slow nod and cleared his throat. "Now for the real reason I came down here. Due to the necessity of meeting the quarterly quota, your requests for vacation have been denied. Corporate and I feel that allowing all of you to take leave at the same time would adversely impact the company's profit margin."

"But, Supervisor Glorp," Ed said in alarm, "we're all of the same clan, and those two weeks are when we go home to celebrate Tunagra with the rest of the clans. The entire planet comes together, and Joongee from all over the galaxy come home. It's almost like part of our religion."

Glorp held up a long, bony finger. "But it is not a religion. It is a Joongee holiday—a holiday not recognized by corporate."

"Do all the other Joongee working here have to stay, too?" Ed asked, his soft, brown eyes wide.

"No," Glorp said in a matter-of-fact tone. "All the other departments have either met their quotas or are on track to do so. This is the only department being denied leave. Coincidently, you all are the only Joongee in this department." He waved a dismissive hand at Ed. "Other than Edward, here. He is the only employee in the custodial department. So, Edward, if you still wish to take leave, you may do so."

Ed looked at the other three with sadness welling up in his eyes, then back to Glorp. "No, thank you, Supervisor Glorp. If they can't go, then I don't want to, either. It would be lonely, anyway."

Reggie clapped him on the shoulder in understanding. He knew Ed didn't have any family back home.

"Good," Glorp said with a slow blink. "Then you won't have two weeks of cleaning to catch up on."

"Is there any way we can work this out?" Harold asked with an edge of desperation. "The numbers can't be that bad."

"You could work 24/7 for the next month," Glorp replied, his protruding forehead wrinkling up impressively. "That might catch your department up. However, please remember you are salaried employees, and Galactic Solutions will not authorize overtime pay at this time."

Maddy's lips pulled back in a sneer, and her paws balled up into fists. The tiny Joongee practically vibrated with rage. Reggie's jaw dropped as her eyes blazed with temper. He didn't stop to think, he just slapped a paw over her muzzle. He knew Maddy. Whatever was about to fall out of her mouth was likely to get her terminated.

His ribs exploded with pain as Maddy's elbow slammed into his side. He whipped his paw away from her face before she could bite him too. *No good deed goes unpunished*, he thought ruefully.

"How *dare* you muzzle me!" she snarled as he bent over and tried to catch his breath.

The *ding* of the lift caught their attention, and they all frowned in confusion at the empty space their supervisor had occupied seconds before. They craned their heads and caught a quick glimpse of his retreating backside a second before the lift doors slid shut behind him.

"For someone who does things so slow, he sure did get back to the lift fast," Ed said with a hint of wonder.

Maddy turned a blistering glare onto Reggie. Her hands were balled into fists, and she looked like she was seriously thinking about using them on him. Reggie held his ground, but he'd be lying if he said the thought of beating a quick retreat didn't cross his mind.

"If you *ever* do that again, I will rip your hand off and feed it to you!" With that, she stormed off to her cubicle, threw herself into her chair, and smashed a fist down onto her desk. Reggie winced at the dent left behind and was grateful for her restraint, however thin it was. That could've been his ribs she'd dented.

"Geez." Reggie rubbed his side and groaned. "Her elbows are so bony."

"She's just Mad Maddy right now," Harold said with the quiet confidence that came from years of experience dealing with Maddy. Out of all of them, he'd known her the longest. "She'll calm down. She always does."

"Don't let her hear you call her that," Ed whispered as his ears flattened in alarm. "You know she doesn't like it."

The gentle giant cringed as a low, rumbling growl drifted across the cubicle farm, and he risked a quick look over his shoulder to make sure Maddy was still fuming safely at her desk.

He turned back to them with a sad expression. "I don't like it when she's so upset. I hope she feels better soon."

Reggie patted him on the shoulder again. "Don't worry about it, Ed. She will. By the way, you didn't have to turn down your leave like that. We won't be mad if you go without us—not even Maddy would be angry with you."

"Don't bet on it," she muttered, but they could hear the lie in her voice.

Ed gave her a hopeful smile before he shook his head. "Nah. It's not really home without you guys. You're my clan."

Reggie looked up at his friend and smiled. "It wouldn't be home to us either, Ed."

"Speak for yourself," Maddy grumbled. Again, nobody believed her.

Ed scooped up the pieces of the broken mop, but Harold was standing in front of the overturned bucket. "Excuse me, Pops."

Harold's ears didn't so much as twitch as he stared off into space, a dejected slump bowing down his narrow shoulders. Ed tried again. "Um, hey, Pops. You're kind of in my way."

Reggie shook his head at the big Joongee. "Just leave it for now, Ed. It's break time anyway."

He clapped a paw on Harold's shoulder, and the older male jumped half a foot into the air. He clutched at his chest and stared wide-eyed at Reggie, but fortunately didn't have a heart attack. Even better, Maddy snickered as amusement broke through the heavy cloak of rage she'd wrapped around herself.

Reggie looked at his small clan and waved a paw. "Let's go, guys."

"I'm not a guy," Maddy snapped as she shoved back from her desk.

Reggie barely restrained an eye roll. "Come on, guys and *Maddy*."

Maddy sniffed. "Better."

Reggie herded his small clan out the door. It was definitely one of those days.

* * * * *

Chapter Two

The four Joongee slumped around the last empty table in the tiny little breakroom on their level. One of the table legs was shorter than the others, and they had to be careful not to put too much weight on it, or the whole thing would tip over. Again.

Reggie rolled his neck in an attempt to ease the tension in his shoulders. He was moderately successful, right up until Chad sauntered over. The Spotted Joongee was the top earner in Sales for the past five years running, and he never let anyone forget it. The expertly trimmed mane on top of his head was slicked back, and he wore a sharp black suit with a red bowtie.

Chad used to wear regular ties until last month, when Maddy tried to strangle him with it. Reggie had barely stopped her in time… mostly because it had been so much fun watching his eyes bulge out of his skull, he'd nearly forgotten it would be bad if Maddy actually killed him.

Reggie held back a smile when he noticed Chad had stopped on the opposite side of the table from the little female. Not that it would save him if he pissed her off. She was more than capable of launching herself over the table. He'd seen her do it before.

The rest of his sales team crowded close behind him. All Spotted Joongee, all dressed just like Chad, though perhaps not quite as nice. It wouldn't do to outshine the ringleader, after all.

Reggie low-key hated them all. He refused to devote the energy needed to truly hate them, but some days it was harder to resist than others.

"I heard your leave was denied," Chad said, voice dripping with false sympathy. "That's a shame. Tunagra is supposed to be truly epic this year. I hear they got Violent Shaggy to agree to play live."

Reggie blinked. They hadn't made a live appearance in years. He forced himself to shrug. "We'll just have to catch the performance on the tri-v. No big."

Maddy spluttered into her coffee. "No big? No big!"

"It's okay, Maddy," Ed said and patted her on the head. He nearly lost a paw for his efforts. "We can get some yummy treats and watch it together. It'll be like a sleepover!"

Chad laughed. His cronies followed suit in a slightly delayed chorus of annoying cackles. He rested his paws on the table and loomed over Reggie. "The big ones are such overgrown children, and the runts aren't much better. You know, Reginald—"

Reggie angled his ears back. "It's Reggie."

"Right, of course, *Reggie*. You'd get a lot further ahead here if you cut lose the dead weight." He cut a derisive look over to Harold, who was still staring off into space, and shook his head. "*All* the dead weight."

A surge of anger rocked through Reggie, but outwardly he maintained a calm appearance. "You first."

A chorus of high-pitched growls echoed through the breakroom, but Reggie just gazed up at the other clan with a slight smile.

"Runt?"

The soft-voiced question raised every internal alarm Reggie possessed. Across the table, Maddy had gone very still. The fur on the back of her neck slowly stood up, and Reggie knew he only had seconds to act. He shot to his feet, the chair legs squealing obnoxiously across the cheap floor, and forced a very surprised Chad to back up.

Reggie gave him a polite smile and pointed at the ancient clock on the wall. "It looks like your break time is up. Best get back up to your own floor. I wouldn't want you to get in trouble and have your leave cancelled. The door is right there. Walk through it. Now."

Chad looked past Reggie. Whatever he saw on Maddy's face made his ears flatten in panic. He spun on his heel and speed-walked through the door. His cronies practically shoved past each other, desperate not to be the last one in the room. Reggie sat back down and did his best not to smile at the vicious things Maddy muttered under her breath. That female needed no encouragement from him.

Ed slumped down in his seat and picked at his snack. Reggie wrinkled his nose in disgust. He had no idea how the other male could eat pickled chinto tail… let alone after dipping it in chocolate pudding.

Harold slammed his paws down on the table. This time, Reggie was the one to jump, though Maddy and Ed weren't exactly unaffected, either.

"What is *wrong* with you, old timer?" Maddy demanded, clawed hands wrapped tight around the coffee mug she'd almost spilled across the table.

Harold slowly looked up, his dark eyes shining. "I have an idea. Wait here!"

They were left gaping in astonishment as the old Joongee literally sprinted out of the breakroom. Ed spoke around the pickled chinto tail hanging out of his muzzle. "I didn't know Pops could run that fast."

Maddy glared down into her nearly full coffee mug. "I need more coffee for Harold's ideas."

She tipped her muzzle back and chugged the whole thing in one long gulp. Reggie blinked a few times and couldn't decide if he was more impressed or appalled. He settled on appalled when she promptly got up and refilled her mug to the brim.

Ed leaned closer, and Reggie fought back a gag at the larger male's rank breath. "If Maddy gets a paper cut, do you think she bleeds coffee?"

Reggie smirked even as he leaned away from Ed. "Wouldn't shock me in the least."

"Zip it, chinto-breath," Maddy said as she sat back down, but her tone lacked a little of its usual bite. Reggie figured it was the caffeine mellowing her out.

A few minutes later, Harold rushed back in with a stack of slates clutched in his paws and a bulging satchel slung over one narrow shoulder. Reggie lunged as the strap slipped and caught the bag before it hit the floor.

"Gently!" Harold blurted, dark eyes wide. "That's my life's work you're crushing in your hand there."

Reggie sighed and carefully set the bag on the table. He knew what this was about now. Maddy groaned and killed her second round of coffee.

She slammed the empty mug onto the table and snarled. "Here we go again."

Harold tilted sideways, unbalanced by the stack of slates, but Ed steadied him before he could fall. Reggie relieved the older Joongee of his burden and set the heavy stack next to the satchel.

He glanced at the clock as he sat down and sighed. "Break time's almost over, Harold. We don't really have time for—"

"What if we had all the time we wanted?" Harold interrupted with a wide smile, practically shouting. "What if we never had to worry about break time, or credit, or anything at all… ever again?"

Maddy stared at the excited male and wrinkled her muzzle in exasperation. "Did you get into Ed's happy stash again?"

Harold darted a furtive glance over his shoulder, but the break room had emptied out, and they were the only beings left. If they weren't careful, they'd be dinged by Supervisor Glorp and have to stay late to make up the lost time.

The old Joongee dropped his voice to an excited whisper that wasn't much quieter than his previous shout. "I figured it out!"

Reggie rubbed one paw between his eyes. "Figured what out, Harold?"

"The first clue!"

Reggie briefly squeezed his eyes shut and held onto his patience by his clawtips. It was absolutely one of those days. "The first clue to what, Harold?"

"Only the biggest treasure in this sector of the galaxy!"

Maddy tilted her head in sudden interest, avarice gleaming in her purple eyes. "Are you talking about an Asur outpost?"

Harold waved a dismissive paw. "Okay, *one* of the biggest treasures in this sector of the galaxy. I'm talking about the Lost Weapons of Koroth!"

Maddy slumped back in her chair and crossed her arms with a scowl. "Not this again."

Ed slurped up another pickled chinto tail and licked his chops happily. "Oh! I like this story. What's the first clue, Pops?"

"It's not a story, Ed." Harold grinned up at the bigger male and dug through his satchel. Despite his care, rolled up polymer star charts and various topographical maps toppled from the bag and rolled across the floor. Reggie bit back another sigh and helped straighten the mess out. Harold selected one of the slates with trembling paws and looked up at them with bright eyes. "It's real, and I figured it out. Me! Harold, a Records Custodian and amateur historian! The Galactic Historical Society thought my ideas were *crazy*, but I'll show them. *We'll* show them."

Reggie arched a brow. "We will?"

"Yes!"

Reggie unrolled one of the polymer maps and frowned as it activated and lit up. "Harold... this is a child's treasure map. There's even an X in red. Are you sure you're feeling okay?"

"I've never felt better in my life! So much time wasted, but I finally figured out where I went wrong." Harold gestured wildly to the stack of slates. "You're looking at digital copies of every *first-edition* book and paper Dr. Bergan Monschtackle ever published. Later editions changed the formatting. That's why I couldn't get the numbers to work! You have no idea how hard it was tracking these down. We're lucky they survived past the paper-age."

Reggie exchanged a wordless glance with Maddy, but Ed was on the edge of his seat, completely enthralled by the show Harold was putting on.

Harold leaned on the table, but abruptly pulled back when it threatened to tip over and scatter his life's work everywhere. "There were coded messages in each one, you see, and I finally put it all together last night. Listen to this..."

Document #2365284965341987325879416832178952836549328471 3724
> To whomever finds this letter:
> Please, I beg of you. Read no further unless the fate of your world—nay, the fate of the galaxy itself—depends on it.
> I like to think of myself as an inventor, a creator, and above all else, a good scientist. This is not the first time my research has led me down a dark path of death, destruction, and misery, but I can assure you, it will be the last. No more can I allow my brilliance to eclipse my moral judgment and good sense.
> My research began innocently enough. Could I create new, innovative sources of power? Could I create new tools to alleviate the strain of labor on my fellow beings? Could I utilize common materials and make them more cost efficient? Not that I, as a pure scientist, cared about such things as cost, but I can assure you my backers did, to a ridiculous degree. Could I change my world?
> The answer to all of those questions was a resounding YES. Unfortunately, as so often happens in times of war, my inventions were only viewed through the lens of the military mind. The questions changed. Could I increase the power? Could I increase the effective range? Could I make them smaller and more easily portable?
> To my ever-lasting sorrow, the answers remained the same... yes. I could do those things. I did those things. And damned my soul in the process.
> The initial trials went well—almost too well. My country's military snatched them up before they were fully tested, so eager were they to win the war against our greedy neighbors. They deployed them on the field of battle, equipping the average soldier with weapons an order of magnitude above anything they'd ever seen or operated before.
> Something went wrong. I'll never know what. All those who were there that fateful day were nothing more than ashes in the wind after the explosions—those

terrible explosions—finally ceased. The battlefield, all those soldiers… gone. Because of my invention, my folly. Never again.

In the chaos that followed, it was a relatively simple matter to collect all my research, to gather up the remaining weapons of mass destruction and tragedy. But what to do with them? I lacked the means to destroy the actual weapons themselves, and I refused to allow any beings on what was left of my home world to lay a hand on them again. They'd suffered enough for my mistakes.

I borrowed a supply ship (I gave it back, so it wasn't theft, regardless of what my government thought) and transported the weapons off-world. I should have launched the vile things straight into the sun. I nearly did. Doubts plagued me, though. The initial trails went so well, it wouldn't take much to figure out what went wrong and correct the error. It was an insidious thought, proof that the long war had affected my own thinking, but… years of my life had gone into their creation. In the end, I could not destroy them.

Instead, I buried them deep in the bowels of an uninhabited planet, hid them so well the devil himself wouldn't be able to find them. Where they have remained ever since.

It was only as old age crept up on me that I began to question my decision. Once I was gone, they truly would be lost forever. The thought pained me, but there were none left alive I trusted with the knowledge the weapons still existed, let alone where to find them. So, I put my considerable intellect to use in solving my dilemma. My young grandson proved a wholly unexpected source of inspiration with his love of pirates and treasure hunts. I latched onto the idea with the desperation of a being who hears death knocking at his door. I published papers in respected scientific journals, contributed to a prestigious history book, scattered clues to hint at the treasure throughout every written work. I went a step further and took one last journey (this time I paid for passage rather than borrow a ship) and left a trail of breadcrumbs to the treasure itself for those smart enough to decipher the initial clue.

I fear I cannot make finding these terrible weapons easy, *brave adventurer, but if your need is great enough, I'm sure you will persevere and triumph in the end. I just pray the cure is not worse than the disease... and may the Creator have mercy on your souls.*

Sincerely,
Dr. Bergan Monschtackle

P.S. Remember, dear friends, as with all good treasure hunts... X marks the spot.

Reggie straightened up in his chair and took the slate from Harold. He read it again as a small tendril of excitement unfurled. He slowly looked up at the older Joongee. "You're serious about this."

"As a heart attack." Harold tapped the document number on the upper left-hand corner of the letter. "And look here. You see these numbers? They match the gate coordinates to the Zoological System. If I'm right, we'll find the next clue there!"

Ed perked up. "I always wanted to go there! They have animals from all over the galaxy."

"How certain are you this is all real?" Reggie asked.

Harold grinned and a small cackle escaped his jaws. "Very."

Maddy gave Reggie an incredulous look. "Reg... you can't seriously be considering this."

Reggie ignored her and focused on Harold. "*How* certain?"

"Certain enough to quit my job and leave as soon as possible for those gate coordinates," Harold answered without hesitation.

Reggie kept his expression neutral as he considered his options. He glanced at the clock. They should've been back to work ten minutes ago. He was honestly shocked Glorp hadn't come down to check on them yet.

"Reggie!" Maddy hissed, ears flickering in uncertainty. "Are you crazy? You're not really thinking of quitting and running off on some kind of wild treasure hunt with this nutty old fool, are you?"

"I wanna go, too," Ed said, his eyes full of wonder as he looked at the maps and scanned over the inventor's letter. "We could be like, discoverers and stuff."

Reggie looked at Maddy. "I am, actually. I mean, we've always made fun of Harold for obsessing over this, but now I'm starting to wonder if we were the dumb ones. Look at all this evidence."

He took the letter from Ed and slid it over to Maddy. The small female's purple eyes held his gaze for a long moment as if she were trying to find the trick in his words. Finally, she looked down at the letter with a little crease between her eyes.

"My gut tells me this is real." He crossed his arms and leaned back in his chair. "Besides, working in this cubicle farm sucks. I know you hate it as much as I do. I'm willing to bet a bad day out treasure hunting is better than a great day in this hellhole of an office."

Maddy growled and pinned her ears back. "I hate it when you're right."

Harold looked like he was about to jump out of his fur with excitement. "So does that mean you're all in?"

The door to the break room creaked open, and Glorp stepped inside. He glanced at his wrist slate and gave them all a look of profound disapproval. Behind him, Chad leaned against a cubical wall with a cocky grin on his face. The little brown-noser had probably told on them.

"You're all fourteen minutes late from lunch," Glorp announced. "You will be expected to work fourteen minutes past your scheduled time to make up for the loss of productivity. This is a perfect example of why your department is so far behind the rest."

Reggie turned from their overbearing supervisor of torment to face Harold again. "Yeah, we're in."

* * * * *

Chapter Three

Later that evening, the four Joongee trekked over to their favorite pub at the neighboring space station. The state-of-the-art Galactic Solutions space station they worked on had everything from entertainment, restaurants, and fitness facilities, to living quarters for employees. Literally everything a being could need—for a price. One that could be conveniently deducted straight out of their paycheck... after taxes were taken out, of course.

For various reasons, they all refused to spend any of their hard-earned credit there. Duncan's Space Station might be considerably more rundown and not nearly as fancy, but the benefits more than made up for that. Benefits like not being anywhere near the office or that absolute waste of space Chad and his lapdogs. He was always lurking around as if he had nothing better to do than annoy them. As if bragging about his penthouse and how he had such a great view and his own private docking ring made him cool.

Ugh. He's such a tool, Maddy thought as she leaned up against the bar. *At least the music is good tonight.*

She moved her hips to the beat as she impatiently waited for the bartender to make her drinks and passed the time thinking of increasingly nasty ways to pay the company golden pup back for calling her a runt. Her pleasant thoughts stuttered to halt when a hand firmly smacked, squeezed, and jiggled her right butt cheek. Maddy's paws balled into tiny, rock-hard fists as she spun around and smacked his hand away, nothing but murder, malice, and carnage on her mind.

"Hey there, sweet thing," a Spotted male Joongee said. He had a smirk on his face like he'd just done something she should be happy about. "How 'bout I buy you a drink, and we find a quiet corner somewhere?"

Rage twisted up with outrage, but she fought for calm with everything she had. She didn't want to get kicked out before she could even get a single drink. She took a step forward, but the fool didn't move back, and she ended up having to crane her neck back to look him in the eye.

"I'm sorry, what was that?" she asked through gritted teeth.

"Oooh, feisty. I heard that about your type."

A red haze descended over her vision. "My *type?*"

"Yeah, fun-sized—"

Maddy's fist shot out and slammed into his throat. She pulled the punch so he wouldn't die, but she left enough there to cause him to go into a choking fit. As he bent over, she rammed her knee between his legs. Somehow, through all the choking, he still managed to let out a high-pitched yelp as she hit the bullseye, and he dropped to his knees.

It wasn't enough. She wanted to utterly destroy him… but then she wouldn't get her drinks, and she reluctantly decided she needed that more than she needed to vent the rest of her rage.

Maddy grabbed a handful of the fur on his head, tilted his face up to hers, and glared down into his eyes. "Who in the *hell* do you think you are, coming up and putting your nasty paws on me? I should rip your throat out right now."

She curled a lip in disgust. The male was simultaneously choking and cradling his tiny intimate bits, and she was pretty sure tears were leaking out of the corner of his eyes, if his damp fur was any indication. *What a loser.*

"Do they hurt? I bet they do," she crooned with false sympathy. Her eyes narrowed, and she bared her teeth with a menacing growl. "If you *ever* lay paws on me or any other female without permission again, I'll rip them off and shove them down your throat." She leaned closer and added, "And if you want to call security, be my guest. I'm sure they'd *love* to hear how you came up and assaulted me before I defended myself in front of all these witnesses. Nod your head if you understand." The wincing Joongee nodded. "Good."

Maddy straightened and turned back to the bartender in time to see her order come up. He looked from her to the whimpering male on the floor and gave her an approving nod. With a savage smile, she grabbed the tray of drinks and walked toward her table, where Reggie, Ed, and Harold were waiting for her.

"I heard someone yelp across the room," Reggie said and arched a brow at her. "Who did you punch?"

"A jerk who thought my ass was fair game," she answered as she slid his beer to him. "He won't pull that stunt again. He's too busy nursing his bruised… pride."

Maddy thought she saw a glint of anger—or maybe concern—in Reggie's blue eyes for a second, but if it had been there, it was gone as fast as it had arrived. He never seemed to let anything get to him. It was infuriating. What kind of being stayed that calm all the time? It just wasn't normal.

"Goodness, Maddy," Harold said as he eyed her drink. "Even your alcoholic drinks are coffee. You're going to give yourself a heart attack with all that caffeine."

"It's the nectar of the gods," Maddy replied as she lifted her glass of iced coffee and Buffalo Trace bourbon cream to her lips. She sipped it and let the silky liquid coat her tongue in all its roasted glory. A happy sigh escaped her, and the rest of her *perfectly justified* rage mellowed out.

Ed screwed up his face and stuck his tongue out. "Yuck. I don't see how you can drink that stuff. Coffee tastes horrible."

"Agreed," Reggie said and wrinkled his muzzle in distaste.

"Blasphemy!" Maddy hissed and took another slow sip.

"I can't say I agree with these two," Harold said as he picked up his beer, "but you take it to a whole new level, my dear Maddy."

Maddy rolled her eyes and sighed, tired of the age-old discussion regarding how much she loved coffee. Didn't they understand that coffee had saved so many lives over the past decade? All those fools she hadn't stabbed or strangled because of sweet, delicious coffee. "Are we going to sit here and talk about my taste in drinks all night, or are we going to discuss this whole quitting our jobs and going off on some half-cocked adventure thing?"

"Half-cocked adventure thing," Reggie said decisively. He wiped foam from his mouth with the back of his paw and cleared his throat. "I say we go for it."

"Me too," Ed agreed.

"Me three," Harold said.

They all looked at Maddy.

"And how exactly are we supposed to afford this?" Maddy asked with considerable exasperation. "We don't have a ship. Not only that, we don't even have an actual plan. What about gate costs, supplies, food, basic day-to-day necessities? How are we going to do all that?"

"We get a loan," Harold answered in that matter-of-fact tone that made her want to claw his eyes out. "And we all have credit in savings. I think Reggie has quite a bit stashed away from his days as a mercenary with Charlie's Commandos."

A look of discomfort touched on the normally impassive Reggie's face, and he seemed reluctant to respond.

Maddy raised her eyebrows at him in surprise. "You never told me you were a merc, Reg. No wonder you always get the new gadgets and never complain about the sucky pay at work."

Reggie sighed and nodded his head. "I've got some credit put away. Probably enough to put a down payment on a smaller, older-model ship. I was saving it for retirement, but it's not enough to live off of, and I'm nowhere near retirement yet, so I figure this is as good an investment as any."

"Why aren't you still a merc?" Ed asked.

Reggie shrugged, that maddeningly calm expression firmly in place again. "Just wasn't for me. I worked two contracts and then came here. You guys have known me ever since." He looked directly at Maddy. "And I didn't tell you because I didn't want to be asked a million questions about it."

"I've got some credit saved up, too," Ed said cheerfully. "I think the last time I looked, it was like forty-two thousand or something."

Everyone gawked at him.

"What?" Ed asked in bewilderment. "Is that not enough?"

Harold spluttered into his beer, and Ed rushed to explain, his words practically tripping over each other. "I mean, I spend credit on chinto tail, chocolate pudding, lunch stuff for work, rent, some recreational herbs, stuff like that. I mean, I do have a pretty epic video game collection, but I leave the rest of my credit in the bank. My old clan always said to do that. It's really funny. When I did that before, I never seemed to have any credit. Now I do!"

Maddy snarled down into her mug. She was pretty sure his old clan had taken advantage of the big idiot. She looked up in time to catch another flash of... *something* in Reggie's eyes, but not in time to figure out what it was.

"You have plenty, Ed," Harold said reassuringly. "I have close to what Ed does. I've been saving for a long time, and it looks like it's about to pay off."

"I can match what you two are putting in combined," Reggie said with a decisive nod. "We'll take my credit and put it toward the down payment for the ship. The rest can be for all the other expenses. And there *will be* other expenses. If we separate the two, though, the Bith can't come after our ship if we ever default on the personal loan."

Maddy's eyes unfocused the way they always did when she was doing mental math. Her round ears flickered, and she snorted. "You fools still don't have enough, even with a loan."

"Would we have enough if you were in?" Reggie asked. When she reluctantly nodded, he gave her a little grin and asked, "So, how 'bout it Maddy... are you in?"

His tone wasn't pushy or expectant, or angsty, or anything. It seemed like no matter what she said, he'd be okay with her decision. Ed and Harold, on the other hand, looked like they might die if she said no. All three males watched her expectantly and waited with varying levels of patience.

She dug at the table with a claw as she weighed her options. *Why the hell is this all coming down to me? It's Harold's stupid idea, anyway, and Reggie is the one who up and decided it suddenly wasn't a bunch of squat. Ugh, on* the other paw, I hate everyone else at the office. If they leave, I'll be stuck there all by myself with Chad. Nope. So much nope. Not happening.

"Fine," she relented and heaved a sigh. "I'm in. You guys aren't leaving me here with that greasy-furred hemorrhoid of Glorp's. But... I've only got about seventeen thousand in savings."

Reggie flashed her a grin. "Like you said, it's enough. That gives us close to a hundred thousand to work with for gate fees and supplies. If we budget right, take out a loan for another three hundred and fifty thousand, and split the gate fees with larger ships going to the same systems as we are, I think we'll be okay. With all four of us on the loan, we should be fine getting it approved. Do any of you have a bad credit history?"

Everyone but Maddy shook their heads.

"It's credit cards, isn't it?" Reggie said dryly and looked at her pointedly.

Maddy huffed and crossed her arms defensively. "I like clothes, music, and good food, Reg. I like them a lot. And just for the record, I don't have a *bad* credit history. Every single one of my cards are paid on time. It shouldn't be an issue."

"All right, then," Reggie said with a slow grin. "That settles it. We're officially doing this. Tomorrow, we'll put in our two-week notice."

"Seriously," Maddy sniffed. "A notice? We're not just going to quit?"

"That wouldn't be very professional," Harold replied with a shocked tilt to his ears.

"Yeah," Ed added. "It'd be kind of mean. And what if we need to come back?"

"Exactly. There's no sense burning a bridge we don't have to." Maddy couldn't help her smirk, and Reggie jabbed a paw at her. "No, Maddy! That's not what I meant, and you know it. No burning anything."

"Whatever, killjoy. I don't know about you guys," Maddy said as she lifted her drink to her lips, "but I have zero intentions of ever going back to work for Galactic Solutions. I'm done there forever… but I'll work out a notice with you nerds."

"Harold," Reggie said and pointed a finger at him, "you handle finding the ship. I'll fill out a loan application online with the Bith bank tomorrow on our lunch break. After we get the loan, Ed and I will go out after work every day and gather the supplies we'll need. I can use the supply list from my old merc ship as a guide. Maddy…you just try not to kill Chad before the end of our notice."

Maddy curled her lip. "No promises."

* * * * *

Chapter Four

The next morning, Reggie stood in front of Supervisor Glorp's door, the rest of his small clan crowded close behind him. It was closing in on lunchtime. Maddy wanted to march straight into his office first thing—and surprisingly, Harold had been right there with her—but Reggie insisted on getting their notice forms in order first. If they were going to do this, they were going to do it *right*. That meant ensuring they filled out every form correctly, which took time none of them wanted to spend.

Maddy had snapped a stylus out of sheer frustration when she was only halfway through, and Reggie'd had to help Ed with his, but in the end, they got it done. Now, they just needed to finish the process. He raised a paw and knocked briskly on Glorp's door.

After a long pause, they heard, "Enter."

The door slid open, and they filed inside. Glorp eyed them from behind his excessively neat desk and slowly raised his eyebrows. "Shirking your duties to speak with me will not help any of you make your quotas."

Maddy snarled. "You can take your quotas and—"

Reggie loudly cleared his throat and tapped a finger against his slate. Supervisor Glorp's slate chimed. "Per company policy, we have sent you our two weeks' notice forms, and we are here to verbally inform you of our intent to seek other employment opportunities."

Out of the corner of his eye, he caught both Maddy and Harold staring at him. He shrugged and kept his focus where it belonged—on their flabbergasted supervisor. Glorp narrowed his eyes and read through each of the forms with painstaking thoroughness. It took everything Reggie had to hold still. Maddy and Harold both fidgeted, and Ed actually sat on the floor.

Glorp set his slate down and glowered at them all. "How will we meet our quotas now?"

"That sounds like a *you* problem," Maddy said snidely.

A loud breath escaped the Torniack, and his cheeks bulged comically. He tapped a few times on his slate, and each of theirs chimed in turn. Reggie darted a suspicious glance at his slate. "What's this?"

An oily smile spread across Glorp's face. "The quotas you are required to meet within the next two weeks to maintain your eligibility for rehiring. Galactic Solutions will not tolerate slacking of any sort."

Reggie skimmed through the requirements, and it took everything he had to keep his muzzle from wrinkling up into a snarl. "This is unreasonable."

Supervisor Glorp's eyes narrowed so much they threatened to disappear entirely. "It is company policy."

Harold spluttered, and his ears flattened in dismay. "We'll have to work over our allotted hours to complete this."

"And let me guess," Maddy said with her fangs bared. "Overtime isn't authorized."

"No. It is not."

Reggie bit back a sigh as the little female spun to face him. Her purple eyes sparked with fury and viciousness. "Are you sure we can't burn the place down?"

"Not right now, Maddy."

"I can dock your pay for making threats like that, Madeline," Glorp said in a warning tone.

Maddy's ears pinned back. "I was *joking*. And don't call me that. Ever."

Glorp stared at her for a long moment, but Ed broke the stalemate. He stood up to his full height, absolutely towering over everyone in the room... and raised his paw. "Excuse me, Mr. Glorp, sir. If you want me to clean all those levels, I need to go get my mop."

Glorp slow blinked a few times and nodded. "Please attempt not to break any Galactic Solutions equipment this time, Edward."

Ed nodded his head vigorously. "Yes, sir."

Glorp waved a dismissive hand. "Your two-week period starts at the beginning of the work day tomorrow."

"What!" Maddy burst out. A low growl rumbled out of Harold's throat, which was rather more startling to Reggie. He held up a paw and they both subsided.

"We followed company policy to the letter. Our fourteen days should begin today," Reggie argued as politely as he was capable of in that moment.

Glorp pointed at the retro clock on his office wall, smug satisfaction in his beady little eyes. "You missed the cut off by three minutes. Please return to your duties, and do not forget to meet today's quota in addition to the notice quotas."

Reggie herded his clan out of the office before one of them snapped and ripped their soon to be ex-supervisor's throat out. He let out a sigh of relief when the door slid shut behind him. Too soon.

Maddy whirled on him, eyes flashing with anger. "Damn it, Reggie. If you didn't have such a giant stick up your ass, we could've started the countdown today!"

Reggie patted the air with both paws. It didn't seem to calm the small female down, but at least she didn't try to bite him this time. "Relax, Spitfire. We can use the extra day of pay, and it'll give us more time to get everything in order. It's a good thing."

Maddy blinked at him a few times and tilted her head slowly. "Spitfire?"

Reggie winced. He hadn't meant to say that nickname out loud. He hurriedly turned to Harold. "I checked with the local shipyard last night. I sent you a few options to check out after work. Comm me if you run into any snags. I'll work on our loan application between service calls today and get our pre-approval in place."

Harold's eyes lit up. "Excellent! I'll be at my desk if anyone needs me. Lots to do if I'm to leave on time today."

The old Joongee trundled off at a respectable pace. Reggie smiled at Ed. "It's you and me tonight, buddy. You ready to help me hunt down the supplies we'll need?"

Ed grinned broadly. "I love shopping! Maybe we can get Mr. Glorp a farewell gift to be nice."

"Uh… maybe. We'll see how our supply run goes, okay?"

Ed nodded agreeably and trotted off to mop the floors, hopefully without breaking another mop. Reggie steeled himself and turned to look at Maddy, but she'd disappeared on silent paws. *Sneaky little female.* He shook his head at his lucky break and headed back to his desk. The sooner he could knock out today's work, the sooner he could focus on better things.

Before he got back to his desk, his slate chimed again. He silently groaned. *Now what?*

He slung himself into his chair, booted up his station, and reluctantly checked his slate. His round ears flickered in surprise. It was a message from Maddy. He clicked it open and studied the spreadsheet she'd sent him. It was a detailed budget, cross-referenced to the old merc supply list he'd shared with everyone last night.

"You don't need to look so shocked," Maddy said sourly from behind him. Reggie twisted around to look up at her. She smirked. "I *am* an accountant, after all."

Reggie's eyebrow twitched. "You handle accounting software issues. That's not the same thing."

"Yeah, but I still had to have an accounting degree for this job." Unexpectedly, Maddy grinned at him. "You asked last night if I'm in. This is my way of contributing."

"Thanks, Maddy. This'll be helpful," Reggie said slowly. He eyed her with a touch of justified suspicion. "You still can't burn the place down or murder Chad."

Maddy rolled her eyes and stalked back to her desk. "I said no promises!"

Reggie rolled the stiffness out of his neck and settled down to work. It was going to be a long two weeks.

***

Seven days. Seven days had crawled past, and it had taken all Reggie's skill and patience to keep his clan together. Out of all of them, Maddy was the only one who managed to remain calm and kept her head down. It only increased his suspicion. He'd never seen her work so hard in the entire four years they'd known each other.

She was planning something nasty; he just knew it.

Every time he checked on her, though, she grumped at him and told him off for messing up her concentration. Wariness threaded through his entire being, but he couldn't babysit her forever. He had his own quotas to meet, and supplies to run down in the few hours he was able to spare before racking out for the night.

He leaned back in his chair and scrubbed his face. Despite combing through every market on Duncan's Space Station, he'd been unable to track down a new starchart interface. Not even Ed, with his uncanny sense of where to find the best deals, had been able to find one. It was critical to get one for their used ship, though, as navigating without an updated chart was just plain stupid. After a full week of searching, he was finally willing to concede defeat. Tonight, they'd check out the marketplace on the Galactic Solutions' station.

Reggie wrinkled his muzzle in distaste and shoved it aside for later. Right now, he had another call to answer. He glanced at his comm and let out a slow, controlled breath. Only seven days, six more hours to go.

* * *

Maddy darted a careful sideways glance over at Reggie. He'd been keeping an annoyingly close eye on her all week, but it looked like he was thoroughly distracted with his latest call. She bit back a snicker that might attract his attention, but it was hard when he was using his extra patient voice. It sounded like his latest customer was demanding he fix something immediately, as if all it would take was a snap of his paws. *If I was Reggie, I'd tell that whiny turd my magic wand was out for repairs. Ugh. Customers suck.*

Her desk chair usually squeaked when she rolled it back from her desk, but she'd oiled the wheels yesterday in anticipation of her stealth mission. Reggie couldn't be allowed to interfere. Chad was about to regret every rude, nasty thing he'd ever said about her. In particular, he was going to regret calling her a runt for the rest of his pathetic little life.

Earlier that week, she'd managed to slap a tiny camera next to the security camera up in the corner of Chad's swanky office. As much of a hotshot as he was, corporate still kept an eye on him—just like they did everyone else. It added an extra layer of challenge to her plan, and the crawlspace in the ceiling had totally sucked, but what was life without obstacles?

Maddy tapped her slate and pulled up the feed to Chad's office. A slow smile spread across her face. He was still there, sitting in his fancy chair without a care in the world, feet up on his desk as he chattered away on his comm. He wouldn't be smiling by the end of the day.

* * *

An hour later, Reggie groaned and rubbed at his eyes as he got off the comm with the Bith bank. He'd suffered through unbelievable wait times to get through to an actual, living representative, but the answer hadn't changed. Their personal loan was approved in full… but at a much higher interest rate than even his worst estimate. He flexed his paws, tempted to strangle Maddy, but he'd read through the credit report himself. She might have a lot of open credit lines, but she hadn't lied when she said she paid them all on time. In fact, she paid them off completely every month. He'd argued that the behavior should *improve* her credit score, not damage it, but the representative had been impervious to his arguments.

He scanned through the documents again, but the numbers didn't change. Instead of the 5 percent interest rate they'd first been promised, they were stuck with a ridiculous 15 percent. At that rate, it would take them *decades* to pay off the loan. Harold's treasure better be the real deal, or they'd be paying for their gamble the rest of their lives.

Reggie's ears flicked back as he registered the low rumble coming from his chest, and he took a few deep breaths until his growl faded away, and he was calm again. They had the loan. That was the important part. Now Harold just had to complete the purchase for their new ship. Any of the three he'd pointed out to him would be a good fit for their new adventure. Small enough to hook up with larger ships to cut down on gate fees, but large enough for the four of them to spread out comfortably without getting under each other's paws. With Maddy onboard, he felt that last point was especially important.

Sometimes she needed a little space, and it was easier to give it to her than risk death by strangulation like she'd nearly done to Chad. He pulled uncomfortably at his own tie before straightening it once more. In just over a week, he'd hopefully never have to wear one again. He might not agree with Maddy's desire to burn down Galactic Solutions, but he could admit the thought of burning all his ties was incredibly tempting.

He glanced over at her desk. Reggie blinked and scrubbed his eyes, as if that would change the fact that Maddy's chair was empty. He whimpered and *thunked* his head onto his desk. "Why me? Just why?"

Reggie debated his options. He could stay here, work down his quota, and get off in time to go shopping for the last thing they desperately needed. Or he could hunt down Maddy before she did something bound to be impulsive, poorly-thought-out, and nasty. He was sorely tempted to do the former, and to hell with what that crazy female did to Chad. In the end, though, he couldn't allow a member of his clan to get into trouble like that, so he shoved himself to his feet and marched over to Maddy's desk.

He didn't really need to check for her scent. He knew what she smelled like, but it didn't hurt to refresh his scent memory. Joongee weren't the greatest at scent tracking, but their noses weren't useless—unlike certain beings he could name. He drew in a few deep breaths through his nose and nodded decisively. Coffee with that sweet honey undertone; that was all Maddy. He had her.

Reggie stalked off through the office. He'd track down that damn female and keep her out of trouble, because that's what a good leader did... even if he had to work late to do it.

* * *

Maddy tapped on her slate again, one last check to ensure Chad was safely in his office. It wasn't that she was afraid of him—she'd proven more than once that she could easily take the larger male in a fight—but getting caught would ruin the entire prank. A satisfied smirk twisted her muzzle when the feed confirmed the clown was still sitting his office, chatting up his latest sales victim. *Good. Keep talking, jerk-face.*

She glanced both ways down the hallway of the glamorous penthouse level, but there weren't any beings in sight. She adjusted her maid uniform and shoved her cleaning cart out with a squeak of poorly maintained wheels. It hadn't taken much effort to secure what she needed. The cleaning staff that worked on this level weren't usually treated well by management or the employees that lived there. All it had taken was a few drinks the other night with a *very* disgruntled Pikith, and Maddy had secured herself a copy of the access card that allowed the holder into any and every penthouse on level five. The same level where Chad lived.

She paused outside his room, looked up and down the hall one last time, and swiped her access card. The green light and off-key *beep* were music to her ears, and she pushed her cart into the room without hesitation.

The door slid shut behind her, but she stayed in the foyer and surveyed the space without moving deeper into the suite. Her muzzle wrinkled up in distaste. *How does anybody* live *like this?*

The penthouse was *spotless*. No clothes on the floor, no dishes in the sink, no dust—though that was probably more due to the cleaning service than anything that waste of space did—and monochrome colors that were probably meant to be sophisticated, but just looked cold and lifeless.

There weren't even any personal touches... if one didn't count the "I love me" wall Chad had going on above the couch. Every picture, certificate, and award was all about him and his overachieving accomplishments. The center picture was a life-size image of Chad. The same image on his business cards. *Ugh.*

Maddy hated the penthouse. She hated the tidiness. Most of all, she hated Chad's face.

A slight cackle escaped before she could hold it back. Time to put her plan into action.

She flipped back the cover on her cart and contemplated her supplies with an evil grin. *Where to start...*

The bottle of lurid orange dye screamed for her attention, and she plucked it out of the cart with a snicker. After thoroughly mixing it into every bottle of fur-wash he owned, she moved on to Chad's bedroom. Her muzzle wrinkled. Even his bed was made. What kind of monster did that? She threw open his closet door and paused in shock and unholy glee. *Huh... never would have pegged him for* that *kind of fetish.*

She whipped out her slate and took pictures from several angles. Those would get posted to the company feed and every social media platform she could find. Anonymously, of course. She checked the time on her slate and pinned her ears back. She didn't have time to dawdle. She hustled to the kitchen and found the salt and sugar containers. Swapping them was an easy task, though she actually had to do some cleaning when some of the white crystals spilled on the floor. Couldn't give the game away, but *damn* did the fact that she actually had to clean—while wearing a maid's uniform no less—rankle.

Next, she dug through his pantry in search of one key item. Nothing. Her eyes narrowed, and her gaze drifted back to the coffee machine sitting all alone on the vast expanse of pristine countertop. It had to be here somewhere. She marched over and threw open the cabinet above the machine. *Bingo.*

Another cackle escaped as she committed sacrilege and switched out every bit of his overpriced coffee for *decaf.* She was fully aware she was probably going to the bad place for that crime, but it was *so* worth it.

Almost able to hear her time ticking down to zero, she rushed back to her cart. She reached for the frozen-shelled waterbugs and hesitated. Her original plan was to hide them in the air vents, but it occurred to her something that smelly and obvious might get the real service staff in trouble. She heaved a sigh and left them in the cart. If half of what the Pikith had told her the other night was true, they didn't need any more crap heaped on them.

Her paw flashed out, and she grabbed a tiny plastic device instead. No larger than her smallest claw and thinner than her slate, it had a sticky backing, and a battery guaranteed to last a minimum of ten years. Its sole purpose was to beep at irregular intervals. She panned her gaze around the room before tracking up to the ceiling. Specifically, to the fancy lighting fixtures. She dragged a chair over, but even with the added height, she was too short to reach it.

She checked the time on her slate and cursed. She could always hide it in one of the vents, she supposed, but everyone online agreed the echo tended to give away its position. She didn't want him to find this, ever. She growled in frustration, but there was nothing taller she could use. *Maybe I can use the mop handle...*

A sharp knock on the door startled her out of her musing thoughts. *Damn it. He found me.*

Her shoulders momentarily slumped before she straightened up and marched to the door. She slammed her paw on the control panel and tilted her chin up defiantly as it slid open.

* * *

Reggie slowed to a stop next to Chad's penthouse door. A sigh gusted out of him. He hadn't needed to follow her scent trail after all. She'd gone exactly where he thought she would. He lifted one paw and visibly restrained himself to a polite knock when all he wanted to do was kick the door down.

He expected to see destruction on a level unknown to most civilians. He expected to see broken furniture, slashed pictures, maybe even unmentionable things smeared across the walls if Maddy was particularly enraged. He did not expect to find a spotless suite, and he absolutely did *not* expect to find Maddy glaring up at him, dressed as a maid of all things.

He bit his lip hard to hold back his laughter and choked out, "What the heck are you wearing? You look ridiculous!"

He thought he caught a flash of hurt in those purple eyes before she ratcheted up her already impressive glare and hauled him bodily into the penthouse. "Who cares what I look like? What do you want, Reggie?"

His amusement died in a surge of frustration as the door slid shut behind him. Why did everything have to be so difficult with her? "I'm trying to keep you out of trouble. Chad's shift is almost over. We need to get out of here."

Maddy snorted and stared up at the ceiling. There was a kitchen chair in the middle of the living area for some reason. "You can go if you want. I'm not leaving until I'm done."

Reggie blew out a slow breath and clawed for every scrap of patience he could muster. He gritted out, "What if I help you?"

Maddy whirled on him and gave him a careful onceover. A slow smile broke out over her face that made her purple eyes sparkle. "You just might be tall enough. Can you stick this inside the light fixture?"

Reggie took the small device from her and examined it critically. He shook his head. "Too easy to find."

He hopped up on the chair, peeled off the plastic protecting the sticky back, and stretched up onto his tiptoes. He allowed himself a smug smile when he was able to secure it to the fixture where it connected to the ceiling. It blended in perfectly, and short of ripping out the entire fixture, there was no reason for any being to mess with that part of it.

"Perfect," Maddy said with a wild cackle. She dashed over to Chad's desk chair, screwdriver in hand. "Just need to remove the air cylinder. He'll have to constantly pump up his chair to the right height."

Reggie twitched an eyebrow. "Don't forget the chair in his office."

Maddy grinned at him. "Already done, with a little help from Ed. We also relocated all the spare air cylinders. Permanently. They'll have to order more."

Reggie was about to jump down from the chair when something on Chad's desk caught his eye. He carefully replaced the chair in the kitchen before he strode over to examine it. The sleek device was exactly what he and Ed had tirelessly searched for—a current starchart for navigation. He whistled soundlessly. It wasn't just any starchart. It was a top-of-the-line StarNav5500, capable of interfacing with any computer on any ship. It was literally the best money could buy... so of course Chad had one. He must have bought it for that fancy new yacht he'd been bragging about the other day. *Consider this my payback for insulting my clan, Chad.*

Without further thought, he slipped it into his pocket and looked up to see Maddy gaping at him.

"You do realize that's stealing, right?"

"I prefer the term 'tactically acquired' myself," he said with a wink. Her vicious smirk would've scared away many a lesser being, but Reggie was made of sterner stuff than most Joongee. He just arched an eyebrow. "Are you done *now*?"

"I don't know, Reg. Anything else you want to *tactically acquire* while we're here?"

He cast an unimpressed gaze around the penthouse. "Naw, I'm good."

* * * * *

Chapter Five

Reggie glared at his slate. He swore time had slowed down. He'd finished the last of his company-mandated quota, and they were down to their final minutes of working in this awful, soul-sucking place. He'd just completed his last call, managed not to reach through the comm and strangle the customer, and now only had to sit through a small eternity of minutes.

He'd already checked on Ed and Harold and knew they were good to go. Maddy was sitting at her desk, frantically working through the last of her tasks. She might have to stay a few minutes later, but he knew she'd finish up her quota, too.

Reggie glanced over at Maddy and snorted. He was wrong. She'd not only finish on time, she might even finish early. He knew when spite was motivating a being, and spite was *absolutely* what was driving that small female right now.

Harold trotted over from the Records area, slate clutched tight in both paws, and a bemused smile on his face. "Have you seen this yet, Reggie?"

"Seen what?"

Ed wandered over from where he'd been patiently waiting for the rest of his clan to finish their day and looked over Harold's shoulder. "Gee, Pops, those are some really fluffy toys. I might have to get one. They look so squishy."

Reggie furrowed his brow in confusion.

Harold tilted his slate so he could see the pictures of neatly displayed stuffed animals in what looked like a closet. "Did you know Chad in Sales has a fantastic stuffed animal collection? It's all over the net. The pink ones in particular are in excellent condition."

Reggie gave Maddy a little side eye, but the sneaky little female kept her head down, supposedly focused on her job. He caught the unholy glee in her purple eyes, though, and had to bite back a grin. Her revenge on Chad had been far subtler and less violent than he'd have ever given her credit for, and he was reluctantly impressed. He lifted his water bottle to her in a silent toast, and her ears flicked once in acknowledgement.

The lift *dinged*, and Reggie glanced over in time to see a furious Chad stride out before the doors were fully opened. His jaw hit the floor as Chad dashed over to their area of the cubicle farm.

"You!" he exclaimed and pointed an accusing finger at Maddy. "I know it was you… somehow, *you* did this!"

It took everything Reggie had not to howl in laughter. The rest of his clan didn't bother to hold back. Ed laughed so hard, he collapsed to the floor, while Harold clutched his slate to his chest and chuckled helplessly. Best of all was Maddy. She cackled and pounded a tiny fist on her desk as tears rolled down her face.

Reggie cleared his throat to divert Chad's attention. He didn't want the other male to get too close to Maddy. Her amusement could turn to defensive rage in a heartbeat if the larger male was stupid enough to physically threaten her.

"That's an interesting color choice, Chad," he said casually. "Did you do it to drive up sales?"

A mad gleam suffused the other male's bloodshot eyes. There were heavy bags under them like he hadn't slept the night before. Chad rounded on Reggie. "Drive *up* sales? This is driving them away! I'm a laughingstock, and it's all *her* fault."

Reggie frowned at Chad and lied with a straight face. "No, it's not. Maddy's been under my supervision for the past two weeks. She couldn't possibly have had anything to do with it."

"Liar! I *know* she did this!" he yelled and indicated his body with both hands. "This isn't even the worst of it! Both my office chair here and the one at home just *happened* to break at the same time. Coincidence?" He jabbed a finger at Maddy again. "I think not. Not only that, but there's something constantly beeping in my penthouse, and it kept me up all night. I didn't sleep a wink! I'm exhausted, despite the four cups of coffee I've had this morning. Five, if you count the one I had to dump down the sink because my sugar container was full of salt!" He turned back to Maddy and spoke through gritted teeth. "I know it was you. I don't know how you got into my penthouse, but I know you did. I know you're responsible for everything, and I also know you stole my StarNav5500. Give it back."

Reggie wrinkled his muzzle and allowed his fangs to slip past his lips. "Be careful with your accusations, *Chad*."

The other male's ears tipped back, an indication he wasn't sure he could take Reggie in a fight. Reggie didn't have to guess. If *Maddy* could nearly strangle him with his own tie, Reggie could wipe the floor with him without breaking a sweat. He held Chad's gaze without blinking.

"Whatever," Chad snarled. "I can afford to buy another one, unlike you fecal stains. Nobody's going to miss you losers. Good riddance."

The furious Joongee turned heel and stalked away, a high-pitched growl trailing after him. The last thing Reggie saw was his lurid tail tip before the lift doors slid closed. He lost it.

"Orange," he said between howls of laughter. "He's *orange*. Maddy, that was glorious."

A sly smile crossed the sneaky female's face. "He is orange, isn't he? How strange."

Reggie chuckled and checked his slate. He shot to his feet. For the first time in years, he could feel it—the call to adventure. A slightly savage grin pulled at his lips, and he looked over his small clan.

"Let's blow this popsicle stand."

Harold tilted his head. "What does that even mean?"

Reggie shrugged. "I saw it in a Human tri-v on the net once. It means let's get the hell out of here!"

Maddy held up one paw and furiously tapped at her station with the other. A few seconds later, she let out a triumphant cry and leapt up from her desk. Her steps slowed as she neared Reggie, and she glanced back over her shoulder once before grinning up at him.

She held two fingers a fraction of an inch apart and said, "Just a little fire? I have a starter kit in my bottom drawer for a special occasion. I think this qualifies."

He snorted and led them out of the office for the last time. "Maybe next time, Maddy." For a moment, he wondered if she was serious, then dismissed the idea. She was obviously joking. Wasn't she?

Harold quickly took the lead after they arrived at the main docking ring on Duncan's Station. "I can't wait to show you our new ship! It's amazing, and I think I got a really good deal for all it offers—"

"She," Ed interrupted and nudged Harold's side. "Ships are called *she*, Pops."

Maddy rolled her eyes. "Stupid tradition, if you ask me."

Reggie shrugged and walked a little faster, hoping the older Joongee would hurry. "Any one of the three I sent you would do the job. Did you go for the Halestorm cutter? It looked like it had decent weapons, even though the shielding would need an upgrade."

Harold shot him a puzzled look over his shoulder. "Why would we need weapons?"

Reggie began to get a bad feeling, and his ears tilted back as he listed off the reasons. "Space pirates, slavers, trigger-happy mercs, greedy government officials...pick one, Harold."

Harold shook his head with a benevolent smile, as if Reggie was a scared pup in need of reassurance. "I think we'll be just fine, Reggie. You worry too much."

Reggie blinked a few times and took a deep breath. By this point he was practically walking on the older Joongee's heels as he led them toward the end of the docking ring. "Okay, so you didn't go with the Halestorm. Did you get the Reaver or the Starset?"

"Neither," Harold replied with a proud grin and grandly gestured out the clear-steel portal inset in the wall. "There it, uh, *she* is. Isn't she beautiful? I had to pay a little more than we originally budgeted for, but they assured me she was worth every credit, and far better than the three you wanted me to look at."

The bottom dropped out of Reggie's stomach, and he groaned.

Maddy shoved past him and scowled. Her voice dripped with venom as she whirled on the older male. "Harold. Please tell me our ship is docked behind that floating piece of space garbage."

Harold's ears flattened in irritation. His tail even twitched with ire as he crossed his arms defensively. "She's not *garbage*. She's got everything we need for our adventure. The nice beings at the shipyard said so."

"Sucker... you are such a sucker. Why did we let *Harold* buy our ship?" Maddy snarled and slammed a paw on the clear-steel portal hard enough to vibrate the metal. "It's painted four different freaking colors! And there are worn-off stickers all over it, like it was used as some sort of delivery shuttle or something. What the hell were you thinking? Never mind. Don't answer that. You weren't thinking. You couldn't have been."

Reggie rubbed the spot between his eyes, but he knew it wouldn't be enough to chase off his impending headache. Maybe he could still salvage this. "Harold, is that ship even space-worthy? The port-side thruster is missing panels, and you can see right inside it. If someone wanted to steal parts, they wouldn't have to try very hard."

"That's intentional," Harold replied. "The sales representative assured me it was a necessary precaution. He said the engine puts out so much power that the thrusters need extra ventilation. And of course it's space-worthy. How else would they have delivered it?"

Reggie sighed. "So, it has a problem with overheating. Great. Send me the purchase paperwork. I need to check for the return clause and see if we can get a better ship."

Harold's muzzle twisted, and he kicked at the deck. "Uh, well, you see, Reggie… they offered to give us a 2 percent discount if I waived the return clause."

Reggie clamped down on the words that wanted to spill out of his mouth. He held onto his patience by his clawtips and quietly said, "So, we can't return it."

It wasn't a question, but Harold answered anyway. "Uh… no."

Maddy slammed a paw into the clear steel again, but Ed just plastered himself to the portal and gazed out at their new ship with wide eyes. "Harold's right, she's *beautiful*."

Maddy gave Ed an incredulous look. "Are you freaking kidding me?" She whirled back to Harold. "Did… did you seriously just spend our credit on this hunk of junk? Please tell me you've finally developed a sense of humor, and this is a joke!"

Harold patted the air down with his paws. "Relax. Just breathe. The interest rate is really low. I talked them down to 37 percent. They assured me we were getting this baby at a steal!"

Maddy let loose a high-pitched shriek. The males all flattened their ears in response. "You have the financial sense of a rotten potato!"

"But Maddy, I got them to agree to coolant refills for life, *and* I got them to throw in all the old mattresses for free," Harold said with a proud smile. "You've got to admit, that's better financial sense than your average potato, rotten or otherwise."

Maddy didn't respond. Her jaw clenched shut, and her whole body shook with rage, but she remained quiet. Probably because if she didn't, she'd say some really horrible things that might cause Harold to have a stroke. She really did have a foul mouth when she wanted to.

Reggie scrubbed his face and blew out a sharp breath. He could deal with this. It was really bad, and it was really going to suck, but he could make it work. "Send me the specs and the ship logs, Harold. We'll have to inspect the ship nose-to-tail before we leave. Then we can work on loading the supplies."

Harold tapped his slate a few times. "Done."

Maddy's demeanor changed in an instant, and she turned a sweet smile on Harold. Every alarm bell Reggie possessed went off, but the older Joongee seemed oblivious.

"Harold," she said in the nicest tone Reggie had ever heard come out of her mouth, "we'll need to register our ship. Have you named her yet?"

Harold brightened as relief plastered itself all over his face, probably because Maddy wasn't yelling at him anymore. "No, I thought we could name her together."

"Oh, please. Allow me! I know you guys have so much to load, but I'm so small, I won't be much help with that," she said with a helpless note to her voice that Reggie didn't buy for an instant. "I can handle all the registration stuff while you big, strong males handle the supplies. I want to contribute equally."

Maddy batted her eyes at Harold, and he patted her head indulgently. "Of course, Maddy. I'll send you the registration forms now."

Reggie bit back a sigh. *Idiot. Not that you don't have this one coming to you.*

As Harold trotted off to the airlock leading to their new ship, he shot out a paw and grabbed her arm. "Keep it clean, Maddy. Nothing that'll get us in trouble."

Maddy blinked up at him, the very picture of innocence. She even patted his paw before gently pulling out of his grasp instead of trying to break it like she normally would have. "Of course, Reggie. I'm not stupid."

"That's what I'm worried about," Reggie muttered as he trailed along behind his clan. His workload had tripled in an instant, and they hadn't even made it off the station yet. He just hoped that bucket of bolts was still capable enough; otherwise, they'd have a much shorter adventure than any of them had counted on.

"Well?" Harold asked a few hours later as he anxiously trailed behind Reggie on his ship inspection.

Ed had mostly gotten in the way and bounced all over the place like a pup in a toy store, while Maddy had point-blank refused to set one paw on the ship until Reggie declared it safe. Every once in a while, he'd check on her, but she was still sitting outside the ship, busily working on the registration. He'd also set her to finding an outgoing ship they could latch onto to cut down their first gate fee… assuming their ship didn't vent atmo the second they got beyond the station.

Reggie scanned the logs again and pinched the bridge of his muzzle. "The engine seems to be okay, I guess, and the powerplant looks solid enough, but I'm not a mechanic or an engineer. I'm just going by the user manual and checking to make sure everything is within the operating parameters. Hopefully no major parts go out because I don't think this model is even made anymore. Finding replacement parts is going to be difficult. There are no shield generators to speak of, zero armaments, the computer system is so old it actually predates what we used at Galactic Solutions—I didn't think that was even possible—and there's only one bathroom, Harold. One."

The older male tilted his head in confusion. "Out of that entire list, it seems like the bathroom is the least important."

"How do you think Maddy is going to react to having to share the head with three males?" Reggie asked dryly.

Harold winced. "Oh."

"Yeah, oh."

Reggie shot him a scathing look. "Also, Harold, this ship doesn't use liquid coolant. It's a bio-recyclant coolant system."

Harold screwed up his face and cocked his head to the side. "What does that mean?"

Ed got excited, nearly bounced out of his seat, and put his hand up in the air like a student in school. "Ooh! Ooh! I know! It uses our poop and pee! It breaks it down and recycles it into the coolant system!"

Reggie shrugged. "Yup, that's basically what it does. It also uses the gray water from when we shower, clean the dishes, do laundry, all that." He turned to face Harold. "So that life-time deal for refilling our coolant was just a way for them to get us back over there so they can take a dump all over us, like they did to you when they conned you into buying this lump of parts."

Harold scratched behind one ear, visibly uncomfortable, and tentatively asked, "Is she going to hold together?"

"Maybe? I think so?" Reggie ran a hand through the tangled mess of fur on his head and down his neck. "Did you even test drive this thing before you bought it? The onboard computer is showing that the starboard engine is only putting out 80 percent thrust, and the port-side engine is only at 25 percent."

"What's wrong with that?" Ed asked from the copilot seat before Harold could answer. "That's like 105 percent. So, it's performing better than perfect."

Reggie looked at Ed as the big oaf stuffed a cheese cracker in his mouth and started chewing with his mouth open. Loudly. Crumbs tumbled to his belly as Ed stared back at him with that same happy expression he always had.

"I can't even right now," Reggie said as he rubbed his temples. He turned his attention back to Harold and added, "To be honest, I'll just be happy if this thing makes it to the gate without exploding."

"Your confidence is overwhelming," Maddy said scathingly from behind him.

Harold jumped, but Reggie, cool and collected as ever, glanced over his shoulder with his eyebrows high. "Finally decided to join us?"

Maddy snickered. "I figured when you didn't die in the first four hours, it was probably safe enough. The registration is complete, and I've got us a ship we can piggyback on. It leaves in three hours."

Reggie felt his eyes bulge. "Three hours! We still have to load all the supplies, plus all our stuff from our apartments!"

"Sounds like a *you* problem," Maddy said with a shrug.

The sneaky little female tried to walk away, but Reggie lunged in front of her. "Where do you think you're going?"

She plastered an innocent expression on her face. "To go grab my gear."

"Oh, no you don't. You're helping us load, Miss 'I'm too small to help.'" Her muzzle wrinkled, but Reggie wasn't having it. Not this time. He held back a sly grin. "Don't worry, I'll only give you the stuff small enough for you to carry. I wouldn't want you to strain yourself or anything."

Maddy snarled. "I can carry whatever you can, jerkface!"

Reggie clapped her on the shoulder. "That's the spirit."

Three hours later, they were fully loaded and ready to go. Reggie brought the engine to life and released the clamps to the docking ring. Before he initiated thrust, he turned to his clan.

"It's 276 light-years to the first clue, we've got a fully functional fusion reactor, six weeks of rations, and we all have new overalls… let's punch it."

Reggie hit the throttle, and the little ship sputtered forward to intercept the hulking cargo ship just beyond the space station. The ship handled better than he'd expected once they picked up speed. They closed in on the cargo ship, and in short order, he had them clamped onto the side, along with a host of other small ships like theirs. Though he was willing to bet none of them were in quite as bad a shape—or as old—and he was pretty sure part of their ship had tumbled off into the black somewhere between the space station and the cargo ship.

On approach, Ed laughed and pointed out the bridge's clear-steel portal to the cargo ship. "That big beastie looks like a mongrel with ticks, and we're a tick! I always wondered what that would feel like."

Maddy blinked at Ed a few times but didn't say anything.

Instead of sitting on the bridge and not being productive, Reggie issued duties to everyone in order to organize the ship. It wouldn't do to live in an unorganized mess for the foreseeable future. He was surprised when Maddy didn't argue with him, or even comment that he wasn't her boss or a real ship captain. She just shrugged and did her part. When it was time to transit through the Bith gate, everyone gathered back on the bridge. They all wanted to see the swirling, opaque portal open up. It was beautiful, no matter how many times you saw it.

Before they entered the gate, Harold turned to Maddy. "What did you name our ship?"

Maddy grinned, purple eyes lit with vicious amusement. "*HI-ADA.*"

Harold's face twisted into a look of confusion. It was quickly replaced with a look of disorientation as they all felt the effects of slipping through the Bith gate and into alter-reality.

* * * * *

Chapter Six

The trip to the Zoological System was a four-day transit. During that time, the small clan spent their time turning *HIADA* into as much of a home as possible, rather than just a dingy old ship.

Ed put his janitorial skills to use and had the whole place spotless. He'd "tactically acquired" some of Galactic Solutions' industrial-strength cleaning products and a few other items. The galley gleamed like it had just been installed, and the floors shined like new. Even the ceiling was clean.

Say what you want about Ed, but none of the rest of us could've gotten this place so clean so fast, Reggie thought as he passed through the common area. Ed was sitting on the couch taking a break, and Reggie clapped him on the shoulder as he passed.

"This place looks amazing, Ed. It's hard to believe it's the same ship as before. If we could get the outside looking like the inside, we'd be in good shape."

"Thanks, Reggie," Ed replied with a kind smile.

The large Joongee had an industrial-sized box of cheese crackers on the coffee table and his ganjaroo vape pen next to it. Reggie chuckled. *It's no wonder he's always in a good mood… and hungry.*

Maddy walked in from the laundry room with an armload of clean towels. She dumped them on the couch next to Ed and began to fold them into perfect rectangles. Each one was the exact same size. She looked up and caught Reggie watching her. Her gaze drifted down to Ed, who was also watching her with a curious expression.

"Take a picture, losers. It'll last longer."

Reggie pointed at the perfect towels. "You, uh, got a thing about towels, Maddy?"

Her brow furrowed, her arms crossed, and she cocked her hips. "Yes, I do. And if I catch any of you just cramming them into the linen storage any which way... I will make you regret it."

The corner of Reggie's mouth lifted. "Aye, aye, queen of the linen. Your wish is my command."

He wanted no part in Maddy's revenge plots. He'd already seen what she was capable of in that regard.

"Why do they have to be folded so neatly?" Ed asked with idle curiosity as he picked up another cracker.

Maddy growled, and her muzzle wrinkled up with what looked like disgust. "It's not about being neat. It's about that stupid linen storage door actually *closing*. I've got a bruise on my hip from the last hundred times I ran into it. So, this is how we're going to fold the towels. You get me?"

Ed shrugged and shoved a cracker in his mouth. "Works for me." He stood, took the box of crackers back to the galley, and came back out with a bucket of cleaning supplies. "I'm going to go try to get more of the ship cleaned up before we exit alter-reality. Can you let me know before we do, Reggie? I want to watch."

Reggie gave him a nod and smiled. "Sure will, Ed. Thanks again for getting this place so clean. If you need me, I'll be down in engineering again."

Maddy snorted as she plopped another perfectly folded towel down on the pile. "Seems like you live down there. Sure, you're not just hiding from basic housekeeping? Even Harold is being useful and putting together all our bedroom furniture. Thank the gods my bed fits in there. And Ed is a saint for how clean he got it before my stuff went in."

"Positive," Reggie replied dryly. "Someone has to learn how to keep this tub flying. I'm trying to learn all I can about the engine, powerplant, and the programming. That way, if there's an issue, we won't just be helplessly drifting in space." He sighed and crossed his arms. "We should look into getting a small replicator to make replacement parts for the ship. We can probably find a used one fairly cheap. Once we have access to the net again, I'll look for one. In the meantime, let's just hope nothing breaks down."

"Whatever," Maddy grumbled as she snatched up the next towel with a quick jerk of her claws. "Don't think you're going to get out of your turn to cook dinner."

Reggie winced. "Maybe we should make that Harold's permanent duty. You know, if you want anything edible. The rest of us suck."

"At least he's good for something," she said with a snort. "I still can't believe he bought this hunk of crap-cooled garbage."

"If it wasn't for Harold, we'd still be sitting on our tails in cubicle-farm hell at Galactic Solutions," he reminded her with a frown. "Cut him some slack."

Maddy heaved a sigh, but she nodded and went back to folding towels. Reggie ran a tired paw through his tangled mane and headed for the hatch. He hadn't remembered adventure being this much work. Of course, the last time he'd been adventuring, he'd done it with an established mercenary company. He'd only been a single part of a dedicated team of beings, not the leader, and he found himself with a newfound respect for his old commander. He'd never understood how much had fallen on the leader's shoulders before this.

"Reggie," she called after him. He glanced back to see her ears flicker once before settling into their normal irritated slant. "I'll see about finding us a used replicator."

Reggie gave her a slight smile and headed down to the engine room. Maybe they'd make a good team after all.

Several hours later, they were all sitting on the bridge and staring out the portal as the emergence countdown hit zero. They all groaned, shook their heads, and fought the odd sensation as they entered normal space in the Zoological System. Reggie contacted the cargo ship and thanked them for the ride before detaching from its hull and heading toward the Zoo.

There were two primary traffic routes in the Zoological System—one for the contractors, vendors, and planetary employees, and one for paying customers. While vast swaths of acreage on both the third and fourth planets had been devoted to food management for the zoo animals, significant amounts of supplies and equipment still needed to be imported on a daily basis, and the traffic on the first route was constant but well-managed.

The second route for tourists was downright insane. The Zoo, located on the fourth planet from the sun, was completely devoted to the conservation of animals from all over the galaxy, and was a major tourist attraction. The massive planet once had a different name, but the government located on the smaller third planet had renamed it the Zoo long ago.

Even parts of the oceans were sectioned off in places and used to hold some of the aquatic life that couldn't survive long-term in the enclosures.

"Wow," Ed said with wonder. "That's a lot of traffic."

Maddy groaned with irritation. "It's going to take forever to get there in this piece of crap."

Reggie shot her a look, and the small female let out a slow breath.

"I mean, it's going to take forever to get there with all that traffic," she amended through gritted teeth. "Obviously."

Ed's tail swished eagerly, and he grinned. "We could always play a game to pass the time! I Spy, Guess the Ship, Alphabet Soup…"

Maddy hid her face in her hands. "Oh, gods, make it stop."

Reggie bit back a smile. "That's a great idea, Ed, but maybe Harold should go over his research again so we can build a plan of attack."

Ed's face screwed up into a worried frown as Harold dashed off the bridge. "Who are we attacking?"

"It's just an expression, Ed," he replied with a reassuring smile.

Harold rushed back onto the bridge with his slate clutched in his paws and a wide grin on his face. "Maddy, would you be a dear and pull up the system map on the display?"

Maddy, who was seated at the outdated nav station, heaved a sigh and did as he asked. The image flickered until the irate female slammed her tiny fist down onto the panel. The use of percussive engineering resolved the issue, and the image stabilized.

Reggie sighed. *Yet another system that needs to be upgraded…*

"Zoom in on the Zoo, please," Harold said, head down as he tapped at something on his slate.

Maddy zoomed in far enough to center the image on the third and fourth planets.

"How do you know the next clue is on the Zoo? How do you know we don't need to go to…" Maddy trailed off as she scanned the data for the third planet and rolled her eyes. "Seriously, they named their homeworld Zookeeper?"

Harold looked up from his slate and cleared his throat. "While it's certainly possible the next clue is on Zookeeper, I believe it'll be located within the Koroth sector of the Zoo."

Maddy rolled her eyes. "Just about every planet in this part of the galaxy has a sector on the Zoo. It's nothing special."

Reggie arched an eyebrow. "She's not wrong. That's not much to go on, Harold."

"Ah," the older Joongee said and raised one finger high, "but I happen to know Dr. Bergan Monschtackle personally sponsored one of the exhibits. The kinkakaijou was his grandson's favorite animal, and it remains a popular exhibit to this day."

Harold turned his slate so the others could see the small, golden-furred animal on the screen. Roughly the size of a Human's housecat, the four-legged beast had a long, prehensile tail with a tuft of fur at the end, large hazel eyes, and an odd mane around its neck. On closer inspection, Reggie realized the mane was made up of thin, fur-covered tentacles. It hung upside-down from a branch, and its head was twisted much further around than most vertebrates could manage.

It was an oddly cute and vaguely disturbing animal.

"What the *hell* is that thing?" Maddy demanded.

"A kinkakaijou," Harold said slowly, as if speaking to a young child. "They're native to Koroth, but much of their natural habitat was destroyed when the Lost Weapons were deployed in battle before they were fully operational. The troop at the Zoo are some of the last in existence."

Ed snatched the slate right out of Harold's paws. He ignored the older Joongee's squawk of surprise and pressed his face close to the screen. "She's so cute! I want one. Please, can we get one? Every ship needs a mascot, Pops."

Harold cleared his throat and gently took his slate back. "Yes, well, as I said, they're nearly extinct. I don't believe the Zoo is selling them in the gift shop."

Reggie snorted at the joke, but he trailed off when he realized Harold was dead serious. He sighed. "So, we need to go poke around the kinkakaijou exhibit and hope we can find the next clue. That about right, Harold?"

"Exactly! How hard can it be?"

"Please don't say things like that, Harold," Reggie replied with a groan and flattened his ears. "That's just asking the universe to mess with us."

They crept along at the slowest speed their ship could go—which was pretty slow by any standard—and inched along in the traffic lane. At the rate they were going, it would be another few hours before they even got to the planet, let alone the additional travel time to get to the Koroth sector.

"Are we there yet?" Ed asked with a bright smile.

Reggie rubbed at that spot between his eyes again. "Gonna be a while, buddy."

"Great! Now we can play some travel games," he said with his tail lashing in excitement.

Maddy whimpered. "Please, kill me now."

* * * * *

Chapter Seven

"Can we go see some of the other animals while we're here?" Ed asked after they landed. He had his muzzle buried in a brochure of all the different creatures housed on the planet. "There are so many cool animals here. I want to see them all!"

Reggie shrugged on his backpack after collecting it from the security officer. "That would take a while. I think I read that only a handful of beings have managed to see every exhibit in one visit. It took them over a month. There's a reason the Zoo has so many hotels and long-term docking. That being said, I wouldn't mind seeing some of the aquatic stuff. I love aquariums."

"I want to see some of the carnivore feeding times," Maddy said with a bloodthirsty glint in her eyes. "You think they kill the feeder animal before, or do the predators get to hunt?"

"We're on a mission!" Harold exclaimed with an air of urgency. The other three looked at him like he'd gone insane. It was very unlike him to be so antsy. "Don't lose focus, everyone. We have to get to the Koroth exhibit and find the clue at the kinkakaijou. We don't have time to dawdle."

Reggie raised a single eyebrow at the older Joongee. "It's not a race, Harold. It's fine. We have time to see a few things. We spent a lot of credit, time, and effort to get here. None of us have ever had the opportunity to visit the Zoo, so we're not going to waste it."

"Yeah, Pops," Ed agreed. "Adventures are supposed to be fun, not all rushed and stuffy with a whole schedule planned out."

"Stop sucking all the joy out of the Zoo," Maddy added with a menacing glare. "I want to see predators fed. Besides, you kind of owe us for screwing up on *HIADA* so badly. We want to have fun, so that's what we're going to do."

Harold let out a defeated sight. "Fine, but can we at least agree to only spend one day here?"

"That's fair," Reggie agreed with a nod. "We don't really have the extra credit to spend on additional admissions anyway. This place is expensive. I'm afraid to see what the food costs. That's where theme parks really get you. The food and souvenirs."

As they entered the park, a massive holographic advertisement caught their attention.

Come see the all-new Earth exhibit and meet our beautiful new clan of hyenas! You're sure to fall in love with our gorgeous alpha female, who rules supreme in this small matriarchy! Photo opportunities and meet-and-greet tickets sold at the exhibit entrance.

The message was followed by a short video of six four-legged animals from Earth. They were a brownish-tan color with light spots. Their muzzles were short on their stubby heads, and they had rounded ears that came to a point at the top. They were obviously carnivorous predators, with their sharp teeth and clawed paws.

"Huh," Ed grunted with a puzzled tilt to his head. "They look like us."

One of the hyenas, presumably the alpha female, snapped at one of the males who got too close, and he scurried away with his tail tucked.

Ed laughed. "Look, Maddy. She's even mean like you!"

"I am not mean!"

All the males stopped and looked at her. Her ears twitched, and her jaw tightened.

"I'm *not*," Maddy snapped. "And we look nothing like them. Do you walk around on all fours and poop in the woods, Ed?"

"Plains," Ed replied.

"Huh?"

Ed pointed at the holo. "It says they're from the plains of Africa on Earth. So, they poop on the plains."

Maddy shook her head in exasperation. "Fine. The plains then. Still doesn't change the fact we don't look like that."

"I dunno," Reggie said. He had his head cocked to the side as he studied the hyenas. "That's a pretty strong resemblance."

"Oh, really?" Maddy said with an evil gleam in her purple eyes and a sly grin on her face. "If we're so alike, then that means I should be the one in charge of this little escapade, doesn't it?"

Reggie's eyes shot wide, and he turned to face her. "You know, now that I've had a moment of further reflection, you're right. We don't look anything alike."

Maddy snorted in satisfaction. "Didn't think so."

"But we do," Ed argued as he dipped a chinto tail into his pudding cup.

"Shut up, Ed," Reggie muttered under his breath as he pushed Ed along. "Do you want Maddy running the show?"

Ed seemed to finally get the gist of it. "Oh."

Maddy gagged as he shoved the whole chinto tail into his mouth and chewed loudly. "Seriously, Ed, that's such a waste of good chocolate. Are you sure you're not pregnant, because that's something a pregnant female would eat."

Ed chewed thoughtfully. "No, I've never done that before."

"You've... never been pregnant before?" Harold asked slowly, a look of absolute befuddlement on his face.

"Nope," he replied as he dipped another chinto tail into his pudding.

Maddy opened her mouth, but Reggie nudged her side and got them moving again. "Let it go. Ed, buddy, I have no idea how you aren't four hundred pounds with the way you eat."

"It's all the ganjaroo," Maddy muttered with a roll of her eyes.

The four Joongee steadily worked their way through the crowd. They finally made it past the massive visitor's center and into the Zoo proper. Reggie was surprised to see the others all look toward him.

"Well?" Maddy demanded after a beat of silence. "Where to first?"

Reggie really wanted to say the aquarium, but the tyranabbit feeding time was coming up, and there were a bunch of interesting animals between them and the closest aquatic exhibit. It wouldn't be right to skip all that just because he was impatient.

"How about we go see the targanveetra first? Then we can check out the tyranabbit. It says in the brochure it only eats live prey," he said with a grin for his bloodthirsty little female.

Maddy's ears perked forward, and her tail swished happily. She punched a tiny fist into the air. "Yes!"

"After that, we can hit up the sea life and aquatic area," Reggie said, for once not bothering to hold back his excited grin. He turned his attention to Harold and added, "If there's anything you want to see, Harold, just speak up."

Harold grumbled, and his ears angled backward. "The only thing I want to see is the kinkakaijou exhibit. But... I'll try not to suck all the joy out of our adventure."

Maddy looked as if she were holding back an inappropriate comment, and Reggie shook his head quickly. The older Joongee was oblivious, as always, and there was no sense riling him up.

They quickly made for the trolley station and hopped on the one headed in the direction of the targanveetra habitat. There were hundreds of different trollies running through the park. There were even aircraft to take you to the other continents. With a zoo spanning the entirety of a planet, motorized transportation was an absolute necessity.

The targanveetra turned out to be less than exciting. The lumbering, six-legged beasts, with their massive, elongated heads and big, puffy lips, were perfectly designed grazing herbivores. However, it seemed all the gray-skinned beasts did was feed on the lush grasses in their field, or occasionally low-hanging leaves or fruits. Reggie's muzzle wrinkled as the closest targanveetra defecated near the fence while its short, stubby tail acted to keep the droppings from hitting its legs. Before the breeze could bring the stench to his nose, a compact robot buzzed out of a hidden underground access port and removed the pile.

According to the holo info plaque, targanveetra manure made some of the best fertilizer in the galaxy. Not only was it used to fertilize the system's vast fields necessary to support the resident animals, it was also sold at a premium to farmers all over the galaxy.

Reggie glanced from the slow-moving beasts to his clan. Maddy's eyes had glazed over, Harold's tail was twitching in barely restrained impatience, and even Ed's enthusiasm was faltering.

He bit back a laugh. "Ready to move on?"

"Gods, yes," Maddy breathed out.

"Yes, please," Harold said fervently.

Ed tilted his head as another robot emerged to vacuum up another deposit. "Maybe just a few more minutes?"

"No!" all three shouted in a chorus.

* * *

"Oh, come on, Reg. You said this was a carnivore feeding." Maddy whined as she leaned up against the fencing. She tried to figure out what she was looking at when a Human child ran up next to her. "This can't be a tyranabbit."

"Mommy, Mommy! Look! They have bunnies here, too!"

"Well, what do you know?" the child's mother said as she walked up to join them. "I guess some animals exist on multiple planets."

"It's so cute!" the child shouted as she bounced in place in excitement.

Maddy wasn't sure what the fuss was all about. The thing was small, white, fluffy, and hopped around on its back legs. There wasn't anything all that impressive about it. Though, she had to admit, there was something about it that screamed adorable.

She shot Reggie an irritated glare. "A bunny?"

"The brochure said it was a tyranabbit," Reggie replied when the Humans stopped being so loud. "Maybe it's a typo."

Maddy glanced away from the cute little animal in disappointment. "Hey... where'd the others go?"

Reggie shrugged. "Ed and Harold said they'd meet us at the aquarium. They didn't want to see the slaughter."

"What slaughter?" Maddy grumbled as she glared at the bunny. "They're not missing anything."

A small rodent popped its head out of a small, camouflaged tube protruding from the ground and scampered out toward a piece of bread in the bunny's enclosure. When it stopped to grab its prize, the bunny reared back on its hind legs and screeched. The two Joongee flattened their ears automatically, while the Humans clamped their hands over their ears a beat later.

The bunny's chest parted to reveal a blood-red interior pocket. A translucent red membrane shot out and engulfed the rodent. The membrane retracted, and the bunny's chest cavity closed again. The screeching cut off abruptly as the bunny dropped back down to all fours and resumed hopping around the enclosure.

A scream of horror escaped the young Human girl. The two Joongee watched as her mother quickly scooped her up and carried her away, leaving a trail of wails and tears.

Maddy slowly looked back at the cute little animal with wide eyes. The overhead speaker came to life and said:

"Welcome to the tyranabbit enclosure. Tyranabbits closely resemble the cute and cuddly bunnies from Earth, but they are anything but harmless. Hidden within their chest is a membrane that will lash out and catch unsuspecting prey. Once caught, the prey is slowly digested alive over a matter of days. It is a slow and gruesome way to go, but nature knows no boundaries. All of this makes the tyranabbit a cute but deadly addition to Galactic Zoo. Don't forget to schedule a meet-and-greet and have your picture taken with the tyranabbit!"

An admiring grin broke out across Maddy's face, and she eyed the tyranabbit with newfound respect. *Now that's one savage bunny!*

"Huh," Reggie grunted, the barest hint of awe in his tone. "I guess it wasn't a typo after all. That was pretty awesome."

A tall Human male walked up and stood behind Reggie with an impressed look on his face. Maddy's ear twitched as he let out a low whistle.

"That thing scared the bejeezus out of my daughter. I thought it was cool as hell." He snorted, and one corner of his mouth rose in a half grin. "I guess your chances of being killed by a bunny are low, but never zero."

He watched the tyranabbit hop around as if it were nothing more than a harmless bunny, chuckled, shook his head, and walked back to his wife and daughter. The little girl still had a terrified look on her face, but the ice cream bar in her hand seemed to have calmed her down. Maddy eyed her treat with interest. *Oooh. Chocolate. I wonder if it comes in coffee flavor?*

* * *

Reggie sat on a bench in the cool, dark room. Waves of blue light danced along the walls and across his face and body. Aquariums always soothed his soul, especially the big ones you could actually sit inside as all the oceanic life swam around you. Something about the experience quieted the storms within his mind. Nobody understood how hard it was to not lose his temper and keep it all together. It was a constant battle. Working for Galactic Solutions had been the worst of it. Since they'd left, he'd felt like some of the pressure was gone, though the constant anger was still there. But not right then, not as he sat there in complete serenity under the life of the ocean.

In that moment, the thunder and lightning ceased, the clouds melted away, and it was all replaced by a feeling of peace and serenity. It wasn't often he was able to feel that relief, so he made it a point to appreciate the moments when they came. This particular moment was better than all the others before. He'd never in his life seen an aquarium as magnificent as the Zoo's.

The room he was in was no smaller than a warball field and completely surrounded by water on all sides and above. It was like they were in a glass bubble at the bottom of an ocean, which wasn't far from the truth. Above and around him, all types of creatures swam, floated, and jetted by. Best of all, every one of the guests seemed to understand this was a place of calm and stayed quiet. Reggie sat there for a long while before getting up to go see his favorite part of aquatic exhibits.

Jellyfish.

Jellyfish were his absolute favorite creatures in the galaxy. They had many different names on multiple worlds, but he preferred the Human term. To him, they seemed like the most chilled out animal ever. Their tentacles just sort of drifted behind them as they rode the currents. The jellies didn't even have to work for their meals—food literally swam into their grasp. Watching them was another part of aquariums that never failed to silence the riot within him.

"Whooooa," Ed said in awe as he stepped up next to Reggie. This particular tank was full of translucent jellyfish, and the backlight constantly changed colors. The light effect caused the jellies to appear to change color, too. "Trippy."

"Yeah, I love this place," Reggie said with a quiet intensity. Ed looked down at him with an odd expression. His ears flickered. "What?"

"This place is special to you, huh?"

Reggie raised an eyebrow. "Why do you say that?"

He wondered if maybe he'd let too much of his emotions show in front of everyone.

"You just seem, I dunno, at peace or something." Ed shrugged. "Like, I know you're wound pretty tight most of the time. You don't want us all to know it, but I can tell. But down here—" he waved a hand at the jellies and toward the big observation bubble "—you look relaxed and calm."

Reggie ears flattened as he cleared his throat and stood a little straighter. The storms started to circle in his mind again. He hadn't realized it had been so obvious. It wouldn't do for the rest of the clan to think he was fighting an internal battle all the time. They might lose confidence in him. He couldn't be like Maddy and lash out all the time. He had to maintain control.

The corner of Ed's mouth lifted in a half smile. He'd obviously noticed the change in Reggie's demeanor. "Don't worry, Reggie. Maddy and Harold don't see it. Maddy thinks you don't have an angry bone in your body, and Harold is more spaced out than me."

The larger Joongee patted Reggie on the arm. The affectionate gesture would've knocked Reggie to the side if he didn't keep his weight balanced as a matter of habit. Reggie tried to force his ears to relax, but they stubbornly remained tilted backward, broadcasting his distress to anyone paying attention. He desperately tried to regain the calm the aquarium had given him.

"Don't stress it. I can just see the difference, that's all." Ed shrugged his massive shoulders. "We all have our special places we like to retreat to. This is yours."

Reggie went to speak, but Ed cut him off. "Oh, and your secret is safe with me. Maddy doesn't need any more ammunition than she already has to mess with all of us." Ed took another look at the jellyfish.

"I like these guys. They just… chill. I'm all about that. Anyway, I'm going to catch up to Maddy and Harold. Take your time and don't rush. The kinkakaijou aren't going anywhere, even if Harold thinks they are."

A big grin crossed Reggie's face, and his ears stood back up on their own. The tension flooded out of his back and shoulders as he relaxed. "Thanks, Ed."

Ed didn't say anything. He just smiled and nodded as he stared at the jellies, then walked toward the exit. Reggie turned back to his jellies, a relaxed smile still on his face.

* * * * *

Chapter Eight

After several hours and three nervous breakdowns from Harold, the clan decided they'd only look at the animals on the way to the kinkakaijou exhibit. There was much more they all wanted to see, but there were only so many hours in the day, and they *did* have a mission to accomplish.

Maddy was completely enamored with the gorkival. They were an avian species with bright, multi-colored feathers and short, red bills. Their most unique feature was their tongue, which shot out and speared smaller animals in the water or in the grass with a barbed spike on the end.

Even Harold, despite his eagerness to move on, stopped at a particular enclosure. It was for a most visually disturbing animal—the araztic. Creepy didn't even begin to describe the twelve-legged insectoid. They came in all shades of brown and green, and they had nine eyes, one large one at the center surrounded by eight smaller ones. The plaque on the wall indicated it fed on whatever smaller animals it could catch. The araztic would latch onto its prey with two long fangs and grind them into mush with the smaller teeth in the mouth on its underside.

However, that wasn't even the most disturbing thing they came across. That title went to the sorvenire, a long, legless, scaled creature with four eyes. Though they started out as tiny creatures, each had the potential to reach up to six feet in length and eight inches in girth. It wasn't their appearance that was disturbing, though—it was their feeding and breeding methods.

The sorvenire would bite their prey and wait for the venom to melt their meal from the inside out. After the poor creature was sufficiently melted, they'd use their hollow tongue like a straw to slurp up the soup through one of the puncture wounds created by their fangs.

According to the plaque, the breeding habits of the sorvenire played a vital role in its natural habitat. Most of the native scavenger species had been hunted to extinction, and the sorvenire was one of the last creatures that fed on rotting carcasses. They'd lay their eggs within dead animals so the hatchlings would have something to eat when they hatched. Though there was no scientific proof to support the theory, there was a popular rumor that they were also constrictors and had killed animals in this manner for the sole purpose of laying their eggs within them. One of the plaques had a rather graphic depiction of a sorvenire slithering in through the mouth of a large herbivore and down the throat.

Even Maddy was disturbed by that one.

Finally, after a long day tramping around the zoo—and only seeing a tiny fraction of what it had to offer—the four Joongee made it to the kinkakaijou exhibit. By that point, Harold was practically vibrating with impatience and dashed ahead through the wide entrance. The exhibit was the kind beings could walk through on a looping path that allowed them to get as close to the animals as they'd allow.

As they walked along the trail, a shockingly-loud, haunting cry echoed through the treetops.

"What the hell." Maddy's hackles stood up as she looked around warily. "I thought these things were tiny. That didn't sound tiny, Harold."

Harold smiled. "The males have throat pouches they can fill with air to make sounds entirely disproportional to their size. Isn't it marvelous?"

"Yeah, super marvelous," she muttered.

Reggie glanced up at the drooping branches of the overarching trees and watched them shiver as a troop of kinkakaijou bounded away. He only managed to catch flashes of golden fur through the leaves but had no problem hearing their chittering cries. He flattened his ears at the shrill screech of one smaller animal as it was left behind. The tiny thing scrambled after its brethren and disappeared into the foliage. Silence fell over the small enclosure.

"Doesn't look like they want to be watched today."

"It would appear not," Harold said as he hurried over to the plaque midway down the path. "But this is why we're really here."

The older Joongee pulled an actual handkerchief from his pocket and wiped the plaque clean. Up at the top right of the plaque was an image of Dr. Bergan Monschtackle. Reggie studied the image closely. Korothians apparently weren't too different from the Humans they'd seen at the tyranabbit exhibit. If not for the horizontal pupils, lack of eyebrows, and the bright red ridge that ran down the Korothian's nose bridge, they could've been the same species. Beneath his image, the plaque read:

The absurdly generous donation from Dr. Bergan Monschtackle has enabled the Galactic Zoo to continue its conservation of the critically endangered kinkakaijou. The good doctor's love for the animal was enough to convince him to donate enough credit in their honor that the animals will never know hunger or fear of poaching. The kinkakaijou you see before you are among the last in the galaxy and serve as a living example of the tragedies and unexpected consequences of war.

Without the love and contributions of Dr. Bergan Monschtackle, it is likely they would have already gone extinct.

"How could he have made a contribution large enough to last thousands of years' worth of food and shelter?" Maddy asked with a puzzled tilt to her head. "That just doesn't add up."

Harold raised a hand in the air. "Do you really think he only donated credit, Maddy?"

She gave him an incredulous look. "Duh. Love and sunshine don't put food in your belly, Harold."

"True enough," Harold replied with what Reggie called his teaching expression, "but while he donated millions in credit, he did far more than that—he donated the royalties from his children's books and the patents for his inventions in perpetuity. He even donated the interest from some investments he made." He pointed up to the tree. "These little kinkakaijou are among some of the richest animals in the entire galaxy. Monschtackle made sure the Zoo owners couldn't touch the credit flow for anything other than the kinkakaijou exhibit and their wellbeing. The good doctor had an excellent contract lawyer."

"He wrote children's books?" Maddy asked as her ears perked forward in interest.

"Yes," Harold answered with a triumphant grin. "They were a key part in putting the initial letter together. However, they were very hard to track down because he didn't publish under his real name. You were my inspiration for figuring out that little detail, Maddy. I remembered that you publish urban fantasy shifter erotica under a pen name, and that made me realize that he would have never made it so easy for someone to find the clues hidden in his books. It took a few years of research, and the reading of hundreds of random children's books, but I finally found the right series—*The Adventures of the Red Herring Pirates*."

Maddy's eyes went wide, her ears pinned back, and her jaw dropped. She shook herself violently and snapped her teeth at the older Joongee. "Harold!"

Reggie and Ed looked at her with smirks on their faces.

"Not a word out of you two!" She whirled back on Harold. "That was supposed to be a secret!"

Harold's hand shot to his mouth, and his tail drooped in shame. "Oh, I-I'm sorry, Maddy. I got so caught up in the excitement that it just slipped."

"Maddy's an author?" Ed asked, his eyes bright. "That's so cool! Good job, Maddy. I hope you sell a ton."

Maddy's anger seemed to wither away, and her ears rose a bit. "Um, thanks. They do okay."

"Ed's right," Reggie said with a firm nod. "That's really cool. When all this is over, I'll have to check out your series." He gave her a smile and a wink before turning back to Harold. "What about Monschtackle's kids? He didn't leave them anything?"

Harold rolled his eyes and sighed. "Do you really think he was able to leave so much for the kinkakaijou and not have other assets to leave his descendants? Come now, Reggie. That's just silly talk."

"Right. That's silly talk," Reggie deadpanned. "Not this whole treasure hunt thing. Got it."

"Exactly," Harold said and went back to the plaque. Below the information about Monschtackle and his contributions to the Zoo was a statement from the doctor himself.

It is with great joy and with no lack of pride that I make this donation to the kinkakaijou exhibit with the Galactic Zoo. These amazing creatures have always been my favorite, as well as that of my children and grandchildren. It gives me great satisfaction to know that, for as long as the Galactic Zoo exists, so will the kinkakaijou. One can always run to the Mall of Malls and grab a stuffed one, but nothing compares to the real thing. I feel in large part responsible for their NEAR EXTINCTION, and hope that in saving them, I can repay a fraction of the debt I owe my people. I hold onto the hope that the conservation efforts of this fine institution will bring their numbers back to the point they can be released into the wild again once the forests on my beloved Koroth recover. Their extinction to me would be like buying a puzzle with missing pieces. The galaxy just wouldn't seem whole.

Ed frowned at the plaque. "Did any of them ever get to go home?"

Harold shook his head slowly. "No. The forests on Koroth still haven't recovered. The trees might never grow again."

The four Joongee fell silent for a moment. Ed's ears drooped. "That's really sad. I mean, it's nice that you can get a stuffed one at the Mall of Malls, but that's just not the same."

"That's it!" Harold exclaimed loudly, causing the others to jump in alarm. "We have to go to the Mall of Malls!"

He pulled his slate out and took a picture of the plaque.

"Oooh," Maddy cooed and rubbed her paws together. "A shopping trip!"

"No," Reggie said firmly and stabbed a claw at her. "Our credit line is tapped out. All the extra credit we have is for whatever we need to find the rest of the clues. If you go spending all our credit on shoes and purses, I swear I'll hide all your coffee."

Maddy locked her hands behind her back, bent slightly at the waist, and looked up at him with the sweetest, most devious look he'd ever seen. Her lips parted into an evil little smile. "Do you really want to start a war with me, little pup? Because that's how you start a war with me."

Reggie narrowed his eyes and didn't let his expression falter, despite the trepidation in his gut. He couldn't back down from her, or she'd walk all over him. "I'm not starting a war, Maddy, but I promise you, if you want a war, I'll win."

The two Joongee stepped closer to each other until their chests brushed up against each other's.

"If you thought what I did to Chad was bad, just wait until I'm caffeine deprived," she said with a warning growl.

Reggie tilted his muzzled down arched a brow down at the smaller female. "No spending credit we don't have, and I won't hide your coffee. Simple."

Maddy narrowed her brilliant purple eyes, but he could see her amusement, too. She was having fun. "Hide my coffee, and I'll rip out your spine and use it to clean the toilet."

Reggie nearly lost it at that one, but somehow managed to keep the laughter out of his expression. He had to admit, her threats were certainly creative.

"Enough squabbling, you two," Harold said as he abruptly shoved his way between them. He flailed his arms like a grandpa tired of his pups bickering. "We need to pack it up and head back to *HIADA*." He gave Maddy a quizzical look. "I still haven't figured out what that means."

Maddy gave him a sly grin, her battle with Reggie momentarily forgotten. "And here I thought you were a historian, Harold! I promise it has historical significance. Would you like me to give you a hint?"

"No! I'll figure it out myself, just you wait, Maddy. I'm a very good historian, you know. I'll just have to expand my search into different areas of interest." Harold walked toward the park's exit, his tail lashing in excitement. "Come on, you three. We've got treasure to find!"

* * *

"I'll catch up!" Ed shouted to the others as they stepped outside the enclosure. "I want to try to see one of these kinkakaijou things. I think the one chasing after the others is still down here somewhere."

"Okay," Reggie replied. "Just don't take too long, or we'll get charged credit for a second day. We'll see you back up at the front."

"Cool."

Ed waited for them to get further away before sitting down on the bench beneath the large limb of the sprawling kinkakaijou trees. While patrons could walk through the exhibit, there were tall fences that kept the animals safely inside. This particular tree, however, was taller than the enclosure, and several branches overshadowed the bench. If the kinkakaijou truly wanted to escape, they probably could.

Ed figured since the enclosure was all they'd ever known, though, they probably didn't want to get out because it was their home. However, he'd noticed something earlier when the others were all talking.

He pulled a bag from his pocket and poured out a handful of crackers. Ed placed the crackers in a small pile next to him on the bench and scooted back from it by about a foot. "You can come down if you want."

A slight rustle of leaves answered him.

"It's okay," he crooned with a gentle smile. "I won't hurt you. I saw how the others were being mean to you and left you all alone. You can come sit with me if you want. I got some snacks if you're hungry."

A small head popped out from a leaf cluster. Big, bright, hazel eyes looked down on him with curiosity. The small kinkakaijou who hadn't been able to keep up with the others earlier slowly emerged. Ed decided, based on its size and delicate features, that it must be a female. Her golden-furred tentacles twitched nervously around her neck as she gripped the limb with her hands and feet. Behind her, a prehensile tail flicked back and forth as she appeared to be considering her options.

"There you are," Ed said in an inviting voice. He motioned to the crackers. "All yours, if you want them."

The kinkakaijou stared at him for another long minute before hunger apparently overcame fear. She leapt from the tree limb and landed next to him on the back of the bench. Cautiously, she slid down and sat next to the cracker pile. Without taking her eyes off Ed, she selected the topmost cracker and took a bite. The little kinkakaijou apparently liked the cracker, because her eyes grew even bigger, and she shoved the rest of the cracker straight into her mouth.

Ed peeked under the kinkakaijou while it was preoccupied with the crackers. "I was right! You *are* a female. I'll call you Boo."

Boo looked up at him, cocked her head to the side, and blinked.

"Do you like that name?"

Boo made a happy chittering sound and went back to her crackers, seemingly fine with the appointed name. After finishing off the last cracker, she sat back on her haunches and cleaned her paws off with her tongue. She turned to run back to the enclosure but stopped at the edge of the bench. Ed thought she appeared hesitant.

"What's the matter? Don't wanna go back?"

The kinkakaijou turned back to face him. To Ed's surprise, she scooted closer to him and sat down again. She looked up at him with the saddest eyes. It really did seem like she was hesitant to go back.

"Do they always treat you like that? Are they mean to you? Like, do they pick on you and steal food from you and stuff?"

Another chitter brought a smile to Ed's face.

"I'd swear you can understand me if I didn't know any better." He scratched the top of his head. "If that's what's going on in there, I know how you feel. My old clan used to make fun of me all the time. They called me stupid, dumb, idiot, moron, and all kinds of stuff. They always liked to point out all the stuff I did wrong, even when I did something right or did nice things for them. I'm pretty sure they stole my stuff, too. I had lots of things go missing, and my credit always seemed to be lower than it should be."

He looked down to see Boo had scooted even closer to him.

"Anyway, that doesn't happen anymore. I left that clan a long time ago. I have a new clan now. A better clan. We actually care about each other. Even Maddy, though she'll never admit it." He gave Boo a sad smile. "But you can't do that, can you? This group of kinkakaijou are all that's left in the galaxy. They're all you have."

Suddenly, Boo jumped into his lap and rose up on her hind legs so she was face to face with him. She placed her little hands on the sides of his muzzle and looked into his eyes. Even her tentacles reached out and felt his face. It tickled a bit, but Ed remained still.

"See? I won't hurt you. I'm your friend."

Boo climbed up his chest, onto his shoulder, and started grooming the fur on his head and neck.

"Hopefully you don't find anything to eat in there. I try to take pretty thorough showers."

To his dismay, Boo pulled a small bug off his neck and ate it.

"That must've landed on me sometime today. I swear I'm clean."

In a flash, Boo shot down from his shoulder, through the open top of his overalls, and curled up into a ball against his belly. Seconds later, he could both hear and feel her purring. The sensation tickled and made him laugh. He leaned back and gently patted her through his overalls, but after a short time, he sat back up with a sigh.

"Come on, Boo, time for you to go back. I can't stay all day. I have to meet back up with my clan."

He unzipped his overalls to find Boo sleeping peacefully on his lap. She'd managed to wrap up in the bottom of his t-shirt like it was a blanket. He gently slipped his hand under her and lifted her up. Her big eyes blinked open, and she gave him a sleepy smile as she wrapped her tentacles around his hand. Ed stood up on the bench and lifted her up toward the tree limb.

"Here you go. Back home now."

She looked up at the tree, and her entire body drooped. Her tentacles fell slack, her shoulders slumped, and her tail hung limp. Boo turned to look at him, and Ed could see the sadness in her eyes. She was unhappy there.

"Is it that bad?"

Boo ran down the length of his arm and nuzzled the side of his face. She chittered sadly in his ear before scurrying back down into his overalls. Excited, she popped her head out, ducked, then repeated the process twice more.

"Are you trying to tell me to hide you in my overalls so you can leave like when I left my old clan?"

She answered him by grabbing the zipper of his overalls and tugging it upward.

Ed grinned at her adorable antics. "I guess that means yes."

* * * * *

Chapter Nine

Maddy blinked at Ed a few times. "Is that a kinkakaijou in your pocket, or are you just happy to see me?"

Maddy and the other two males had been waiting on Ed for a while at the Zoo's exit so they could continue their expedition. They'd begun to joke about sending a search party for him when he'd jogged up with his signature goofy grin firmly in place.

Ed gave her a funny look. "How did you know?"

He gently unzipped his overalls a quarter of the way and pulled them aside. A tiny little head with bright hazel eyes popped up and looked at her. Maddy stared back in shock for a few seconds before she found her voice again.

"Huh. It's a kinkakaijou. Not sure why I'm surprised," she said with a slow shake of her head.

Reggie's eyes bulged with alarm, and he rushed over to Ed. The backpack in his hands dropped and landed on Ed's feet. The bigger Joongee didn't even seem to notice the impact.

"What the hell are you thinking, Ed?" Reggie hissed.

"They were so mean to her, Reggie," Ed replied, sadness and old memories twisting his expression. "She's so sad and miserable in there. I swear I tried to get Boo to go back, but she wouldn't. She kept hiding in my overalls and wouldn't jump back over the fence."

"Boo?" Maddy asked.

"Yeah, Boo," Ed said with a smile.

Maddy gave him an astonished look. "You named it already? Great."

An alarm suddenly sounded in the air, and security guards rushed around, as well as zoo workers. Ed promptly zipped up his overalls and knelt to search for something in Reggie's backpack. One of the security guards, a female Yalteen, walked straight up to them.

"Excuse me, folks. If I could have a moment of your time, please."

"What can we do for you?" Reggie asked, determinedly keeping his ears tipped forward as if his clanmate didn't have a stolen animal in his shirt.

The security guard held up a photo of a small kinkakaijou. "Unfortunately, we're missing one of our kinkakaijou. They're extremely endangered, and it's important we find her."

"Oh," Reggie said evasively as he accepted the photo. "Are you sure she's missing? Maybe she fell asleep in a tree somewhere."

"No," the Yalteen replied with a shake of her head. "It was feeding time, and the zoologists went in to do the daily count, only to discover this little female missing. They said she was mostly shunned by the rest of the group, so it's possible she escaped the enclosure." She pointed at Ed. "You were the last one the cameras picked up in the area. Did you happen to see her? The bench you were sitting on is mostly blocked from camera view, but you were there for quite a while. Is there anything you can tell me that might help?"

Ed shrugged and shook his head. "No, ma'am. I'm sorry. I saw her with the others when we first got there, but that's it. They were all running away from the visitors, I think. I never saw one after that. I was really disappointed."

"They're very skittish," the guard explained with strained patience. She pulled out a clear, plastic card and handed it to Reggie. "If any of you happen to spot her, please call security. Thanks for your time."

The Yalteen gave a hurried tip of her hat before she rushed off to continue her search for the missing kinkakaijou.

Reggie whirled on Ed and in a harsh whisper said, "You just lied to her!"

Ed looked up at him with sad puppy eyes.

"What was he supposed to do, Reg?" Maddy asked. Her tone was less than friendly. "Stand up, unzip, and be like, 'Here it is. I tried to smuggle it out, but since you asked me nicely, I'll give it back.'"

"Yes!" Reggie snapped.

Maddy advanced on him with a snarl as Harold looked on nervously and wrung his paws. "In case it escaped your notice, you lied to the guard, too! So don't act all high and mighty, oh fearless leader."

Reggie paused and quietly admitted, "Yeah, I lied, too. I didn't want Ed to get in trouble."

She rolled her eyes, but the wrinkles in her muzzle smoothed out as some of her anger faded. "That's sickeningly sweet, but we need to get the hell out of here, or we'll *all* be in trouble. I don't feel like getting arrested today, so how about we stop standing around arguing like a pack of idiots?"

"Damn it." Reggie rubbed that spot between his eyes. He really wished he could go back to the jellyfish in the aquarium. "Okay, fine. Ed, carry my backpack in front of you so nobody sees that bulge. Everyone else, form up around Ed. We gotta get all the way to *HIADA* without getting caught. Go. Now."

They made the trip back to the docking facility in what had to be record time. As soon as everyone was in, Reggie sealed the hatch and locked the ship down. He pressed both palms and his forehead against the cool steel and counted to twenty before turning around.

"Ed, what in the heck were you thinking?" he asked in a calm, level tone.

Ed unzipped his overalls, and the kinkakaijou leapt to the large couch in the common area. She looked around the ship, her large eyes full of wonder. In a flash, she jumped from the couch to the coffee table, then straight up to the crossbeam on the ceiling. Using her hands, feet, tail, and tentacles, she shimmied across it and directly over to Ed. Once there, she dropped down to his shoulder and curled herself around his neck. She caressed him with her tentacles as she laid there with her eyes closed.

"See?" Ed exclaimed. "That's pretty much what she did before. Except she jumped down my overalls and wouldn't come back out. I didn't mean for this to happen."

Maddy cocked her head to the side with a smirk. "So, you *accidently* stole a kinkakaijou. One of the most endangered species in the zoo. Badass, Ed. I didn't know you had it in you."

"I didn't steal Boo," Ed protested. "I liberated her." He reached up and scratched the little sleeping creature. "You all should've seen how sad she was and how much she didn't want to go back. I promise you would've done the same thing. Besides, it wasn't my choice, it was hers."

"Regardless of how and why it happened," Reggie said with a sigh, "it appears we have a new ship mascot after all. One we've got to keep the zoo from finding out about. She's your responsibility, Ed. You're in charge of taking care of her."

"I can do that," Ed said with a smile.

"You'd better," Maddy snapped with a grumpy expression. "Because I've got enough to deal with without a creepy little tree monster getting into everything. Keep her out of my room and my stuff, Ed." She pointed a claw at him. "I'm serious. I don't care how cute she is, keep that thing away from me."

Ed turned his shoulder away and put a defensive hand up to block Boo from Maddy. "Okay, Maddy, geez. She hasn't done anything to you or anything. Why are you so mean?"

"I'm not mean! I'm just setting expectations." With that, Maddy turned and headed to the bridge. "Come on, Reg, we gotta get the hell outta here."

Reggie shook his head. "Harold, can you help Ed research what he'll need for Boo, please? Download the files before we exit the system." He went to leave but stopped short and turned back. "Hang on a second. Exactly *where* do we need to go now? You said something about the Mall of Malls."

Harold, who'd stood back as if trying to distance himself from the whole argument, beamed with excitement, and his ears perked straight up. "Precisely! We need to go to the Brahmin System. The second planet is host to the largest mall in the galaxy, nicknamed the Mall of Malls. It was right there on the plaque. Plus, the Brahmin System is the only authorized dealer of the official stuffed kinkakaijou toy. Combine that with the previous clue leading us to the galaxy's largest zoo, it only makes sense that our next takes us to the galaxy's largest mall!"

Reggie frowned and lowered his ears a bit. "Seems a little odd. I mean, can it really be that simple? Maybe he was just saying that to throw us off whatever other clue might be hidden in his statement."

"Nonsense," Harold said with a shake of his head and a somewhat condescending pat on his shoulder. "Trust me, my pup. I've been working on this all my life. The Mall of Malls is our destination. I'll download everything I can about that as well before we leave this system."

"All right then." Reggie heaved another sigh and shrugged. "Guess we're going to the mall. I'll go see about connecting with a cargo ship or something."

Maddy got off the comm as Reggie entered the bridge. He gave her a half smile and sat down in the pilot's seat. She was in the copilot's seat, white coffee mug in hand.

"I got us a good deal with a freighter headed out of the system," she said as she leaned back in her seat. "They said we should leave in about twenty minutes to intercept and clamp down. They take all the Galactic Zoo merchandise to the Mall to sell."

"How much are they charging us?" Reggie asked as he ran through his pre-flight checklist.

"Five percent of the total gate fee," she replied nonchalantly.

Reggie's eyes went wide. "Wow! Why such a good deal?"

"Said they make the run all the time, and the Zoo pays for their gate fees," she said with a small grin. "They weren't trying to take advantage of us. Apparently, the 5 percent is Galactic Zoo policy. As subcontractors, they have to adhere to it, or they would've just let us ride along for free."

"Awesome," Reggie said and went back to his checklist. "That saves us some credit for other expenses."

"Yup, like your parts replicator." Maddy snickered at his expression. "Don't look so surprised, Reg. I'm not as mean as you all seem to think I am. It's waiting for us at the mall. I found us a good used one for a decent price. We can grab it while we hunt for whatever clue we're supposed to find next. Speaking of... did Harold say what it was we're after?"

"Nope," Reggie answered with a twitch of his eyebrow. "He said to trust him."

"Wonderful," she said dryly. "Good thing it's a seven-day gate transit."

"Yup. Plenty of time for him to figure it out." Reggie hit the intercom. "Get ready for liftoff, you two!"

With that, he fired up the lift thrusters, oriented them in the right direction, and initiated forward thrust. An hour later, they were clamped down on the freighter and headed to the gate. Traffic on the way out seemed to be much faster than coming in, and it wasn't more than a few hours later when Reggie announced they were ten minutes from gate entry. Ed—accompanied by his new shoulder companion—and Harold quickly entered the bridge to watch the gate come to life.

* * *

"All right, Harold, spill it," Maddy said as they sat in the common area. "What in the hells are we looking for at the mall that could possibly be from our guy?"

Harold grinned as he set his slate down on the coffee table. He tapped in a few commands, and a massive holographic schematic appeared. "This is the Mall of Malls."

"Impressive," Reggie said in a tone that implied the opposite. "Are we supposed to be noticing something?"

"Is there a coffee shop marked on there?" Maddy asked as she scanned the map. With the seven-day transit ahead of them, she'd need to replenish her stock. Plus, it was always fun to try local varieties.

"It's not what you see," Harold replied, completely ignoring her question. "It's what you *don't* see." He entered another command, and a second set of schematics illuminated beneath the mall. "This is the city of Querth. The owners of the mall built it right on top of the old city. It's all tunnels and passages now. Building on top of it was cheaper than demolishing it. I believe there are cities on Earth built in this same manner. New York City, Paris, and a few others had tunnel systems and cities beneath them. I believe Dr. Bergan Monschtackle hid the next clue within this city. All we have to do is get down there and find it."

"Not it," Maddy said promptly. "There are supplies and things we need that I can get at the mall. I will one hundred percent be doing that instead of crawling around in some old tunnels and getting all dirty. You two strong males can handle that. Leave the shopping to me."

Reggie frowned at her. "Two?"

She hesitated, then reached out and placed a hand on Ed's shoulder. The larger Joongee's ears had been flickering in unease from the moment Harold brought up the underground tunnels. It was obvious to her that he didn't want to go down there, either. "Ed stays with me. I need someone I trust to watch my back. Malls can be dangerous places."

Ed tilted his head down to Maddy, eyes wide. "You trust me?"

"Of course," Maddy replied without thought. She backpedaled a little at the smiles on the males' faces and added, "Plus, I need a pack mule to carry all the stuff. Duh."

Reggie's eyes darted from her to Ed, then back to her. He must've noticed the relieved look on Ed's face and the tension disappear from his shoulders because he just nodded and said, "Okay, cool. Can you also see about getting some games or something? I didn't realize how much downtime we'd have on this trip. They can help us pass the time and keep us from getting too bored. We had a well-stocked game room in my old merc unit for a reason."

"Sure," Maddy agreed easily. "Not that any of you are going to win any of them."

She sauntered over to the galley and opened the pantry where she kept her coffee. A pair of luminous hazel eyes blinked back at her. Empty coffee containers tumbled every which way as Boo launched herself out of the pantry and up into the pipes crisscrossing the ceiling. Maddy's eyes bulged as she stared after the little animal and slowly turned back to the pantry with an awful feeling in her gut.

"No, no, no, nooooo!" she shrieked as she pawed through the empty containers with increasing desperation.

Reggie bolted into the galley, fists clenched as if he expected to find something to fight. Maddy slowly crumpled to the floor, and he dashed over. "What is it? What's wrong?"

Maddy couldn't answer at first, too caught up in the devastation to form a coherent response.

The larger male crouched down next to her, eyes bright with concern. "Are you hurt? Come on, Spitfire, answer me."

Harold and Ed crowded close, both as worried as their clan leader. Maddy cleared her throat and focused on Reggie like he was an anchor in a storm. "It's gone."

Reggie placed his paws on her shoulders and gave her a gentle squeeze. "What's gone?"

"The coffee, it's gone. All gone," she said with a sniffle as a big tear rolled down her cheek.

Harold threw his paws in the air. "Is that all that's wrong? For star's sake, Madeline, we thought you were injured with all that screaming."

Maddy was too busy fighting back sobs to snap at him for using her full name. "Seven days, Reg. I have to go *seven days* without coffee."

Reggie's normally stoic expression twitched as if he were holding back laughter, but that couldn't be right. Why would he laugh at a time like this? This was a disaster!

Boo crept back into the galley, her tail held close to her belly, and her eyes apprehensive. Maddy shrieked and pointed a clawed finger at the tiny kinkakaijou.

"I'll kill you, you little furball!"

Ed gasped as Boo leaped for the safety of his arms. "Maddy! Don't joke around like that, Boo is very sensitive."

Reggie was damn perceptive, which was something Maddy usually appreciated in a male… just not when he got in the way of some well-deserved revenge. His hands clamped down on her shoulders as she tried to lunge to her feet. She ended up sprawled in his lap, but she was too enraged to really notice anything other than the fact that she couldn't get where she wanted to go.

"Who said I was joking?" Maddy snarled when she couldn't free herself from Reggie's grip. "I told you to keep her away from my stuff, Ed!"

Ed hugged Boo tight to his chest. "She didn't mean it, Maddy."

A deranged cackle escaped her lips. "She ate all my coffee. If I eat *her*, I'll get my coffee back!"

She tried to squirm out of Reggie's arms, but he wrapped her up in a bear hug and spoke low in her ear. "Easy, Spitfire. Calm down.

You can't kill her, and you definitely can't eat her. She didn't know any better, and you're scaring her."

"But, Reggie—"

"You keep saying you're not mean. Prove it," he said with a lot of challenge in his voice.

He opened his arms and let her go. Everyone froze and watched her with bated breath—even Boo. She could feel the weight of all that expectation, all that hope, and it just pissed her off even more. All she wanted to do was lunge off Reggie, hopefully stomp on something precious of his in the process, and snatch Boo off Ed's shoulder. She wouldn't actually hurt her, she just wanted to vent a little… with lots of yelling and maybe some cursing. She glared into those hazel eyes, and bit by bit, the fear in them penetrated the red haze of her rage.

Maddy flattened her ears and slowly, *carefully*, extricated herself from Reggie and stood up. She clenched her fists, lifted her chin, and quietly said, "If anyone needs me, I'll be in my bunk."

* * * * *

Chapter Ten

Five days later, Reggie and Ed stood outside Maddy's quarters. The tiny female had refused to come out of her room except to use the facilities and occasionally eat whatever meal Harold was brave enough to force on her. Reggie had had just about enough of her little pity party. Even during a gate transit, there were still duties that needed to be attended to, and Maddy had shirked hers long enough. It was time for her to suck it up.

He raised his paw to knock, but Ed grabbed it before it made contact. "Are you sure about this?"

"Yes," Reggie answered with the slightest snap to his voice. "She's sulked long enough. Besides, how bad can it be?"

He knocked, but there was no answer. He knocked again, and again, until his paw ached, but there was still no answer. His ears twitched. Alarm shot through him at the faint cry he heard through the thick hatch. He quickly checked the keypad, but she hadn't bothered to lock it.

"Maddy, if you can hear me, we're coming in!"

The door slid aside, and his heart sank. Apparently, it was much worse than he'd thought.

Ed peered over his shoulder and asked in a hushed voice, "What's wrong with her? Is she gonna die, Reggie?"

"No, Ed, she's not going to die," Reggie said with a wince. "She's just going through caffeine withdrawal."

He kicked himself for not checking on her sooner, but in his defense, he'd never really been a coffee drinker. He'd forgotten about the time his merc unit had been stranded with nothing but decaf for two weeks. The side effects from the sudden loss of caffeine on those who imbibed high quantities on a regular basis were quite severe. It was like watching substance abusers go through a detox.

Maddy was in her bed, staring at the ceiling. When she spoke, her voice was hoarse from disuse. "The universe is just an endless expanse of emptiness. A void where hopes and dreams are sucked from your soul to drift away forever. It is the dark and cold embrace of death, ready to snuff out the warmth and light within us. It is all there is, all that has been, and all that will ever be. And… it is nothing."

Maddy whimpered again, that same faint cry Reggie had heard through the door previously.

"Holy crap," Ed said in a low voice. "Like, are you *sure* she's not dying?"

"Yeah, Ed," he said and fought back a gag at the rank wash of the other male's breath. Ed had been eating pickled chinto tails dipped in pudding again, and he was pretty sure there was still some stuck in his teeth. "She's just being dramatic. Those are the lyrics to one of the songs she loves."

Reggie picked his way through the clothing-strewn floor to Maddy's side, partly because he needed to check on her, but also to get away from Ed's breath. He glanced around her room with interest, as it was the first time he'd been inside since he'd inspected the ship. There were empty coffee mugs and fur products all over the small dresser, and she'd written lines from her favorite songs on the walls in a surprisingly elegant scrawl. Some of the letters were even dotted with hearts, and the colors were all in shades of pink, purple, and a light blue.

Maddy, sprawled out on her bunk, had one leg dangling off the edge and the other bent at the knee. He was pretty sure she was in the same stretchy pants and tank top she'd worn the last three days. All her earrings had been removed, and her feet were bare. She slowly turned her head toward him, and he cringed at her bloodshot eyes. Even though she was looking directly at him, there was a vagueness to her gaze he didn't like. There was no life in those eyes, no rage, no amusement, no viciousness. She was just—empty. It was wrong, and it raised the hackles on the back of his neck.

There was an icepack on the floor next to her bunk, but when he knelt down to touch it, it was room temperature. He looked back at Ed, who still hovered by the door. "Can you go grab her an icepack for her headache?"

"On it, Reg!" Ed's ears perked up, and he smiled reassuringly. "Don't worry, Maddy. We'll help you!"

Maddy winced at Ed's overly-loud proclamation and flattened her ears in abject misery. "Ouch."

"Have you taken anything for the pain yet?"

"Yes. Only two hours and eighteen minutes until I can take more," she said in a rasp. Her eyes focused on him with a hint of wry amusement lurking in their depths. It was a bit of a relief. Maybe she wasn't as far gone as she appeared. "Reg? I really hate that furball."

He patted her shoulder with a chuckle. "Yeah, I know, Spitfire."

Maddy gave him a quiet snort. "You're lucky I tolerate you, otherwise I'd have to throat-punch you for that nickname."

Reggie grinned. "Come on, Maddy. We've been friends for over four years. I think I've earned nickname privileges."

Her eyes narrowed. "You would think that."

Ed burst back into the room with an icepack clutched in each hand. "I didn't know if one would be enough, so I grabbed two!"

Maddy screwed her face up in pain. "Please stop shouting, Ed."

"Sorry!" Ed whisper-shouted as he handed her one of the icepacks and dropped the other on her forehead.

"My hero," she muttered and slowly placed a paw over the icepack to hold it in place. She cracked one eye back open and added, "Thanks, Ed."

The big Joongee scuffed one foot against the deck and cleared his throat. "Boo would like to apologize later, if that's okay?"

"The furball wants to apologize." Maddy blinked at him a few times. "Sure—"

"Great!"

Ed rushed back out of the room.

"Because that makes sense." Maddy shook her head and pressed the icepack tighter.

Reggie gave a low chuckle as he stood to leave. "That little kinkakaijou is distressingly smart. It might be a good idea to make friends with her."

"Yeah, sure. Whatever," Maddy muttered and closed her eyes. "I'll make friends with the furball."

Reggie strode to the door but paused to glance over his shoulder at Maddy. "I'm kind of proud of you, you know."

Surprise flickered across her face and her ears tilted. "Really?"

"You did good."

With that, he walked out, leaving a visibly baffled Maddy behind.

* * *

Maddy wasn't sure how to feel about Reggie being *proud* of her. It gave her a warm, disgustingly fuzzy feeling. Her immediate reaction was to claw it out, stomp on it, and possibly light it on fire for good measure. Fire seemed to be the perfect solution to most of her problems, except someone was always stopping her from doing it. It was annoying. Her second reaction was to lock it up in a chest, weld the lid down, wrap it in chains, and bury it in the deepest depths of some next level denial. After the blessed chill of the icepack took the edge off her pounding headache, her last reaction was to poke at it, like an annoying scab that wasn't quite ready to fall off. It was the least desirable of the three, but oddly the one that called to her most.

He was *proud* of her. What the hell was she supposed to do with that?

A faint scrabbling in the ducting above caught her attention, and she cracked her eyes open to glare at the ceiling. *Now what?*

The air vent above her bunk popped open, and Boo cautiously dropped her head down. Her large, hazel eyes focused on Maddy with apprehension, and the tiny creature chirped in an inquisitive manner.

Maddy sighed. "Yeah, sure. Come on in. Apparently, it's bug Maddy day. Just... keep the noise down, all right?"

To her surprise, the kinkakaijou seemed to take extra care in dropping out of the vent and climbing down the wall. Outside of the faint scratch of her claws, she was about as quiet as could be. The little furball slowly crawled onto Maddy's bunk, every muscle tensed as if she were poised to jump away at the slightest movement.

Maddy let out a slow breath and forced herself to relax, though the muscles in her neck remained stubbornly tight with pain. "I'm not gonna hurt you, furball. Promise."

Boo chirped again and held out a small bag. Maddy's breath caught. "Is that... it is! It's my missing bag of chocolate-covered espresso beans. I thought I lost that on the last gate transit."

Even though Maddy wanted nothing more than to snatch it out of the little creature's paw, she forced herself to sit up slowly. She didn't want to startle her, or worse, make her run away before she handed over her salvation.

Boo dropped the bag into Maddy's outstretched paw and let out a sad chirp. She watched with those expressive hazel eyes as Maddy poured out a generous handful and popped it straight into her mouth. *Oh, sweet chocolate coffee heaven!*

Maddy ate another handful before the greedy haze lifted enough for her to notice the sad look on Boo's face. Her tail and her mane of tentacles hung limp, and she looked rather pathetic. Reggie's admonishment to make friends with her echoed in her mind, and she wrinkled her muzzle and clutched the bag close. But... he was *proud* of her.

"Damn it." She poured out a third handful and held it out to Boo. "Want some?"

She watched as Boo crammed all of it into her mouth at once. The little kinkakaijou's cheeks bulged comically, and a reluctant laugh escaped before she could hold it back.

"I still don't like you," she muttered as she poured out another handful for Boo, "but maybe we can share the coffee. *Share.* You understand?"

Boo chirped happily but froze with her handful of beans halfway to her mouth. She tilted her head and studied the small pile. Her tentacles flexed, and she let out a low grumble as if arguing with herself. Then she split the pile and held out half to Maddy.

Maddy's ears angled back. "Reggie's right. You *are* distressingly smart."

She accepted Boo's offering, though, and munched on the espresso beans thoughtfully. "Maybe we can come to some sort of arrangement, furball. Truce?"

Boo crammed the last of her treat into her mouth and purred. Her tiny paw patted Maddy on the shoulder before she scampered back up into the air vent. As the grate was pulled closed once more, Maddy ate one last handful of pure happiness. Already she could feel her headache fading. She leaned back on her pillow and plopped the second icepack on her face. Maybe after a nap she'd feel up to helping around the ship again. Maybe Reggie being... *ugh*, proud of her wasn't a bad thing after all.

* * *

The four Joongee and Boo sat on the bridge and suffered through the brief disorientation as they emerged back into normal space. Reggie gripped the flight controls and wrinkled his muzzle as he guided them into one of the traffic lanes.

"Good grief," Maddy muttered. "I thought the Zoo traffic was bad."

She messed around with the nav console. After a few minutes, she let out a triumphant cackle. "Oh, Chad, I always knew you'd be good for something."

"I always thought he'd make an excellent butt-wipe for Glorp," Reggie quipped. "He was always up there anyway."

"Yeah, that, too." Maddy snickered. "Check this out."

Reggie narrowed his eyes and studied the new image on the main screen. Traffic lanes for personal ships were highlighted in green, commercial routes in orange, and off to the side was a secondary route in red.

He zoomed in on that route and tilted his head. "It's marked hazardous."

"Don't be such a wuss, Reg," she said snidely.

Reggie stared at her. "It goes through an *asteroid field*, Maddy."

"And your point is...?" Maddy said dryly. "Who cares if we pick up a few extra dings? Nobody would notice with all the other dents in this POS. Hell, if we're lucky, we'll smack something big enough to total this thing, and we can collect the insurance. But even better, there's almost no traffic on this route! We'd be there in half the time."

At that, Harold perked up. "That does sound rather nice, Reggie. Do you think *HLADA* can handle it?"

Reggie studied the route, especially where it intersected with the asteroid field. There didn't seem to be much in the way of smaller debris, and most of the larger asteroids were slow-moving. The outdated sensors picked up a few ships along that route, so it wasn't completely abandoned, though most seemed to be small ships like theirs. His ears tilted back with uncertainty, and he debated the merits of risking damage to their ship versus sitting in traffic for the next however many hours.

"Come on, Reggie, I *need* to get to that coffee," Maddy begged with the most pitiful look he'd ever seen. Her eyes were still bloodshot, but she didn't seem to be in anywhere near as bad a shape as before. "Please, I'm begging you."

Ed raised his paw. "Hey, if we take the safer route, we can always play more road trip games!"

Reggie eyes went wide, and he shot up straight in his seat. "Whelp, that settles it. Alternate route it is. Everyone, say, 'Thank you, Chad.'"

There was a chorus of "thank you" as Reggie guided them toward their new route. Harold sounded confused, Maddy snide, and Ed genuine.

"Why are we thanking him again?" Harold asked tentatively as Ed ambled off the bridge with an absent wave.

Maddy patted the nav console possessively and pointed at the StarNav5500 plugged into the side. "We have Chad to thank for this baby."

Harold clutched his slate to his chest and gasped. "Are you saying you stole that, Maddy? You should be ashamed of yourself!"

Reggie raised his hand before Maddy could explode. "Yeah, that was me. And it's called 'tactically acquired,' not stolen."

Harold gaped at him and spluttered for a couple of seconds before he pulled himself together. "I expect better behavior from my clan leader, Reginald."

"It's *Reggie*," Maddy said sharply before Reggie could correct him. She arched an eyebrow and added, "We wouldn't have gotten this far without it, Harold. That means no clues, no treasure hunt, no Lost Weapons of Coronado."

"Lost Weapons of *Koroth*," Harold corrected with a sniff. His ears flickered once, and he nodded stiffly. "Well, so long as it doesn't happen again. I'll be in the common area studying the underground tunnel system if you need my assistance with anything."

The older Joongee walked stiffly off the bridge, his tail twitching in indignation. Reggie met Maddy's eyes, and they both burst into laughter.

"The look on his face!" Maddy managed between gasps for breath.

"Yeah, that was pretty good."

Maddy gave him a devious smile. "From now on, I think I'll call him Harry whenever he uses our full names."

"He'll hate it," Reggie said flatly. He winked at her. "Do it."

Maddy kicked back in her seat, apparently content to hang out while he flew the ship.

He gave her a little side eye. "Don't you have anything better to do?"

"Nope," she replied easily as she propped her feet up on the console.

"You sure?"

She crossed one foot over the other. "Yep."

Reggie sighed and decided the best thing to do was ignore her and focus on flying the new route. It seemed to be the equivalent of a country road back home, all gravel and potholes, with random twists and turns along the way. He was willing to bet that the other ships along this route were system locals, and he paid attention to how they maneuvered.

A small smile tugged on his lips. Maddy was right. They'd be at the mall in no time flat.

They were halfway through the asteroid field when his sensors cut out. He frowned and tapped a few commands on his console, but nothing happened.

Maddy tilted her head, eyes half-lidded and idly asked, "What's wrong?"

Reggie ran a quick diagnostic, ears flattened with irritation. *Of all the times for their sensors to crash, it had to be in the middle of an asteroid field.* Once again, he mentally cursed himself for allowing Harold to purchase their ship. That was yet another system that needed a complete overhaul.

He growled and applied a little percussive engineering to the console, but the system refused to come back up. Worse, the diagnostic returned no errors.

He raised his fist to bang on it again and froze as realization hit him. "We're being jammed."

"*What?*"

His muzzle twisted up far enough he knew his fangs were visible, but he was too worried to care in that moment. He glared out the clear-steel portal, but he couldn't see anything. He knew that didn't mean squat.

The fur stood up on the back of his neck, and he smacked the intercom on. "Everyone, get to the bridge now. We're about to have a problem."

* * * * *

Chapter Eleven

Maddy dropped her feet to the floor with a *bang*. "What kind of problem?"

Reggie didn't answer her directly. "Come here, Maddy. *Now*."

Maddy squashed her initial instinct to tell him to go pound sand and sauntered over as he stood up. He grabbed her arm and slung her into the pilot's seat. He ignored her squawk of indignation and jabbed a finger at the controls.

"I need you to keep *HIADA* on course. Can you do that?"

Maddy blinked at him a few times before she slowly said, "Yeah, sure. How hard can it be?"

Reggie gave her a grim look. "And Maddy? Fly as fast as you can."

"You're scaring me, Reg," she replied as she tentatively increased thrust. She scowled up at him. "I don't like being scared. It pisses me off."

"Good," he snapped. "Hold onto that. I'll be right back."

Maddy snarled as Reggie took off at a sprint. "Damn it, Reg. What are you so afraid of?"

His answer was shouted over his shoulder, and it raised the fur on the back of her neck. "Pirates!"

Reggie darted around a confused Harold and was gone. Harold shuffled onto the bridge and looked at her with wide eyes. "Did he say *pirates?*"

Maddy swallowed hard and tightened her grip on the controls. She glanced over at Harold as Ed shambled in with Boo clutched in his arms. "Yeah, Harold. He said pirates. You know, one of those reasons he wanted a ship with weapons and shields!"

The older Joongee winced. "I apologized for that!"

Ed tilted his head, and Boo grabbed onto his ear to hold onto her perch. "You know, Pops, I don't think you really did."

Maddy snarled as a small asteroid pinged off the starboard side. She fought the controls and tried to get them back on course. "You guys might want to strap in. I'm an accountant, not a pilot!"

A second, larger chunk of rock slammed into the top of the ship. An ominous scraping sound shivered through the bridge, and Maddy winced. An alert popped up on the console, and she quickly scanned it.

"Damn!" She growled and finally managed to correct their flight path. "There goes our comm array."

Ed patted her shoulder before he dropped into his seat. "It's okay, Maddy. We can fix it when we get to the Mall."

"*If* we get to the Mall," Reggie snarled from behind them.

Maddy craned her head around as Reggie stormed back onto the bridge. She was fairly certain her jaw hit the deck. Four years. She'd known that male for over four *years*, and she just realized she'd never seen him in anything but long sleeves.

Reggie rushed up next to her with a rifle in his hands, a pistol strapped to either hip and a tactical vest hugging his torso. His arms were bare, and he was absolutely *ripped*.

"Damn, Reggie. I didn't know you had guns like that," she said with an appreciative look.

Harold frowned in disapproval. "I didn't know you'd brought any guns aboard, either."

Maddy bit her lip and fought back an entirely inappropriate comment. She hadn't exactly been talking about the rifle held in Reggie's hands.

Reggie gave Harold a cold, pointed look. His muscles tensed, and Maddy had to do a quick drool check, because *damn*.

"And I didn't think anyone as smart as you would be stupid enough to traipse around the galaxy unarmed and completely at the mercy of anyone who wanted to take what's ours." He turned to Ed. "Go hide Boo in the ventilation. If they see her, they'll take her. She's bound to be worth a fortune on the black market."

Ed threw off his straps and rushed off the bridge with Boo cradled protectively in his massive arms.

Reggie turned back to Maddy. "You need to go and hi—"

Maddy's ears pinned back, and her lips peeled back into a snarl. "Finish that sentence, and I swear *I'll* be what you need to worry about. Not the pirates."

"Fine," Reggie said as he grabbed her arm, pulled her effortlessly from the pilot's seat, and dropped her into the copilot's. It happened so fast, she didn't even have time to get mad. He placed his rifle on the console where he could grab it quickly and retook the controls. "But don't say I didn't warn you. This might get bad real fast. Hold tight, everyone."

Maddy hurried to snap her restraints on and gripped the armrests so hard her claws bit into the leather as Reggie pushed the thrusters to their max and navigated the asteroid field visually. She winced and squeezed her eyes shut as *HIADA* brushed up against one of the smaller asteroids. She frowned in confusion. She could swear they were slowing down. Her eyes flew open, and she darted a concerned glance at the flight console, but the thrusters were still maxed out.

"Damn!" Reggie shouted.

"What?" Harold asked, eyes wide and ears flat.

"They locked on with their tractor beam. We can't get away. This bucket of bolts doesn't have enough ass to break their hold. If I push any harder, our engine is going to blow." He growled, released the controls, shut the engine down, and grabbed his rifle from the console.

Maddy stared up at him, her jaw agape. "W-what the hell, Reg? You're giving up?"

He looked down at her with an expression she'd never seen on his face before. It was pure determination. Reggie the customer service agent had left the ship. Reginald the mercenary sergeant was here now, and he wasn't playing games.

"No. I'm going to make sure I give these asshats a proper greeting. You should find a place to hide." He held up a paw to forestall anything she might say. "Do it, Maddy. I don't want you to get hurt… or worse." He turned and sprinted toward the miniscule cargo hold where the main hatch was located.

"Maybe you should listen to him, Maddy," Harold said tentatively.

Maddy rounded on him with a snarl and paused. The older Joongee looked *terrified*, with his ears flattened and tail tucked. She bit back her original words and softened them as much as she was able.

"Go hide, Harold. I'm going to help," Maddy said with a rumbling growl as she ripped off her restraints and chased after Reggie.

Along the way, she snatched up a hefty wrench nearly as long as her arm. She carried it on her shoulder like a club and stopped next to Reggie in the little cargo hold at the rear of the ship. Reggie popped out the rifle's magazine, checked the ammo count, slapped it back in, and chambered a round. Maddy sternly reminded herself this was no time for drooling, but holy hell. Male Joongee were typically like Harold, not whatever badass mercenary Reggie had just turned into.

He gave her a crooked grin. "Guess it would've been a miracle if you'd actually listened to me."

"I'm not always a good being, Reg—" Maddy snorted and lifted her muzzle defiantly "—but I'm not going to let you face them alone. I told Harold to go hide."

"Good. Hopefully Ed does the same," he replied grimly. His head tilted, and he looked at her with a little smirk. "Since you insist on being here, how do you feel about being the center of attention?"

Maddy shot him a wild look. "The *what?*"

Reggie's smirk turned into a great big grin.

* * *

Captain Edward Teach grinned as the little ship was pulled into the forward bay of *Queen Anne's Revenge* by the tractor beam. He'd named his ship after finding out he had the same name as the most feared pirate in the late 17th and early 18th century on Earth. It just seemed appropriate. The week had been slow, and the only ships to pass through the back way to the planet were the locals who paid him not to mess with them. He could've gone after one, sure, but then he'd lose a source of steady credit flow. That was no way to do business.

"Ship secured, Captain," Floyd Barnes, his tactical officer, reported.

Teach ran a hand over his long, black beard. "Excellent. You've got the bridge, Barnes. Keep us on the straight and narrow, and watch out for that blasted mall security patrol."

"Aye, aye, Captain," Barnes replied crisply.

Teach gave a slow grin. "As for the rest of you sorry lot, let's go see what prize we've won today. All hands, weapons ready."

"Aye, aye, Captain!" the crew roared with enthusiasm. A lack of profits and boredom from the slow week had taken a toll on everyone, and they were more than ready for action. They snatched up their weapons and dashed to the forward bay.

"Blast you all, where your heads be at?" Teach bellowed in irritation as he trotted after them. He was just in time, too. In their haste, they'd nearly opened the entrance before pressurizing the bay. "What, are you new at this?"

Properly chastised, the crew of *Queen Anne's Revenge* cautiously opened the hatch to the forward bay after pressurizing it. Inside, the tractor beam had placed the small ship in the center of the bay. It was ugly, to say the least. There were even panels missing on the portside thruster housing, and none of the paint matched.

"Bugger," Captain Teach grumbled. "Looks like this might be a bust, gents."

Randy Vortz squinted in the dim light of the bay. "Is that spray paint on the side? What does *HIADA* mean?"

"Probably some alien word for knowledge," Thomas Gorn replied. "Bunch of bloody wankers, aliens."

Randy shrugged. "I don't think so. They're the same as us, just different."

Thomas rolled his eyes. "Whatever you say, chum."

"Shut it, you lot," Teach snapped. "Vortz, get in there and crack that thing open. We'll cover you." He turned to Eric Qualth. "Qualth, you go with Vortz."

"Aye, Captain," Randy and Eric answered together.

Teach scowled as he searched for his last crew member. "Where's that blasted idiot?"

Randy and Eric darted for the main hatch to the ship while Teach and Thomas took cover behind some steel crates and aimed laser pistols at the entrance. If anyone came out shooting, they'd be eliminated quickly. Randy ripped open the hatch's control panel and pulled a kit from the small of his back. A short second later, he turned and gave Teach the thumbs up, signaling he had control of the hatch. Teach gave him the nod to proceed, and Randy entered the command to open the hatch.

The hatch spiraled open, and the ramp extended to the bay floor. Inside, Teach saw a lone female Joongee. She was petite little thing, who stood with her hands behind her back and a bewildered expression on her face. Teach grinned and stood from his place of cover. This little female would be no problem for him. If she gave him any issues, he'd simply pick her up and stick her in the brig. It wasn't like someone that small could fight him off. He was over six feet tall and weighed an easy 225 pounds.

He walked toward the ship's ramp. Once he got close, he looked up at the Joongee and smiled at her. Now that he was closer, he could see she was wearing overalls over a short-sleeved shirt and work boots. She had a unique look, with her spikey, stark white mane, but she seemed harmless enough. Fortunately for her, she hadn't made any sudden movements, or run.

"And what have we here?" Teach called up to her. "A damsel all alone on this rusty old ship?" He gave her a slight bow and dramatic wave with the hand holding his gun. "Captain Edward Teach, at your service."

The female narrowed her eyes in defiance, but her ears flickered, and she slowly backed away from him. "Damsel? You got me all wrong, Captain Ass Munch. And if you're at my service, why the hell did you drag me and my ship into your hellhole?"

Teach's smile melted away in an instant. "I'd watch my tongue if I were you, lass."

He stalked his prey up the ramp and into the crappy ship. The female backed away until she bumped up against a crate in the middle of the hold. She looked around wildly before setting her feet and baring her cute little fangs at him.

"Bad things happen to mouthy little wenches around here." He stopped within arm's reach of the insolent female. "So, does the mouth have a name?"

She gave him a savage grin as her nervousness seemed to melt away. "They call me Mad Maddy."

Teach laughed and glanced back at his crew. "We've got a live one here, boys! Name's Mad Maddy, she says!" He waved them up the ramp. "Get up here and search this tub!"

As Teach turned back to Mad Maddy, something cold, hard, and unforgiving smashed into the side of his head. The pain was immeasurable, and he found himself on the floor. Behind him he heard a clatter and a crash, followed by yelling and growling.

* * *

Reggie grinned from behind the wall as Maddy smashed the pirate captain in the head with the wrench she'd hidden behind her back. The man crumpled to the floor, and Maddy raised the wrench again with a wild growl. He silently groaned. She was supposed to get to cover. Instead, she stood in full view of a bunch of pirates who could and would shoot her in a heartbeat.

The sound of rushing footsteps prompted him to emerge from his hiding space, and he butt-stroked the first man onto the ship with his rifle. As the man collapsed to the deck, two more pirates rushed up the ramp. One raised his gun, but Maddy chucked her wrench across the hold before he could fire. The wrench not only knocked the weapon out of his hands, but judging by the *snap*, it also broke bones. The man howled in pain and clutched at his arm.

The second pirate jabbed at him with a knife, but Reggie jerked back and heel-stomped him in the gut. When the man doubled over with a gasp, he cracked him on the back of the head with his rifle stock. He was trying not to kill these idiots, but they were making this way too easy.

The first pirate got the drop on him while he was off balance and punched him square in the muzzle with his off hand. His eyes watered, the man's face blurred, and he caught another punch to the face before a pistol appeared between his eyes. Reggie froze. *Shouldn't have gotten cocky...*

Before the man could fire, a steel grate fell from above them, and Ed dropped down onto the pirate. The pistol tumbled out of his hands, and Ed flattened him to the floor. Harold had apparently found his courage and tumbled down after the larger Joongee. He landed on top of the pirate with the injured arm, mostly by accident, but it worked out in his favor. As the pirate tried to curl up in pain, the older Joongee snatched up his gun from the deck and trained it on him with shaking hands.

Ed shoved the much smaller pirate up against the wall and used his size, weight, and strength advantage to hold him there. His ears angled back. "Hey, man, that wasn't cool. Like, you could've hurt my friend."

Reggie redirected his focus to the pirate he'd cracked over the head, but the man was on his hands and knees, shaking his head vaguely. He grinned. They just might make it out of this all right.

"Reg!" Maddy snarled.

Reggie jerked his head around in time to see the pirate captain on his feet once more. Teach had a laser pistol aimed directly in Maddy's face. The smaller female was weaponless and far too close to the pirate to dodge out of the way. If he fired, there was no way he'd miss. Reggie snapped his rifle up and set the sights on the captain. *Screw not killing these guys.*

* * *

Teach rolled to his back in time to see the Joongee female raise a rather large wrench over her head to strike him again. Before she could, his men charged onto the tiny ship and began fighting with a male Joongee. Instead of finishing him off like a smart being, she threw away her only weapon to save the male. *Stupid wench. Now you're mine.*

He lashed out, grabbed her behind the knee, and yanked her off her feet. She hit the floor on her back, and he rolled on top of her. Despite his throbbing head, he easily overpowered the startled female and shoved his laser pistol in her face. That got her attention. Her eyes went wide, and she stopped struggling.

"That's what I thought, little Mad Maddy," he said as he panted through the pain in his skull. "Now, get up nice and slow like."

The little female did as he instructed. As he regained his feet, she pinned her ears and snarled. "Reg!"

He didn't take his eyes off the female. The sounds of fighting were dying off, and he knew he didn't have much time to regain control of the situation. He knew exactly how to do that. Threaten the smallest, the youngest, the females, and the males always caved.

"Now then," he said with an oily smile, "give me one good reason why I shouldn't burn a hole through your pretty little face?"

"Because I'll blow a hole in yours before you can," a menacing male voice growled. There was real hate and malice in that voice.

Teach slid a sideways glance across the hold. A larger, muscular male Joongee had a kinetic rifle trained on him. The barrel didn't waver an inch, and the Joongee's eyes were cold and hard. He meant what he said—he'd kill him without hesitation or remorse. Now *this* was a being worth fighting.

His smile didn't waver. He knew something the Joongee didn't.

Thomas rose up behind the male and pressed a pistol to the back of his head. "Drop it, dog-man, or I'll blast your brains all over that wall."

Teach panned his gaze around the small hold and frowned. Randy was smashed against the wall by an even bigger male Joongee, and Eric was held at gunpoint by a much older one. It was like they'd just appeared out of nowhere.

"That's fine," the male with the kinetic rifle replied coldly. "I'll die knowing I killed a scumbag pirate captain before I ate it. Works for me. I hate pirates."

Thomas didn't seem to know what to do with that. He looked past the male Joongee to Teach. "Bit aggressive for Joongee ain't they? Don't they normally take office jobs and stay out of fights? These two seem like they *want* the smoke."

Mad Maddy's muzzle wrinkled up, and she bared her teeth despite Teach's laser pistol in her face. "We want *all* the smoke. So, bring it on, *matey*."

With a shout, another man rushed onto the ship. As he topped the ramp, he tripped on a dangling boot lace and toppled head over heels. His momentum carried him face-first into a cabinet, and he knocked it over.

"I'm okay!" He scrambled back to his feet and drew his pistol. The man immediately lowered it again, checked the safety, clicked it off, then aimed it at the Joongee with the rifle. "Freeze, jerk!"

Teach rolled his eyes and let out a heavy sigh. "Blast it, Oops Moops. If you weren't my sister's son, I would've spaced your useless ass years ago."

"Sorry, Captain," Oops Moops replied. "I was in the head, and the door got jammed when I tried to get out."

"Shut up, you idiot," Teach snarled. He turned back to the male with the rifle, who'd ignored the antics of his nephew like the useless distraction they were. Whoever this male was, he had training. "Lower your weapon. You can't win here. You'll all die. First, I'll kill her, then you'll kill me, then Gorn will kill you, Oops Moops will kill the big one, and then they'll both kill your elder." He gave the male a smug grin. "You really don't have much of a choice here, Joongee. You're beaten."

"There's always a choice," the male growled. "Maybe today I woke up and chose violence and death. You do realize your little equation still leaves you dead, right? Sure, I'll be dead, too, but I'll take out a scumbag pirate in the process. Good enough for me."

He gave Teach a vicious grin, and the crazy little female let loose a hair-raising cackle. There was a mad gleam in her eyes that promised the situation was about to spiral out of his control.

"Uhm… Reggie…" the biggest one said as his ears drooped, and his tail tucked in close. "I don't really want to die."

"Reggie?" Randy said. His voice was a bit muffled from being smashed face-first into the wall by the bigger male. "Sergeant Reginald from Charlie's Commandos?"

The male with the rifle raised an eyebrow, and his ears flattened even further.

"Ed," he said without taking his focus off Teach, "pull that pirate of yours off the wall and walk him out here so I can see his face."

Teach felt a cold shiver run down his spine as the Joongee narrowed his eyes at him and bared his fanglike incisors. "You or your men attack my friend or make a stupid move, and you're dead."

The one he'd called Ed slowly pulled Randy away from the wall and held his arms firm behind his back. He frog-marched him into Sergeant Reginald's line of sight, somehow without spoiling his aim on Teach. Oops Moops followed him with caution and kept his weapon trained on his head.

"Randy?" the Joongee sergeant said in disbelief. "I'll be damned. Another good merc turned pirate."

Randy's face flushed red with shame. "It's not like that, Reggie."

"Save it," Reginald snapped as the fur on the back of his neck rose.

"Hold on just a damned minute!" Teach roared. Everyone turned their attention to him. "Vortz, you know this Joongee?"

"Yeah, Reg," Mad Maddy growled. "You know this pirate? What the hell?"

Teach gave her a quick nod of approval. "Indeed. We deserve some answers, I think."

Mad Maddy gave him a quizzical look. "When exactly did we get to be on the same side?"

Teach shrugged, and his body language relaxed a hair. His pistol didn't waver from her, though. "Just go with it, lass. This is a first for me, too."

The little female shrugged, her ears flicked once, and they both turned their attention back to Reginald and Randy.

"Reggie here was the supply sergeant of Charlie's Commandos, and I was the executive officer," Randy answered. "That was about four years ago now."

"And look how far you've fallen," Reggie spat.

"*Ha!*" Mad Maddy shouted, her eyes full of mischievous glee. "You were the *supply sergeant*, Reggie? And here I was, thinking you were some badass merc or something. Oh, this is great. If we actually live through this, I'm never going to let you live this down. Mr. I-Was-A-Merc, I-can-be-the-leader."

Randy shot a look of disdain at her. "Don't be so quick to judge. He was a merc, same as me. Training and everything that comes with the job. Our ship was boarded by pirates more than once. He did his part and then some." He gave his head a rueful shake. "Damndest thing I ever saw. We actually had to save them from *him*, not the other way around."

Maddy wrinkled her muzzle but nodded once. Teach caught her eyeing the male with renewed interest and filed it away for later use.

Randy grinned at Reginald. "That was the one and only time I ever saw you lose your head. Well, today not included." Randy rubbed the side of his head. "You really cracked me good."

"That's what you get for piracy!" Reggie roared.

Randy lowered his eyes to the deck. "You don't understand, mate."

"All right, all right, enough, you two," Teach grumbled. "Sergeant Reginald, if you'd be so kind as to lower your weapon so we can get this nasty business over with…"

"Screw you, Captain Asshat," Reggie snarled. "You drop *your* weapon."

"Back to this, are we?" Teach huffed. "Listen, son, we're not animals. Nobody has to die here. We just want to steal anything of value, and then you can be off."

"Captain," Randy said cautiously, "maybe if you let his friend go, Reggie here might be more inclined to lower his gun, and then maybe we could all do the same?"

"Then nobody would get hurt," Ed said with a smile and nodded his big head. "That would be good."

Teach grinned at Reggie. "Yes, it certainly would. Don't you agree, Reginald? Your large friend seems to think so."

"Come on, Reggie," Randy pleaded. "This doesn't have to end badly."

Reggie wrinkled his nose in disgust. "Fine. Him first."

Randy looked back at Teach. "Captain?"

Teach narrowed his eyes at Mad Maddy. "No tricks, little princess."

She gave him a dirty look. "I'll play as nice as you do."

He could tell she meant it and mentally noted that she might make an excellent addition to his crew. Teach looked back to Randy and Reginald.

"We have an accord." With that, he backed away from Mad Maddy and holstered his gun on his hip. "There, you see?"

An obviously reluctant Reggie lowered his rifle and allowed it to hang from the sling clipped to his tactical vest. His ear flicked toward the elder Joongee. The trembling male cautiously backed away from Eric and dropped the gun with a clatter. Anyone who knew anything about weapons cringed at the blatant lack of gun safety.

Ed released Randy with a grateful swish of his tail and patted the smaller Human on the shoulder.

"There," Reggie snapped. "Now, have your men do the same."

"Nephew, Gorn," Teach said in a calm, authoritative voice, "lower your weapons."

"But Uncle Teach, I—"

"*Now*, you blasted waste of space!" Teach snarled and once again mentally cursed his sister for saddling him with her spawn. Oops Moops sighed and lowered his rifle. As he was backing away, he tripped over that dangling boot lace again and landed on his rear end. Teach sighed.

For a moment, everyone just stared at each other, unsure of what to do next.

The biggest Joongee cleared his throat. "Hey, something I've always wondered. Do space pirates make people walk the plank?"

Mad Maddy snorted. "Better question… do space pirates drink coffee? Because I'm dying for a fix."

* * * * *

Chapter Twelve

A broad grin creased Captain Teach's face. "Ah, it's coffee that you need? Well, no reason we can't be civil out here in the black. If you'd all accompany us off your fine vessel, we can conduct our business over beverages, and you can be on your way. Much better than shooting it out, wouldn't you agree, Sergeant Reginald?"

Reggie flattened his ears. "It's just Reggie now, thanks. How about you just let us be on our way, no harm, no foul."

Reggie might've allowed his rifle to hang from its sling, but he didn't trust this pirate further than he could pick him up and throw him—something that might be possible for Ed, but certainly not for him. And Randy... what the hell was his old battle buddy thinking? Joining a pirate crew, robbing innocent beings, injuring or killing where they'd once sworn an oath to protect with their own lives if necessary. His muzzle wrinkled as he shot a glare at Randy. Whatever his reasons were, they couldn't be good enough to justify this new life of his.

Randy winced as his captain bellowed a laugh. The man even clutched at his sides like it was the funniest thing he'd ever heard, but Reggie didn't buy his act for a second. Harold drifted closer to Reggie's back, tail tucked with fear, but Ed smiled along with the captain. Maddy just looked bored, but there was a slight tension in her ears that belied her expression.

Teach gave him an oily smile. "That's not how this works, boyo. You want to use this route, you pay the toll. Same as everyone else."

"Wait, hold up." Scorn twisted Maddy's expression, and she snickered. "Are you trying to tell me a bunch of badass space pirates are nothing more than glorified toll collectors? Really? That's the best scheme you could come up with? Did you build your own bridge between two asteroids, too?"

Rather than take offense, Teach chuckled. "Oh, I like you. No bridges. I don't know the first thing about construction. As for our current endeavor, it's low risk, high reward. What's not to like?"

Reggie curled his lip up in disgust. "Plenty."

"I don't suppose you have the credit to pay the toll?" The expression on Teach's face said he already knew the answer.

Reggie really wanted to wipe it off his face with some applied violence, but there were still too many variables. He also didn't like how close Maddy was to the captain. It wouldn't take much for him to lay hands on her again.

"Maddy, come here," Reggie said with a calm he didn't currently feel. Maddy narrowed her eyes, but for once complied without fighting him. He waited until she stood at his shoulder before asking, "What's the toll?"

"Twenty thousand credit," Teach replied with cold eyes. Reggie felt his eyes bulge in shock, and Harold actually cursed behind him. A slight smirk that did nothing to dispel the ice appeared on Teach's face. "Unless you have that kind of credit lying around, we'll be taking our cut from what you have onboard. Savvy?"

Maddy scowled. "If you touch my fur products, I'll gut you like a space fish. You savvy?"

Randy turned his face to hers with a conciliatory smile. "That's not really the kind of thing we look for."

Reggie felt his lip curl up past his fangs, and a growl rumbled out of his chest. Oops Moops backed up a step, and even Randy looked wary. The captain just grinned and waited.

Ed tugged on Reggie's arm. "Let them look, Reg. What can it hurt? We don't have the treasure yet, remember?"

All eyes snapped to Ed, and Reggie had to bite back a groan. He forced himself to roll his eyes at the bigger Joongee. "Yes, Ed, they're well aware we haven't made it to the mall yet."

"Treasure, you say?" Teach said with blatant interest. He smiled jovially at the large male. "Why don't you tell me about this treasure of yours, Ed?"

"We're, like, on an adventure," Ed replied with a broad grin. "We went to the Zoo and looked at the animals, and now we're on our way to the Mall."

The pirate's interest visibly dimmed, and Reggie started to relax. But Ed kept talking.

"We're going to search for—"

"Ed." Maddy heaved a sigh and rubbed her paw over her eyes. "They don't give a crap about our flea market treasure hunt. Unless you boys are avid bargain hunters?"

Teach rolled his eyes and gestured for them to start walking. "That sounds like work, lass. As we've established, we really don't like to work too hard. Now, how about that coffee I promised you?"

Maddy rubbed her paws together as her eyes lit up with unholy glee. "Now we're talking. I'd like a whole pot, please. And a straw."

Oops Moops furrowed his brow. "Uh, would you like a mug, too?"

"Nope. Pot, straw, done," she said, dusting her paws sharply, and pointed a clawed finger at the clumsy pirate. "What're you waiting for?"

Teach frowned and opened his mouth, but before he could say anything, Oops Moops took off at a sprint. The captain blinked a few times in amazement. "I don't think I've ever seen my nephew move so fast in all my life."

Reggie didn't like the appreciative look Teach sent Maddy's way, and he resolved to get this over with as quickly as possible. There wasn't much on their ship worth stealing, so the sooner they let the pirates search, the better. He just hoped things didn't turn violent again. The reassuring weight of his rifle comforted him, and he vowed if it did come down to violence, the first thing he would do was shoot Teach. It was possible the others wouldn't press things without their captain.

Teach shot him a sly grin as if he could sense the direction of his thoughts, but then gestured everyone down the ramp. "If I know my nephew, he'll trip halfway back with the coffee. Best we go to the galley and try to head off disaster. My word as a pirate, you'll have your coffee, Mad Maddy."

Maddy sniffed and walked down the ramp first. "Oh, I'll get my coffee. I don't need your word on it."

Harold scuttled after her. His wide eyes darted everywhere, his tail still firmly tucked. Reggie really hoped the old Joongee didn't choose this particular moment to finally have that heart attack. He doubted the pirates would be too helpful. He watched the pirate with the injured arm stumble off his ship through narrowed eyes and noted his comrades didn't offer to help—not even Randy. The guy had to be in some serious pain.

Reggie nodded for Ed to go next and waited for Teach to make his move. He just wasn't sure if that move was going to be walking off his ship to get Maddy her coffee fix, or if he was going to try to shoot him in the back. Teach, however, simply walked over to Gorn and ordered him to relieve someone named Barnes from the bridge.

As Teach strolled down the ramp, he glanced over his shoulder at Reggie. "Barnes is my tactical officer, but he's not my best pilot. I'd rather he didn't accidentally steer us into an asteroid."

Reggie pointed at the injured man. "You may want to get your man's arm checked out. I think I heard something break."

"Ahh," Teach crooned, his eyes bright. "A being of compassion, you are." He turned to the injured man. "Get to the med bay and see to it. Nanite shot and back down here to do your duty. Hop to it, lad!"

"Aye, Captain!" Eric shouted. He gave Reggie a quick look of thanks before running from the bay.

Randy slowly eased up next to Reggie and winced. "The captain ain't wrong about Barnes, Sarge."

Reggie pinned his ears flat. "Don't call me that."

The two former comrades-in-arms walked off the ship, one visibly contrite, and the other spitting mad. Reggie lengthened his stride to catch up to his clan. Maddy was nearly to the hold exit, and he didn't want her walking into a trap in her eagerness for caffeine.

He wrinkled his muzzle as Randy matched his pace. "Look, Reg, it's not what you think."

"Sure, it's not," Reggie snarled. Ed looked over his shoulder, his expression twisted in concern. Reggie clawed his way back to a facsimile of calm and gave his friend a reassuring smile.

Randy launched into a stuttering explanation, but Reggie wasn't interested in hearing it. He was so angry at his old friend, so determined not to listen to his excuses, that he made a mistake. He caught up to his clan. For a brief moment, the four of them were bunched together.

Teach slid off to the side with a triumphant grin and uttered a single word. "Now."

An energy barrier snapped into place between the Joongee and the pirates. Reggie whirled toward the exit of the hold with a snarl, but the energy barrier stretched all around them in a perfect circle. His eyes shot to the deck, and he mentally cursed himself. *How did I miss the containment markers?*

Maddy slammed her fist into the barrier and reared back with a startled *yowl* of pain. The fur on her paw was singed, and his nose twitched at the bitter stench of burned fur. She shook her hand as a steady rumble leaked out of her clenched jaws, and her eyes gleamed with hate.

Ed dropped a large paw on her shoulder. "Are you all right, Maddy?"

She shook him off without taking her burning gaze off Teach. "I'm fine."

Reggie winced. When a female said the word 'fine,' it was never, ever fine. Teach strolled closer to his captives, a satisfied smirk on his despicable face. Harold visibly trembled and pressed against Ed's side. The older Joongee just wasn't made for this sort of situation.

"We had an accord, Teach," Reggie said with as much calm as he was capable of in that moment. He fought back a surge of wild anger, stuffed it back down, and locked it up tight. He controlled his anger. It didn't control him—never again.

Randy drew his shoulders back and frowned at his captain. For a brief instant, he looked like the man Reggie remembered. "We gave them our word, Captain."

"Aye, that we did," the pirate captain agreed easily, "but we never set a time limit for our little truce."

Randy went to protest again, and Teach dropped him with a single, powerful blow to the head. Reggie snarled with hatred as his old friend staggered and fell.

"If you weren't so good at what you do, I'd never tolerate your moral bullshit on my crew," Teach said to the downed pirate in a conversational tone. He looked up at Maddy with a sly grin. "I meant what I said before. I really do like you, Mad Maddy. You wouldn't like a new career, by chance, would you?"

Maddy snarled and spat at him, but the energy barrier prevented it from reaching his face. Teach twitched an eyebrow and shook his head in mock sorrow.

"I'll take that as a no. Pity. You would've made a fine pirate." Teach snapped his fingers at the still standing pirate who'd just arrived. "Search the ship. Strip it of anything of value."

Reggie and Maddy snarled as one, and even Ed rumbled a tentative growl. The pirate froze with one foot in the air. Teach cuffed him upside the head.

"Quit yer lollygagging and move your rear end, Barnes. Vortz will join you as soon as he picks himself up off the floor, as well as Qualth." Teach shot the Joongee a smug grin. "As we agreed, if you'll recall. Bloodshed may be bad for business, but I still get my pound of flesh."

As Barnes trotted off, Eric returned from the med bay. He appeared to have full use of his arm back, and he shot Reggie another grateful look before Teach waved him toward their ship.

All Reggie could do was watch as they hustled back up the ramp into *HIADA*. He couldn't stop Teach from taking what he wanted. He couldn't stop him from hauling his old friend back to his feet and shoving him toward his ship. He couldn't fix Maddy's paw or reassure Ed they wouldn't find Boo.

But he could help Harold.

Reggie deliberately turned his back on Teach and placed both paws on Harold's trembling shoulders. "Look at me, Harold. It's going to be okay."

The whites were showing around Harold's light brown eyes, and a steady whine whistled along with his breath. The older Joongee looked two steps away from expiring from fear alone. "S-should have listened to you about those other ships, Reggie."

Reggie snorted a laugh. "Naw, you got us the best ship in the galaxy. Isn't that right, Ed?"

The bigger Joongee smiled gently at Harold. "I told you from the beginning, she's beautiful, Pops."

"Y-you did say that, didn't you," Harold replied, his ears rising the tiniest fraction from his skull.

Maddy snorted, and Reggie tensed for whatever nasty thing was about to fall out of her mouth. But all she said was, "Don't forget, she's got the best name in the galaxy, too."

Harold darted a nervous glance toward their ship as something *clanged* loudly from inside. "Yes, what did you say *HIADA* means again?"

"Trust me, it's truly historic. You'll figure it out one of these days." Maddy smirked and breathed a sigh of relief as Oops Moops dashed back into the hold waving a full coffee pot over his head. "Finally."

Reggie was positive the man was going to trip again, but he stumbled to a stop just shy of the energy barrier without incident. A confused frown drifted across his face before he looked to his uncle.

"How am I supposed to get her coffee when you've trapped them in the barrier?" he demanded with a hint of petulance.

"Blast it, nephew, who cares about coffee?" Teach bellowed so loudly Oops Moops jumped. Steaming hot coffee sloshed over the edge of the pot and splashed onto the edge of his hand, but he didn't drop it, despite his reddened skin. The blasphemous waste of the caffeinated liquid gold caused Maddy to whimper. "Get your useless ass in that ship and find me some treasure to make this whole waste of a day worthwhile."

Reggie thought he caught a flash of irritation in Oops Moops' eyes before he ducked his head and obediently set the coffee pot down on a nearby shelf. He bit back a grin when the young Human carefully set a straw next to it, and Maddy strained closer to the barrier with another truly pathetic whimper.

Before Oops Moops made it all the way up the ramp, Randy jogged back down. Reggie wasn't sure if the trickle of blood on the side of his head was from the fight or from Teach hitting him. Either way, it stirred the rage coiled deep within. Once upon a time, when he'd been at his lowest, he'd considered Randy and the rest of the Commandos his clan. It rubbed his fur the wrong way to see him hurting, even if he was a scumbag pirate now.

Randy trotted across the hold but stopped out of immediate reach of his captain. He rubbed the back of his neck and appeared genuinely nervous.

Teach grunted and crossed his arms. "Out with it, Vortz."

"Their supplies are low, their weapons and ammo are nonexistent, and their technology is so outdated, I'm amazed they didn't end up lost in a black hole or something," Randy said with an apologetic wince at Reggie. "As for their ship, I have no idea how it's even space worthy."

Teach rubbed at his jaw. "What if we resell it, scrap it for parts?"

"We could try, but it'll be a tough sell," Randy said and showed his captain something on his slate. "That model was recalled over fifty years ago."

"*Recalled?*" Maddy muttered before raising her voice to an ear-splitting shriek. "Harold, you are such a dumbass!"

Her outburst caused Reggie to wince in pain and flatten his ears to his skull, while Harold tried to shrink back behind Ed's bulk.

"Blast!" Teach roared and kicked a nearby crate. His eyes caught on the hopping mad Maddy's face, and he went from angry to amused in less than a heartbeat. His bellowing laugh echoed around the hold.

Randy tucked his slate away and tried to placate Maddy. "The good news is, you guys probably paid next to nothing for this hunk of space junk."

The small female laughed with a razor's edge of hysteria and glared daggers at Harold through burning purple eyes. Her claws flexed in midair as if she were envisioning strangling the old Joongee.

"The bad news is, you guys own this hunk of space junk," Randy added before he turned back to Teach. "We'd have to break the ship down to its base components to get away with selling it. We don't have the equipment or expertise for that, and we don't have anyone on the hook for that kind of operation. It'll cost us more to keep them than let them go."

Teach shook his head in disbelief. "It's a wash. The whole blasted day is a wash."

Oops Moops drifted closer and pointed at the coffee pot. "If we're going to let them go, can I give Mad Maddy her coffee first?"

"Who said I was going to let them go?" Teach asked with a low growl as he prowled closer to the trapped Joongee. "Maybe we should have some fun with them first, make them pay for wasting our time. Afterwards, we can sell them to some slavers. Too bad the Bieratang recently got out of the slave business. I don't particularly want to deal with a Gritloth. They make us look like saints."

Randy clenched his fists. "That's not how we operate, *Captain*. We don't deal in slavery."

Qualth and the new pirate Barnes moseyed out of *HLADA* and stood at Randy's side.

Teach eyed them both speculatively. "What say you two?"

Before either could say anything, Ed drew himself up to his full height. "No offense, man, but I don't think we want to play your kind of games."

Teach grinned, nothing but malice and rage in his expression, and said, "No offense, but we hold all the power here—"

Alarms blared, and the lights in the hold flashed red in time with the strident cacophony. All the Joongee pinned their ears, but the alarm abruptly cut out, which was somehow much worse. The pirates all tensed.

"Not again," Oops Moops said on a drawn-out groan.

"Brace yourselves!" Randy snapped.

The lights flickered and failed, leaving them in stygian gloom. Long seconds passed before emergency lights kicked on and cast a dim red glow over the bay.

Teach glared around at his ship. "Maybe that's the worst of it this time."

As if his words were a catalyst, the gravity plates failed. Harold wailed in fear as their feet left the deck, and Maddy clutched at Ed. She reached out for Reggie, but before their hands connected, the gravity plates kicked back on. The Joongee landed in a heap within their energy cell, but the pirates all managed to keep their feet.

Oops Moops actually glared at his uncle. "Don't tempt fate like that again. It's bad luck."

"I'll show you bad luck," Teach muttered and raised a fist. He looked to the decrepit ship and sighed with relief. "At least one of you idiots engaged the magnetic struts."

"Captain!" Randy cut in. "We need to reboot the system before our ship accidentally vents atmo or somehow spaces all of us."

Teach glared at him for a drawn-out moment. His eyes gleamed with something akin to madness in the red glow of the emergency lights, but at last he nodded sharply. "Barnes! Go reboot."

Barnes took off at a dead run, while Randy directed an imploring gaze at the silently raging captain. "Sir, if we don't get new software soon, or fix what we have, we're going to die out here."

Teach kicked the crate again and growled under his breath. His shoulders slumped, and he sighed. "Aye, I know."

Reggie narrowed his eyes, but if this was a trick, it was one of the best he'd ever seen. And if it *wasn't* a trick, that meant it was an opportunity. He cleared his throat. "What software are you using?"

Randy and Teach exchanged a glance before both shrugged. It was Oops Moops who said, "StoneAge 9.0."

Reggie choked on a laugh. "Are you serious? That's older than what we used at Galactic Solutions. I didn't even think that was possible! Well, aside from the crap-lousy system on *HIADA*."

"Watch your tongue, lad," Teach growled, "or I'll cut it out of your head."

"Wow," Maddy said with a roll of her eyes. "Way to go all dark there." She wiggled her claws at him. "We're so scared."

Reggie held up a hand, silently begging her to stop talking. She subsided with a low growl. He'd probably pay for that later, but this was their shot, he could feel it. "I know that software. I've worked with it before. I might be able to help you out with your little problem. For a price."

Teach grunted. "Let me guess. You want me to let you all go."

Harold peered around Ed, his expression a mix of fear and determination. "And our ship."

"Yeah," Maddy snarled and punched a fist in the air, "and all your coffee!"

The pirate captain's mouth quirked up in a grin. It seemed he really did like her. "Now, lass. Let's not get carried away here. If your man—pardon, your male—can fix our ship, we'll let all of you go, along with your ship. But you're not getting my coffee."

"You gave your word I'd get coffee," Maddy snapped.

Teach spread his arms. "Pirate."

"Also, he's not my male!" she added with bared fangs.

Reggie pinched the bridge of his muzzle. This was getting out of hand. "Can we come to an accord *before* your ship kills us all? Please?"

* * * * *

Chapter Thirteen

Maddy watched with wary eyes as Reggie settled in at the main computer terminal. This time he'd pinned the pirate captain down to specific terms and a time limit for their new accord, but she still didn't trust Teach to keep his word. Fortunately for them, the pirate crew seemed more interested in not dying than in screwing them over, but that could change in a heartbeat once Reggie fixed their ship.

She tried to keep her eyes moving, to watch everyone at once, but her gaze stumbled on Reggie's face. This weird, stoic, *bored* expression settled over his face like a mask, and it took her a minute to remember where she'd seen that look last—when they worked at Galactic Solutions. It had only been a few weeks, but already that expression was so foreign, so *wrong* on his face, that the fur on the back of her neck rose in protest.

Reggie paused with his finger pads resting on the keyboard and calmly looked at Teach. "Will you allow me access to your terminal?"

Everyone just kind of stopped and stared at him, Maddy included. She rolled her eyes. "Idiot."

Reggie's ears flickered in embarrassment, and he muttered, "Sorry, old habits."

His fingers flew over the keyboard, and he hummed to himself as he dove into the system code. She tried to remember ever hearing him hum before, but she couldn't recall it, and she didn't recognize the tune. It wasn't half bad. She'd have to ask him later what it was so she could find the song and download it. If the lyrics were good, she could add some to her walls. Too much time passed by before she realized she'd gotten lost in her own thoughts and snapped her head around to check their surroundings. Teach and the others were still standing in the exact same spots they had been.

"Some systems are going to flash on- and offline," Reggie informed the captain. "Your problems are nearly all software, not hardware, though I would recommend purchasing some new motherboards and updating the hard drives soon. You can get universal ones that'll work." He reached up and scratched behind an ear. "I'm having to update a lot of systems and rewrite some of the coding. Luckily, most of it's available on the net. This system is so old, it's all free, too. Should have you fixed up soon."

Teach nodded and smiled. "Free is the best price. Capturing you lot just might have been worth getting cracked in the head with a wrench."

He shot Maddy a grin, and she rolled her eyes.

"I should have swung harder."

"Still say you'd make a fine pirate, Mad Maddy."

"All right," Reggie said before Maddy could reply. "Everyone hold onto something. I've got to do a full-on hard reboot. Everything is going to shut down for a few seconds, then come right back."

Teach raised an eyebrow at him. "You're sure about this?"

"Yeah," Randy said from behind the captain. "Dying in a dead ship isn't exactly the way I want to go out."

"Positive," Reggie replied in a monotone. "Ten seconds at the most. After that, the ship's systems should run like new."

"Do it," Teach said.

Maddy gripped her armrests and prepared to hold herself down in zero gravity. Reggie entered the command, and the entire ship went dark and silent. She felt herself rise in her seat, and the circulating air on the bridge ceased. Silently she counted to ten in her head. By the time she got to eight, the lights flickered on, and the command console lit up as all the ship's systems came back to life.

The pirates let out a triumphant yell, and Maddy relaxed in the seat. Her muzzle wrinkled up as Reggie appeared unfazed by the success. She watched in disbelief as he raised a claw up next to his ear.

"Thank you for choosing Galactic Solutions. Your business is very important to us. Would you like to take a short survey at the end of the call to let us know how our service was?"

"*Reg!*" Maddy shouted in exasperation. "Snap out of it!"

Reggie seemed to snap out of a daze and shook his head. "Sorry. I think it's engrained in my brain now."

"Mate," Randy said, bewilderment in his eyes, "most mercs end up with PTSD from combat. You got it from working in customer service and tech support. You truly are the single most unique individual I've ever known."

Reggie let out a long sigh and nodded with a blank expression. "It really was hell."

Maddy buried her face in her paws. "My clan is so weird."

* * *

Reggie stood at the edge of *HIADA*'s ramp as the other three trudged up into the ship. He kept his eyes on the pirates, Teach in particular. His rifle hung on its sling, and his pistols were on his hips, both safety snaps undone. So far, he'd kept to his end of the deal, but that didn't mean much. He was a pirate, after all. If he decided to act like one, Reggie would put a lot of holes in him.

Once everyone was loaded up, Reggie backed up the ramp, one methodical step at a time. Turning his back on them now could result in tragedy. As he entered the ship, he reached over and placed his paw over the control panel. Before he closed the hatch, he turned his attention to Randy and gave him a single nod. Randy returned the nod with a half-smile a second before Reggie sealed the ship.

Before he headed to the bridge, Reggie turned on the monitor at the rear hatch and took a look with the rear-facing cameras. He watched as the pirates exited the bay, and the doors sealed behind them. As soon as the lights on his side of the doors turned red, he ran to the bridge.

"Everyone, get strapped in!"

He unclipped his rifle and set it on the dash as he leapt into the pilot's seat and ran through the start-up sequence. Maddy was already there and strapped in to the copilot's seat. She had a pot of coffee clutched in her paws as if it were her most precious possession.

She glanced between her coffee and the rifle. "Do you need me to hold the rifle?"

He shot her an incredulous look. "Do I look like an idiot? Have you ever even *seen* a gun in real life?"

Maddy shot him a dirty look back. "No, but it looks pretty simple to me. Point the bang end at the bad guy and pull the trigger."

"Little more to it than that, Maddy," Reggie said with a huff. He paused as the engine ramped up into a steady, reassuring hum and stared at the coffee pot in her hands. "Where did you get that?"

Just then, Ed and Harold entered the bridge and strapped into their seats. Ed was munching from a box of cookies, and Boo had a small bag of crackers as she sat on his shoulders.

Harold narrowed his eyes on the coffee pot before strapping in next to Maddy. "Madeline, *what* did you do now?"

Maddy gave them all a smug grin and stuck a straw into the top of the pot. "Teach was right about one thing—I'd make an awesome pirate."

Reggie bit back an incredulous grin as he finished the start-up sequence. "Did you… did you *steal* that from the pirates?"

"Why does everyone look so surprised?" she muttered around her straw before her eyes rolled back in bliss. She sighed after she'd drained half the pot in one go. "I told that bastard I'd get my coffee."

Beyond the viewing portal of *HIADA*, the doors to *Queen Anne's Revenge's* forward hold slid open. Reggie held his breath as he spun the engine to full power and released the magnetic struts. As soon as the doors were open wide enough, he initiated thrust, and the small ship shot from the bowels of the much larger pirate ship.

"We're free!" Maddy shouted with an odd mix of savagery and glee.

Reggie frowned as he watched the sensor readings. "Maybe."

"What?" Maddy asked as her ears angled backward.

He pointed to the large blip behind them. "They're coming after us again."

"*What?*" Harold yelped.

"Hold on."

Reggie banked the ship hard to starboard, and *Queen Anne's Revenge* matched his trajectory. He turned it back to port, and she did the same.

With a sly grin, Reggie straightened out and activated the rear viewing cameras.

"Look," he said and pointed a claw at the screen. "They left the forward hold door open. Teach is coming after us again."

"He lied?" Ed asked. Boo chirped on his shoulder and cocked her head. Their expressions were nearly identical.

"You just can't trust a pirate to keep their word," Harold said with a mournful shake of his head.

Reggie grinned even wider, and he looked at Maddy. "No. No, you can't. That's why I left a little surprise in their computer system."

Maddy's eyes went wide, and she gave him an appreciative look. "And what little surprise might that be?"

"I reprogrammed their tractor beam to be able to lock onto anything *except* this ship," Reggie replied. "Also, every time they get within three hundred meters of *HIADA*, their auto-pilot kicks in and decreases their thrust. I denied their missile guidance system the ability to lock onto us as well. They can't catch us."

"That's brilliant, Reg!" Maddy said with an admiring smile.

Reggie's ears perked up, and his tail wagged a bit. "Thanks. I realized about halfway into the job that I forgot to make Teach agree not to recapture us. He agreed to the terms super-fast, and it was bugging me. Once I realized my mistake, I did the only thing I could to keep us safe." He glanced over his shoulder at Harold and Ed. "Never screw with the tech guy." He turned his attention back to the asteroid field. "But just to be safe, let's take a detour."

With that, Reggie dove *HIADA* at a medium-sized asteroid and into the field itself. He used every bit of the minimal piloting skills he had to keep them from crashing into a rocky death.

Maddy clutched at the armrests and tapped her boots on the floor with anxiety. Despite how well she'd done during the fight, she was looking a little frayed around the edges now.

"What the hell are you doing, Reg? You're going to get us killed! Watch it!" She hugged her coffee pot to her chest and growled. "Dear gods, why the hell did I ever agree to leave with you morons? I'm going to die. This is so stupid. A galactic treasure hunt? What the hell was I thinking? A pyramid scheme masquerading as an MLM would've been a better idea than this!"

"Can it, Maddy," Reggie said, his tone flat, yet commanding. "I'm driving."

He didn't look at her, but he could feel her death-stare boring into the side of his head. She could glare all she wanted. He needed to be able to concentrate, and her incessant complaining wasn't going to help them right now.

"I like pyramids," Ed said abruptly in a soothing voice. "They have triangles. Anything with more sides than a triangle is too confusing, and you can't trust it. Those things are super old, too. You ever seen a regular house after a few years of someone not living in it? It's falling apart. Nobody's lived in a pyramid in literally forever, and they're still super stout. Triangles are totally better than squares."

That made Reggie tear his eyes from his screens and look at Maddy.

Maddy blinked rapidly at him with a dumbfounded expression and turned to face Ed. "What in the actual fu—"

"Madeline!" Harold snapped and pointed a claw in her face. "Such language is not appropriate. We are civilized beings, not riffraff who say such things."

"Remove your finger from my face, or you will lose it," Maddy growled in response.

Harold snatched his back, obviously fond of keeping all eight digits. "I'm just saying. Such language isn't really necessary. I let enough go, but I won't tolerate that one."

"I'm with Pops," Ed said as he dug through his bag of cookies. "That's a pretty harsh one. I said it once when I was a pup, and my mom made me chew on a bar of soap." He shuddered. "So gross."

Reggie made a sharp correction to their flight path, and Maddy groaned miserably. "You guys make me want to use the worst words imaginable sometimes. Whatever, fine. Go on with your weird shape rant, Ed. Distract me from this insanity."

"Circles," Ed continued with a happy smile as he held up a cookie, "totally shady. They don't have sides. So, like, you don't know if they're coming or going, or where the front is." He shoved it into his mouth whole and chomped down with a pleased mumble. "But some circles are cool. Like cookies. Cookies are awesome. I wonder if there are triangle-shaped cookies."

Boo tentatively held a triangular-shaped cracker toward Ed's mouth with an inquisitive chirp.

Ed smiled gently. "No thanks, Boo. That's a cracker, not a cookie."

The little kinkakaijou tilted her head to the side as she studied the cracker's shape, then crammed it into her mouth.

"Stars save me," Maddy said. "There's two of them now."

* * *

"Blast!" Teach roared as he slammed his fists down on the command console. "Why the bloody hell can we not catch that decrepit excuse of a ship?"

"It's weird, Captain," Randy said, his voice perfectly calm. "Every time we close in on them, the engines lose thrust. It's the autopilot. The stupid thing keeps engaging and shutting them down."

Teach gnashed his teeth and ran a hand over his beard. "Then can someone explain to me why the tractor beam failed?"

"No clue, Captain," Barnes answered. "It won't lock on. I tested it out on some small asteroid chunks, and it worked fine then, but it won't lock onto the ship. I can't figure it out."

"The hell with it," Teach growled. "Blast them to bits before they get out of range."

"Captain?" Eric asked from the offensive weapons station.

"You heard me, Qualth! Fire! *Now!*"

Eric grimaced and reluctantly said, "Aye, sir. Firing missiles."

"Let's see them get away now," Teach said with a savage grin as he leaned forward in his chair. "We can scoop up the scraps and…"

His eyes bulged, and his jaw dropped as both missiles went flying in opposite directions and impacted on two different asteroids. Oops Moops' jaw dropped, and Eric muttered curses under his breath as he checked his weapon system.

"What the devil is going on here?" Teach roared.

Eric shook his head, obviously confused. "I specified the correct target, Captain. The missiles' guidance system should've carried them right to the ship."

"It's a curse," Oops Moops said in a trembling voice. "Ever since we robbed that old Caimanin lady, everything's gone wrong. She cursed us!"

Randy grunted, his expression unimpressed. "There's no such thing as curses."

Oops Moops crossed his arms defensively. "Oh, yeah? Then why was she shaking that beaded staff at us and mumbling in some weird language our translators couldn't understand?"

Teach rubbed at his face and thought for the millionth time in a week that if Moops wasn't the son of his favorite sister, he would've spaced him ages ago. While it was true the Caimanin were an odd-looking race, with a distinctly crocodilian appearance, dusky green scales alternating with a blood-red stripe running from snout to tail tip, and eyes set just below their necks, they were nothing special. He privately admitted that old wench in particular had an odd fashion sense, with her smattering of veils and chains instead of proper clothes, but the fact that she'd been muttering gibberish didn't make her creepy. It just made her senile. He should've stolen her ship as well as her goods.

"Do you think maybe, just maybe, it was because we were liberating her of her valuables?" Teach ground out.

His idiot nephew rubbed at his jaw thoughtfully. "Maybe it was something on her ship, then. A cursed object of some sort... like a banana!"

"There is no bloody curse!" Teach bellowed and slammed a fist down on his console.

"Hey, Captain. You think maybe it has something to do with what that bloke was doing all up in our systems?" Gorn asked absently as he expertly guided the *Queen Anne's Revenge* through the asteroid field.

Teach clenched his jaw so tight it popped. "Damn that little Joongee scoundrel! If I ever see him again, I'll have his guts for garters and his pelt as a new coat. Mark my words, gents. Mark my words." He turned to Gorn. "Get us out of this asteroid field and back to base, Gorn. The day is theirs."

Teach stalked to the bridge's exit and turned to face his crew. "Sloppy. All of you. Ashamed to be your captain, I am. Four untrained Joongee bested you, and we're deeper in the hole for it. I shall retire to my quarters and decide what type of punishment is best suited for this absolute Charlie Foxtrot of a day. In the meantime, I want this ship spotless. Get this deck swabbed, the walls washed, and I want the head so clean, Oops Moops can eat off it." He eyed his nephew, who did his best to shrink into his station. "Because he just might be doing so."

* * *

Reggie checked the radar. "Looks like we lost them. They can't maneuver in this cluster like we can." He piloted *HIADA* to a mostly clear zone and set the autopilot. "Now to see where the hell we are and where we need to go to make it to the Mall."

He leaned up to activate the StarNav5500, and his heart fell to his feet. Where the device had once been plugged into the nav console, there was now just an empty port. It was gone, and with it, any hope they had of successfully navigating the stars.

"Oh, no. Please, no. No, no, nooo…" he groaned miserably.

Maddy frantically searched all along the console and on the floor around her seat. "It has to be here somewhere, Reg. It has to."

"The pirates must've stolen it," Reggie said in a defeated tone. His ears drooped, and he turned his gaze out to the asteroid field. The whole bridge fell silent, and he could feel the weight of all those eyes on him. "Our nav system is too old to work without that interface."

Maddy snorted. "So we just use the net. It'll get us pointed in the right direction at least."

"There's too much interference out here for our slates to connect, and our comm array is down, remember?" Reggie said with a shake of his head.

Maddy winced, but there was no judgement in his voice. "So, we can't use the net or the gate to navigate back to the main traffic route?"

"No."

Harold gave him a kindly smile and gestured out the clear-steel portal at the front of the bridge. "My dear pup, I think you're overreacting. Simply point us toward the system's sun. That should get us close enough our slates can connect, and we'll be just fine."

Reggie lifted an eyebrow. "Be my guest, Harold. Which star should I fly us toward?"

Harold strode over to the portal and peered out. Reggie obliged him and slowly turned the ship so the old Joongee could get a nice view of all the asteroids and the stars scattered like pinpricks of light against the deep black of space.

"There!" Harold said triumphantly and pointed at a star that was brighter than the rest.

Reggie kept turning the ship, and Harold tilted his head.

"No, there! No... that one? Or maybe..." The old Joongee cleared his throat and returned to his seat. "I see your point, Reggie."

Reggie gripped the flight controls and fought back a surge of helplessness. "I have no clue where we are. I can only get us as far as the sensors can reach at a time, and that isn't far. We're so turned around right now, we could search for months before we get back to the main traffic route."

Maddy let out a shaking breath. "We're low on supplies, Reg. We don't *have* months."

"I know," he said calmly enough, but that wild rage fought against his control. He'd failed his clan. He kept his shoulders back by sheer force of will. They needed him to be strong. His mind raced through their options. "We could try navigating the old-fashioned way, but we need the proper charting tools." He turned to Harold. "I don't suppose you have any star charts and some of the equipment?"

Harold's ears drooped and his chin lowered. "I'm afraid not. I didn't know we'd be coming to this system. Even if I'd known... astronomy was never my forte."

Reggie hung his head. "Then we're screwed. The only real chance we have is to radio for help. And being that we're deep in Teach's territory, the chances of a local actually helping us without screwing us over are slim to none."

Suddenly, Boo leapt from Ed's shoulder and landed on the main console. She chirped and chittered frantically and waved her little hands and tentacles in all directions.

"Uh, what's she doing?" Reggie asked.

"Interpretive dance?" Maddy suggested sarcastically.

Ed ignored her and looked over Reggie's shoulder. "Like, I think she's trying to tell you something." He leaned in further, and Reggie tried not to gag at his rank breath. "What's up, Boo? Need to use the potty or something?"

The little kinkakaijou jabbed a finger upward. She screeched in excitement, and her eyes seemed to get brighter and wider. It was almost as if she was smiling, too.

"The furball is definitely excited about something," Maddy said cautiously. She picked up her nearly empty coffee pot and slurped from the straw as if it comforted her.

Reggie furrowed his brow, leaned in close, and said, "What is it, Boo?"

It was the first time he'd actually tried to communicate with her. The little thing had jumped on his shoulder and lap numerous times and been rewarded with rubs and scritches, but he'd never actually tried to speak to her as if she could understand his words.

Boo jumped from the console to his shoulder, climbed up onto his head, and sprang toward the ceiling. She latched onto a crossbeam and clambered to a small air vent she promptly popped open and disappeared through. Above them, they could hear the faint sounds of her little feet pattering through the vent and away from the bridge. Silence fell once more.

The Joongee all looked at each other in bewilderment. Maddy slurped on her coffee again and muttered, "Well, that was anticlimactic."

A few moments later, they heard the tiny footsteps bounding through the vent as Boo returned. A slight scaping sound announced she'd reached the access point again, followed by her dropping straight down onto the console in front of Reggie.

A huge grin overtook Reggie's face as the weight of his failure fell away. "Clever girl."

Clasped in Boo's prehensile tail was the StarNav5500. She held it high like a trophy with an expression of pure accomplishment on her little face. Those hazel eyes had never seemed brighter than they did in that moment.

"Good job, Boo!" Ed shouted and nearly caused Reggie to go deaf in one ear.

"Well done, little one," Harold said in a loving tone.

Maddy nodded and kicked back in her seat with a smirk. "Not bad, furball. Not bad at all."

"She must've snuck up here and taken it out before Teach's men could find it," Reggie said, his voice full of wonder. "I knew she was smart, but I didn't think she was *that* smart."

Boo gave him an odd look and crossed her little arms. It was almost as if she'd understood what he'd said—and taken offense to it.

Reggie put up his paws in defense. "No, no. I didn't mean it as an insult. I just meant that it was a surprise. I'm very appreciative. Thank you, Boo."

Boo leaned in with her eyes closed and chittered as her tentacles curled all over the place. He couldn't be certain, but it seemed as if she was saying thank you and reveling in the light of her accomplishment.

"Ed," Reggie said, turning to look at his friend. "I want you to do some research with Harold and find out as much as you can about the kinkakaijou's intellect. Either Boo's a special case, or the zoologists have missed a huge find with this species."

Maddy eyed the little kinkakaijou suspiciously. "Or those little furballs pulled a fast one on everyone. I mean, you saw their enclosure, right? The only way it could've been fancier was if they used gold for the fencing."

Ed smiled sadly. "It was still a cage, Maddy. One Boo didn't want to be in anymore."

Harold nodded eagerly. "We'll find out what we can about our little companion as soon as the array is fixed, or we can connect our slates to the net."

Reggie reached a paw out to Boo and held it open. "May I have it now so we can go?"

Boo chirped and dropped the device into his paw. It was a comforting weight. He immediately plugged it back in and brought up the system layout.

"Looks like we got lucky." He smiled down at Boo. "In more ways than one." Maddy snorted, and he shot her dirty look. "We were headed in the right direction. If I take it slow and careful, we should exit the asteroid field directly in front of the planet. Shouldn't take more than a few hours to get there."

Reggie looked around the bridge, smirked, and added, "From now on, we just deal with the traffic. No more shortcuts."

* * * * *

Chapter Fourteen

The mall was busy. Obnoxiously busy. There were beings *everywhere*. Imagine an introvert's worst nightmare, then double it, then double it again. It still wouldn't come close to the absolute nightmare that was this massive, multi-species herd of retail connoisseurs.

Reggie curled his lip in disgust. "I thought the tunnels sounded sucky, but after seeing this crowd, I think we got the better end of the deal."

With a grunt, he hoisted his pack off the ground, slipped the straps over his shoulders, and snapped the waist buckle. Harold stood next to him with his own pack. In his hands was a medium-sized slate that held the layout of the underground tunnels of the dead city below the mall.

Harold sniffed and wrinkled his muzzle. "I agree with Reggie. We get to have an adventure, while you two deal with the public and run errands."

"Whatever you say," Maddy snipped with a roll of her eyes. "You two go dig around underground all you want. Ed and I will stay up here in the light with all the food and all the not getting nasty and dirty."

Reggie leaned closer to Harold and studied the map on the slate. "Looks like the closest entrance to the tunnels is to the east in the next wing. We should start there." He looked at Maddy and Ed. "Essentials only, you two. Get the stuff on the list, like the parts to fix our comm array—not a bunch of junk. And please make sure to be on time to pick up that replicator." Not forgetting his manners, he gave Maddy a smile. "Thanks again for finding it, Maddy. We really need it."

"I know. I'm awesome," she replied with a smug grin. "Now get going. The sooner we get this clue, the sooner we get the treasure. The sooner we get the treasure, the sooner I get rich. The sooner I get rich, the sooner I can buy a tropical island on a distant planet in a distant system far away from society and sip my coffee on a beach somewhere with the beach breeze blowing in my mane."

Reggie raised an eyebrow at her. "Dream big much?"

"Sometimes," Maddy replied and shooed them off with an enthusiastic wave. "Have fun storming the tunnels, boys!"

Alarm shot through Reggie at the innocent smile on Maddy's face. He didn't trust that smile for an instant, and he suddenly second-guessed his decision to split the team. He trusted Ed, but Maddy was a self-proclaimed shopping addict. And he was turning her loose in the largest mall in the galaxy. *Maddy's right... I really am an idiot.*

"Please don't mess this up," Reggie said quietly, staring down into those purple eyes of hers, trying to convey how serious he was without sending her flying into a rage.

"Relax, Reg," Maddy said confidently and gave him a wink. "We've got this, right, Ed?"

"Right," Ed agreed with a gentle swish of his tail.

Reggie sighed and followed Harold toward the next wing to the east. He knew his ears were flat, betraying his doubt, but he didn't have the energy to fight it. It was a battle he couldn't win. He'd just have to trust them. Both of them.

* * *

"**F**inally," Maddy gasped as Reggie and Harold turned the corner. "Let's go, Ed. We got some shopping to do!"

Ed scratched under his chin. "Uh, Maddy, didn't Reggie just say not to go on a shopping spree?" He turned toward the docking area where *HLADA* was parked. "Do you think Boo will be okay all by herself for the day?"

Maddy rolled her eyes and backtracked to stand in front of him. She had to crane her neck to make eye contact with the overgrown ox, even when he looked down at her. "Look, Ed, I didn't come to the galaxy's biggest freaking mall not to go shopping or get overpriced coffee and a big-ass doughnut with it." She glanced over her shoulder toward the ship. "And the furball will be just fine. She's already shown she can take care of herself."

"Yeah," Ed relented. "I guess you're right."

"Of course I'm right!" Maddy shouted gleefully and grabbed his arm. She pulled him with all her tiny might and managed to turn him a bit. The big lug didn't fight her. He never did. "Come on. I'll get you a chocolate-covered, cream-filled doughnut with sprinkles and powdered sugar on it."

Ed licked his chops. "Mmm, that sounds awesome."

"Freaking right it does…"

* * *

Reggie darted his eyes around as he and Harold got closer to the area where the tunnel entrance was supposed to be. So far, he'd only noticed a single security guard in the vicinity.

The middle-aged Caldivar had been sipping a giant cup of coffee and enjoying a pastry, and appeared oblivious to their presence. He'd also been pretty overweight and seemed to have exchanged the typical powerful Caldivar physique for a softer, more rotund figure. That probably had a lot to do with the two-wheeled, motorized, stand-on scooter thing he had parked next to him. All he had to do was stand on it and lean in the direction he wanted to go. Reggie guessed that was usually in the direction of the nearest deli or bakery.

At least we don't have to worry about him coming after us.

* * *

Blahrt took a bite of his jelly-stuffed eclair as he did his best not to let the young Joongee see him watching him and the older male at his side. He looked nervous and kept shifting his eyes back and forth like he was looking for someone or something. The two Joongee had caught his eye immediately, as they stood out from the crowd. Nobody came to the mall in work overalls, boots, and loaded down with backpacks unless they were up to no good. It was suspicious, and he didn't care for it one bit.

Every year, dozens of beings would come and try to get into the tunnels beneath the mall. It was senseless and dangerous. There was nothing down there but dust, dirt, and debris from a city long since dead. Most important of all, it was off limits to the public. That's what really mattered. He wasn't going to allow a single soul down there. Not on his watch, and certainly not in his sector of the mall.

East Wing 23 had been his turf for more than thirty years now, and nobody had ever gotten the best of him. Nobody. He held a perfect record. There were commendations on his wall and a big patch on his left sleeve to prove it. As far as security guards went, he was the best of the best. He might've gotten soft around the middle in the last decade or so, but he was just as sharp as ever.

Blahrt reached over and removed his security slate from the pouch on his Treker 3000. Years of experience and intuition caused his suspicion of the pair of Joongee to rise as he tapped his password in. He darted his third eye in their direction as he pulled up the layout of E23. Door alarms had long ago been placed on the interior of the old tunnel entrances. They weren't connected to the actual door handles, or even the access panels. They were simple devices at the top corner of the doorway that would send a signal to the security guard on duty in that sector. That little idea had been his own. Blahrt smiled as he remembered his supervisor pinning a small medal on his chest for his innovation.

All four tunnel alarms in E23 still showed green, but those two were nearing the closest entrance. Blahrt casually stood and prepared to board his Treker.

* * *

"I don't like it," Reggie said as his internal warning siren sounded the alarm. He reached out, grabbed the cuff of Harold's sleeve, and redirected him from the first tunnel entrance. The older Joongee momentarily resisted, but ultimately followed.

"What is it, Reggie?" He twisted his head side to side. "Is someone watching?"

"Gut feeling," Reggie replied without looking at him. "Keep going. That security guard back there didn't appear to be watching us, but that doesn't mean anything. There are cameras everywhere, and

Caldivar can look in two places at once. He very well could've been watching us."

Harold put a paw up to his mouth. "Oh, dear. You're quite right. What should we do? I didn't even consider the cameras."

"Neither did I," Reggie replied in an irritated tone. "Too much time behind a desk has made me tactically stupid."

They stopped next to a vending machine, and Reggie pulled out his credit card. He sorted the various items as he thought aloud. "It's a mall. Sure, they have cameras and security guards, but it's still a mall. There are bound to be blind spots or damaged cameras near the tunnel entrances. How many more entrances are in this area?"

Harold checked his slate. "There's this one, plus three more."

Reggie nodded decisively. "Then let's check them all. If we're lucky, there'll be a blind spot or a busted camera. If not, we'll need to come up with a plan B. As we walk, look in the storefronts and act like you're looking for something. Shouldn't be that hard, considering we actually *are* looking for something."

"As you say, my pup," Harold said with his ears perked up, nothing but confidence in his clan leader in his bearing. "As you say."

* * *

"You have sugar and sprinkles in your face fur," Maddy said with her muzzle wrinkled in disgust. She handed Ed a napkin. "You know, you could've eaten it in more than two bites."

Ed accepted the napkin and wiped his muzzle clean. "Couldn't help it. It was too delicious." He picked up his hot chocolate and took a sip. His ears immediately perked straight up. "So good. I love this place. I want to live here."

Maddy took a generous sip of her overly complicated and expensive mocha. Little tingles of ecstasy shot through her body at the perfect combination of coffee and chocolate, and she sighed happily. "Same. This is amaaazing. All we're missing is my tropical beach island and umbrellas."

She glanced at her wrist slate and frowned. They'd already been there half an hour, and time wasn't slowing down despite her need to drink her treat slowly.

"We need to get going," she said reluctantly before she drained the rest of her mocha in one glorious pull. "We're due to pick up the replicator in twenty minutes, and we still need to get the other supplies. I want to get that done so we can walk around for a while and check out the other stores."

"Sounds good to me," Ed replied as he turned his cup up. His ears drooped a bit when not a single drop of hot chocolate landed on his tongue. He set down his empty cup with a sad expression.

Maddy smiled. She understood that look down to her bones. "Don't worry. We can get one to go."

"And a donut for Boo?"

"Yeah, sure," Maddy replied with an easy shrug. It was easy to be generous with that glorious mix of caffeine and chocolate dancing on her tongue. "Why not?"

After they collected their to-go order, they checked one of the interactive maps for the nearest hover-cart depot. It took a little longer than Maddy anticipated to work their way through the crowd, and only the occasional sip of her second mocha kept an impatient snarl off her face. It helped to have Ed there, as most beings stepped aside for the large Joongee. All she had to do was stroll along in his shadow.

"Seriously?" Maddy said when they finally reached the depot. Her ears pinned back in annoyance as she read the sign. "Twenty credit to use the stupid hover carts for a day? That's space-way robbery."

"Yeah, but we need it," Ed replied. "I'm strong, but I don't want to carry that replicator by paw all day. I bet it's heavy."

Maddy rolled her eyes. "Well, duh, Ed. I wasn't going to make you do that." She slipped her card into the reader, and the light turned green as the cart's magnetic lock released. "But it's still ridiculous. The malls back home charge less than half that."

Ed shrugged as he pulled out the hover cart. "Supply and demand determine prices, not the actual worth of something. If, all of a sudden, red pants were the big thing, and everyone started buying them, the price would skyrocket. Doesn't mean the pants are any better than they were before. It's just that beings want them and will pay the price asked for them, even if it's too much. That's the demand part. On the other paw, merchants have to have enough on hand to sell. There's your supply part. The stores make credit as well as the companies who actually make the product."

Maddy looked up at him in wonder. "When did you become an economist?"

Ed shrugged again. "Doesn't everyone understand that?"

"Ed, you're so much more complicated than you let on." Maddy slow blinked and shook her head, causing her earrings to clink. "Anyway, let's go get the replicator."

Ten minutes later, they exited the used appliance store with a slightly used, new-to-them replicator. Maddy was really proud of the purchase. The machine was barely used, and she'd gotten a great price for it. Reggie was going to be thrilled. She paused as that thought hit her and angled her ears back. *Why the hell does that matter?*

She dismissed the uncomfortable thought and turned to look into the next store. Her eyes went wide, and she took a step toward the window. From front to back and wall to wall, the store was filled with every shade and color of nail polish imaginable. They even had the newest shade of black that was said to absorb all light and looked more like a black hole than a color.

But what her eyes snagged on was the section of purples. Every shade imaginable, and more than a few that looked like they'd match her unusual purple eyes. She took another step without even thinking about it, so close to the window now that her breath fogged the pane.

Ed stepped up beside her. "You wanna go in, Maddy?"

Maddy snapped out of her daze and gave him a haughty look. "What the hell would I do with all that froufrou crap?" She flexed her paws out to show him her claws. "Does it look like I wear that junk?"

Ed's brow furrowed, and he looked from her and back into the store, then back to her. "Are you sure? You looked pretty excited, and I think a lot of those colors would look great on your claws."

"I said I didn't want it," she said and glared down at the floor. "Let's go."

With that, she turned and walked off at a brisk pace toward one of the supply chains. Her ears drooped despite her best efforts to keep them upright, but she at least managed to keep herself from looking back. *If I start wearing froufrou crap like that, they won't take me seriously anymore. I'm tough, and I have to look it. I'm Mad Maddy, Pirate Maddy... no, Pirate Queen Maddy. A badass like me doesn't need nail polish. Even if it was really pretty...*

"Okay, Maddy, if you're sure," Ed said as he pushed the hover cart after her. "I hope Reggie and Harold are having as much fun as we are."

"Yeah, whatever," Maddy grumbled. "I'm sure they're having a blast."

* * *

"Well, that didn't work out. At all," Reggie grumbled as they reached the end of the section. "Every single camera works, and the ones near the tunnel entrances all have perfect views."

"What do we do?" Harold asked. His tail flicked from side to side with anxiety, and his ears drooped slightly.

"I need to think," Reggie said as he pulled off his pack and sat on a nearby bench.

Harold did the same and studied his slate. "Perhaps if we went to another corridor?"

Reggie shook his head. "No. I'm betting they're all the same. Even if we did happen to find an entrance that didn't have a working camera, it would probably be too late in the day to do us any good. We need a solution fairly quick."

Across the way, a mass of yelling and laughing younglings ran out of a toy store. All of them clutched balloons on a string. Reggie narrowed his eyes as an idea formed.

"Harold, did you ever get balloons as a pup?"

The old Joongee gave him a warm smile. "Oh, yes, I did. I particularly loved it when they were in the shape of some sort of animal. My parents would take us to the circus when it was in town, and I would beg them to let me get one from the clowns."

A shudder shook Reggie's entire body. "Clowns. They creep me out." He pointed to the toy shop. "How much credit do you think a hundred balloons would cost?"

* * *

Blahrt parked his Treker to the side of the busy corridor and stepped off it. Immediately he had to jump out of the way of a herd of younglings on a field trip from the neighboring system. The group had been terrorizing the mall for the last three days, and he'd be happy when they left. He'd promised himself a dozen cupcakes from that new bakery as a reward for surviving the week. Only two days left to go. He could almost taste the chocolate chinto tail special of the week.

Fifty meters away, his targets entered a toy store. It was the first store they'd entered since he'd spotted them. He furrowed his brow and huffed. Maybe he'd misjudged them. It was possible they were just two working-class Joongee. A father and son stopping by to get a gift for a family member's birthday or something of the sort. He decided to wait a few more minutes. If they didn't do anything by then, he'd move on with his day.

* * * * *

Chapter Fifteen

"Ok, that's everything on Reggie's super stingy list except for games," Maddy said tiredly as they exited the last store. She looked at the hover cart piled high with supplies. "Good thinking on filling the inside of the replicator with stuff, Ed."

"It just seemed like an awful waste of space."

Maddy paused and looked up at him. "Pretty sure I've heard that somewhere before, but I can't put a claw on it."

Ed tilted his head. "Me neither."

She shrugged and let it go.

"Oh, well. Look," she said and pointed at a big map on the wall. "There's a gaming store in the next section. Let's head over and see what we can find."

He grabbed the hover cart and pushed hard until he walked beside her again. "Okay, Maddy. Maybe they'll have *Intergalactic Red Ops 6*. I already beat *5* like three times. I heard that in this one, you can get an anti-gravity gun and make your enemies float up into space. That would be, like, epic."

The two of them entered the store. It didn't look like much from the outside, but inside it was massive. There was everything from the latest virtual reality systems, to video games, to old-fashioned board games. There was something from, and for, every walk of life in the galaxy.

"Whoa," Ed said, his eyes full of wonder. A slow smile spread across his face. "This is my happy place."

Maddy grinned up at him, feeling rather like a pup herself in a place filled with nothing but items meant solely for fun. "Of course, this would be the store that held your heart."

"Nah," Ed replied with a broad grin. "The doughnut shop took that, but this is definitely a close second. Ooh, I see *Intergalactic Red Ops 6*. I'll be right back."

Ed left the hover cart on one side of the aisle and tromped off, his sights set on *IRO6*, and his tail wagging excitedly. Maddy grinned after him before looking up and down the aisles for some multiplayer games that all four of them could play during transit time. She was careful to keep their hover cart within sight at all times. She didn't trust anyone in this galaxy not to steal her coffee, let alone a cart piled high with a crap-ton of supplies, an expensive replicator, and a new comm array.

A short time later, Ed rejoined her. She shot him a grateful look as he took the armload of games from her. She'd had to stand there and wait for him, since she was too short to reach the top of the pile on their hover cart. Unfortunately, when Ed loaded their games onto the cart, his knee bumped the side, and it scooted sideways into a large display of old-fashioned puzzles. Both Joongee flattened their ears as the whole display came crashing down. One particularly large box landed corner-first on her head, and she snarled in irritation as her temper flared.

She bared her fangs and whirled on her companion. "Damn it, Ed! I can't take you anywhere! Maybe I should start calling you Oops Ed!"

"Sorry, Maddy," Ed replied as his tail tucked, his shoulders slumped, and his ears drooped to the sides of his head in despair. Softly, he added, "It was an accident."

A store clerk rushed over and asked, "Are you two all right?"

Maddy rubbed her sore head and muttered, "We're fine."

The Pikith breathed a sharp sigh of relief. She had the short, white hair females of her race typically maintained and wore a smock with the store's logo on it. "These displays are so easy to knock down. I don't know why they keep having us build them." She picked up one of the boxes. "Probably because this thing sells more than anything else in the store."

"Really?" Ed asked, interest perking his ears back up, though his posture remained wary, as if he expected Maddy or the clerk to yell at him again. "Why? It's just a puzzle, right?"

"Yes and no," the Pikith answered in a friendly tone as she gathered the fallen boxes and began stacking them again. "This is the Impossible Puzzle. It has forty-two variations that ultimately create the same sculpture. None of them are the same, but none of them have a different outcome. It's pretty insane. Nobody has ever solved them all."

Maddy let out an irritated huff. She knew she'd hurt Ed's feelings when she'd yelled at him, but the big dope needed to pay more attention to his surroundings. The fact that she was more irritated with herself for losing her temper *again* just made her even more irritated. She couldn't take it out on Ed, though, because she wasn't mean, damn it. She wasn't! That didn't mean she couldn't accidentally-on-purpose stomp on the box that had hurt her.

She casually lifted her foot and glanced down to make sure her aim was true. Her gaze snagged on the cover of the puzzle box, and she froze as all thoughts of revenge on an inanimate object fled right along with her irritation. She snatched up the box and read the words twice to be sure she hadn't been hit in the head harder than she thought.

When the words didn't change, her jaw dropped, and her eyes doubled in size.

"*Ed!*" she shouted so loudly, the startled Pikith clerk knocked over the display again. "Uh, sorry. Look, Ed! Look at the name on the puzzle!"

Maddy practically shoved the box into his muzzle in her excitement. She danced from paw to paw impatiently as he slowly scanned the front. Ed's posture straightened fully as he seemed to realize she wasn't angry with him anymore, and he tilted his head in confusion as he slowly read out loud.

"From the brilliant mind of Dr. Bergan Monschtackle, Grizno Toys brings you the ultimate challenge. This three-dimensional, colorless, edgeless puzzle will have you scratching your head for hours, days, weeks, possibly years! Take your pick from any one of the forty-two brain-teasing versions and see if you have what it takes!"

"Exactly!" Maddy practically shrieked. Her stupid tail wagged in elation, but she was too happy to put the effort into holding it still.

The big male looked at Maddy and flicked his ears in confusion. "I don't get it, Maddy. What's so important about tha..." Realization fluttered into his expression. "Oh! That's the same doctor—"

"That set up the kinkakaijou research and preservation center at the Zoo," Maddy hurriedly finished for him before he could give too much of their secret away.

The Pikith smiled as she gathered up the boxes again. "Oh, I've been there. Adorable little things. It was kinda sad the day I went, though. There was this little one that the rest of them sort of ignored. I think it was a female. I felt so sad for her and just wanted to wrap her up in a hug and take her home with me. I really hope the rest of her troop stopped being mean to her like that. My heart broke for the poor little thing."

"I'm fairly certain things worked out for her," Maddy replied easily. She looked over at Ed and winked. The big moron grinned like an idiot, but she couldn't hold that against him for even a second when she was barely holding back a smirk of her own. She turned her attention back to the Pikith and pointed to the box in Ed's hands. "We'll take one. I think we've got what it takes, right Ed?"

"Right! Do you need some help stacking these back up?" Ed asked as he grabbed several of the boxes from the floor. "It's kinda my fault they fell."

"Nah," the clerk said with a dismissive wave as she took the extra boxes from him. "This happens at least three times a week. I'll have it back up in a few minutes. You two carry on, and have a nice day."

"You, too, and thanks again." Ed waved at her as they walked to the checkout counter. He looked down at Maddy. "Do you think that puzzle is the clue?"

Maddy grinned big and bright. "Oh, I know it is. I bet you have to solve the puzzle to figure out what the actual clue is, though."

"Should we call Reggie and Harold?" he asked as he stacked their purchases on the counter.

Maddy's grin turned mischievous. "Naw. They said they wanted an adventure. What kind of friends would we be if we took that away from them?" The cashier handed her card back to her. "Besides, I still want to go to the music store."

Ed shrugged and stacked everything back on the hover cart. She noticed this time he was extra careful not to bump into it, even though he had to strain to reach the top of the pile. She winced and promised herself she'd do better. She could control herself. She wouldn't drive away *these* friends.

"Okay, Maddy," he said with an accepting smile. "Maybe they'll find a second clue down there. This could be like a double clue stop or something."

Maddy waited impatiently as Ed oh-so-carefully backed the hover cart through the door and out into the main thoroughfare of the mall. He stopped suddenly, let go of the cart, and walked over to pick something up off the ground next to a bench. Maddy wrinkled her muzzle and snarled as a trio of young Prithmar eyed the cart and casually edged closer. She stalked over to the cart with the fur on the back of her neck standing tall, and the trio scattered. She blew out a breath and watched Ed pick up some random piece of trash next to the bench. She knew the big Joongee hated littering, but they really didn't have time for his altruism if they were going to check out the music shop before the others got back.

Maddy tapped her foot with mounting impatience as he slowly stood and studied the small, square piece of trash in his big paw. She huffed in exasperation as he walked back so slowly he seemed to be going backwards because he couldn't take his focus off whatever it was he'd found.

Ed drifted to a halt in front of her, his eyes as wide as they would go as he handed her the piece of trash. Her annoyed growl cut off abruptly as he said, "I think I found a winning scratch ticket for a thousand credit."

"No. Freaking. Way." Maddy studied the images on the polymer ticket, and, to her astonishment, he was right. It was a winning ticket for one thousand credit. "Ed, I'm starting to think you're a good luck charm."

* * *

Reggie and Harold exited the toy store with two bundles of twenty-five balloons each. They'd waived the weights normally given to the younglings to keep them from floating off. As they exited, Reggie glanced in the direction of the first tunnel entrance. The security guard was nowhere to be seen.

"Let's go." He turned in the direction of the last entrance. "We're short on time."

Harold struggled to match Reggie's pace but managed to reply between his harsh breaths, "Yes, yes, I know."

When they reached the last tunnel entrance, Harold looked at his wrist slate and gasped. He slipped one strap of his pack off and took out a bottle of pills. As he struggled to get the lid off, he absentmindedly lost hold of one of his balloon bundles. The bundle floated up to the ceiling, and Harold cried out in dismay.

Reggie stopped and craned his neck back at the balloons. He looked back at Harold with a fierce scowl. "Are you kidding me right now? Do you know how much credit you just decorated the ceiling with?"

Harold winced but pointed to his pill bottle and snapped back. "Well, I'm sorry, but I must take my medicine on time without fail, or I really will have that heart attack you constantly worry about!"

Reggie seemed to barely hear him as he looked around at where they were. His muzzle wrinkled up in scorn. "We went the wrong way, you senile old fool!"

The younger Joongee stormed off in the direction of the first entrance without looking back once. Harold hurriedly took his medicine and struggled to put his pill bottle back in his backpack. He nearly lost the other bunch of balloons before he managed to tuck the bottle away. Bag half-zipped and barely hanging on one shoulder, Harold chased after Reggie.

* * *

Blahrt sat in the food court and was about to dig into his lunch when he got a notification from his security slate. Grumbling about eventually starving to death, he reached over and pulled it from his pouch. The notification stated one of the cameras on E23 was obstructed. He accessed it and saw nothing but different colored balloons. He let out a sigh and set the slate back down.

"I'll be so glad when that field trip is long gone. Dang younglings causing me more and more work each day." He dismissed the notification and returned his attention to the sandwich on his tray. "The balloons can wait until after lunch."

* * *

Harold finally managed to catch Reggie's faster stride and tried to slip his pack back onto the other shoulder. In doing so, his other bundle of balloons slipped his grasp and floated up to the ceiling.

"Uh, Reggie?"

Reggie stopped short and turned around with an irritated look on his face and ears pinned. "What now, Harold? Did you lose the other..." His eyes narrowed, and he turned his face to the ceiling. "You actually lost the other bundle, too. Seriously? How hard is it for someone your age to keep up with freaking balloons? Honestly, Harold, it's a bit ridiculous."

Harold looked down in shame and embarrassment. "Should we go back and get more?"

"No!" Reggie shouted, so much frustration in his voice, the crowd parted around them rather than get near the enraged Joongee. "That was all the extra credit we had to spend. It doesn't grow on trees, you know." He shook his head angrily and turned around. "Let's just go."

* * *

Another notification sounded from Blahrt's slate as he was mid-bite. He slapped his half-eaten sandwich down on the plate and picked it up. Another camera was blocked. Again, it was a bundle of balloons. He arched the brow above his third eye as his famous intuition pinged. One bundle was an accident; two in the same sector was suspicious activity. He accessed the other camera in the vicinity of the second one and watched the video from five minutes prior. He chuckled as he watched the older Joongee struggle with his pack, then felt bad for him as the younger one spoke to him rather indignantly.

"If he were my offspring, I'd show him who was the boss," Blahrt muttered as he accessed the video of the camera neighboring the first blocked camera. Again, he chuckled as the older male lost hold of the first set of balloons while going after his pills.

"I know your struggle, friend." He glanced at the four medicine bottles on his lunch table. "Getting older is hard on the body. Some things even nanites can't fix. Either that, or the treatment costs more than we can afford."

Blahrt let out a heavy sigh as the younger male yelled again—or rather for the first time, as he was watching the recording in reverse order.

"Whippersnapper needs to be taught some manners. You should respect your elders."

A passing Rincah female with a small herd of younglings in tow paused and looked at him quizzically. He gave her a friendly nod. "Just talking to myself, ma'am."

She snorted in irritation and shook her horns at her younglings to get them moving again. He kept his smile in place until they were well past his table. The end of the week and those delicious cupcakes couldn't come soon enough. He dismissed the second alarm and set the slate down again.

"Just some bad luck befalling a fellow senior citizen. I'll take care of it after lunch," he said to his sandwich before taking another bite. He was still chewing when he added, "Hopefully he takes care of that disrespectful pup of his. I don't care how old they get, they're never too old to be put in their place."

* * *

Harold pushed his old legs as hard as they'd go and managed to get ahead of Reggie. His tongue hung out in a most unbecoming way, and his mouth was dry from all the panting. He spotted salvation and made an abrupt right turn in front of Reggie in an attempt to get to the water fountain. It didn't work out. Reggie tripped and toppled over the old male. Luckily, the younger Joongee had the presence of mind to put his hands out and catch most of his weight before landing on Harold.

The growl coming from Reggie's chest and the sneer on his face made Harold wince and shrink back in fear. He dipped his chin down to hide his throat from the sharp fangs exposed by Reggie's peeled back upper lip.

"I'm s-sorry, Reggie. Honestly. I was just so thirsty from all this walking back and forth and…"

"Save it," Reggie snapped before he gracelessly clambered back to his feet. He looked down at his empty hand and snarled before craning his head back.

Harold followed his gaze and saw that one of Reggie's bundles had floated up to the ceiling. That made him cower even worse than before.

"Son of a—" Reggie appeared to bite his lip and took a deep breath. "Get up, Harold. We don't have time to sit here and argue."

He turned his angry eyes back in the direction they'd been walking and stepped over Harold without bothering to offer him a hand up. Harold whimpered, but he scrambled to his feet and followed his clan leader.

Reggie slowed as they neared the first tunnel entrance at the front of the wing. He allowed the last bundle of balloons to slip from his grasp with a faint smile. He waited until they hit the ceiling to spin into the small cove that held the doorway. Harold was in right behind him a second later.

In one swift movement, Reggie had his pack off and open. From within it, he pulled out a small canvas pack and unzipped it. Inside was an electronic device with several wires attached to it. Attached to each wire were different types of connectors for different types of devices. One even had a blank access card on it. Harold marveled at the small device. Even more so, he was impressed with how calm Reggie appeared to be in comparison to only moments before.

"You put on quite the performance, pup," Harold said, his smile warm, with no trace of the previous fear in his body language. "For a moment there, I thought you were actually angry with me."

Reggie snorted a soft laugh as he connected one of the wires to the access panel of the door. "Being angry isn't really that hard an emotion to fake. But thanks."

The lights on the device in Reggie's hand flashed different colors, and coding Harold didn't recognize scrolled across the screen. After a few seconds, the lights all turned green, as did the access panel. There was an audible *click* as the door's magnetic lock disengaged.

"That's a handy little tool," Harold said with an admiring lilt to his voice.

"Yup," Reggie replied as he stuffed it back into his pack. "Randy and I built two of them. I did the coding, and he put the hardware together. That's how he was able to open the ramp to *HIADA*. He can code, too." He shrugged. "I'm just better at it. They come in handy when trying to rescue beings from wrecks or hostage situations and stuff."

Harold looked at Reggie in a new light and smiled. "You'll have to sit down with me one of these days and tell me some of those stories. I'd very much like to hear them."

"Sure thing," Reggie replied as he opened the door. He stepped inside and grabbed Harold by the arm.

Harold grunted as Reggie yanked him through the door and swiftly closed it behind them.

* * *

Two more notifications had gone off on Blahrt's slate during his lunchbreak, but he'd ignored them in his irritation and hunger. They were probably just reminder notifications from the previous two. Once his sandwich was gone, he finished off his soda, wiped his mouth, and tossed his trash away.

Only then did he pick up the slate and unlock the screen. His heart skipped a beat at the two brand new notifications. Two more cameras were blocked. Both by balloons. He watched the replay of the third one and relaxed a bit. It was on the fourth one that his suspicions rose sharply. The younger Joongee had just let his balloons go. No tripping, no accident, no nothing. He just let them go. With a *smile*.

Another notification came through his slate. This one made him shoot up from his seat and hop onto his Treker with a snarl. He'd been played. It had all been an act, a distraction. The door alarm to the first tunnel access had been triggered. They'd gotten past the security panel and unlocked the door. That meant it was time for Blahrt to go to work. The idea of calling for backup crossed his mind, but he quickly dismissed it. Backup was for rookies. He could handle the situation on his own. E23 was his turf and his responsibility. He'd show those trespassers who was boss.

* * * * *

Chapter Sixteen

The music was loud and angry, just the way Maddy liked it. After a few songs, she removed the headphones and looked around the music store. She'd needed the few sacred moments of eardrum-splitting bliss to clear her head.

While not quite as large as the gaming store, the music shop was big enough to have a massive selection of music from countless systems and styles. The front area consisted of all the various music offerings available on the different devices and formats, with rooms branching off to either side. The room on the left was for musical instruction, with everything from live to virtual instructors, and even a section of music books. To the right was a room bursting with musical instruments and various beings testing them out.

Maddy poked her head through that door and flattened her ears at the discordant cacophony of sound that immediately assaulted her senses. It was so loud, she could feel as well as hear it. She jerked her head back, and the music from the main room's speakers replaced the sound of incompetent musicians. She eyed the doorway with new appreciation.

"That's some impressive soundproofing," she said idly to Ed as her ears cautiously came back up.

When there was no response, she jerked her head around, but the big lug was nowhere in sight. She cursed and dashed back to their hover cart. Fortunately, it appeared nothing had been stolen in her short absence. She grumbled at her lack of height, something that normally didn't bother her, and boosted herself up onto a shelf to look for him.

Nothing.

"I swear to the gods, we're ditching this stuff on *HIADA* as soon as he gets back," she growled to herself as she pushed the cart along. She ambled along the aisles and looked for her next musical obsession. In the time since they'd quit the cubical farm and been on their little adventure, she'd listened to her entire music collection and needed something new to spice it up a bit. Sure, she still had her undying favorites, but there were new favorites just waiting to be discovered.

Her feet drifted to a halt as an unfamiliar melody from a small speaker assaulted her ears in the best way possible. She tilted her head as her eyes drifted closed, and she gave herself over to the music. When the song ended, she scanned the information with eager eyes.

"Grunge?"

A slow grin broke out over her face, and she dove into a new genre. None of the lyrics seemed to make sense, but that was half the fun.

"Humans back in the day had some good taste," she mumbled as she scanned the code for digital downloads.

Between one song and the next, Ed reappeared as stealthily as he'd vanished. Maddy squawked in surprise. "It should be against the laws of physics for someone as big as you to move that quietly."

Ed flicked his ears in amusement. "It's easy when the music is this loud, Maddy."

"Where'd you go?" she demanded irritably, the high from her new music fading somewhat with the reminder that he'd essentially dumped all their stuff on her without so much as a warning.

"I remembered there was something I needed to pick up," Ed said with a wide grin.

Maddy gave him some side eye, but he refused to elaborate, so she let it go with a grumble. "Fine, keep your secrets. We need to get this stuff back to the ship before it gets stolen. Besides, it's a real pain in the tail to haul it around in the smaller stores. We can come back to do the real shopping."

Ed tilted his head. "Real shopping? I thought we got everything Reggie said we needed."

"Oh, we did," Maddy said with a slow grin, "but you found us some fun credit that's just begging to be spent on fun things."

Ed frowned and shifted his weight. "I dunno, Maddy…"

"We can start with another round of donuts and coffee," she said in a singsong tone.

Ed looked from the cart to Maddy and back. One side of his mouth curled up onto a smile. "After the ship?"

"After the ship."

They exchanged a fist bump and trundled out of the store as fast as their feet and the hover cart could go.

* * *

Darkness engulfed Reggie and Harold in a suffocating embrace the instant Reggie pulled the access door shut. He clicked on the high-powered flashlight he'd removed from his rifle and panned it around the narrow corridor. There was nothing to see but dust and webbing from some sort of bug in the corners near the ceiling. He eyed the size of some of the webs and sincerely hoped whatever had made them was long dead.

Harold dug through his pack and slipped his headlamp on. He clicked it a few times before the warm yellow light beamed out—directly into Reggie's face. At his automatic sound of protest, Harold angled his face down so he wasn't blinding him anymore.

"Sorry, Reggie," he said with an eager chuckle. "It's been quite some time since I had cause to use one of these."

Reggie decided not to tell Harold he looked ridiculous, and spared a moment to be thankful Maddy was up above with Ed. There was no way she wouldn't have fallen over cackling at the owlish look on Harold's face or the archaic contraption on his head. The miner jokes would have been never-ending.

"No problem," he said instead and set off down the corridor. There was no telling how much time they had before someone caught on to them. Even with the cameras blocked, he wouldn't put it past mall security to have a way to know the old access door had been bypassed and unlocked. He slowed to a stop as they reached a three-way intersection. "Which way?"

The light from Harold's headlamp angled down and to the right. "Uh… yes?"

Reggie had to fight to keep some very real anger from showing in his expression as he slowly turned to face a very sheepish Harold. "What do you mean, *yes*? That's not an answer."

"Uh, well, you see, Reggie," Harold said quickly, "it's a maze down here. Streets on top of streets, partially collapsed buildings, tunnels dug every which way by authorized government expeditions and intrepid explorers such as ourselves. Nobody's sure how far or how deep it goes. The diagram I have is only the bit that's been explored and recorded. Some say those who've tried to map the outer edges never returned."

Reggie felt his eyes bulge. "And you're just mentioning this *now?*"

Harold waved away his concern. "No need for panic, my pup. We shouldn't need to go quite as far as those lost souls ventured."

"Back to my original question, then," Reggie said through gritted teeth as he gestured to the three different tunnels. "Which way?"

"Right?" Harold asked after a brief pause.

"Are you asking, or telling?"

Harold winced. "Telling?"

Reggie sighed and tromped down the right-hand tunnel. "You have no idea where to go, do you?"

"Not a clue," Harold admitted cheerfully, "but that's part of the adventure!"

Reggie rubbed the bridge of his muzzle and hoped Maddy and Ed weren't spending all their remaining credit up above.

* * *

Unloading all the supplies, the comm array, and the new replicator had taken far longer than either Maddy or Ed wanted, even with Boo's enthusiastic help. Both Joongee were itching to get back to the mall proper, but with the limited space on *HIADA*, they had to put all the supplies in their proper places rather than dump it all on the deck like Maddy would've preferred. On the plus side, when they were *finally* done, Ed was able to present Boo with a somewhat squished, but still delicious, chocolate-frosted, mocha-filled donut with raspberry sprinkles from their first trip to the donut shop.

Boo's hazel eyes had gotten big as she clutched the donut in both paws. The giant confection was bigger than her head, and her tentacles splayed wide in joy. She chirped a thanks that included both Ed and Maddy and bounded off with her prize.

The cart unloaded, and the ship-pet fully sugarized, caffeinated, and placated, Ed and Maddy headed back to the mall, returned the hover cart, and made a beeline straight for the donut shop. As they stood outside the shop and munched on their latest sugar rush, they gazed out at the vast expanse of stores with equally excited gazes.

"What should we do first, Maddy?" Ed asked as his tail swept back and forth happily.

Maddy shrugged, a little overwhelmed herself as she licked her finger pads clean and scrolled through the interactive map on her slate. She shook herself sternly. She was no shopping noob, and they had credit to burn. Targets acquired, Maddy put her slate away and rubbed her paws together in unconcealed glee.

That scratch-off ticket had turned out to be valid, and they'd had the credit deposited to their joint account. She wanted to spend all of it in a blaze of shopping glory, but she remembered that disgusting warm fuzzy feeling she'd gotten when Reggie had said he was proud of her. She also remembered the pleading look in his eyes when he'd practically begged her not to mess this up.

She sighed, some of her enthusiasm deflating. "We should probably save half the winnings for emergencies."

Ed nodded his big head. "That's smart, Maddy."

There was a chunk of sugar glaze stuck to his cheek, but before she could tell him, he flicked his tongue out and licked it off. He looked down at her expectantly with his eyebrows raised high.

Maddy had a feeling Ed was waiting for her to say something in particular, and she scrambled for what a good friend would do. Her shoulders slumped and she groaned. "*And* we should probably start with getting those two idiots something before ourselves."

Ed patted her gently on the shoulder. "That's a really nice idea. I know just the thing to get Reggie. Do you have any ideas for Harold? You've known him the longest."

Maddy winced and kicked at the ground. "Maybe? Let me think about it while we go get your thing for Reg."

* * *

"Again?" Reggie said flatly as they ran straight into their fourth dead end. The pile of jagged boulders and rusted girders stretched from floor to ceiling with no way past, and it seemed to mock him as he played his flashlight over the slope.

Harold was undeterred. He simply made a notation on his slate-map and turned back the way they'd come. When they reached the last intersection of tunnels, they paused while Harold figured out the next best way to search. So far, the few buildings they'd come across had been nothing but rubble and had clearly been picked clean of anything of value long ago. There had been no sign of any clues from the long-dead doctor, and Reggie was starting to believe they were on a wild chinto chase.

A faint tremor shook the ground beneath their boots, and dust spilled down from the rock overhead. Harold hunched over his slate protectively, and both coughed as the dust found its way inside their noses. Reggie's ears perked up, and he clamped a paw over Harold's mouth.

The older Joongee jerked back with an irritated glare, but Reggie held his paw up for him to stop. He kept his voice to a low hush and asked, "Did you hear that?"

Both Joongee perked their ears up and listened intently, but whatever sound Reggie had heard didn't repeat itself. Reggie rolled his shoulders and wished, not for the first time, that he'd figured out a way to smuggle his rifle down with them.

He sharply gestured for Harold to continue on. "Let's move it, Harold. The less time we spend down here, the better."

* * *

Blahrt sniffled and tried to hold back a second sneeze as he blinked his eyes clear. "Dratted quakes. Getting dust in my nose and my eyes. I hate it down here."

He hesitated at one of the larger intact buildings and shone his flashlight around the bottom floor, but outside of some scattered boot prints in the dust to indicate the Joongee had been and gone, there was nothing there.

Blahrt sighed and thought longingly of those cupcakes as he eased his Treker down the corridor. Maybe he'd reward himself early after all this. He hit a bump that rattled his teeth, but his faithful Treker handled it just fine.

"I *really* hate it down here," he said to the machine. He gritted his teeth as he hit another bump. "I'm going to make those Joongee regret making me chase after them."

* * *

Reggie counted out slow breaths as he waited for Harold to consult his map. Every time he reached ten, he started his count over. It was either that or break the slate over Harold's head, and that just wasn't something most friendships could come back from. Besides, if he broke the slate, he'd likely be stuck down there forever, with only Harold for company until they died. Knowing the older Joongee, he'd want to keep searching for clues the entire time, too.

"Are you sure we're in the right spot?" he asked for the third time as Harold actually turned his slate sideways and squinted around the cavernous building.

Judging by the decaying partial walls crumbling all around them, this had once been an office with a cubicle farm like Galactic Solutions. The similarities practically gave Reggie hives, and he barely resisted the urge to claw at his fur. *Come on, Harold. Figure it out before I scratch myself bloody.*

"I don't understand," Harold said querulously. "According to the map, there should be an intersection of five tunnels right here."

"You're saying we're lost," Reggie replied dryly.

"No, I'm saying the blasted map is wrong!" Harold shouted in a rare fit of temper.

He stomped over to Reggie with his slate clenched in one paw but stopped as another quake hit. The floor shook under their boots, and an ominous groan split the air.

Reggie's eyes widened. "Run!"

He took one step toward Harold, and the section of floor they stood on collapsed under their feet. They barely had time to shout before they hit the ground. Reggie landed perfectly balanced on his feet with one hand down to steady himself, whereas Harold… did not.

"You okay, Harold?" Reggie asked as he helped the older Joongee to his feet.

Harold coughed miserably and dusted himself off. His eyes bulged, and he dove back to the ground. Frantically, he threw chunks of rotten flooring aside until he uncovered a badly dinged slate.

Alarm punched through Reggie. "Does it still work?"

Harold's paws visibly trembled as he dusted the slate off and tapped the screen. His sigh of relief told Reggie everything he needed to know, and he panned his flashlight around the new space. As the dust settled, a chuckle escaped him.

"What's so funny?" Harold asked, wide-eyed with his headlamp sitting askew on his forehead.

"How many tunnels do you see?" Reggie replied with a wide grin.

Harold turned and looked up. The light from his headlamp illuminated five separate tunnel entrances.

"Now we're getting somewhere," the older Joongee said with a small snarl of triumph. The excitement of the hunt gleamed in his eyes again, and he jabbed a clawed finger at the centermost tunnel. "That's definitely the way."

Five minutes later, they sprinted back out of the tunnel.

"It's possible I was wrong," Harold panted as he braced his paws on his knees.

"You think?" Reggie demanded as he danced around the intersection, frantically ripping off chunks of webbing and *very* determined chitinous creatures with way too many eyes and mouths. He stomped repeatedly, but most skittered back into the tunnel. The few he managed to smash practically exploded into a yellow goo that splattered his boots and flooded his nostrils with a horrific stench.

Reggie gagged and wiped his boots off as best he could while Harold backed away from him with his hand clamped over his muzzle.

"I think that's the tunnel we really want," Harold said with half his previous confidence and pointed at the tunnel on the right side of the centermost.

Reggie gave him a grim smile. "You lead this time."

* * *

Blahrt zipped along on his Treker until he found the caved-in section of the old S-Mart Office building. He heaved a sigh and flipped a switch on the handlebar, which diverted power to the downward thrusters. With the ease of years of practice with the enhanced hover feature, he carefully guided it out over the gaping hole and descended into the dark. He wrinkled his nose as he picked up a faint whiff of something foul and resolved to spend as little time down there as possible.

"Honestly," he said to his Treker with a faint whine of complaint. "How hard can it be to track down two little Joongee? After all, I'm the top guard in the whole company."

The light mounted to the front of his Treker showed boot prints going into and out of the center tunnel, but there were two trails of boot prints heading into the tunnel to the right and none coming out.

"Got you," he said and twisted the throttle to the max. His faithful Treker spluttered twice before puttering down the tunnel at a pace just a little faster than he could walk. He grinned and leaned forward into the gentle breeze. "Nobody gets the best of Blahrt. Nobody."

* * *

Reggie dragged Harold to a stop again. "I hear something."

"Again? Are you sure you don't need to get your hearing checked?" Harold asked with a concerned swish of his tail. "You know, as you get older, Reggie, it's important to see a doctor at least once a—"

Reggie clamped a hand over Harold's muzzle again. "Quiet."

He clicked off his light and batted at Harold's headlamp until he gave up on finding the switch and just moved his hand over it to block most of the light. His eyes quickly adjusted to the gloom, and he strained his ears.

A faint light reached his searching eyes at the same time he picked up the hum of a hover vehicle. He grabbed Harold by the shoulders, spun him around, and removed his hand from the headlamp so the comforting yellow glow illuminated the way ahead again.

"Time to go!"

Harold stumbled into motion again, but much too slowly for Reggie's taste. "But the map shows there's some kind of hazard ahead."

"Yeah, well, there's definitely some kind of hazard behind," Reggie snapped and gently shoved at Harold's back to get him moving faster. "We're not alone down here."

The two Joongee trotted down the tunnel, but the hum grew louder. Reggie pinned his ears back and extended his stride into a run. Harold's breathing grew ragged, but he managed to keep the pace— for the moment. The tunnel sloped downward beneath their boots, and running became easier. The hum grew fainter.

Reggie crushed the sense of relief before it could spread too far. Whoever it was, they were still following. His nose twitched as he caught a new scent. He took his eyes off the tunnel ahead long enough to glance at Harold. "Why do I smell spoiled eggs, Harold? *Why?*"

"Uh… maybe… some kind of buildup… of sulfuric bacteria," he said between panted breaths.

"In the air?" Reggie demanded incredulously.

Harold stumbled, and Reggie darted out a hand to steady him as the slope steepened even more. Now they were practically flying ahead, almost faster than the light could illuminate the path. A faint glimmer reflected the light back to them.

"No," Harold gasped out. "Usually it's in ground water."

Reggie's eyes widened. "Oh, no."

It was too late to put on the brakes. Between one step and the next, they sprinted straight from solid ground into slimy water that reached their waists. The sudden resistance of the water killed their momentum and balance, and both plunged under the water with a great splash.

Reggie got his boots under him and surfaced, coughing up stinking water, desperately hoping whatever bacteria was floating in it didn't kill them before they could get a round of antibacterial meds in their systems. He reached back down and hauled Harold to his feet. The older Joongee wheezed and spat out a mouthful of water into Reggie's face by accident.

"Sorry, Reg." Harold's headlamp spluttered out and died. "Oh, bother."

It didn't matter. The hum had grown louder again, and light flooded the tunnel behind them. Reggie could make out a suspiciously familiar overweight Caldivar on a hover scooter. He twisted around and, thanks to the Caldivar's light, he could see the tunnel sloped back up enough to climb out of the water.

"Come on, Harold," he said and tugged on Harold's arm until the old Joongee moved. "We can't get caught now. We're too close. We *are* close, right?"

"Uh… right," Harold said as he slogged through the water beside him.

Reggie glanced sidelong at him and could just make out the wince on his face. He bit back a sigh and moved faster.

"Stop! In the name of Mall Security!"

Reggie glanced over his shoulder in time to see the old Caldivar putter forward into the water. Unfortunately for him, it was deeper than he must have anticipated, because the front end of the scooter dipped into the water and flung the Caldivar over the handlebars. He landed with an enormous splash.

Reggie gritted his teeth. "Faster, Harold."

The security guard resurfaced with a bellow of anger like some overweight leviathan of the deep.

Harold flinched and actually pulled ahead of Reggie. "Faster is good."

* * * * *

Chapter Seventeen

"There!" Maddy shouted and jabbed a finger to the left of the wide shopping concourse. "Faster, Ed!"

The bigger Joongee barreled ahead, and Maddy tucked herself close in behind him as he cut a path through the endless crowd. Just as they cleared a noisy group of Humans, a bunch of Caimanin loaded down with shopping bags and dragging a hover cart burst out of the crowd.

Maddy locked eyes with the lead female and pinned back her ears. "Oh, no you don't."

The lead Caimanin female wrinkled her snout, an impressive amount of curving fangs slipping free, and lengthened her stride. Maddy shoved against Ed's back and pushed him to go faster. This was their third attempt. They wouldn't fail this time. *Almost there… almost…*

"Ha!"

Maddy grinned in a mix of triumph and relief as she slid onto the cool syntho-wood bench next to Ed. She looked up into the frustrated face of the Caimanin female and gave a little finger wave.

"Better luck next time," she said with a smirk.

"Maddy, be nice," Ed admonished even as he propped his feet up on one of their bigger bags with a happy sigh. He smiled at the

Caimanin and added, "I think the group at the next bench down was getting ready to leave."

The female snapped her jaws twice in thanks and hurried off with her friends trailing dejectedly behind her.

"Can we be done now, Maddy?" Ed asked plaintively. His ears drooped, and his tail hung limp with exhaustion. "My feet hurt, and all these bags are getting really heavy."

Maddy smiled fondly at the pile of shopping bags on the bench and clustered around their feet. It had been a long time since she'd been able to shop like that. Oddly, she'd almost had more fun buying stuff for Reggie and Harold than she had for herself. Her gaze caught on one of the heaviest bags. It had a prominent golden logo of a rounded, winged Nilta within a stylized mug.

"Yeah, I think we're done," she said reluctantly.

Finding something for Harold had turned out to be easier than she'd first thought. The old Joongee loved honey ale, and Maddy was certain he'd love the variety pack they'd bought him. It had his favorite flavors, plus three brand-new seasonal brews.

Ed rolled his head toward her. "Should we comm the others *now*? Just to check in at least?"

Maddy rolled her shoulders to release the tension from carrying her own share of the bags and waved a lazy paw. "Be nice, Ed. Let them have their fun."

* * *

"This is quite possibly the worst day of my life," Reggie said in a conversational tone as he trudged along next to Harold. He slowly turned his head to the older Joongee and narrowed his eyes. "And I used to be a mercenary, Harold. A *mercenary*. That means I've been shot at and nearly died on multiple occasions."

Harold gave him a weak smile. Drying mud flaked off his muzzle and pattered on the ground as he said, "It could always be worse."

"Dear gods, he didn't mean it." Reggie squeezed his eyes shut and angled his head backward. "Please, universe, don't punish us for his blatant disrespect."

Harold chuckled as if he were joking and forged ahead with a bounce in his step.

Reggie flicked his ears back in annoyance and shook his head violently as a chunk of mud slid into his left ear. After their impromptu bath, they'd had to cross a long section of deep, powdery dirt. Not only had it taken considerable effort to walk through, Harold had tripped and pulled Reggie down with him while they were still soaking wet. The stinking water had combined with the dirt to form a disgusting crust of mud that was going to take forever to get out of his fur.

Harold had finally found something in the last partially-collapsed building they'd searched—a mark low on the inner wall that vaguely resembled a kinkakaijou. Harold had recorded the image and hustled along, more certain than ever that they were on the correct path. Reggie thought the fact the picture had clearly been drawn by a pup in faded colored ink of some sort negated any superficial resemblance to Boo, but there was no talking to Harold in that moment.

Reggie grumbled under his breath and held onto his fraying calm with everything he had left in him. Which wasn't much. He was tired, sore, hungry, and beyond filthy, but he refused to let this situation break his control. Painstakingly, he bit back a sigh at the sound of rocks tumbling down somewhere behind them and held on a little tighter. *This won't break me... even if that Caldivar hasn't given up.*

Ahead of him, Harold slowed to a stop. His ears flicked back, and flecks of mud shot straight into Reggie's eyes. He swiped a dirty paw across his face and blinked his vision clear in time to see Harold running a hand over a fractured wall.

"No-no-no," Harold muttered as his tail swished frantically. "There must be a way through."

Reggie panned his flashlight around the tunnel, but the ground was solid dirt, and the walls were giant slabs of rock, probably the remains of industrial buildings. The fractured wall blocking their way looked like a partial collapse of the tunnel that had been somewhat cleared by previous explorers. Their efforts had left jagged chunks of rock piled along the base of the tunnel walls and a mostly vertical interlocking mess that completely plugged the tunnel.

There weren't even windows they could crawl through this time to continue to work their way forward.

"Harold, I think it's time to admit—"

"That you're rule breakers and should be punished to the full extent of mall law?" a winded voice panted out of the darkness.

The Joongee whirled around as the Caldivar security guard limped into the light cast by Reggie's flashlight. All three of his eyes squinted shut when Reggie accidentally jerked his light up into the guard's face. He pointed it at the floor with a muttered apology.

"Time to give up and accept the consequences of your actions," he said in a slightly firmer tone.

The Caldivar squared his shoulders and marched closer. If anything, he was covered in even more mud than they were. Great chunks fell to the ground with each ponderous step, and it was difficult to tell where the mud stopped and his gray, mottled skin began.

Reggie opened his mouth to argue with the guard, but Harold beat him to it with a wild cackle. "No! We're not giving up! Not now, not when we're so close."

The older Joongee launched himself at the wall and clawed at it in desperation. Small chunks of rock broke free and bounced off the ground and his boots. A familiar scent reached Reggie's nose, and his eyes widened in alarm.

"Harold, stop—"

"Sir, please cease and desist," the Caldivar said over Reggie.

Harold didn't listen to either of them. The guard reached out and gently tugged on Harold's arm, but the old Joongee dug his claws into a particularly deep crack and refused to let go. He wrinkled his muzzle and let out a truly impressive snarl. It was almost as good as Maddy's.

The guard tugged again. "Sir, please let go of the wall."

"No," he grunted and yanked on the stone. An ominous groan echoed from the walls, and all three of them froze.

"Harold," Reggie said in a low voice, "please let go of the wall."

A trickle of dust drifted down from the ceiling, and Reggie slowly looked up to see cracks spreading like the forked branches of lightning. He took a cautious step toward Harold but froze as the ground shook beneath his boots. The Caldivar lost his footing and stumbled backward into Reggie. He tripped over the shorter Joongee and tumbled onto his back with a startled shout... and pulled Harold away from the wall, the chunk of stone still clutched in his claws.

Harold staggered but, for once, kept his footing. He stared down at the damp rock in his hands before he looked back at the wall and the empty place in the center where it used to be. "Oh, dear."

Reggie tensed and stared at the wall. Nothing happened. He made the mistake of breathing out a sigh of relief just as a second, louder groan filled the tunnel. He flattened his ears instinctively at the rumbling sound, and Harold dropped the rock like a pup who'd just been caught stealing candy.

Reggie reached down, grabbed the overweight guard's wrist, and yanked him back to his feet. "Time to go, Officer."

A sharp *crack* echoed off the tunnel walls. Small rocks tumbled out of the fractured wall. A second, larger rock thudded to the floor. The cracks in the ceiling deepened, and a shower of dust rained down on them. They all coughed and squinted through the haze. Another *thud*, another rock, and this one just barely missed Harold's boot. Worst of all, the scent deepened.

"Cave in," Harold whispered, fear threading through his voice, and a tremble shaking his body.

Reggie yanked on Harold and the guard. "Run. *Now!*"

They turned and ran. Reggie mentally cursed the older beings as pebbles and small rocks hit their heads. Slow. They were both too slow. The smart thing, the *logical* thing, would be to run at his own pace, to leave them behind.

Nobody gets left behind.

He gritted his teeth, tightened his grip on his clan brother and the security guard, and pulled them along with him. Still slow, but not as slow as before. He kept one eye on the path ahead and one on the ceiling.

Then the next quake hit.

The ground shook beneath their boots, and they stumbled more than ran, but Reggie made sure they didn't stop. They couldn't stop. Not with that scent flooding the tunnel. A rumble heralded the collapse of the fractured wall behind them, followed by the roar of untold gallons of trapped, stinking water escaping its prison. That wasn't the problem.

The low point in the tunnel up ahead, where there was already a pool of stinking water, was the problem.

If they weren't fast enough, the water would flood the tunnel. They'd drown in horrible, stinking water. Reggie clenched his jaw and let out a defiant growl. *I'm not going out like that.*

He pulled his companions along even faster, but both beings were already doing their level best to keep up. Seconds later, they crashed through the pond at the low point in a great spray of water. None of them went down, though it was a close thing for the Caldivar. As they climbed out the far side, he stretched out a hand for his hover scooter.

"My Treker," he gasped.

"No time!" Reggie yelled and dragged him harder.

The wall of water that gushed out of the tunnel did more to persuade the security guard than anything he did, and together they sprinted for the wide intersection. There were a few support columns at the far end, remnants of some kind of pavilion, back in the long-ago days when this was the surface. Reggie dragged Harold and the guard toward them. *If we can get behind the pillars, we'll be fine.*

The Caldivar tripped over the rotten flooring from the collapse that had brought them to this level in the first place and faceplanted. Reggie shoved Harold ahead of him and turned back for the guard.

"Reggie!"

The roar of the water drowned out anything else Harold might have said.

* * *

"**M**addy, either you comm them, or I will," Ed said with unusual directness. "They've been gone, like, way too long."

Maddy blinked in surprise and checked the time on her slate. Her ears angled back, and she twisted her mouth to the side. "You're right."

The big Joongee watched her intently as she tried to comm them. Maddy grumbled when she got no response and tried again, and again. Finally, she slammed her comm down in frustration.

"We'll give them a little more time," she said with a low growl. "They might be too deep for the signal to reach them."

Ed scratched behind one ear, his eyes alight with concern. "What if they don't answer again?"

Maddy took a deep breath and shook out her fur. "We'll burn that bridge when we get to it."

"Isn't it 'cross that bridge,' Maddy?" Ed asked with a curious tilt to his head.

"Nope," she said and took a slow sip of her iced mocha in the hope it would calm the unease twisting in her gut. It didn't work, but at least it tasted good.

* * *

Reggie ignored Harold's cry and latched onto the Caldivar's arm just as the wall of water gushed out into the intersection. It hit him like a flying brick, a stinking deluge that stole his breath and swept his feet out from under him. The guard grabbed his arm in return and kept him from being swept away. A heartbeat, two, three, and it was over. The water level dropped as the flow from the tunnel trickled off to a stream, and he was able to breathe again.

Reggie clumsily lunged to his feet. "Harold!"

"Here," a miserable voice replied. Reggie whipped his head around to see the older Joongee poke his head out from behind one of the columns. His headlamp was gone, but other than muddy, bedraggled fur, torn overalls, and a thoroughly soaked backpack, he appeared to be fine.

Reggie sighed in relief. "Let's get out of here."

"Back to the mall?" Harold asked dejectedly.

"Yes," Reggie replied firmly, ears pinned flat to his skull in irritation.

"Best idea you two have had all day," the Caldivar grumbled as he wiped water out of his eyes.

* * *

Nearly an hour later, they trudged out of the access door and back into the mall proper. The Caldivar reached up and reset the trip sensor.

Reggie glared at the trip sensor as his shoulders slumped. "I knew I missed something."

The guard *harrumphed* as he closed the door and locked it again. He turned to the Joongee, drew himself up to his full height, and glared at them with all three eyes. "All right, down to business, you two. Breaking and entering! Trespassing in a restricted area! Not obeying the orders of a duly appointed member of Mall Security!"

Reggie gave him an incredulous look and pulled his upper lip back, exposing his fangs. His ears pinned to his head, and his paws balled into fists. It was difficult, and he mostly failed, but he tried to keep his voice neutral. "Are you freaking kidding me? I just saved your life!"

This was the first time he'd seen the Caldivar in the light and was able to see his name tag. It read Blahrt. That was it. No rank or any other title. His uniform sleeves had patches with the mall security emblem, and there were several pins on his chest, but Reggie had no clue what they symbolized.

Blahrt *harrumphed* again as he reached behind him to grab at something on his belt. Reggie could only guess he was going for handcuffs.

"You wouldn't have needed to save my life if you hadn't been down there in the first place." He pointed a chubby finger at Reggie. "You should learn to respect those in authority as well as your elders. You think you know everything, but you're still wet behind the ears!"

Blahrt looked him up and down, then chuckled. A glimmer of humor sparkled in his old eyes. "Literally, at the moment."

Reggie looked down at his soaked overalls and boots, then over at Harold. The old Joongee was caked in mud and every bit as soaked as he was. He had to admit, it was pretty comical, given Blahrt's last statement.

"All right, you have me there," he relented with a nod. He spread his arms wide as Blahrt fumbled around with the back of his belt. "Isn't there some way we can work this out?"

"Afraid not," Blahrt replied. "Rules are rules, and you two trampled all over some of the more serious ones."

With a grunt, he finally yanked a small slate from the back of his belt. It had a soft, black leather case on it that he flipped over like an old-fashioned notebook. From his shirt pocket he pulled out a small stylus that nearly disappeared in his large hand. Blahrt mumbled under his breath as he tapped the slate. After several awkward, silent moments, standing there dripping filth all over the mall floor, he looked back up at Reggie and Harold.

"Seventeen violations in total. That's the mall record to be given to any single individual, much less two at the same time. Comm sequence, please."

Reggie's eyes narrowed, and his head cocked to the side. "Excuse me?"

"Your comm sequence, please."

Reggie darted his eyes over to Harold, who just shrugged, equally confused. He scratched behind an ear and cursed as his claw came away packed with stinking mud. "Why, exactly, do you need my comm sequence?"

All three of Blahrt's eyes narrowed. "To send you this citation, of course."

Reggie's eyes slammed shut, and he took a deep, calming breath as he fought for every scrap of patience he had left. "A *what?*"

Blahrt huffed and shifted his weight. "A citation, pup. Now, give me your comm sequence."

Flabbergasted, Reggie recited his comm sequence as Blahrt tapped on his slate. After the sequence was entered, Blahrt asked Harold for his. Both numbers entered, he held the slate and stylus out to Reggie. "Sign and date here, please."

Reggie, unsure of what else to do, accepted the slate, signed, dated, and handed it back to Blahrt, who then handed it off to Harold to do the same. Once he had the slate back from Harold, Blahrt signed it with an elaborate flourish.

A second later, Reggie's slate dinged in his pack, as did Harold's. He set his dripping wet backpack on the floor, reached in, pulled the slate out, and checked the notification. It was a copy of his citation.

He read it twice in growing disbelief as he shook his head. "That's it? All that? The chasing, running, almost being crushed, nearly drowning in rank water... all for a written warning? No actual ticket or being taken into custody for all this stuff?"

Blahrt snorted so hard, his ample belly bounced up and down. "I'm a mall security officer, pup, not a law enforcement officer." His eyes narrowed again, and he pointed at the slate in Reggie's hand. "But don't go thinking that isn't a serious matter. I take my job *very* seriously. If you get two more, you'll both be banned from the mall for a period of six months. I'd mind myself, if I were you."

Reggie worked his jaw up and down until he finally found the words. "If you're just mall security, why chase us at all? You could've literally just waited up here for us to come back out!"

"Maybe," he replied with a thoughtful expression, "but you could've died or gotten lost down there, and I felt it was my duty to go."

"Not exactly," Harold replied dryly and held up his slate. "We have the previously mapped areas, and I was tracking our every step."

The Caldivar's brow furrowed, and his shoulders slumped. "Huh. Well, then... yeah. I guess I could've just waited for you to come back." He shook his head and stood straight again. "No, no, I couldn't have. How was I supposed to know you had all that? Besides, that entire area is restricted. Authorized personnel only."

Unsure of how to reply, and feeling extremely confused at the whole unorthodox situation, Reggie slipped the slate into his pocket and kicked at the ground with the toe of his boot. He cleared his throat and said, "We're sorry about your Treker."

Harold nodded. "Yes, very sorry about that."

The Caldivar shrugged but couldn't quite hide his misery. "I'll put in a requisition for another. I'm the top employee, after all. It should only take a few… months to get another."

"We could all use the exercise, right?" Reggie said with a small grin.

The corner of Blahrt's mouth rose in a half smile. He patted his belly and laughed. "I don't suppose it's going to kill me to walk a little bit more for a while. Besides, I just burned all the calories I'm about to scarf down when I get my hands on my cupcakes."

* * * * *

Chapter Eighteen

"Reggie!"

Reggie turned from Blahrt with a wave and felt his jaw hit the floor as Maddy and Ed barreled up to them. They were loaded down with shopping bags, none of which appeared to be from the kind of stores that had the supplies they were supposed to buy. Even worse, there was no sign of the replicator they so desperately needed.

"What happened to you guys?" Maddy asked with a smirk. Her nose twitched, and she took a hasty couple of steps back. "You stink."

The *snap* of the last of Reggie's control shattering was nearly audible, and a snarl ripped its way free. He stalked toward the smaller female with measured steps until he was right in her face.

"Yes, Madeline," he said in a low growl, "we stink. We're covered in filthy, stinking mud, we fell through filthy, stinking floors, and we nearly drowned in filthy, stinking water. For nothing! We didn't find the damn clue, and we wasted a whole day—just like *you* apparently did!"

Maddy's ears flicked back, and any amusement in her purple eyes died. Her tiny fists clenched around her shopping bags. "What's that supposed to mean, *Reginald?*"

"It means you messed it up!" he snarled. He thought he caught a flash of hurt in her eyes, but his control was gone, and he couldn't stop the words from pouring out of his mouth like a river of frustrated rage. "After I practically *begged* you not to, you went ahead and did whatever you wanted, just like you always do. And you dragged Ed right along with you."

Unable to trust himself so close to Maddy, he paced away from her, shedding chunks of stinking mud as he went.

Harold crossed his arms and shook his head at the other Joongee like a disappointed parent. "You should both be ashamed of yourselves."

Reggie took a deep breath and tried to drag a hand through the short mane on top of his head, but his claws snagged in the mud, and he ended up ripping a chunk of fur out. The stinging pain helped ground him again, and he whirled back to face Maddy and Ed.

"I trusted you both," he said in a low voice. "We needed those supplies, we *needed* that replicator, and you blew it on what? Junk? Coffee? I hope it was worth it, because we're screwed."

Maddy flinched. She actually *flinched*, and Reggie suddenly felt like he was the one who'd messed up. Ed glanced between them, and his tail flicked back and forth as an anxious whine escaped his muzzle. At that, rage twisted Maddy's expression, and Reggie felt like he was on more solid ground. He knew how to handle her rage.

"Are. You. Kidding me!" she shrieked at the top of her lungs. Her chest heaved, and Reggie wasn't sure whether she was about to scream again or murder them all. She ground her teeth audibly and said, "We bought your damn supplies and picked up the replicator. They're on the ship!"

Reggie scowled right back at her and stabbed a finger at the shopping bags. "Then what's all this? I told you we didn't have the credit to blow on a shopping spree!"

Maddy threw the bags in his face and snarled. "Presents for you two, though I'm having a really hard time remembering why we did anything nice for you jerks!"

The tiny female whirled around and stalked away from them before she paused. Her shoulders heaved, and she spun on her heel, every sharp tooth on full display. All three males flinched back from her.

She stabbed a clawed finger at Harold and roared, "And we found your stupid clue, *Harry!*"

Harold spluttered, and his ears flicked back in shock. Ed nodded his head emphatically and said, "It's true, Pops. We found it!"

Maddy growled under her breath and turned away again. She stalked into the crowd, which had given them a wide berth, though Reggie wasn't sure whether it was because of the fighting or the stench.

"Where are you going?" he bellowed after her, fully aware he was acting like an enraged lunatic and far past the point of caring. "We're not done fighting yet!"

"Oh, we are *so* done!" she snapped back over her shoulder as she headed toward *HIADA*.

The crowd swallowed her small form, and she was gone.

The three males stood around awkwardly for a moment. The crowd drew a little closer now that they weren't fighting, but they still had a little bubble of space thanks to the thick stench that hung in a near visible cloud around their group. Harold coughed and scratched at the back of his neck, while Ed sidestepped the resulting shower of dried mud.

The silence gave Reggie the time he needed to gather up the shreds of his control. He sighed and muttered a curse under his breath.

"Think I made her angry?" Reggie asked with a wince.

Harold sighed. "She's just being Mad Maddy again. She'll get over it."

"No, you hurt her feelings." Ed frowned at them both. "Mine, too. We both worked really hard to get all the supplies we needed and the replicator and comm array."

Reggie spread his hands helplessly at all the bags. "If you bought all that stuff, how do you explain this?"

Ed pinned him with a flat stare, and his ears angled back in annoyance. "Because, like, I found a winning scratch-off ticket for a whole bunch of credit. We saved half of it for emergencies and bought stuff for everyone with the other half. We're on an adventure, Reggie, not a mercenary mission. This is supposed to be *fun*."

Reggie and Harold exchanged a glance, and he wondered if his expression was as stricken as the older Joongee's. His shoulders slumped, and he scrubbed his face as a wave of exhaustion slammed into him.

"I'm sorry, Ed." He let out a heavy sigh. "And you're right. This *is* supposed to be a fun trip. I'll try not to be so demanding and impatient with you guys. I should've asked you about the bags instead of jumping down your throats like that."

"Yeah, you should've," Ed said with a forgiving smile. He gathered up the bags Maddy had thrown and jerked his head. "Let's get back to the ship. You guys can clean up."

Harold cleared his throat as they maneuvered through the crowds. "Sorry, Ed. I'm afraid I lost my temper, too."

"Did you, Pops? I didn't notice." Ed chuckled and looked down at the old Joongee. "How about you and I hang out with Boo tonight? We can try out some of the new games Maddy and I picked out."

Reggie's ears drooped despite his best efforts not to let his hurt show. He lengthened his stride so he walked beside Ed. "Can I play, too?"

"Nope." Ed's happy grin took away any sting from the instant rejection, and his tail lashed playfully. "You gotta deal with Maddy first. Just apologize. She's not as hateful as you guys seem to think she is. But right now, you're what she'd call a 'jerk-face.'"

Harold winced and patted Reggie on the shoulder. "Have fun with that, pup."

Reggie groaned. It was going to be a long night.

* * *

Maddy stomped up the ramp, entered *HIADA*, and sealed the hatch behind her. Once inside, she let out a fierce growl that turned into a frustrated roar. Slightly relieved, she marched to the galley and made some coffee in the largest mug she had available. Boo dropped from the ceiling and landed on the countertop. Her tentacles writhed with anxiety, and her eyes were wide and fearful, but more than fear, they showed concern and empathy. She held out a small square of chocolate in her tiny little paw.

The sight of the little kinkakaijou's obvious attempt to console her made a large portion of Maddy's anger immediately subside. Slowly, a small smile formed on her face, and she reached out to accept Boo's gift. "Thanks, furball. I need that right now. Stupid Reggie and his stupid face and his stupid assumptions."

She gently plucked the chocolate square from Boo's paw, tossed it in her mouth, and took a swig from her mug. It paired perfectly with the coffee flavor. Content for the moment, she exited the galley and headed for her room. As she passed through the common area, the exterior hatch opened, and the others entered, their arms full of all the gift bags. Maddy gave Ed a slight smile, but completely ignored Reggie and Harold. Once in her room, she locked the door and turned her new music up as loud as it would go.

Across the way, in her closet, a sleek little black dress screamed, "Wear me and take me to a bar!" A grin split her face, and she grabbed her makeup kit. A night out sounded amazing and exactly what she needed. That and a few drinks. They didn't plan to leave until the next day, so she could do whatever she wanted.

* * *

After a long, scalding-hot shower, Reggie dried his fur off and dressed himself in jeans and a tight, black V-neck t-shirt that showed off his hard-earned muscles. It was nice to wear normal clothes again. He slipped a silver chain around his neck. It wasn't overly thick or gaudy, but simple and sleek. His grandmother had given it to him as a gift after he'd completed his training to become a mercenary. In fear of it getting broken or lost, he only wore it every now and then.

Considering the day he'd just had, he needed a drink, and finding a bar sounded like just the thing to do. Going out gave him an excuse to wear it. Doing so always made him feel better. His grandmother had always supported his decisions, even through the hard times. Her death had struck him harder than anyone else in his family.

Reggie shook his head to rid himself of the thoughts of his family and turned his attention to the bags on the floor. They contained all his favorite snacks and drinks, as well as some fun little knickknack type things for his room on the ship. Maddy and Ed had really gone out of their way to make sure they got him and Harold the perfect gifts. One bag in particular held a large, rectangular box. He pulled it out, and his eyes went wide.

"Ed," Reggie said as he rushed into the common room, "are you crazy? These things are super expensive!"

Ed had just exited the galley and was headed to the couch. He stopped and faced him, looked down at the box in Reggie's hands, and smiled.

"I knew you'd been wanting those for a long time, so I got them. There was a store called Vintage Humanity, and they were on sale for, like, 20 percent off. They had your size, so I grabbed them." He shrugged. "I guess we got lucky. All the Converse shoes were on sale."

Reggie looked down at the Converse logo on the black shoe box and lifted the lid. Inside were a pair of black and white Chuck Taylor Converse high tops, fully equipped with self-tightening laces and color control. The color of the fabric, toe tips, and the soles could be changed with the touch of a button on the inside of the shoe's tongue. Reggie had wanted a pair since he was a young pup but had never been able to afford them. As a merc, he'd had the credit to buy them, but always assumed they'd get messed up and never pulled the trigger, so to speak. Once he'd swapped careers and joined the Galactic Solutions workforce, all his left-over merc pay went into his retirement fund, and he was again unable to afford them—not without hurting his retirement funds, anyway.

He looked back up at his big friend. "I... I don't know what to say, Ed. Thank you." He felt a surge of emotion and had to fight back happy tears. "How did you know?"

Ed grinned down at him. "Like, I lost count of how many times I came to talk to you at your cubicle, and you had those shoes pulled up on your monitor. I really wanted to buy them for you last year for your birthday. I even had the extra credit saved up, but then I accidently dropped a whole box of light bulbs at work, and Glorp took the cost out of my pay. I had to use the credit I had saved up for your birthday to pay for that. Today, I found the ticket, and they were on sale. It was totally fate, and I couldn't pass up the opportunity."

Ever grateful to have a clan mate like Ed, Reggie stepped forward and wrapped him in a one-armed hug while holding the shoe box at a safe distance. Ed chuckled and returned the gesture with vigor.

"Thanks, Ed. You're really the best. I love them."

"No worries, Reggie."

They released each other, and Ed turned to Harold and asked, "You wanna work on that puzzle, Pops?"

"Actually," Reggie interjected, "I was going to go get a drink. You guys want to come, too?"

Harold looked down at the puzzle and back up to Reggie. "As much as I want to dive right into this, I think a break is in order. Let's go have that drink." He stuck a claw in his ear and scratched, his expression mournful. "I don't think I'll ever get all the mud out of my ears."

Ed looked over Reggie's shoulder and jutted his chin at the hallway that led to Maddy's door. "What about Maddy?"

Reggie sighed as his shoulders slumped.

"I guess it's time to face the music." The sound of loudly playing music drifted through the crack under Maddy's door. "Literally."

He sat down, slipped the Chuck Taylors on his feet, and smiled as the auto-laces snugged the shoes to a comfortable pressure. They were a perfect fit. He messed with the color schemes, but decided to leave them classic black and white for now. Satisfied, he stood and walked to Maddy's door. Each step felt like he was back walking through the water under the mall. He'd almost rather do that again than what he was about to do. Reggie summoned up all his courage and knocked on her door. Nothing. He knocked again. Again, nothing.

"Come on, Maddy," he pleaded through the door. For a moment he wondered if the music was too loud. Hoping that was the case, he knocked again, louder this time.

The music stopped.

"What." Maddy's tone was flat through the door.

"Can we talk?"

"You said plenty already."

Reggie's shoulders slumped. "Please, Maddy? I feel horrible about earlier. Can you just open the door?"

* * *

Maddy stared at the door and considered. *You should feel horrible, you ass.*

"Why should I open the door for you? So you can yell at me some more?"

She walked toward the door and noticed something on her dresser. It was a small, pink bag she didn't recognize. She picked it up and peered down into it. There were three small vials inside and a plastic card. Remembering proper gift etiquette, she pulled the card out first and read it.

Thought you would like these. I think if you use the Vanga Black first, then the clear one with the sparkles, your claws will look like little pieces of space.

—Ed

"That sneaky, giant twerp," Maddy mumbled as she pulled the vials out. One was Vanga Black, one was a clear coat with glitter, and the last was a glittery purple that perfectly matched her eyes. *Aw, that lovable goofball. So that's where he snuck off to when we were at the music store. He must've slipped these in here when we dropped off the first load of stuff.*

"I don't want to yell at you," came Reggie's answer through the door. "I want to apologize. I'm sorry. You were right, and I was wrong. I'm an idiot, an ass, a moron, a loser, a... a..."

Maddy carefully set her gift back on the dresser. She stalked across her small room, smacked the panel to open the door, and glared at him. "A total jerk-face?"

Reggie smiled at her, crossed his arms over his chest, and leaned against the frame of her doorway. "Yeah, that, too."

* * *

It took all of Reggie's inner strength not to let his jaw drop when Maddy opened the door. She was wearing a tight little black dress, combat boots that somehow worked with the dress—though he wasn't sure how—and had all her earrings in, along with some spiky bangles on her wrists. She'd even done something to make her purple eyes pop. She looked amazing and fierce. He had a feeling her outfit was meant to intimidate, but he just thought she looked adorably gorgeous.

Her immediate insult didn't even bother him. In an attempt to hide how her current look affected him, he leaned against the door frame, crossed his arms, and smiled at her.

"Yeah, that, too."

* * *

Maddy had to take a second to collect her thoughts after her initial insult. Reggie's shirt was way tighter than she was used to, and his short mane had a stylish, messy look to it that really worked for him. She was pretty sure she'd never seen that necklace before, either, and the way he had his arms crossed really accentuated the muscles in his arms.

She felt her eyes lingering on those muscles for way too long and gave herself a mental shake. *Focus! You're mad at him! He hurt your feelings. Wait, what? No, no, we don't let ourselves get hurt. We just get mad. We're mad, not hurt.*

She narrowed her eyes at him and crossed her own arms. "Don't come in here, being all Smiley McSmileyFace, thinking I'm just going to forget about it."

Reggie's smile got even bigger, and for some reason it completely flustered her. *How dare he smile at me like that! Stop making me not hate you!*

The bigger male straightened up and walked toward her. The fur on the back of her neck rose because he wasn't walking so much as stalking. She couldn't decide if she hated it or liked it. *Both? Can it be both?*

He didn't stop until he was inside her little bubble of personal space. He looked down at her with those deep, ocean-blue eyes of his, nothing but complete sincerity swimming in their depths.

"I'm sorry, Maddy. You guys did everything I asked you to, and more. You went above and beyond to do something nice for me and Harold, and I just stomped all over it. Not only that, you actually found the clue we needed while the two of us ran around under the mall like a couple of lunatics." He chuckled and looked off to the side slightly as his ears flattened a bit in embarrassment. "Hell, we even got chased by a chunky security guard and actually got *caught*. I've got the citation to prove it, too."

Maddy snorted an involuntary laugh at that, even more of her anger dissipating. He looked back into her eyes again, and her laughter trailed off. *Damn those blue eyes of his.*

"I acted like a real—what's the word humans use… Jack? Something Jack?"

Maddy's ears perked up, and her mouth curled into a half smile. "A jackass."

"Yup, that's the one," he said with a laugh. "Color me not surprised you knew exactly what I meant."

A hint of nervousness touched his expression, but it was quickly erased by determination. Maddy found herself holding her breath as he clasped his hands behind his back.

"I really am sorry for yelling at you, Maddy," he said earnestly, his ears perking forward. "I'm sorrier that I hurt your feelings more than anything. I can't promise it won't happen again. I'm not perfect—"

"Well, you are a male," Maddy said with more than a touch of snark and earned a quick grin from Reggie.

"Last time I checked," he said with a wink before his voice dropped into a lower, almost husky tone. "Can you forgive me?"

The last of Maddy's anger vanished in a heartbeat. He meant it. This was as sincere, as *real*, as she'd ever seen him. In four years of friendship, she'd never seen him so vulnerable. He was always so guarded, so locked away. The irritating male was one giant mystery wrapped up in an enigma. Sure, she'd seen him go all badass on the pirates—which had been hot, because she wasn't blind, damn it—but this was different somehow. Her first instinct was to tell him to shove his apology up his ass, but she hesitated. There it was again, that baffling desire to not disappoint him.

More than that, she wanted to forgive him more than insult him because... because... hell, she didn't really have an answer for that. She just knew that was what she wanted. This was Reggie, after all. He was her clan mate. Their leader. And... maybe more? Her ears flicked back at that last thought. *Friend. He's my friend. Good lord, I need a drink. Clearly there's something broken in my brain.*

She pointed a claw up at him and scowled. "You get this one time, Reg. *One.* You ever treat me like that again, and I'll rip your male-hood off and shove it down your throat. Got that?"

Amusement shone bright in his eyes, but his expression said he took her threat seriously. "Yes, ma'am, I got it. Loud and clear."

"Good, you freaking jerk-face," Maddy said with a quick nod. She went to turn away, but stopped and added, "And thank you for apologizing."

"Thanks for accepting it," Reggie replied. His whole demeanor seemed to perk up, and his ears stood straight up on his head. "So, me and the guys were gonna go to the bar and have a few drinks to blow off some steam. You want to go, too?" He indicated her with an open palm. "By the looks of it, you were planning to go out anyway."

Maddy snorted. "You're right, I was already headed that way, but, yeah, I'll come with you guys. Just give me a few minutes to finish getting ready."

"Did you just admit I'm right about something?"

"Don't push it."

Reggie smirked and stepped out of her room. Before her door closed, he stuck his head back in and said, "You look really nice, by the way. That makeup really makes your eyes stand out."

He gave her an appreciative smile and disappeared before she could respond. *Something* shot through her as she stood there in shock. She tried to shake it off, but she ended up replaying the whole conversation in her head as she finished getting ready. That look in his eyes at the end… she must've imagined it. *Yup… definitely need a drink.*

* * * * *

Chapter Nineteen

James and Ann's Rat Hole was hopping. It was one of many bars adjacent to the Galactic Mall. Someone had been a real genius and built a strip mall stretching the entire length of the big mall for the sole purpose of filling every single section of it with nightclubs and bars. It took barhopping to a whole new level. It had a fancy, official name, but everyone just called it The Strip.

The Joongee had hopped around for a while before settling in at their current location. They'd been in there for a couple hours, and they were several drinks in and having a good time. Reggie and Ed were deep in a conversation about Ed's new video game when he realized he hadn't seen or heard Maddy in a while. He scanned the crowd and spotted her sitting at the bar with another Joongee male.

The male was Spotted, like him, and dressed in a nice, but casual suit. His mane was that perfect mix of styled and messy, and his watch looked like it cost more than Reggie made at Galactic Solutions in a year. Reggie pretty much disliked him on sight.

The male said something that made Maddy laugh and smile brightly up at him. A sudden feeling of discomfort wedged itself into Reggie's gut, and he had to fight to keep his muzzle from wrinkling up.

"I think I'm going to go check on Maddy," he said to Ed as he took a sip from his glass.

Ed leaned back and looked at the bar. "She seems fine to me."

Reggie shook his head. "I dunno, that male is giving me a weird feeling. I want to make sure."

"Okay," Ed replied doubtfully, "but, like, don't punch him out or anything. Be cool, Reg."

Reggie snorted. "I'm not going to punch him, Ed. Geez."

He set his glass down with a *thump* and stalked over to the bar. Maddy turned to him and smiled big and bright at him. "Hey, Reg!"

Reggie could tell she'd had more than a few drinks. Her purple eyes were just a little too glassy, her smile just a touch too wide. She was definitely tipsy, but he didn't think she'd crossed the line into outright drunk territory.

"Hey, Maddy," he replied and returned the smile cautiously. "You doing all right over here?"

She sipped from her drink and nodded her head a little too vigorously.

"Yup!" She waved a hand at the other male. "Bruce was just telling me about how he works as a, um... words are hard. Oh! An investor. He works with mercenary companies and helps them invest their profits from their contracts."

That was all it took for Reggie's dislike for Bruce to shift to outright hatred. A low growl saturated his voice as he said, "You're a Mercenary Investment Broker."

Bruce pointed at him and winked. "Nailed it, sport."

Great, another freaking Chad.

Reggie's ears angled back slightly. "It's Reggie, not sport, Bruno."

Bruce's ears also tilted back, and a hint of fang slipped free from his muzzle. "I think you meant Bruce, *Reggie*."

Reggie gave him a cocky grin. "My mistake."

He turned to Maddy, who was noisily sipping what was left of her drink through a straw.

"You wanna come and sit with us?" He pointed back to where Ed and Harold were anxiously watching from their table.

"I think she's just fine where she is, friend," Bruce said before Maddy could answer. His oily smile and the possessive hand he placed on her shoulder nearly broke his control.

"Don't think I was asking you, *pal*," Reggie snapped as his grin fell away. "Say, do you MIB guys still screw mercenary companies out of all kinds of credit by charging your ridiculous rates of 70 or 80 percent? I always despised those lowlife bastards for that."

Bruce's eyes grew cold, and the smile disappeared from his face. "It's not ridiculous, considering I do all the work, and they just sit there and make credit paw-over-fist from the investment."

"Just sit there?" Reggie growled as his control slipped further. "Mercenaries do not just sit there, Brooke. We go out and risk our lives to earn the credit you make your living off of."

The smile reappeared on Bruce's face. "I see. You're a merc, huh? And it's Bruce, buddy."

"He was," Maddy said. Reggie started and snapped his attention back to her. He'd almost forgotten she was there. "But he quit and came to work with us at Galactic Solutions. Then we all quit. Now we're just out having fun."

"Quit, did you?" A mischievous light shone in Bruce's eyes, and his ears perked up. He cocked his head to the side and smirked at Reggie. "Couldn't hack it, I guess. Don't worry, there's a reason our kind stay away from the battlefield."

He took a slow sip from his drink and set it back down, holding Reggie's gaze in challenge the whole time. "But then again, some of us are more cowardly than the rest."

Maddy frowned vaguely at him. "Reggie isn't a coward."

"Of course, he isn't, sweetie." Bruce patted her hand with a condescending smile. "There are a number of Joongee still employed by mercs. I guess Reggie just didn't measure up to them. No shame in that."

Fire ignited in Reggie's belly, and his claws dug into the bar top. It took everything he had not to punch Bruce in the face and slam his head through the bar. "You don't have a clue what you're talking about, Brandon. Why don't you just shut your mouth while you're still ahead."

"Reg!"

Reggie looked down to see Maddy glaring up at him. Her ears angled backward, and her tail lashed in anger.

"Why do you keep calling him by the wrong name?" she demanded. "You're being a jerk, and he's just trying to have a conversation."

"You're drunk, Maddy," Reggie replied with as much patience as he could muster. "You'd hate this turd-in-a-suit otherwise. He's Chad, made over again."

"Nuh-uh," Maddy said before she tried to sip more of her drink. A vague frown crossed her face when she realized it was empty. "Chad's orange. Bruce is brown… ish." She tilted her head to the side and smiled at him, her mood shifting so fast, he almost got whiplash. "Kinda like you."

"Chad sounds like a stand-up being," Bruce interjected. He stood, wiped his muzzle on a napkin, and tossed it onto the bar. "Maddy, I think I'm going to find another place to sit. Would you like to come with me?" He eyed Reggie like he was something nasty on the bottom of his shoe. "This spot has become quite crowded."

Maddy grabbed her bag, but Reggie held a paw out to stop her. "She's not going anywhere with the likes of you, Briggle." He gave him a slight back-pawed wave. "Feel free to leave all on your own."

"*Excuse me?*" Maddy snarled. She hopped down from her stool and glared up at him. "Who the hell do you think you are to say who I can and can't talk to or sit with? You're not my father, and even if you were, I don't listen to him, either!"

Several beings at the bar tried to hide in their drinks, but there was no escaping Maddy's drunken wrath.

Reggie drew in a deep breath. "Maddy, I don't think you should—"

"Should what?" she shouted. "Have a good time? Enjoy talking with another male? Do anything that isn't on your itinerary?"

"Maddy, please," he started through his clenched jaw.

"No, Reg!" she said with an accusing finger pointed at him. "Go away. I can handle myself. I don't need you hovering over me like some sort of protector." She brushed past him, took Bruce's arm, and pointed to an empty table in the middle of the bar. "Let's go over there, Bruce."

"It would be my pleasure," Bruce replied with a greasy smile. He looked at Reggie and flashed him finger guns and a wink. "See ya later, partner."

Together they turned and walked away. Maddy looked over her shoulder and shot him a dirty look. All Reggie could do was stare back at her and drown in his own frustrated anger. Feeling the eyes of everyone at the bar on him, Reggie snarled and made the walk-of-shame back to his seat next to Ed.

Did I go too far? Why did I care that she was talking to him so much? That shouldn't have bothered me. I've never cared who she spoke with before. Ugh, I'm such an idiot. I guess I owe her another apology. I'll be a professional at it by the time this treasure hunt is over.

"That didn't go over well," Ed stated. He took a pull from his vape pen and blew two trails of smoke from his nose. "Like, I tried to warn you."

"I know," Reggie replied, sullen and hating it.

"Maddy will be just fine," Harold said in a reassuring tone. "She's more than capable of taking care of herself."

"She is," Reggie said and smiled at him as his ears came back up a little. "I just don't want her to find that one time when she can't."

Harold gave him a knowing smile. "Admirable, pup, but she's fine."

A loud *crash* of shattering glass erupted across the bar. All three of them stood to see what was going on, but Reggie couldn't see past the group of Humans who'd also turned their attention in the direction of the crash. A shocked scream sounded over the crowd, and he jumped up on his chair without hesitation. That was a Joongee's cackling cry. His eyes widened as he saw Maddy slam a glass bottle over Bruce's head and knee him in the face.

Reggie jumped down and shoved his way through the crowd to get to her. Harold was close behind him, and Ed presumably was right behind Harold. Down among the crowd, his line of sight to Maddy was cut off, and he pushed beings aside without regard or care. None of them mattered, only Maddy did.

Nearly there, Reggie tried to push aside a Leethog.

"Hey!" the Leethog growled. He shoved Reggie back into the crowd and snarled, every one of his teeth on display. "Who're you shoving?"

"I need to get through," Reggie snapped without an ounce of apology in his tone. "My friend's over there."

"Screw you," the Leethog snapped. "Nobody shoves me. You can find another way around."

Reggie didn't have time for this. He gritted his teeth and held back the rage. Mostly.

"I. Need. To. Pass." He squared up and leveled his gaze on the Leethog. "Please, move."

Another *crash*, and a different being shouted. Reggie craned his head past the Leethog and managed to catch a glimpse of a female Pikith as she took a punch to the face from a tiny fist that looked an awful lot like Maddy's.

"*Now*," he growled.

The Leethog stepped up to him and poked him in the chest. "Screw you."

He then did the single most stupid thing he could have ever done. The Leethog picked his shoe up off the floor and dragged the dirty sole across the perfectly white toe-tip of Reggie's brand-new Chuck Taylors.

Reggie bared his teeth at the Leethog. "Big mistake."

Reggie feinted with his left shoulder, causing the Leethog to flinch back. That angered the Leethog, and he struck out with a right hook. Reggie leaned back a couple inches and let the punch sail past him. As he leaned back in, the Leethog followed through with his strike, leaving the side of his face open and his left arm useless to attack. Reggie seized the opening and struck him with a left jab to the jaw, followed by a hard right uppercut to the chin. The Leethog dropped, out cold before he even hit the sticky floor. Reggie stepped over him and into the fray.

On the floor lay Bruce with a trickle of blood down the side of his face. A Pikith female sat on the floor with a hand to the side of her head. Maddy was currently wrestling with a female Prithmar. Reggie stepped over to break them apart when a hand gripped his upper arm. He turned to see the hand belonged to a male Prithmar.

"You keep your handsss off my mate," the Prithmar said in low-voiced warning.

Reggie shook his head. "No, I need to break them up. Maddy's going to hurt her."

The Prithmar bellowed a laugh. "Yeah, right. Merinith can handle herssself just fine. You just ssstay right here with me and watch the ssshow."

"No." Reggie narrowed his eyes at the Prithmar. "Let me go, or I'm going to make you."

The slightly taller being looked down at him, and the corners of his mouth rose. "I'd like to sssee you try."

In the blink of an eye, Reggie twisted his arm under and around to the back of the Prithmar's and pulled down hard. He felt the shoulder pop out of its socket and slammed his left elbow down into it. A scream of pain escaped the Prithmar, and Reggie silenced him with a knee to the face. As he stepped toward Maddy and the female, he heard the loud crunching sound of breaking wood directly behind him.

He turned to see Harold holding the remains of a wooden stool in his hands and an unconscious Yalteen on the floor next to the Prithmar. Harold looked up at him with shock in his eyes, as if he couldn't believe what he'd just done.

"He was going to attack you from behind," he said faintly before his eyes narrowed. "I didn't think that was very fair."

Reggie pointed at the stool. "And that was?"

Harold looked at the broken wood in his hands and shrugged. "Call it an equalizer."

A squeal and a snarl tore through the air, and Reggie snapped his attention back to Maddy. She had the Prithmar pinned to the floor and was bashing her face in with her tiny little fists. The speed of her punches was impressive as hell. Reggie tilted his head. *She'd make a great feather-weight boxer.*

Before she could beat the female to death, Reggie rushed over and wrapped his arms around Maddy's upper arms and chest, locking her into a tight bear-hug. With some effort, he lifted her off the Prithmar and stepped to the side. She fought with more ferocity than he'd anticipated, and he nearly dropped her.

"Let me go, Reg!" she shrieked. "Let me finish her off!"

Reggie couldn't help it. He laughed in her ear. "She's done, Spitfire. You won."

He spun her around so she could see the other bodies on the floor. After a second, she quit struggling and leaned back against his chest. He tried not to notice how nice it felt.

"Did Harold take a Yalteen out with a bar stool?" she asked in a conversational tone between panted breaths. "Nice."

The floor vibrated. No. The floor *shook*. Then it shook again. And again. Someone—or some*thing*—enormous was walking up behind them. The looks on the faces of those in the crowd told him whatever it was, it was something he didn't want to mess with. Reggie set Maddy back on her feet and held onto her until she had her balance back.

Together, they slowly turned around. Neither of them said a word. Neither of them moved.

An enormous, red-scaled being glared down at them with menacing orange eyes. He was at least eight feet tall and had massive, leathery wings folded up on his back. Behind him, a muscular tail rested on the floor. His hands and feet both ended in long, razor-sharp claws that could easily make short work of them both. The tight, black shirt he wore read Security.

Reggie swallowed hard. "Um… s-sorry about the mess."

The massive being continued to glare down at them. He crossed his arms over his chest and growled.

"Oh, dear," Harold murmured as he dropped what was left of his bar stool. "I think we're in trouble this time."

Maddy groaned. "I'm way too drunk for this crap."

* * * * *

Chapter Twenty

The jail cell was filthy. Reggie and Harold sat on the steel bench, while two Pikith, a Caldivar, the Leethog from the bar, and a Hariboon slept on the floor. The Hariboon snored like nothing Reggie had ever heard before. Maddy was in the cell next to them. She sat on the floor with her head against the bars. Her pretty black dress was torn and tattered from the fight, and her fur was all in tangles. She kept massaging her temples as if she had a raging headache.

Reggie felt bad for her. Tonight was supposed to be a fun night out after a long, miserable day. Instead, she'd been clocked good a few times and had had more to drink than Reggie had originally thought.

"Freaking dirt-bag Chad impersonator," Maddy grumbled from her cell.

Reggie turned his head to look at her. It was the first time she'd spoken since they'd been thrown in here. The sun was coming up, and a narrow sunbeam cut across the floor of her cell, highlighting the faint stripes in her fur.

He cleared his throat. "Wanna tell us what happened now?"

Maddy groaned as she pushed herself up to a full sitting position and leaned back against the wall. "I should've listened to you. That male was a total creep. After we left you at the bar, he ordered us more drinks. When they showed up, I saw him drop some powder into mine as he picked it up and handed it to me."

Reggie wrinkled up his muzzle as a snarl tore out of his throat. He knew he should've bashed that male's head through the bartop when he had the chance.

"He'd already bought me three drinks before that. There's no telling how much of whatever that was I'd already ingested before you came over. Any more, and I would've been completely out of it." She thumped her head back against the wall and squeezed her eyes shut. "So stupid… I *knew* I shouldn't have been that drunk already."

Reggie nodded carefully. "I thought you looked a little further gone than you should've been."

"Is that why you came over?" Maddy asked with a weak smile. "To protect me?"

Reggie struggled to find the right answer. He didn't really want to admit he just hadn't liked her talking to the other male. She might get mad about that. "Yup, that's it. I could tell you'd had too much, and he was being a creep."

"Oh, okay. Thanks for that, Reg."

Reggie thought he caught a hint of disappointment on her face, but it was gone too fast for him to be sure.

"Anyway," she continued after a beat, "after I saw that, I freaking lost it. I punched that bastard right in the face and tossed the table aside. I'm pretty sure I bashed him over the head with at least three mugs. Then some Prithmar jumped on me because some of the drink in one of the glasses got on her dress. I think there was a Pikith, too…" She looked around the cells and jabbed a finger at the Leethog. "How come he's the only one who got tossed in here with us?"

"The rest were all taken to the hospital," Harold said with a backward tilt to his ears. "We were the only ones who didn't need medical attention."

"False," Reggie said with a vicious snap to his tone. "If Maddy was drugged, she needs medical attention and nanites." He stood and marched to the cell door. Before he could yell for the guard, a Yalteen in a law enforcement uniform came around the corner. "Hey, I need to speak with you."

"You can talk to me, or you can go home," the Yalteen replied calmly. "You three are free to go. The officers on call last night just finished reviewing the bar's camera footage. You all acted in self-defense, and the owners aren't pressing charges." He pointed at Harold. "Your little stool stunt was questionable, but they let it slide because he was about to attack your friend, there. I'm guessing you never saw the knife in his hand?"

Harold swallowed hard, and his hand shot to his mouth. The Yalteen smiled.

"Guess not. Lucky break for you." He set his gaze on Reggie. "And for you."

Reggie turned to Harold and smiled warmly. "Thanks, Harold. You really saved my ass."

"I… I guess I did," Harold replied as his ears perked up. He smiled and shoved his hands into his pockets. "Think nothing of it, pup. You'd have done the same for me."

The officer unlocked the cell door and let them out. He shut and locked it before letting Maddy out of hers. Once she was out, he put a hand on her shoulder.

"We also saw what happened to you. I'm so sorry, ma'am. We do our best to prevent such things, but there are bad beings all over the galaxy," he said in a firm voice. Maddy swallowed hard and nodded sharply. He gave her a professional smile that did nothing to hide his satisfaction as he added, "You'll be happy to know that we'll be prosecuting him to the full extent of the law. There's a doctor waiting for you in our clinic."

"You have your own clinic?" Reggie asked.

The Yalteen nodded. "Sure do. Our precinct sees this sort of thing on a too-regular basis, so we're prepared for everything. Our doctor can tend to her and give her any medications needed. James and Ann have also agreed to pay any medical bills she acquires, as well as waive everything on your tab. They'd tell you themselves, but they're off-planet on a business trip. We had an emergency conference call with them as soon as we gathered all the evidence." He motioned down the hall and looked at Maddy. "Ready, ma'am?"

Obviously shaken, Maddy nodded meekly and walked ahead of them. Reggie and Harold fell into step behind her and the Yalteen.

Before entering the waiting room, they stopped and retrieved their property the officers had confiscated during their arrest and booking. Relief washed over Reggie as he slipped the silver necklace back over his head. He'd been terrified he wouldn't get it back. Harold stuffed his personal slate into his pocket and slipped his wrist slate back on his arm. Reggie grabbed Maddy's bag, and they stepped out into the front waiting room.

Ed, complete with a box of crackers, sat patiently in a chair as he scrolled down his slate. He looked up at them and smiled. "Hey."

"Hey, yourself," Reggie said as he plopped down in the seat next to Ed. "I didn't expect to see you out here."

Harold sat down on the other side of Ed with a soft sigh of relief.

"Someone had to come pick you criminals up," Ed replied with a wide grin. "I got here a few hours ago to post bail for you, but the officers told me it might not be necessary and to just wait a bit."

"How come they didn't arrest you, too?" Reggie asked with a curious tilt to his head.

"I didn't get into the fight."

Reggie gave him a funny look. "You didn't want to help us? You fought the pirates."

"I did want to help," Ed said with a firm nod. He set the slate down on his lap and looked at them earnestly. "But then Pops clocked that Yalteen with the stool. I knew all three of you were going to end up going to jail. If I went to jail, too, there wouldn't be anyone to bail you guys out. Also, if all of us went to jail, the parking meter for HI-ADA would've run out, and we'd have gotten impounded. Then we'd have had to pay four bail fees plus impound fees. I just figured not getting arrested was the best option. Besides, it looked like you all had it handled."

Impressed, Reggie shook his head and smiled. "You thought all that through that fast?"

Ed shrugged. "Yeah. Didn't you?"

"Uh, no," Reggie said wryly, not quite ready to admit he'd pretty much stopped thinking the second Maddy was in danger. "I was more worried about keeping Maddy from committing murder."

"Oh. Fair enough."

An hour later, Maddy walked in from the clinic, apparently already feeling better.

"Everything all right?" Reggie asked as she approached. He handed her the bag with her things in it.

"Yeah, I'm okay," she said with a nod, but her eyes were a little distant. "A little… freaked out something like that happened, but I'm all right."

Reggie put a hand on her shoulder. "I would never have let anything happen to you."

She looked up at him and smiled. "I know, Reg."

There wasn't as much confidence behind her answer as he would've liked. Didn't she know he'd never taken his eyes off her? Didn't she know he never would've let her leave the bar with that creep? Even if she'd hated him forever...

Maddy cleared her throat and shuffled through her bag. "Can we go now? I need some coffee."

"I second that," Harold grumbled. "I didn't sleep a wink in that cell."

"Me, either," Reggie added.

"I slept great," Ed chimed in with an innocent smile. "Me and Boo watched vids and played video games before passing out on the couch."

All three of them stopped, turned, and glared at him.

"What?"

When the group entered the parking lot, they all stopped and looked at Ed again, this time with astonishment and confusion.

"Ed, is that *HIADA*?" Reggie asked.

"Yeah?" Ed said, though it came out more as a question than anything. He frowned at Reggie in concern. "Don't you recognize it? You weren't in jail that long, Reggie."

"Of course, I recognize it, Ed," Reggie said in exasperation. "I meant, how the hell did it get *here*?"

"I flew it."

Reggie's eyes bulged. "You *flew* it?"

"Totally," Ed replied easily.

"How?" Maddy asked, her ears practically sideways in shock. "You've never flown anything before."

"I just, like, did what Reggie always does when he flies," Ed said casually. "It was kinda bumpy at first, but I got the hang of it after a few minutes. Landing was the hardest part, but I got it between the lines pretty good."

Reggie couldn't believe his ears. "You flew the ship just off your memory of everything I do when I fly?"

"Well, yeah. I paid super close attention, because I figured since we go everywhere in a ship, I should, like, know how to do it if there's ever an emergency. Totally paid off today." He looked at Harold and Maddy. "You guys can't fly the ship, too?"

"Not in atmo!" Maddy shouted. It wasn't an angry shout. If anything, she sounded proud and impressed. "Ed! That's awesome!"

Reggie clapped him on the shoulder. "Great job, Ed. If you want, you can be the copilot sometimes and fly with me. I didn't know you wanted to learn. I'd have absolutely taught you how."

Ed smiled down at him. "You did teach me, Reggie."

Reggie chuckled. "Yeah, I guess I did." He looked at Maddy. "Well, since you have coffee on the ship, do you guys just wanna go? We can get up into the black and figure out the next clue."

"Yeah," Ed said and looked at Harold. "I didn't open the puzzle, Pops. I wanted to wait on you."

Harold smiled up at him. "Thank you, Ed. I can't wait to get started."

Maddy shook her head adamantly. "Nope. I want coffee shop coffee made by someone else for way too much credit."

Reggie didn't even bother to argue. After what she'd nearly experienced, she deserved whatever kind of coffee she wanted. Rage boiled in his blood as they walked toward *HIADA*. Bruce was lucky Reggie hadn't known what he was up to the night before, and he was already in custody. Otherwise, Reggie might have beat him to death. Literally. *Scumbag.*

"The mall is only about a ten-minute flight from here," Ed said as they entered the ship.

"Awesome," Reggie said as the hatch shut. "You drive."

* * *

As they entered the coffee shop, the clan heard a deep, rumbling voice say, "I want an extra-large triple mocha Frappuccino with three espresso shots, caffeinated whip, chocolate sauce, and extra sprinkles."

To their surprise, the being standing at the counter was the massive security guard from the bar.

He slammed an enormous red fist down on the counter. "Todd, I swear on my honor that if you do not put an adequate amount of sprinkles on my beverage this time, I will drag you over that counter and stuff you head-first into the nearest trash receptacle."

"Y-yes, sir," a skinny, red-headed Human male squeaked. "S-sorry that your last drink didn't meet our standards, Murockal."

He scurried away to make the giant's drink with shaking hands. They all watched raptly as Murockal accepted the drink with critical eyes. He snaked out his tongue and licked a portion of whip and sprinkles from the top. His eyes lit up, but his expression remained stoic.

He looked down at Todd and nodded gravely. "You will not be stuffed in the trash today, Todd."

Murockal turned around and saw them staring at him. "I see you were all allowed to escape permanent incarceration." He pointed a large claw at Reggie. "You fought well. I can see training in your moves. A tad sloppy, but nothing more training will not correct." His orange eyes moved to Harold. "You... should probably refrain from future fights. There will not always be a stool to use as a weapon." Murockal's gaze landed on Maddy last with considerable approval. "You showed great potential. I enjoyed watching you destroy your foes very much."

"Um, no offense," Maddy said, "but what race are you, and why are you critiquing our fighting?"

Murockal chuckled. "I am not offended, little bruiser. I am a Sheingal, from Sheinrah."

Reggie shook his head. "I've never heard of either of those."

"Me, either," Harold and Maddy both said at the same time. Ed watched with interest but didn't comment.

"Not surprising," Murockal said as he plucked a handful of napkins from the dispenser. "My system was just re-opened to the public for the first time in seven thousand years about six months ago."

"And your first thought was to become a security guard in a bar?" Maddy asked incredulously.

A deep snort escaped Murockal. "I saw the opportunity to see the galaxy, little bruiser. So I took it. Security is only one of my jobs. I am also attending online college courses to gain a business degree. On the side, I fight in underground cage matches. There is very good credit in that, and it keeps me in shape."

"Holy crap," Maddy gasped and spun to Reggie. "Please tell me we have time to go to an underground cage match. Please?"

Reggie shook his head rapidly at her. Murockal shrugged and backed his wings up to the exit.

"I do not believe I have ever seen perforated feces, little bruiser," he said with a deep chuckle. "Perhaps my translator is broken. In any case, I must be off now. I have much homework to get finished before work. Do your best not to get into any more fights." He paused as he was halfway out the door and looked back at her. The direct sunlight gave his scales a mesmerizing opal sheen. "But if you do, keep your left hand up when you throw your right cross. You have a habit of dropping it to your waist and leaving yourself unprotected. It is an easy chink in your armor to fix. Good day to you all."

With that, he shoved his bulk the rest of the way out the door and was gone.

Ed swished his tail and grinned. "I want to be a Sheingal when I grow up."

Harold clamped a hand over his eyes and groaned, but Reggie chuckled and elbowed his bigger friend. "Me, too, buddy. Me, too."

Maddy marched up to the counter. "Okay, Todd. I want exactly what you just gave Murockal." She dipped her chin and narrowed her eyes at him. "And if you want to keep your non-trash receptacle streak going, I suggest you make sure I have as many sprinkles as he did."

Todd swallowed hard and grabbed an extra-large cup. Reggie bit back a snort of amusement. The Human appeared just as intimidated by the tiny Joongee female as he was by the giant Sheingal. *Smart little Human.*

* * * * *

Chapter Twenty-One

"**T**hree days. You've been working on this stupid puzzle for *three* days, Harold," Reggie said as he rubbed the spot between his eyes. "Maybe you can let the rest of us have a go at it?"

Harold glared at him with bloodshot eyes, hunched over the scattered puzzle pieces on the table, and growled. Reggie sighed.

Rather than burn up all their extra credit on docking fees, the Joongee had taken *HIADA* on a slow course toward the gate. The hope was, by the time they reached the gate, they'd know what system they needed to go to next and could work out a ride to cut down on the transit fee. With all the traffic coming in and out of the Galactic Mall System, that wouldn't be a problem.

What was a problem was the fact that Harold was no closer to solving the Impossible Puzzle than he was when he first started. Ever since the plastic wrap had been taken off the plastic puzzle box, Harold hadn't allowed anyone to help. The old Joongee was bound and determined to figure it out on his own. The tactic had yet to work out for him, as all the pieces still sat on the coffee table, unattached to one another.

Harold's fur stuck up in greasy clumps, and Reggie was fairly certain he'd neither showered nor slept since he first sat down, all brighteyed and bushy-tailed, three days prior. If it weren't for the scattered empty snack bags and dirty plates shoved to the other end of the table, he'd question whether Harold had even eaten.

Ed ambled over with a fresh round of snacks, Boo riding high on his shoulder and a vape pen between his fingers. "Come on, Pops. Let us help. Like, I bet if we all put our heads together at the same time, we'll knock it out quick."

Harold snarled with a slight edge of madness. Reggie took a quick step back and set his feet, his body gearing up for a fight without stopping to consult his brain, but Ed just rolled his eyes and patted the older Joongee on the shoulder.

"Aw, don't be like that, Pops," he said with gentle reproof. "Here, eat this. You'll feel better."

The big Joongee had the puzzle moved aside and a plate of various meats, cheeses, and crackers in front of Harold before Reggie could do more than blink. The fur on the back of Harold's neck rose, and his muzzle wrinkled, but his growl died away the second Ed set a bottle of Nilta honey ale in front of him.

Harold let out a long breath and flicked his ears twice. He guzzled half the bottle before he gently set it back down and said, "Um, sorry about that. Perhaps you all would care to assist while I eat?"

"Sure, Harold," Reggie said cautiously as he pulled the puzzle box closer to study it.

There wasn't much to go on, however, with not even a hint of the final shape. All he knew was there were forty-two variations, and somehow they all created the same abstract shape. All the pieces were perfectly clear with random edges and cutouts. There was no pattern to them he could discern. He fussed with it while Harold inhaled his food and polished off a second bottle of ale.

"Are you sure this is the real clue?" he finally asked Harold in frustration.

He repressed a wince and darted a glance at Maddy. He expected her to bite his head off for daring to say she'd made a mistake, but she just sat motionless on the couch. She was curled up in a tiny ball, and while her gaze was focused on them, it didn't seem like she was really paying them any attention. She'd been quiet and just… *off* for days. Ever since the bar. Ever since Bruce.

A deep, rumbling growl started in his chest, but he cut it off almost before the sound escaped. She didn't need his anger, and it wouldn't have done any good, anyway. With considerable effort, he pulled his attention back to the puzzle.

Harold belched and patted his belly in satisfaction. "Thank you, Ed. That really hit the spot, as they say. And yes, Reggie, I'm sure it's the clue. I'm sorry again for nearly dragging you to a muddy, stinky death beneath the mall for nothing. Not to mention getting us covered in those creepy little insects."

Reggie shuddered. Sometimes, when he was right on the edge of sleep, he could still feel those chitinous creatures as they tried to burrow into his fur. "Please don't mention it, Harold. Ever."

"Right. Well, I'm sure we can figure this puzzle out together," the older Joongee said with a hint of his former enthusiasm.

"Just look it up on the net," Maddy said in an indifferent tone.

"Don't be ridiculous. This is an *impossible* puzzle. We'll just have to be the first." Harold's gaze drifted over to the galley, and he added, "Perhaps after another drink…"

Maddy abruptly stood and stalked away. "I'm going to bed."

Reggie stared after her as his ears flattened with dread. That wasn't good. Harold was as oblivious as ever. He stood, swayed slightly, and belched again.

"Oh, dear," he said with an embarrassed smile. "I believe Maddy has the right idea. I'm going to bed as well. I'll attack the problem again tomorrow with fresh eyes. Good night all."

Boo *chirped* and waved a paw from her perch on Ed's shoulder.

Ed waited until Harold was gone before he turned to Reggie. "Don't worry, Reg. Maddy will be okay. We'll make sure of it."

"Of course, she'll be okay." Reggie forced his ears back up and nodded firmly, as if his confidence would make it happen sooner. "My Spitfire doesn't have any quit in her. She'll bounce back… and we'll be there for her until she's steady on her feet again."

"That's what clan does." Ed smiled gently and gestured to the multitude of snacks spread out on the table. "Boo and I are going to stay up for a bit and get our snack on. Want to join us?"

Reggie stood slowly and stretched until every vertebra in his back popped with varying degrees of pleasantness. "Thanks, buddy, but I've got to check a few things on the bridge, then I'm going to get some sleep, too. See you in the morning?"

"'Course," Ed said easily as he sat back in his chair and kicked his feet up. "Night, Reg."

* * *

After Reggie was gone, Ed looked at Boo and grinned. "*His* Spitfire, huh? Like, how long do you think it'll take them to figure things out?"

Boo chittered, shrugged her narrow shoulders, and reached for his vape pen. Ed chuckled when her little nose twitched rapidly as she examined the small device.

"Take it easy with that, little girl." Boo gave him a low, angry screech, and flared her tentacles into a wide mane. Ed patted the air gently. "I'm not saying you can't use it. It won't hurt you. I'm just saying go slow, okay?"

Boo relaxed her tentacles, flicked her tail at him dismissively, and clutched the vape pen to her chest possessively.

An hour later, the little kinkakaijou was sprawled out on her back on the table, cooing a gentle song to herself, and flicking her prehensile tail to the beat. She clutched a different snack in each paw, and four more in her tentacles. Every so often, she'd take a break from her song to nibble on her snacks. Ed glanced over from his work and bit back a chuckle. Her belly was so distended, he wasn't sure how she could fit anything else in there, but she was a determined little thing, and he could appreciate that kind of dedication.

The puzzle had stumped him at first, but he'd always been good at them. He'd found that patience and a steady dose of ganjaroo usually helped. Puzzles were simple when you got down to it. Put the right piece in the right place. Beings like Harold always made it too complicated. Just put the puzzle together. Keep it simple, stupid.

He nibbled on the edge of a cookie as he pondered the massive construct spanning most of the table. Ed turned the last piece end over end, getting a feel for the shape, before he set it back down on the table with a gentle *click*.

"What do ya say we save that last piece for tomorrow, hey, Boo?"

The kinkakaijou just flopped her head sideways and gave him a goofy grin. This time he didn't hold back his laughter. Still chuckling, he scooped her up like a newborn and carried her to bed. He checked on the bridge, but Reggie had done everything that was needed, and he knew his clan leader had routed all the computer stuff to his personal slate. If anything went wrong, Reggie would be the first to know. Everyone was asleep now, and it was past time to join them in catching those Zs.

Tomorrow was going to be a big day.

* * *

Maddy rubbed at her eyes as she shuffled into the common area. She needed coffee in the worst way. Maybe if she drank enough caffeine, her brain would finally wake up. It felt like she'd been mired in sludge for days on end. She didn't feel angry about... things. She didn't feel anything, really. Nothing but sludge and exhaustion.

She made it halfway through the common area before her tired eyes focused on the impressive sculpture on the table. She tilted her head to the side in an attempt to make sense of the shape but came up blank.

"Hey, Maddy? Have you seen—" Reggie stumbled to a halt next to her. His ears stood straight up in shock, and his blue eyes widened. "Did you do this?"

Maddy thought about snapping at him, but that seemed like it would take too much effort. She just shook her head and went back to trying to figure out what the dratted shape was supposed to be. *How is this a clue?*

Harold stumbled in next, his fur marginally less greasy than the day before, but his eyes still bloodshot. He clearly needed more sleep, but Maddy didn't think he'd be getting any more today.

His eyes bugged out as he whisper-shouted, "It's finished?"

"Almost," Ed's deep voice sounded from behind them. They all whirled to face the bigger male, and he smiled at them. Boo chittered a greeting from her favorite perch on his broad shoulder. "I thought we could put the last piece in together. You know, like, as a clan."

Maddy's tail slowly swished behind her, and a curl of excitement cut through the sludge. "You did this, Ed?"

Ed grinned proudly and stroked Boo's silky golden fur. "I had some help."

A small smile tugged at her lips. "Ed, you did good. You too, furball."

Reggie nodded his head sharply in agreement. "Great work, both of you."

"Thanks." Ed ducked his head. His tail wagged happily as he gestured excitedly to the puzzle. "Go ahead, Pops. You put the last piece in!"

Harold picked up the last piece with visibly shaking paws and turned it over several times. He gazed at the abstract sculpture helplessly. "Where…"

Maddy shuffled to the side as Ed moved closer to the table. The big Joongee pointed out where the piece should go, and Maddy shook her head slowly. She could've stared at that puzzle for a million years and never picked that spot. Ed backed up so he stood next to the couch and gave Harold space. Boo chittered, jumped up onto Ed's head, and grabbed onto his ears to steady herself.

They all held their breath as the old Joongee slotted the last puzzle piece home. Brilliant color exploded to life throughout the clear structure—purples, baby blues, soft greens, and every shade of pink imaginable against a backdrop of endless night speckled with gold.

Maddy caught her breath in wonder. It was beautiful... but it still made absolutely zero sense. She growled and thought about that coffee again. Maybe that would help. Before she could take even a single step toward the galley, Boo shrieked in excitement and jumped up and down on Ed's head.

Ed flattened his ears protectively and reached up to pat the tiny kinkakaijou. "It sure is pretty, isn't it, Boo?"

Maddy tilted her head at the little pest. Boo smacked Ed's hand away and jabbed a finger repeatedly at the puzzle sculpture. For once, the big male didn't seem to know what to do with her. He shushed her a few times, but she screeched at the top of her lungs and flared her tentacles wide in agitation.

Coffee was calling her name, but there was no way she could enjoy her precious first cup of the day with all that racket going on. Maddy heaved a sigh and forced her feet to move.

She stalked over to Ed and Boo and wrinkled her muzzle at the pest. "Would you shut up already, furball? It's way too early, and I'm not nearly caffeinated enough for all that noise."

Shockingly, Boo did. She peered down at Maddy with her bright hazel eyes and beckoned her closer. Maddy sighed again. Ed, lumbering ox that he was, had two feet in height on her. There was no way she could reach Boo from the floor. Grumbling under her breath, she hopped up onto the couch so she was eye-level with the furball.

Boo jabbed a finger at the puzzle and let out the most exasperated chitter Maddy had ever heard. She was pretty sure she'd made similar sounds about the males of her species before, and a smile twitched on her face. Boo placed a tiny paw on her cheek and turned Maddy's face toward the puzzle.

Maddy eyes widened, and her body froze. "Harold."

The older Joongee stood at the table, one paw cupping his chin, and the other braced on his hip. "Maybe it's in code?"

Maddy growled. She hated being ignored. "*Harold.*"

Reggie arched a brow at Harold. "Are you saying we need to solve a code before we can unlock the clue?"

"Perhaps, my pup, perhaps," Harold replied vaguely, ears tilted sideways in uncertainty as he studied the puzzle.

Maddy's frustration boiled over and shattered the sludge smothering her. "*HAROLD!*"

She leaped off the couch, grabbed Harold by the arm, and dragged him bodily over to the couch. He yelped and scrambled to keep his feet under him as she jumped back up onto the couch and yanked him up after her.

"Look!" she snarled over his spluttering protests.

Maddy twisted him around so he faced the puzzle. Harold shut his jaw with a *click*, and his ears stood up straight.

Reggie frowned up at them. "What is it?"

Ed stood up on his tiptoes and let out an awed gasp. "So cool."

Reggie leaped up onto the couch next to Maddy. The cushions squished beneath his boots, and while he easily kept his balance, Maddy slid sideways into him. Reggie steadied her with a warm, confident hand against her back as she grabbed onto Ed's shoulder.

"Sorry, Mads," he said with a quick smile before he turned his attention to the puzzle. His eyes widened. "It's a solar system. Harold, can you pinpoint which one?"

Harold already had his nose buried in his slate and was mumbling to himself.

"Maybe the Prithmar system. No... Shippo? Definitely not," he said with a snort. "It's not Sheinrah, I checked into that system after the coffee shop. It's not Salvage..."

Maddy quickly lost interest, but she couldn't quite bring herself to leave. Something in her that had been strung tight the past few days finally relaxed. While not as physically affectionate as certain beings—like Humans—Joongee still enjoyed tactile contact with their clan mates.

She abruptly hopped off the couch, her ears angled back in irritation. *What is wrong with me? I don't need them to feel better.*

Reggie leaped lightly to the floor after her and cleared his throat. "Harold, we should probably use the StarNav5500, don't you think?"

"Oh... yes, yes, that would be easier," Harold muttered vaguely as Reggie placed a paw on his shoulder and steered him out of the common area. Ed followed happily along. Maddy snorted at all of them and trudged to the galley as she mentally berated herself.

She'd hesitated to go get coffee because she'd enjoyed the feeling of Reggie's hand on her back. It had felt... safe. And that was right the hell out. She didn't need a male to make her feel safe—she needed to make *herself* feel safe.

By the time she reached the galley, she was stomping along with her hackles raised high. The remnants of the sludge in her brain flash-boiled away as her anger burned bright. Too enraged to go to the effort of starting a fresh batch, she snatched up yesterday's coffee and chugged it straight from the pot without pausing for breath. After slamming it back down to the counter, she wiped her muzzle dry and snarled to herself. *Stupid Reggie. Stupid coffee. STUPID BRUCE!*

Boo hopped up onto the counter next to the empty coffee pot and chittered at her. Maddy frowned at the questioning lilt to the furball's voice and tilted her head. "Oh. Sorry, did you want some?"

Without waiting for a response—because what sane being wouldn't want coffee—Maddy scooped out some fresh grounds into Boo's little bowl. She'd discovered that while the little kinkakaijou wouldn't actually drink coffee, she loved to eat it.

Boo let out a pleased *chirrup*, and her tentacles rippled in happiness as she munched on the dried grounds.

Harold's cackle of excitement reached them all the way from the bridge, and she flattened her ears at his bellow of triumph. "Of course! The Ahkal-Tiki system!"

"Thanks, Chad!" all the males shouted together. Maddy rolled her eyes as she busied herself making a fresh pot of coffee.

"Yeah, thanks Chad," she said sourly. *Great. The happy, bouncy, pretty pony system. Could my life get any worse?*

"Hey, Maddy?" Reggie called out just before he strode into the galley. "I've got a job for you."

Maddy cast her eyes upward. *Seriously, universe?*

She heaved a sigh and turned her gaze back to Reggie. "What?"

Reggie rubbed the back of his neck at her lack of enthusiasm but forged ahead. "Well, you got us such a great deal on gate fees the last time, I thought maybe you could find us another cargo ship going in the same direction. I mean, you're practically our quartermaster, anyway, so…"

Maddy's ears perked up despite herself. "Quartermaster?"

Reggie smirked at her. "Yeah, you'd be in charge of our supplies, our budget, all our purchases—"

"You mean I get to go shopping as my *job*?" Maddy demanded incredulously, her tail stiff with shock.

"Absolutely." Reggie gave her a slow grin, and his blue eyes were approving. "I took a look at the supply purchases you made at the mall. You got us some great bargains and really stretched our credit. That's what a good quartermaster does. I'd say you earned the job."

Maddy was speechless for several long moments. Reggie trusted her with their credit. He trusted her to go *shopping*. She wrinkled her muzzle in disgust as that warm, fuzzy feeling spread throughout her being again. *Ugh, gross.*

Reggie just watched her with amusement in his eyes and waited patiently.

"The title is acceptable," she finally decided as she lifted her muzzle imperiously. "Pirate Queen Maddy sounds better, but I can live with Quartermaster Maddy. I'll see what I can do about transport."

"Thanks, Spitfire," Reggie said quietly. "I knew I could count on you. I'll see you on the bridge."

He strode back out with a wave, leaving Maddy alone again. Well, alone except for the furball, who'd managed to get coffee grounds all over her face. She fought back a smile as she dropped a damp rag in front of Boo.

The coffee machine *beeped*, indicating the fresh batch was ready to go. Maddy poured herself a proper mug of coffee and smiled. *Maybe today won't completely suck after all.*

* * * * *

Chapter Twenty-Two

The gate travel time between the Mall of Malls and the Ahkal-Tiki System was the longest yet, at eight days. Maddy had done a great job finding them transport with an outgoing luxury cruise vessel packed to the gills with tourists hitting up all the highlights in this sector of the galaxy. Apparently, that included the Ahkal-Tiki, which made a great deal of its credit from the tourist industry. Maddy had looked beyond disgusted when they found out the pretty pony beings traded off their sparkling good looks and typical bouncy personalities to support their economy. They'd even created a booming theme park and resort for those who wanted to admire and spend time with them.

Reggie personally thought it sounded like an awful way to live, but to each their own.

They were seven days into their journey through alter-reality, and they were all bored to tears. Except for Ed, who was having a blast playing his new game, *Intergalactic Red Ops 6*. He'd even roped Harold into co-op mode gameplay, which was probably a good thing for the older Joongee's sanity. He'd spent far too much time obsessing over the next clue for Reggie's taste, and he'd given Ed a fist-bump when Harold wasn't looking. Ed's wink said he knew exactly what he'd been doing.

Reggie had tried to get Maddy interested in some of the new games she'd helped pick out, but she was still moody and withdrawn for the most part. He'd played Ed's game for a while, but he couldn't sit still long enough to get into it properly. He needed to move. More than that, he needed to train.

The Sheingal security guard, Murockal, wasn't wrong. He'd allowed his training to lapse—allowed himself to get sloppy—which was fine when he was an office worker in a safe environment. It was absolutely *not* fine out in the black, with pirates, slavers, and nasty bar fights. Back in his mercenary days, that Yalteen never would've had a chance of sneaking up on him. Yet, if not for Harold and his bar stool, he would've gotten a knife in the back. All because he'd lost all manner of real self-discipline.

The fur on the back of his neck stood up, and he shook himself abruptly. *Time to change that.*

Fortunately for him, he'd brought along all his gym equipment when they'd left Galactic Solutions. Ed had helped him set everything up in the smallest of the rooms intended for crew quarters. There was enough room for all his free weights, a compact total body machine, and a punching bag they'd hung in the back-left corner. Best of all, if they stored away the free weights and the machine, there was just enough space for careful sparring. Reggie wanted to get some proper padding for the floor and possibly the walls first, though.

No sense accidentally breaking anything when they didn't have anyone really trained in first aid.

After changing into baggy gym shorts and an old, ratty t-shirt, Reggie headed for his sanctuary, only to find it had been invaded by a very tiny, very angry female.

It took everything Reggie had to keep his jaw from hitting the floor. Maddy wore cutoff shorts, a tight sports bra, and outside of the neon purple wraps around her hands, not a damn thing else. It didn't really matter to Reggie what Maddy wore—whether it was her normal baggy attire or that cute little dress—he'd always been well aware she was female.

This was different somehow. He'd never realized just how fit she was, and he found himself leaning against the doorframe, mesmerized as she worked over the bag with fierce concentration. He frowned as she threw that wicked right cross and transitioned into a smooth left hook.

Murockal was right. She dropped her left paw on the cross and left that side unprotected.

Maddy seemed to realize it, too, because she snarled in frustration and pounded her fist into the bag with zero finesse and one hundred percent rage. She thunked her forehead against the bag and sucked in air, shoulders heaving. Reggie wondered how long she'd been at it.

Maddy pushed herself upright and ran a hand through her spiky, white mane. Without turning around, she muttered, "Not a good time, Reg."

Before he could think better of it, he snorted and asked, "Is it ever?"

Maddy whirled around, purple eyes blazing with rage, with *life*, and Reggie decided to stick with his gut. He'd treated her with kid gloves too much since the bar incident, and it wasn't helping. Time to try a different tactic.

He slowly stalked closer to her, ears perked up to show he wasn't truly angry. Without breaking eye contact, he reached down, grabbed the target pads he'd tucked away behind the free weights, and set his feet. There might not be enough room for sparring with all the equipment out, but there was more than enough to work on that chink in her armor.

"Come on, Spitfire. Show me what you got," he said with a challenging grin.

Maddy hesitated, and his heart sank. Maybe he'd pushed too hard. Maybe she wasn't ready. He huffed out a shocked breath. *And maybe she'll sucker punch you while you're distracted.*

Reggie straightened back up and flicked his ears mockingly. "Is that it? You got nothing left?"

Maddy snarled and slammed a jab straight into the pad—but only because he'd moved it in time.

He *tsked* and shook his head. "Temper, temper." He tilted his chin down and peered at her over the target pads. "Do it right, Mads."

"Fine," she gritted out between clenched teeth and pinned her ears flat.

She lashed out with a right cross. Reggie caught the hit on one pad and used the other to smack her in the head.

"Hey!" She gave him a hate-filled glare that would've wilted flowers, fangs on full display.

"You dropped your left paw. Keep it where it should be, and I won't be able to hit you," Reggie replied calmly. "Again."

Maddy wrinkled up her muzzle and shook her head sharply. Her pure white mane flared out before a stray piece settled over one eye. She blew it out of the way, reset her feet, and tried again. Her tiny fist slammed into the pad… and Reggie smacked her face with the other.

"Again."

Smack. Growl.

"Again."

Smack! Snarl.

"Again."

SMACK.

"Still dropping the left. Protect yourself. Adapt and overcome."

Again and again, Reggie popped her on the left side of the head, until Maddy screamed in frustration and unleashed a fierce barrage of lightning-fast punches. Almost faster than he could see, her tiny fists slammed into the pads over and over. Reggie grunted, impressed at both her speed and the power behind the blows. His shoulders bunched as he absorbed the hits, but he said nothing as she vented her rage. She needed to get it all out.

At last, she spun away from him, her upper body heaving as she recovered her breath. She set her back to the wall, slumped to the floor, and bowed her head.

"Just leave me alone, Reg," she said, voice so quiet he had to strain his ears.

"I'm not going anywhere," he replied without hesitation.

He let the target pads fall to the floor and sat next to her with his shoulder pressed against hers. He waited. Patience had never been Maddy's strong suit, but she held out longer than he thought possible.

Finally, she let out a broken little sigh. "What are you doing, Reg?"

"I thought that was obvious, Mads," he said softly.

Maddy raised her head enough for him to see her eyes. A small spark lit in those purple depths, and her ears twitched. "Spell it out for me. And if you say 'boxing' or 'sitting,' I swear I'll break your face."

Reggie snorted a laugh. "You could try. All I need to do is wait for that right cross. Then, *smack*, right upside your noggin. I win."

The fur on the back of Maddy's neck rose. "Are you saying you don't think I'm strong enough? You think I don't have what it takes? That I'm just always going to be some helpless damsel who can't defend myself?"

Reggie bit back his first response. She wasn't talking about boxing anymore, and his instincts warned him to tread carefully. He selected and discarded a dozen responses, but in the end, he went with blunt honesty.

"I think you're one of the strongest, smartest, most driven beings I know," he said firmly. He hesitated, but decided she needed to hear more. "I'm here because you're my clan mate, my friend, and I care about you." He gave her a sly grin and nudged her with his shoulder. "And because you're too damned stubborn and hard-headed to ask for help."

Maddy blinked rapidly and sniffled.

"I know you're not okay right now," Reggie continued, "but you need to know I'm here for you, in whatever way you need." His grin turned rueful, and he added, "If that means you need to whale on me some more, that's fine. I can do this all day. Just let me get the pads first, okay?"

She snorted a laugh and leaned into him. She was quiet for so long, he glanced down to make sure she hadn't drifted off to sleep, but her eyes were open.

Without warning, she slammed a fist into the floor with bruising force. When she tried to do it a second time, Reggie caught her hand in his and stopped her. He wrapped his calloused fingers around her tiny fist and gave her a reassuring squeeze.

"I messed up, Reg," she said with a bitter rasp to her voice as she yanked her hand free.

"No," he said immediately. "That creep *Brenda* messed up, and if I ever see him again, I'm going to mess up his face."

"Get in line," she muttered before her ears flattened with misery. "I was careful. I watched my drink. I did everything right, everything

I was always taught to do in a bar to protect myself... and it didn't matter."

"It matters," Reggie said with a frown.

"You tried to help me, and I just pushed you away," she continued as if she hadn't heard him.

Reggie opened his mouth, but the words caught in his throat. He couldn't say it. He couldn't tell her he hadn't gone over there to *help* her. He'd gone over because he'd wanted to pound Bruce's face through the bartop before he'd even known anything was wrong. Because he'd been... *jealous*.

"Well, I *was* being an ass," he said instead.

"It's part of your charm," she shot back with a wry grin. She clenched her jaw. "It could've been so much worse. If it wasn't for you, it probably would've been."

"You saved yourself, remember?" he said with a snort. "It wasn't me. I was just your backup. Well, me and Harold."

A smile spread across her face, and her ears rose a fraction. "Yeah, and Harold. Who took out a Yalteen with a *barstool*. I wish I had a vid of that."

Reggie grinned. "We can always comm Murockal and see if he can get us one."

Maddy nodded and grinned back, her eyes lit up with amusement. "That'd be the perfect birthday gift for Harold."

She blew out a sharp breath and rose to her feet. She tightened the wraps on her hands and arched a brow. "Help me fix my right cross?"

"Thought you'd never ask," he replied with a grin as he hopped up. "Let's try something a little different this time."

A few minutes later, Maddy stood before him with a thunderous scowl on her face. She gently tugged on her left hand, and the lock of mane he'd tied to her hand wrap went with it. She winced at the resultant pull on her scalp, and if anything, her scowl deepened.

"Is this really necessary?" she growled.

"Yup. It's not your right cross that's the issue. The strike itself is wicked mean and on target. The issue is, your blocking hand keeps dropping. This will help you remember to keep it up." Reggie rolled his shoulders and held up the target pads. "Old boxing trick. Pain is the best teacher."

When she just stood there, he lashed out with one of the pads and smacked her in the side playfully. "Let's go, slowpoke—"

Maddy snarled and slammed her right cross into the pad. She winced when she nearly ripped that little piece of her mane out of her head as her left hand dropped too low. This time, Reggie didn't have to tell her to do it again. She wrinkled her muzzle, reset her feet, and threw a straight jab at the pad, followed by a right cross. Again, she dropped her left hand. Again, she snarled.

The next time, he watched as she halted the motion of her left hand mid-drop. After that, her left hand hovered next to her face, exactly where it should be. Jab and cross, over and over, and that left hand didn't move an inch. Reggie let her work on it a few more minutes before he grinned and stepped back.

"Now you've got it, Mads," he said with warm approval.

Maddy panted, but beamed, with triumph shining bright in her eyes. She wiggled her left hand at him. "A little help?"

Reggie stepped close and unbound the tiny lock of her mane from the wrap. As careful as he was, he still accidentally pulled on it, and Maddy winced again. "Sorry."

Without stopping to think about it, he smoothed her mane back with gentle fingers over the sore spot. When he realized what he was doing, his ears flickered in embarrassment, and he stepped back abruptly.

Reggie cleared his throat but couldn't meet her eyes. He wasn't sure what he'd see, wasn't sure he wanted to know what she thought of that accidental tender gesture. Because he was almost positive Maddy had leaned into his touch… just a little.

"You should practice that combo more before you stop for the day. Really get it set into your muscle memory," he said as he quickly put the target pads away.

"Yeah," she said after a heartbeat too long. "That's a good idea. Thanks for the help, Reg."

"Any time, Mads," he replied and darted a glance at her face, but the tiny female had already turned back to the bag, the muscles in her back tense with anticipation. He noticed she kept one ear turned toward him, though, and he felt a smile curl his muzzle as he walked to the door.

He looked over his shoulder at the sound of fists hitting the bag, and he grinned when that left hand stayed exactly where it was supposed to on her right cross, solid and unwavering in its defense of her head.

Reggie went back to his room and did a quick stationary workout before he showered and changed back into normal clothes. When he walked past the small gym on his way to the common area, his steps slowed at the angry music blasting through the closed door.

Relief swamped him in a heavy wave, and he breathed out a silent *Thank you.*

Maddy hadn't listened to music since the bar incident. Not even once. He knew that didn't mean everything was fixed, but he thought maybe she was on the path to feeling better. It would be nice having her tiny, angry, sarcastic self back again. He never thought he'd miss her quick snaps of anger, but he now found they were part of what endeared her to him.

He listened for a moment and found his head nodding to the beat before he finished the short trek to the common area. *What did she call that style again? Grunge music? Not bad.*

Ed and Harold greeted him cheerfully as they battled it out on *Intergalactic Red Ops 6*. He sat next to them on the couch and propped his feet up on the table. He was prepared to watch them play, but Ed hit pause.

"What's up, Reggie?" Ed asked with a friendly smile and offered up his controller. "You ready to play again?"

Reggie took the controller with a grin. "Yeah… I think I am."

* * * * *

Chapter Twenty-Three

None of them knew what to expect when they arrived in the Ahkal-Tiki System. However, brightly colored asteroids were certainly the last thing on their list of possibilities. Nevertheless, that's exactly what they got. Not only were the asteroids painted in vivid colors, they were also polka-dotted and arranged in enormous, specific shapes that ships entering the system had to travel through. The first arrangement was a pink-and-purple polka-dotted heart, the next was a blue and green star, and then what appeared to be an artistic rendition of an actual Ahkal-Tiki.

"Dear gods," Maddy croaked in disbelief. "I'm in hell. This is hell."

"How do they keep the asteroids in those shapes?" Ed asked, his eyes bright with wonder.

"Small automatic thrusters running on a synchronized orbit would be my assumption," Harold replied. "Relatively simple, honestly."

"How do they get the asteroids painted like that?" Reggie asked as he steered them under the arch of a massive eight-banded rainbow.

Before Harold could answer, a video hail came through on the comm. Reggie punched the answer command, and they were assaulted by an overload of color and an overly happy, shrill voice. On the screen was a hot pink Ahkal-Tiki. From the knee down on all four of her legs, she was a neon purple, and her meticulously braided mane and tail were electric blue. As if the colors weren't enough, her mane and tail also had various colors of jewels and beads woven into them.

The long, pointed horn protruding from her forehead was gold and sparkly.

"*Welcome to the Ahkal-Tiki system, new friends! We are so happy to have you here, and we just know you'll have the best time ever with us!*" She pranced around in a happy four-legged dance, reared up on her hind legs, and shook her head side to side.

Maddy flattened her ears and dragged her paws down the side of her head. "Reggie…"

Reggie paused the pre-recorded message, looked over at her, and snickered. "Yeah?"

"Is your gun still loaded?"

He glanced at the rifle on the wall next to him and arched an eyebrow at her. "Yes. Why?"

"I think I need you to put me out of my misery."

Reggie snorted. "Nah, it's not that bad. You'll live to be miserable another day."

"Traitor," Maddy grumbled as Reggie restarted the message.

"*In order to make sure we give you all the most awesomest time ever, please select the appropriate option so we can totally take the best care of you! If you're here to visit the amusement parks, paint stores, join the weekly dance contest, have a birthday party or wedding scheduled, or if you just want to tour our super amazing planet and to hang out with your new bestest friends in the whole wide galaxy, press one! If you're a bunch of adventure-seeking super awesome explorers and you're here for the Clue Song, press two!*" The Ahkal-Tiki giggled and pranced around some more, causing the jewelry in her mane and tail to jingle. "*We just can't wait to meet you and give you a big, warm hug before we make all your wishes come true! See you soon, new friends!*"

The screen transitioned to a new screen with a continuous show of multicolored fireworks. Layered on top of the fireworks were

Option 1-Tourism and Option 2-Clue Song. Boo hopped down from Ed's shoulder and watched the display with her tiny mouth agape.

Everyone turned a questioning look to Harold. He sank back in his seat and shrugged with his paws up. "I-I really don't know what's going on."

Maddy narrowed her eyes. "They said they have a clue song, Harold. What are they talking about?"

"Yeah," Reggie piled on. "What's the deal? Do they know about the Lost Weapons of Koroth?"

Harold shook his head vigorously. "I don't know, pups. I've never been here before. You know just as much as I do. This is all new to me as well."

"I think you're full of targanveetra manure," Maddy deadpanned.

Ed's big hand clapped down on Harold's shoulder. "Come on, guys. Like, he said he didn't know. We didn't know, either, and we all put the same clues together as Pops did. I'm sure he'd let us know if there was more." He looked down at Harold with his oversized puppy eyes. "Right, Pops?"

Harold cleared his throat and patted Ed's hand. "Right you are, my pup. Right you are."

Not completely convinced, thanks to the slightly shrill note to Harold's voice, Reggie turned his attention back to the screen. "Well, we aren't here for the tourism, that's for sure. I guess we should just choose option two."

"If it's really a song, I'm going to shoot myself," Maddy grumbled as Reggie selected the second option.

Immediately, a different Ahkal-Tiki popped up on the screen. This one was blue with pink stripes and a black bejeweled mane and tail. Her horn was a glittery emerald green.

"*Greetings, brave adventurers of the cosmos! In order to receive your super awesome helpful clue, please come down to the main planet and land in the indicated landing zone on the screen! The next step in your quest awaits, and we have just the information you need!*"

The screen went blank for a second before the landing coordinates popped up in eye-searing colors. Everyone turned to face Harold again.

"Pops?" Ed asked. "Are you sure there's not more to this than you're telling us?"

Harold shifted in his seat and cleared his throat. "No, no, I'm not hiding anything. Everything is fine. As I said, this is just as surprising to me as it is to all of you."

Reggie huffed and rubbed the spot between his eyes. "Guess we're headed down to the planet."

He entered the landing coordinates and engaged *HIADA's* thrusters. As they headed toward the planet, they gazed at it in wonder.

"How in the galaxy did they paint all the landmasses different colors?" Maddy asked. "It's like a giant tie-dye ball."

Ed took a drag from his vape pen and blew vapor out his nose. "Trippy."

* * *

"Everyone ready?" Reggie asked. He patted his hip to make sure his concealed sidearm was properly secured. He didn't think he'd need it, but if the previous events of their trip were any indication at all, anything was possible, even on the pretty pony planet. Everyone said yes except for Maddy.

"No," she said miserably as she clutched her travel coffee mug in front of her like it was a shield. She'd wanted to stay on the ship to protect her sanity, but she'd been outvoted by the whole clan. This was an adventure, and she had to participate, too. "Are you sure I can't stay on the ship with Boo?"

"Sorry. You've got to suffer with the rest of us," Reggie said with a snicker.

Reggie opened the exit hatch, and the ramp extended to rest on the deep-purple tarmac. The air-control tower was yellow with green stripes. All the other buildings, aircraft, and ships parked around them were also painted in various eye-searing patterns. It was a bit startling at first. Maddy groaned and took a bracing drink from her coffee mug.

"Is that…" Reggie trailed off, unable to articulate what his eyes were seeing.

"Yes, Reggie," Maddy said before he could finish, her tone dry as a desert. "It's a giant freaking gift box fully equipped with a big pink freaking bow."

Sure enough, at the end of the tarmac was an enormous gift box with a big pink bow on the top. Printed on the front of the box was a puzzle piece with a question mark on it.

Again, everyone turned to glare at Harold.

"I swear I don't know what this is all about!"

All of a sudden, the lid on the gift box blew open, the front panel fell to the ground, and all manner of sparkly confetti was blasted into the air as dozens of Ahkal-Tiki galloped toward them. Above the charging wave of multi-colored Ahkal-Tiki, streamers flew through the air amidst the fluttering confetti. The charging ponies came to an abrupt halt with smiles on their long, colorful faces. Gigantic speakers rose from the floor of the gift box, and music filled the air. The Ahkal-

Tiki pawed the ground in time to the thunderous beat with their three-fingered forepaws.

Maddy's ears drooped, and a whine escaped her throat. She turned to Reggie and said, "Please, Reg? Please? Just put a bullet in my head. It would be so much better than this. You said you'd never let anything happen to me. Well, this is happening to me, and it's horrible! Make it stop, Reg! Make it stop!"

Reggie looked down at her and chuckled. "Bar creeps, pirates, jerks in the store, I'll save you from them all." He nodded toward the dancing ponies and grinned. "But a happy clue song from colorful, friendly, bouncing ponies? No way. If I punched something that cute and adorable, the universe would never let me live it down. Or Ed, for that matter."

Maddy turned, and they both watched as Ed bobbed his head and swayed with the music, his eyes full of wonder as he watched the dancing Ahkal-Tiki.

Maddy groaned. "Oh, no. We've lost Ed."

In unison, the Ahkal-Tiki sang in Earth Common.

> *Hello new friends, this is where your adventure begins*
> *And we're so glad to help you on your journey!*
> *Across the stars, you traveled to where we are*
> *And we're so glad to help you on your journey!*
> *Now listen close with your ears and your heart*
> *And remember to sing it with the Ahkal-Tiki!*

As the chorus ended, a pink Ahkal-Tiki with a golden mane and tail stepped front and center and sang alone in a soaring soprano. Her voice was almost angelic.

All treasure hunts must come to an end
Don't hold a grudge, you've made it this far
But in order to persevere and triumph remember to sing it boldly
New friends are the key to where you want to be
And remember to sing it in Ahkal-Tiki!

As the pink and gold female finished her verse, the rest of the herd joined in again with the chorus. When they finished, a loud explosion of fireworks and colored smoke erupted from the ground. As the thick clouds of pinks, purples, blues, and greens dissipated, all that remained of the Ahkal-Tiki song-and-dance crew were the glittery pieces of confetti on the tarmac.

"Holy hell," Reggie said in disbelief. "They disappeared."

"Even the gift box is closed again," Maddy said and pointed.

Sure enough, the gift box was completely reset with bow on top.

"They're ninjas," Ed said in awe.

"No, we're just really organized and very good at our job," said a high-pitched, bubbly voice from the side.

Everyone jumped and turned to see the pink and gold Ahkal-Tiki who'd sung lead in the song. She sat back on her haunches and held out a paw with a friendly smile.

Reggie could see that, rather than hooves like her back legs, her front legs were equipped with flexible paws with three fingers and an opposable thumb. It explained how a primarily quadrupedal species had managed to develop into a space-faring race.

"Hi, new friends! I'm Aurelian, president and over-all leader of the Ahkal-Tiki System. It's nice to meet you!"

Stunned that the planetary leader herself was greeting them, Reggie stepped forward and accepted the proffered hand. The thick pads on the underside of each finger and her palm rasped across his fur, and the glittering gold nail polish on each blunt nail perfectly matched her horn.

"It's nice to meet you, President Aurelian," he said respectfully. "I'm Reggie, and these are my clan mates—Maddy, Ed, and Harold."

"Please, just call me Aurelian!" she said as she released Reggie's hand and trotted over to Maddy. "Oooh, your eyes are so pretty, Maddy! And I love your white mane! It's all so pretty! I just know you and I are going to be the best of friends!"

Maddy, clearly unnerved, shot Reggie a wide-eyed glance before giving Aurelian a skeptical look. "Uh, sure, whatever you say."

"President... er, Aurelian," Reggie said in an effort to distract her from Maddy, "shouldn't you have a security force or something with you?"

She giggled and waved his question off. "Don't be so silly. Why would I need one of those? The Ahkal-Tiki are friends with everyone! Nobody wants to hurt me." She pranced back to stand in front of them. "So, what did you think of the song? Did you love it? You loved it, didn't you?"

"It was great," Ed answered before anyone else could. "Like, I'm glad I recorded it on my slate. I'll watch it again later. You sing really good, Aurelian. Are you sure I can call you that? President Aurelian sounds so fancy."

"Aw! Thank you!" Aurelian gushed as her tail swished behind her. "And no, you don't have to call me President. That's just my title. Not who I am."

"Why do you guys have a clue song?" Maddy asked, eyeing Harold with a whole lot of suspicion in her purple eyes.

"Why, for the race to find Dr. Monschtackle's treasure, silly!" Reggie slowly turned his head to pin Harold with a fierce stare, and the older Joongee squirmed as the Ahkal-Tiki continued her enthusiastic explanation.

"A lot of beings used to come through here to get our clue to the Lost Weapons of Koroth. But ever since that race started, whole *bunches* of beings come to our system." Aurelia dropped her voice like she was giving away a state secret as she added, "That's what gave our race the idea to commercialize ourselves and capitalize on tourism. We were already getting a ton of traffic through here for the clue he left our ancestors to pass along. No point in not taking advantage of it!"

Reggie tilted his head at Harold, and in a deceptively casual tone of voice, asked, "A race? Do you know what she's talking about?"

Harold wrung his hands together nervously. "Uhm, well, you see…"

"Harold!" Maddy wrinkled up her muzzle in impatience. "Spill it! Now!"

"It's easy!" Aurelian said before Harold could speak again. "Dezmire Assadh has hosted a competition every year for over two decades now. Hundreds of teams race to find the Lost Weapons of Koroth and win half a million in credit. It's been so much fun! Originally, we just had the boring old clue from Dr. Monschtackle, but we turned it into a fun song to share with all our new friends!"

"*Hundreds?* A race? It's a freaking *contest?*" Maddy growled, her voice climbing in pitch as she glared daggers at Harold.

Reggie rubbed the spot between his eyes and breathed slowly. He sank mental claws into his self-control and held on with everything he had. It wouldn't do to strangle Harold in front of the nice system president. "How many times have you guys performed this week, Aurelian?"

Aurelian tapped her lower lip with a stubby finger. "Hmmm. I think this made the thirty-fourth time this week. I don't do all the performances, of course, but we've never had Joongee come here before, and I just had to meet you all!"

Reggie ground his teeth so hard he thought he felt something crack. He pinned his ears as he stepped closer to Harold. "Did you know about this?"

Harold cleared his throat and raised his muzzle, his nervous demeanor all but gone. "Yes. Yes, I did."

Maddy stomped up to him, rage igniting her purple eyes. "And you didn't think to share that important little tidbit of information with the class?"

"No, I did not," Harold replied defiantly, despite everyone crowding him.

"Why not, Pops?" Ed asked without a hint of anger, only genuine curiosity in his eyes. "Seems like it was something we should've all known about from the beginning."

"It's quite simple, really," Harold said as he smoothed the frazzled mane on his head. "We aren't part of the contest. We're searching for the treasure for ourselves, *not* Mr. Assadh. Besides, we have something none of the teams searching for the weapons of Koroth have."

"And that is?" Reggie asked with a hint of a growl.

"The very first clue, pup." Harold grinned pointedly at Maddy before he shifted his gaze to him. "Specifically, the clues I picked up from the good doctor's *other* writings."

Reggie really hoped he wasn't talking about the hints from those children's books. The sinking feeling in his gut said otherwise.

Harold gestured the other Joongee even closer and dropped his voice low. "What I pieced together from those publications was what led us to our first stop on our adventure, and I don't believe any other beings ever correctly deciphered that clue. The popularity of the second clue negated the first in some ways, but there was more to it than simple coordinates. I believe we'll need that later, and that gives us an edge the other teams lack."

Reggie raised an eyebrow at him. "Are you saying there's more to what we have already in our possession than we've used so far?"

"I am," Harold replied with a brisk nod. "This is simply our next stepping stone, pup. For the other hunters, it's their last."

"So, that explains why you were in such a hurry at the—" Reggie stopped himself before he said too much. "At the first stop on our trip." He laughed. "And to think, I actually said this wasn't a race. Guess I was dead wrong."

"Ah, yes, well, I just didn't see any reason to put unnecessary pressure on all of you, and I believe you said this was supposed to be fun." Harold rubbed the back of his neck. "I was, and still am, very confident that none of the other teams will find it before we do because of that first clue."

"Oooh, how exciting!" Aurelian squealed. All the Joongee jumped. Somehow, the bright pink Ahkal-Tiki had inserted herself into their huddle without anyone noticing.

"Ninja," Ed breathed out.

"Nobody's ever talked about finding a clue before the Impossible Puzzle!" Aurelian said as she perked her ears forward in interest. "They usually just talk about putting the puzzle together and seeing our system on it. I mean, not all of them actually put the puzzle together themselves, they just get the info off the net. I think only like thirty-one of the forty-two variations have been successfully figured out."

Maddy stared at Harold with a deadpan expression. "They just go to the net. Odd. If only someone had thought of that."

Harold winced and hurriedly said, "Anyway, Assadh has been holding his annual race for the last twenty-three years, and nobody has ever come close. In a hunt like this, every single clue is a crucial part of the overall scheme. Especially with a brilliant mind such as Dr. Monschtackle's. Admittedly, I never knew about this Ahkal-Tiki Clue Song. I'd heard rumors that other clues had been discovered, but I never gave them a second thought—there are always rumors with treasure like this."

"Oooh, I *love* rumors. So much fun! I have a question," Aurelian said with a shake of her golden mane. "Why are we standing so close together?"

Reggie stepped back and pulled Maddy along with him when it looked like the tiny female was going to say something… undiplomatic. "It's a Joongee thing."

Now that Maddy was at a safer distance, Harold flicked his ears back and bowed his head to her. "Maddy was correct. In hindsight, it might've been easier to look up videos of the completed puzzle on the net. I honestly didn't think there would be any, but it makes sense with it being so popular in the mall."

"What's the fun in that?" Ed asked with a dismissive wave of his paw. "I'm glad you didn't look it up. Boo and I had a blast putting that thing together. And seeing the looks on all your faces… it was priceless, and something I'll never forget. Besides, this trip wouldn't have been nearly as much fun if we hadn't started from the very beginning."

Look at how much closer we all are because of it." He shook his head. "I wouldn't have it any other way than how it is right now."

"That is *so* sweet!" Aurelian squealed. She reached up and wiped a tear from her cheek.

"Seriously. Shoot me." Maddy locked eyes with Reggie, but he just grinned at her. She took a swig of coffee before she turned that pleading gaze on Harold. "Please tell me that song told you where we need to go next. And can we go there now? Like right now?"

"Good question," Reggie agreed, but couldn't resist adding, "Regardless, we can stay for a little longer, Maddy. Really stretch out our legs, you know? What do you think, Harold?"

"Staying for a little longer may not be a bad idea." Harold rubbed his chin in thought while Maddy flexed her hands like she was contemplating strangling him. "I may need to listen to the song a few more times. I have some ideas, of course, but I can't say for sure where we need to go next."

"You can all totally come to my house and listen to the song!" Aurelian pranced in a quick circle. "I love to host guests, and you can meet all of my bestest friends!"

Maddy groaned and caught an elbow from Reggie for it. She snapped a death glare up at him, only to receive one from him in return.

In a voice so low she could barely hear it, he said, "Don't piss off the damned *system* president, Mads." Reggie stepped forward and smiled. "We'd love to come meet your friends and see your home, Aurelian. Thank you so much. I promise we won't be there for too long."

"Yay! I love having new company over." Aurelian's eyes brightened, and she did a little hoppy, happy dance in a wide circle around them. Her rear hooves clicked and clacked on the tarmac. "It's going to be so much fun! Come on! Follow me!"

* * * * *

Chapter Twenty-Four

Everything Maddy saw made her cringe as they walked down the main thoroughfare of the capital city. Everything was so, so… *cute*. It was disturbing. *Everything* was brightly colored, with stripes, polka dots, swirls, hearts, stars, and a multitude of annoyingly adorable stencils. Even the other race that seemed to do all the maintenance was adorable. The meter-tall, fluffy, bipedal beings had small, rounded ears on their heads and short muzzles. They reminded of her of the stuffed teddy bears she'd seen back in the Vintage Humanity store at the mall—the ones that were dyed in an assortment of colors.

"What's up with the rainbow bear patrol doing all the work around here?" Maddy frowned as she looked around the city. "I don't see any of your race doing the work."

Aurelian skip-hopped and twirled in the air. She landed daintily, and without missing a beat, began to walk backward as she smiled at Maddy. "That's because the Vol'Dare are contracted to do all the maintenance and painting of the planet. We manage the tourism and run the parks and attractions, while they make sure everything stays pretty and operational. It's a beneficial relationship between our two planets, and everyone is very well paid."

"They're not from Ahkal-Tiki?" Reggie asked. Like a lot of systems, the system and the primary planet shared the same name.

"Nope!" Aurelian turned her body to look at him. Maddy wondered how the hell she could walk backward like that on four legs and not fall or run into something. "They live on the fourth planet in our system, Zergron. It's the only planet in our system that isn't painted or dyed. It's all green and brown trees, or blue water. So boring!"

"How is it you're able to paint the asteroids and the entire planet? And why?" Reggie tilted his head. "Sorry if I'm asking too many questions or bothering you."

"It's no bother at all!" Aurelian spun herself around to walk forward and shook her mane. Her tone shifted from bouncy to professional in the space of a heartbeat. "Space-worthy paint is our biggest export and nearly brings in as much credit as tourism. We paint the asteroids, the planets, and buildings as part of our marketing strategy. We do something similar with our second biggest export as well!" She did a spin and swished her tail. "The best hair and fur dye in the galaxy! Obviously, we only use the brightest and most eye-catching colors."

"Obviously," Maddy muttered with a roll of her eyes. She darted to the side before Reggie could elbow her again. Aurelian just grinned at her.

"We have the boring stuff, too. Black, gray, white, and so on. As far as how we do it, the Vol'Dare are very good at what they do. You should see them in space. They move around like they were born in the black," she said with what appeared to be genuine awe. She tossed her head in the Ahkal-Tiki version of a shrug. "I think it has something to do with how small they are. Anyway, the painting is accomplished in small shuttles equipped with wide sprayers to apply the main colors, and smaller, more precise nozzles to create the designs. Tiny thrusters on the asteroids keep them in the proper position and make it easy to adjust the shapes when needed."

Maddy watched through narrowed eyes. The pink princess had far more brains behind her golden horn than she let on.

The Ahkal-Tiki tossed her head again and added, "It's not as complicated as you'd think."

"Interesting," Reggie said with a flick of his ears. Maddy bit back a grin—of course that giant nerd was interested in how space painting worked.

They stopped short as a massive group of laughing and screaming younglings ran in front of them. Aurelian reared up on her hind legs and let out a loud whinny followed by lots of giggling. The younglings stopped and stared at her with wide-eyed wonder. She appeared to revel in it as she pranced around in a circle, allowing the kids to run their grubby little hands down her sides, neck, and mane.

"Are you all having a wonderful time?" she asked, her tone back to that bubbly, excited squeal that grated across every nerve Maddy possessed.

"Yes, President Aurelian!" the younglings answered in unison.

"Wonderful!" The Ahkal-Tiki pranced in place, careful of her hooves around the younglings. "I'm so happy your school was able to expand your field trip from the Mall of Malls to our super fun planet! Enjoy your stay and remember to have lots of fun!"

The younglings screamed and yelled with joy and ran off like a herd of sugar-high chintos. A trio of adults stumbled after them, their expressions shell-shocked and exhausted.

Aurelian let out sweet sigh and turned back to them. "I just love little ones. Don't you?"

"Oh, yeah," Maddy replied with a smirk. "Especially when they stay far, far away from me and don't make any noise."

Reggie nudged her, and she returned the favor with a hard elbow to his ribs. He'd apparently been ready for it, though, because he moved his arm just enough to take the brunt of the blow. *Damn it, he's learning my tactics.*

Something caught her eye, and she stepped away from the group as hope surged in her chest. "Is that a coffee shop?"

"Oh, why yes, it is!" Aurelian trotted up next to her and winked. "Sparkles and Sprinkles is our major coffee chain. There's one on practically every street! It's my absolute favorite place to get a sweet treat and a delicious drink. The Vol'Dare claim their coffee is better, but they're just grumpy-pants and wouldn't know a good sparkling drink if they drowned in it!"

Maddy stopped walking and stared at the bubbly Ahkal-Tiki. Despite the delivery, she'd actually managed to sound snarky. Also, the thought of drowning one of the colorful bears in coffee was hilarious. She snorted a laugh.

"You've convinced me," Maddy said as she hooked her mostly full travel mug to her belt. Ordinary coffee was great, but she loved trying fancy new drinks. Reggie cleared his throat, and she darted a glance at him. He gestured sharply at the president behind her back and mimed taking a drink. Maddy sighed and reluctantly asked, "Would you like to get a drink with me?"

"Oh, no thanks, you go ahead, new friend!" Aurelian said with a toss of her mane. "I already had my morning fix. You go get an extra-large cup, on the house!"

"Thanks," Maddy said slowly. She dropped her voice to a mutter as she moved out of range of Reggie's elbows and added, "I'm going to need it if we're going to be here for any length of time."

She entered the building and was immediately floored. Even the coffee beans were different colors and sparkly. *Why? Why the hell does everything have to be so... so... cute? This is beyond disturbing.*

She walked up to the counter and was immediately greeted by an overly happy attendant. "Hi! Welcome to Sparkles and Sprinkles! What can I get started for you?"

Maddy blinked a few times. Coffee shop employees seemed to come in two varieties—dead-eyed zombies or enthusiastic samplers of their own wares—but this was over the top even for the second variety. *This planet is hiding something, or they're on something stronger than Ed's ganjaroo. Nobody is this happy all the time. It's not normal.*

"Um, I need a second."

"Take all the time you need," the barista said with a small bounce. "Just let me know if you have any questions about anything on our super awesome menu!"

None of the items painted on the board over the counter looked even remotely familiar. They all had weird fairytale names. Rainbow Surprise, Happily Ever After, Dreams Come True, Sparkles and Sprinkles, Dash of This/Dash of That, Love And Friendship, and a dozen more stupid names that didn't tell her anything about what was actually in the drink.

"Just give me an extra-large Sparkles and Sprinkles," she finally grumbled. She figured the signature drink was always a safe bet, even in a crazy place like this. She jerked her thumb over her shoulder, where the pretty pink princess Aurelian was visible out the window. "She said it'd be on the house."

"Oh, Aurelian has new friends, how wonderful!" the Ahkal-Tiki sang out with a larger smile and more enthusiasm than was actually necessary. "Coming right up!"

Maddy rolled her eyes and crossed her arms as she watched pink, blue, and purple coffee beans drop from a clear tube above the grinder. *At least it's freshly ground.*

A few minutes later, the attendant handed her a massive cup with pink and purple whipped cream on top and silver and gold sprinkles. The cup was clear, and she could see the blue coffee inside, as well as a swirling array of multi-colored glitter.

"Uh, excuse me," she said in alarm. "There's glitter in this. How am I supposed to drink it? Are you trying to kill me?"

The Ahkal-Tiki giggled at her, but somehow kept it from sounding mean or condescending. Maybe that was the Ahkal-Tiki superpower. "Not at all, silly! Everything is one hundred percent edible! Just try it. I guarantee you're going to absolutely love it!"

Maddy put the cup to her nose and sniffed cautiously. The whip even smelled like pink and purple. She wasn't sure how exactly that worked, but that's what registered in her brain. With nothing but doubt and suspicion in her mind, she put the cup to her lips and sipped. The flavor hit her tongue, and her eyes went wide. She couldn't believe it.

It was... *amazing.*

It infuriated her. She'd expected all the cuteness to be some sort of mask to hide the fact that it was sucky coffee. The fact that she absolutely loved something so cute and adorable in such an overly cute and adorable place irked her to her very core.

She gave the attendant a forced shrug but couldn't stop her tail from swishing. "It's not bad. Thanks."

"You're very welcome," the barista replied enthusiastically. "We're so happy you stopped in, have a sparkling day and come back soon!"

Maddy exited the coffee shop and rejoined her group as they waited outside patiently for her. She sipped on the ridiculously good drink as they walked, thoroughly enjoying the flavor. She was nearly halfway through when her eyes narrowed suspiciously.

"Is there anything wrong, new friend?" Aurelian asked with immediate concern.

Reggie glared at Maddy from the Ahkal-Tiki's other side. "I'm sure Maddy's just fine. Right, Maddy?"

Maddy took a sip of coffee to buy herself time to think about how to rephrase the harsh words that initially came to mind. She settled on, "This coffee is defective."

There, nice and diplomatic. Reggie groaned and rubbed that spot between his eyes. If he thought that was bad, he probably didn't need to know what she'd originally planned to say.

"Oh, no," Aurelian replied, her ears drooping to the side. "What's wrong with it?"

Maddy kicked at the ground as they walked and pinned her ears back. "I'm not getting my normal rush."

The Ahkal-Tiki brightened. "You used the wrong 'D' word, silly. The coffee isn't *defective*, it's *decaffeinated*."

"You mean it has no caffeine?" Maddy stared down at her delicious, treacherous drink in horror. "How can it be coffee without caffeine!"

"Oh, that's easy peasy, lemon squeezy," she replied and launched into a detailed explanation on how the decaffeination process worked and blah blah blah. Maddy tuned her out after ten seconds and trudged along with the group. *I should've known something so pretty would be sucky coffee.*

They walked a few blocks further and reached the center of the city, where lush purple, pink, and turquoise grass dotted with picturesque trees provided an expansive park for beings of all sorts to play and relax. On one side of the park was a huge, pink home with gold accents.

"Got a thing for pink and gold, don't you?" Maddy asked in a despondent tone, still beyond miffed about the coffee trick.

"They're my favorite colors!" Aurelian said with a wide grin. "Isn't it so pretty? Come on in, everyone!" She turned to face Maddy. "I can give you a tour of the house while they listen to the song! You're going to love it!"

Maddy did *not* love it.

It was like some sort of pink and gold explosion happened inside the house and nobody had cleaned it up. All the furniture was oversized and poofy with feathers, beads, and sequins, yet it still somehow managed to look incredibly comfortable.

Harold, Reggie, and Ed took seats on a large couch and pulled up Ed's recording of the Ahkal-Tiki's song and dance routine. Maddy, on the other hand, was being brutally punished for some unknown reason via an unwanted tour of Aurelian's home.

"And this is where I do all my mane and tail braiding in the morning!" Aurelian explained excitedly as she trotted over to a low vanity. It was painted a brilliant white with gold and pink accents and had a huge mirror and a large light ring around it. She pulled open the lowest drawer and proudly gestured at the dozens of different kinds of brushes and combs, jeweled clips and barrettes in every color of the rainbow, as well as a pair of golden shears for mane trimming.

"Cool," Maddy said in a flat tone. She hoped the others figured out the clue quickly so she could get the hell out of this prison of cuteness.

"Well, that's about it," Aurelian said and plopped down on her haunches. "Do you like it?"

Maddy took a long sip from her travel mug of *real* coffee and nodded. "Yup. It's… big… and pink and very, uh, homey. You must be very happy here."

"Oh, yes, I am!" Aurelian replied with a huge smile. "I'm so happy you like it! Maybe after your adventure, you could come over sometime for a sleepover! I bet our horn and nail polish would look great on your claws."

Maddy wasn't exactly sure how to respond to that. On the one paw, no way in hell. On the other, Reggie had warned Maddy not to piss her off, because she was the president and leader of the whole system. Also… those little bottles of nail polish she'd left sitting on her dresser in her room popped into her mind.

She couldn't help but wonder if Aurelian had some cool colors that weren't pink or gold as she slowly said, "Uhh, sure. Maybe. I'll have to check my schedule and let you know."

"Yay!" Aurelian shrieked and literally bounced in place.

Maddy took another sip of her coffee and stoically waited out the happy, bouncy storm.

The pretty princess tilted her head and eyed the plain, boring old travel mug clutched in her paw. "What's that?"

"Real coffee." She hesitated, but Reggie had told her to be nice, damn it. She reluctantly held it out. "You want to try it?"

Aurelian fidgeted and tapped one of her thick fingers on the floor. "Maybe. It certainly smells good, but I've never had real coffee before."

Maddy's ears perked up, and a hint of liveliness threaded through her voice. This was one of her favorite subjects, after all. "Real coffee is *amazing*. It perks you up, gives you an extra boost of energy, and it even saves lives."

"Really?" Aurelian asked, shooting the travel mug a look of respect.

Maddy grinned. "It sure does. It makes me happy enough I don't commit murder or beat the squat out of people who annoy me... I've also never tried to drown anyone in coffee before, either, so there's that."

Aurelian snorted a laugh. "That is occasionally tempting, but it would be a waste of good coffee."

"Exactly," Maddy agreed with a grin. She shook the travel mug enticingly. "Give it a try. Once you go to real coffee, you'll never go back to the fake stuff."

Cautiously, Aurelian sniffed the drink, then put it to her lips. Her eyes bugged out immediately, and she guzzled the entire travel mug.

"Oh, wow!" she exclaimed. "That was amazing!"

She belched and handed the cup back to Maddy.

"I'm glad you liked it," Maddy said, shaking her now empty travel mug with an annoyed swish of her tail. "I'll get more when I'm back on my ship."

She expected to hear an overly-enthusiastic response from Aurelian, but it didn't come. She looked up and saw that the Ahkal-Tiki's whole demeanor had changed in mere seconds. Her eyes looked heavy, and she swayed back and forth.

Alarm shot through Maddy. "Aurelian? Are you okay?"

"Hmm? Oh, yeah, just super sleepy all of a sudden," she mumbled groggily.

"I guess caffeine makes you sleepy rather than wakes you up. That's so freaking *weird*." Maddy hurried to Aurelian's side and braced her shoulder against her to keep her from faceplanting. "And you're a lightweight, too. Come on, let's get you to a bed."

"No, I'm okay," Aurelian replied mid-yawn and abruptly spun around, leaving Maddy bracing her hindquarters instead of her shoulder. "I'll just lay down right here."

With that, she collapsed—right on top of Maddy. She tried to hold her up, but the Ahkal-Tiki was more than twice her size, and she was squashed down into the plush carpet by a bright pink butt with a golden bejeweled tail smothering her face.

"Can't... breathe," Maddy gasped out and shoved Aurelian's tail off her face. It moved enough for her to suck in a deep breath, but it snagged on something before she could get her eyes clear. "Oh, you've got to be kidding me."

She squirmed and heaved, but every time she managed to wriggle out from under Aurelian's butt even a little bit, her head jerked sideways in a painful tug. Rage and panic at being trapped shot through her, and it took several long breaths before she regained control of herself. She carefully jerked one arm free and dug her claws through the tail until she reached the side of her head. The thick, golden strands had somehow entwined themselves with her hoop earrings, and no matter how she tugged at them, she couldn't get them free. She couldn't even get enough slack to see properly.

"Okay, no big deal. I can call for help," she muttered, but the thought of the others seeing her like this was humiliating. Worse,

Reggie was sure to blame her for this predicament, even though she'd been trying to be *nice* by sharing her coffee. She let her head thunk back down on the carpet and groaned miserably. "Even when I'm trying to be nice, I can't win."

She gave serious consideration to just ripping the earrings out, but her ear was sensitive, and it would hurt. A *lot*. Plus, it might tear her ear enough she'd never be able to wear jewelry in it again. *Think, Maddy, think. I can't call for help, I can't rip my earrings out… but maybe I can cut myself free?*

Maddy stretched her arm out blindly and knocked her claws against the still-open vanity drawer. A grin twisted her muzzle as she remembered those shiny gold shears inside, and she tried to lift her arm enough to dig into the drawer.

A frustrated growl escaped her when her arm wasn't quite long enough, and Aurelian snorted. Maddy held her breath, hoping the damn pony princess would wake up and help her out of her extremely embarrassing predicament. Unfortunately, Aurelian's breathing just shifted into a steady snoring that rivaled Ed for volume, and if anything, settled more of her weight on Maddy. Her lungs wheezed, and desperation drove her to wrap her claws around the drawer handle and *heave*.

The whole drawer tore free of the vanity with a loud tearing sound. Maddy froze. If anything was going to get Reggie's attention, it was the sound of something breaking. After several agonizing minutes when nobody charged in and laughed at her, she dug around inside the drawer until her hand landed on the shears.

Relief surged through her, and she maneuvered her arm until she could begin carefully snipping through the thick strands near her ear.

She didn't want to cut more than she had to, but if she didn't get free soon, she was going to scream… or suffocate.

Panic and breathlessness drove her to cut faster, and she cursed viciously as she nicked the side of her ear. She moved the shears a little farther away from her vulnerable skin and finished cutting herself free.

Once the tail was no longer pulling on her ear, it was easy to wiggle out from under Aurelian's pink butt, and she scrambled away on all fours.

She shook her head vigorously, but the tail had come with her. She froze in horror. *The tail had done* what *now?*

"No, no, no," she chanted as she frantically untangled the tail from her earrings. She accidentally pulled too hard and ended up ripping one out completely. She snarled at the flash of pain, but the loss of that one earring was what allowed her to finally get the thick strands of hair out of her eyes.

The bottom dropped out of her stomach. She was clutching most of Aurelian's beautiful tail in her hands, leaving the Ahkal-Tiki president with a ragged stub barely a quarter of its previous glorious length.

"Reggie is gonna *kill* me," she whispered in horror.

* * * * *

Chapter Twenty-Five

Loud, fast-paced steps coming down the stairs tore Reggie's attention from the Clue Song playing on Ed's slate. The three of them had listened to it no less than a dozen times, and he still didn't have the first idea what the hidden clue was. He turned toward the commotion in time to see Maddy trip and tumble down the last five steps on the staircase. Her purple eyes were wide and wild as she scrambled to her feet.

"What's wrong, Mads?" he asked as he leapt to his feet.

Maddy looked up at him, looked back up the stairs, then back to him again. "It's time to go. Like, now. We need to leave."

Reggie raised an eyebrow and looked up the stairs. He didn't see anything out of the ordinary, but with his clan, that didn't mean squat. "Something happen up there with you two? She didn't try to take your coffee or paint you pink and you killed her, did you?"

Reggie meant it as a joke, but Maddy flinched and wrung her paws in an uncharacteristic gesture. His eyes narrowed as her ears flicked back and forth, and her tail swished in a tight arc. She was anxious, maybe even... scared?

"Uh, no, no, I didn't kill her," Maddy replied as she shifted her weight from one foot to the other. "But she did fall asleep, and I think we should just go. It's a little weird for us to stay here while she's um... sleeping."

"Asleep?" Reggie asked through narrowed eyes. "Did you do something to her?"

Maddy glowered back at him and pinned her ears. "No, Reggie, I didn't do anything to her. She just said she was really tired from her day as president, doing the Clue Song, and then giving us the royal treatment. Feel free to go check on her if you don't believe me." Maddy jabbed a finger up the stairs. "She's in the third room on the right in the second hallway."

Reggie instantly felt bad for doubting Maddy. Being the system president must be stressful and exhausting for Aurelian to take a nap in the middle of the day.

"No," he said, "I believe you. I just thought it was weird for her to go to bed like that without a word after she's been so courteous to us so far."

Maddy shrugged, but the gesture seemed a little forced. "I guess courtesy only goes so far on Ahkal-Tiki. Come on, let's go."

"Okay," Reggie replied with a shrug of his own. He turned back to the oversized couch where Ed and Harold were still watching the video. Ed was humming along with the tune as he swayed back and forth. "Come on, you two. Time to go. We can figure it out on the ship."

Harold looked past them to the stairs. "Shouldn't we say goodbye?"

"Nope," Maddy snapped, her eyes still a little wild, and her tone just this side of frantic. "Aurelian is passed out from exhaustion. We should leave before we wear out our welcome."

"Odd," Harold said and slowly leaned forward. He let out a surprised *oof* when Maddy grabbed his arm and hauled him to his feet. "Go easy on an old Joongee there, Madeline."

"Like, I hope she's not getting sick or anything," Ed said as he hopped off the couch. "That could totally mess with her awesome singing voice."

"I think she'll be fine," Maddy replied.

Reggie looked at her a little sideways as she did her best to herd them all out the door. Something about the whole situation seemed… off. She didn't even seem to notice Harold had called her by her hated full name. Her tail was still doing that anxious little swish, too. Ears weren't always easy to control, but tails were nearly impossible.

The trip back to *HIADA* took about half the time as the trip to Aurelian's home due to Maddy rushing them like a tiny drill sergeant. She didn't even want to stop back by the coffee shop, which raised all sorts of red flags in Reggie's mind until he remembered it was all decaf.

All she wanted to do was get to the ship and get gone. Reggie tilted his head and studied her as they neared their little junker of a ship. He'd never seen her quite so motivated, though he supposed she might've just finally snapped with all the pony cuteness overload.

As soon as everyone was in, Maddy slapped the control panel and sealed them inside. After the eye-searing colors of the Ahkal-Tiki city, the dull grays and browns of the ship were a bit of an adjustment, but Maddy didn't hesitate for a second. "To the controls, Reggie!"

"But, Maddy," Ed said as he scratched behind one ear, "we don't even know where we're going yet."

"He can still get us in the air headed toward the gate," Maddy snapped. "Now get your tails moving!"

Reggie narrowed his eyes at her before he turned and headed for the bridge. "Come on, Ed. You can be copilot."

"Cool!" Ed grinned broadly and followed.

* * *

As soon as the engine fired up and Maddy felt *HIADA* lift off the ground, she rushed to her room. She shut the door, kicked her boots off, unzipped her overalls, and pulled them completely off. It left her in nothing but her underwear and sports bra, but she was a little too freaked out to care. Besides, it was *her* room.

Frantically, she turned the overalls upside down and shook them with a little more force than was probably necessary. A braided, golden Ahkal-Tiki tail embedded with precious stones, beads, and pearls practically flew out of the baggy garment and hit the deck with a loud *thunk*.

"Squat, squat, squat!" she harshly whispered through gritted teeth. "Where the hell am I going to hide this thing?"

She whimpered as she looked around her room with wild eyes. *If Reggie finds it, he's going to space me!*

* * *

"Okay, Ed, you take over," Reggie said as they exited the atmosphere. "Remember everything we talked about on the way here?"

"For sure, Reg. Like, I got this," Ed replied with a confident nod. He took hold of the controls and checked his instruments. "Looks like smooth sailing to the gate. Be a few hours before we get there."

"Awesome," Reggie said and stood to leave the bridge. "I'm going to go check on Maddy. She was acting sort of weird."

Ed chuckled and waved him off. "Girls are always sort of weird, buddy. That's the secret."

Reggie snorted a laugh as he left the bridge and marched to Maddy's door. He knocked, but didn't get an answer. He knocked again. This time he was answered by a loud crashing noise followed by a shrill curse word.

Without thinking, and worried something had happened to Maddy, Reggie overrode the control panel and darted into her room. What he saw brought him to a screeching halt with his jaw firmly resting on the deck.

Maddy stood in the center of her room with a drawer from her dresser lying broken at her feet. Clothes were scattered all over the floor, but Maddy herself was damn near naked. He was torn between backpedaling out of her room, begging for forgiveness, and demanding to know if she was okay. Instead of doing either of those useful things, he just ended up staring like an idiot.

Reggie's brain tripped over itself, because *Damn*.

It slowly dawned on him that Maddy wasn't shrieking at him to get out, or doing anything at all really. The tiny female seemed frozen in place and just stared at him with wide, fearful eyes. The awkwardness of the situation slammed into him, and he nearly turned around out of respect for her state of undress… but then his eyes landed on the golden Ahkal-Tiki tail clutched in her hand.

A very familiar golden Ahkal-Tiki tail.

Anything close to a lustful thought disappeared and was immediately replaced by anger, and worse, disappointment. He reached back without breaking eye contact with Maddy and slapped the control panel to close the door.

She shot out a paw imploringly, desperation threading through her voice as she said, "It's not what it looks like, Reggie! I swear!"

She'd apparently forgotten she was all but naked, because she made no effort to get dressed. Either she had zero modesty issues, or she was exactly as freaked out as she looked. Regardless, Reggie kept his gaze pinned to her face and refused to look lower. Again.

"Maddy, what in the hell is wrong with you?" he demanded as he bared his fangs and pinned his ears back. "Did you seriously cut Aurelian's tail off and steal it? Are you freaking kidding me? Have you got any freaking idea how long it takes for an Ahkal-Tiki to grow their tail back?"

"No," Maddy replied in a meek tone and dropped her eyes to the floor.

"A long ass time!" he roared. The familiar burn of rage threatened his self-control, but at Maddy's flinch, he managed to throttle it back enough to speak somewhat calmly. "What the hell are you going to do with that thing, anyway? Keep it on a shelf like a trophy?"

"It was an accident!" Her tone was pleading and slightly on the pitiful side, and her purple eyes held none of their usual fire.

Reggie jabbed a finger at the tail. "How in the blue hell could that possibly happen by accident?"

"Because clearly the universe hates me!" Maddy said in a wail as her ears drooped. "I *swear* it wasn't on purpose."

"No wonder you were in such a hurry to get out of there." He cocked his head to the side, narrowed his gaze, and asked, "Did you leave her tied up in a closet somewhere? Please tell me you didn't leave her tied up in a closet."

Maddy swallowed hard, and her hands tightened on the braided, slightly ragged tail. She didn't answer right away, and Reggie nearly lost it again.

Reggie squeezed his eyes shut and rubbed at the spot between them. "Maddy, I swear, if you left the president of the Ahkal-Tiki system tied up in a closet with some sparkly gold and pink rope, I'm going to make you watch me space all your coffee, then leave you on Ahkal-Tiki, where all you can get is decaf for the rest of your life."

Maddy shot both hands, along with the tail, out in front of her as if to stop an oncoming force. "No, no, no! I swear, Reggie! It wasn't like that! She really did fall asleep!"

Reggie formed a mental cage around the anger sharks swimming through his mind and counted to ten. He forced his ears back up, though he couldn't quite manage to stop the angry lash of his tail. "Okay, Maddy, tell me *exactly* what happened."

Maddy jumped over the dresser drawer and came uncomfortably close to him, given her current lack of clothing. He swallowed hard and valiantly kept his gaze locked on hers.

"So, we got to her stupid vanity room, and she was showing me all her mane and tail brushes." Maddy spoke so quickly, her words blurred together, and her ears wouldn't stop flickering in anxiety. "I was doing the whole act like I liked her house thing, because you told me not to piss her off, and I swear to the gods Reggie, I did my best. Then she started eyeballing my coffee mug from the ship, and I asked her if she wanted to try my coffee because it's different from here since it has the caffeine. She liked it so much, she drank the entire mug!"

Maddy threw her hands in the air, and Reggie had to jerk backward to keep from taking a severed Ahkal-Tiki tail to the face. Maddy didn't even notice and began to pace back and forth as she continued her story. Reggie did his best to keep his eyes up, but it was, to say the least, difficult. *The universe hates me. Seriously. Hates. Me.*

"Well, come to find out," she said in a shrill voice that hurt his ears, "the freaking Ahkal-Tiki have the absolute opposite reaction to caffeine that we do. It knocked her out. Really fast. One minute she was groggy, the next she fell right on top of me and pinned me to the floor with her massive rump! I couldn't move, couldn't hardly breathe, and she was so freaking heavy."

Maddy rubbed at her ribs with her free hand as she paced, and Reggie could tell from the hitch in her stride that she was sore.

"Then, when I finally managed to move her a little, my damned earrings got all tangled in her tail. It would've ripped them *all* out and torn my ear to pieces if I'd just snatched it out."

Reggie's eyes darted up to her ears. One of her larger gold hoop earrings was gone, and her ear looked swollen. He kicked himself for not noticing the blood-stained fur and torn skin sooner.

"I remembered the scissors in her drawer, so I cut myself free." Maddy stopped pacing abruptly and her shoulders slumped. "It wasn't until I got up and looked in the mirror that I realized I accidently cut nearly all her tail off. I was horrified. So… I panicked and ran. I was afraid of what the Ahkal-Tiki would say or do to us, and I was afraid of you getting mad at me again."

Reggie's anger wavered as she looked up at him with tear-filled eyes. She blinked them clear, but he'd seen them. She was seconds away from bawling her eyes out.

"Come on, Reg! I gave her my *coffee*! I was trying my best to be *nice* to her!" Maddy pointed at the damaged dresser. "I was going to hide it in there, but you came in before I could. I was really hoping we could leave the system before she woke up and threw a princess hissy fit or whatever she's going to do. They don't know where we're going yet, and I figured we'd never see them again… and you'd never have to find out about what happened."

"I wish you'd told me what happened while we were still at Aurelian's! Maybe we could've fixed things if you hadn't tried to keep secrets from me. Damn it, Maddy, we're clan. We're *friends*. We're—"

Reggie cut himself off and took a deep breath "We're not supposed to keep secrets from each other."

She winced, and it was his turn to pace as he turned things over in his mind. Her story floored him, and he was a bit skeptical. It was outlandish and nearly unbelievable.

Reggie drifted to a halt in front of her and stared into her eyes. *If it is true, she accidently drugged Aurelian the same way Bruce tried to drug her. I just don't see Mads doing that to anyone. Especially after what happened to her. She's not even fully over her own experience yet. There's no way. She has to be telling me the truth. She's done some crazy stuff before, but never anything like this.*

Reggie crossed his arms and looked down at the floor. A smile tugged at his lips as he remembered one other, very important fact about his little Spitfire. She never lied to him. She might not tell him about something, but she never outright lied to his face.

"You... believe me, right, Reg?"

That voice. That tiny, pitiful, worried voice asking him if he believed her with such sincerity was what broke him. All the anger, the disappointment, and panic just melted away as the anger sharks swam back into the deepest depths of his mind.

He looked up, met her pleading eyes, and gave her a soft smile as he nodded. "Yes, Mads, I believe you. I don't think even you would do anything this crazy." He looked at the tail and let out a reluctant chuckle. "Well, I guess technically you would, just not on purpose. Why didn't you just call for help?"

Maddy's ears flattened, and her lip curled in disgust. "And have you three make fun of me forever for being stuck under a stupid pink and gold, happy, prancy, bouncy pony princess? Hell no!"

Reggie snorted. "Yeah, I can see your point. Okay, Mads, let's get this song figured out so we can haul ass. If she drank all your coffee, and the caffeine hits them that quick, my credit says she'll be out for a while, and we'll be long gone."

In a flash, Maddy was on him and had her arms wrapped around his neck in a tight hug. Shock ran through him in two different ways. First, Maddy had *never* embraced him before. Second, he was even more aware of just how little she had on with her body pressed against his. In an attempt not to touch anything he shouldn't, he placed his palms directly on the center of her back and squeezed her gently.

He cleared his throat after a long moment. "Um, Mads?"

Maddy kept her face tucked into the crook of his neck, and her breath tickled when she answered. "Yeah?"

Reggie drew in a deep breath. "You do realize you're almost naked, right?"

"What?" Maddy pushed off him, looked down, and jumped back with an ear-splitting shriek. "Reg! Why didn't you *say* anything?"

She snatched up her overalls, slipped her legs in, and bounced up and down to get them up. The bouncing wasn't helping his self-control in the least, so Reggie spun around to face the door.

"It was an intense moment, and it didn't seem like the most important thing in the room at the time," he said defensively.

"Uh huh. You just wanted the show to keep going."

He could hear the playfulness in her voice, even though she tried to hide it. He was pretty sure she was smiling, too. "I really didn't notice anything."

"Oh, so you're saying there's nothing there worth looking at? I don't meet your standards?"

The sound of shuffling clothing stopped, and he turned back around. Maddy was standing there expectantly with her hands on her hips and a playful tilt to her ears.

"Not saying that at all," Reggie replied with a slow grin. "Just that I wasn't standing here ogling you like a brute. I only busted in here because I heard you cursing, and it sounded like you were in pain."

"My hero." Maddy bit back a smile and gently kicked the broken drawer. "It fell on my toes."

Reggie nodded sheepishly. "I'm sorry for getting mad without listening to your story first. And I'm sorry you weren't dressed… I hope I didn't make you uncomfortable."

Maddy smirked at him and crossed her arms. "You make me a lot of things, Reg, but uncomfortable has never been one of them."

They stood there for a moment longer in a strange sort of silence until Reggie remembered something. He arched a brow and said, "So… cherries?"

Maddy's ears angled back in embarrassment. "It was a matched set, and it was on *sale*. Don't judge me!"

"No judgement here," Reggie said in a strangled tone as he valiantly held back laughter. He clapped his paws together. "Well, should we go see what Ed and Harold have figured out?"

Maddy reached down and picked up the tail. "First, we need to do something with this."

"Just stick it on your dresser. We can tell Harold and Ed the story in alter-reality. They'll get a kick out of it." Reggie tilted his head with a frown. "Ed might be a little upset. He really seemed to take a liking to the Ahkal-Tiki."

"Noticed that, did you?" Maddy asked dryly. "Did you see him dancing when they performed? He was in Joongee heaven."

Maddy dropped the tail on her dresser and managed to force the damaged drawer back into place with a minor application of percussive engineering and liberal amounts of swearing.

Reggie stepped to the side as he opened her door. He gestured with an open paw and a gallant bow that had Maddy giggling, though he suspected it was more from relief than his antics. "After you."

*****

Chapter Twenty-Six

Maddy sauntered onto the bridge as if she hadn't just had a mental breakdown in her room... in front of Reggie... in her underwear. *Fake it 'til you make it, right?*

In all honesty, the underwear part bothered her the least. That particular set actually covered more than her favorite swimsuit, so it wasn't that big a deal. She bit back a smug smile as she took her customary seat at the old nav station. In the middle of a breakdown she might've been, but even a blind being couldn't have missed Reggie's reaction to her. That combination of male interest and chivalrous behavior had been something else.

Something she *liked*.

She shook off the thought as unimportant but couldn't help but glance out the corner of her eye as Reggie took his place in the captain's chair like he was born to command.

"Any sign of pursuit?" he asked Ed as if it were a perfectly reasonable thing to say.

Ed tilted his head. "Naw, like, why would anyone be chasing us? We didn't steal anything, and there's no pirates in this system."

Harold, for once, wasn't nearly as oblivious as she would've preferred. He cast her a suspicious glare. "Yes, Madeline, why would anyone be chasing us?"

"No reason," she said with forced casualness and a dismissive flick of her ears. "And don't call me that, *Harry*."

Harold sniffed in distaste and went back to listening to that obnoxiously cute Clue Song on his slate. Reggie checked their course and gave Ed a double thumbs up.

"Great job flying, Ed," he said with that quiet, encouraging tone that somehow never sounded condescending. He turned to Harold. "Any luck figuring out where we're going next?"

"No," Harold said as he spread his paws helplessly. "The song is so... so..."

"Annoyingly cheerful?" Maddy suggested with a smirk.

Harold sighed and ran a hand over the fur between his ears. "I was going to say banal."

Before Maddy could ask what that meant, Ed shook his head and said, "It's not trite, or boring, Pops. It's fun!"

"Yes," Harold replied dryly. "Because 'across the stars, you traveled to where we are, and we're so glad to help you on your journey' is so fresh and original."

"No, no, no!" Ed said with a big grin. "You've got to sing it, Pops."

With that, he broke into song. Maddy flattened her ears at his off-key rendition and groaned at the stupid lyrics.

Reggie flashed her a wicked grin. "What's the matter, Maddy?"

He joined in on the next verse, singing the ridiculous song in a shockingly good voice. Maddy froze and slowly turned to stare at him. He put a lot of those grunge singers she'd been listening to lately to shame.

When they came to the end of the second chorus, Ed grinned at Reggie. "Wow, Reggie. I didn't know you could sing like that. Could you sing Aurelian's verse again?"

Reggie shrugged and sang the solo verse. The smooth timbre of his voice gave Maddy goosebumps, and she decided then and there that she loved that stupid song. It was her new favorite, so long as Reggie was the one singing it.

When Harold shouted for him to stop, Maddy nearly threw her comm at his head. "Why, Harold? Just why."

Harold's ears stood straight up in excitement. "It's right there in the song. You've got to sing it *in* Ahkal-Tiki. Not in their world or system, in their *language*."

He pulled up a translation on his slate and muttered the words in what Maddy was sure was a terrible accent. He tried singing it, and everyone flattened their ears before he made it past the first line.

"Please, for the love of the gods, *stop*," Maddy grumbled.

Harold scowled at her and shoved the slate in Reggie's face. The other male grabbed it before it ended up squashed against his muzzle. "Sing it again, Reggie. Slowly."

The older Joongee listened intently to the words, but Maddy just leaned back and let Reggie's voice wash over her in a soothing wave. She could listen to that male sing gate coordinates.

Harold's eyes lit up with excitement when Reggie got to the solo verse. "Of course!"

He waved for Reggie to stop, and Maddy gave serious thought to strangling him. Harold was right back to oblivious, though, and seemed blithely unaware of how close he'd just come to death by angry female.

"The Ahkal-Tiki language has a pronunciation shift between the spoken and the sung," he explained as he snatched his slate back from Reggie. "*Ere'shya* normally translates to grudge, but when you sing it, it translates to *grunge*."

Maddy perked her ears up. "Grunge... like the music?"

Harold looked at her as if she were being deliberately obtuse. "No, silly, as in the Grunge System! That's where we need to go next, I'm sure of it!"

Everyone looked to Reggie. Their clan leader picked up his slate and scrolled through something on the screen with his brow furrowed. Even before he spoke, Maddy could read the doubt in the set of his ears.

"There's nothing in that system except for garbage," Reggie said with a touch of exasperation. "Seriously, every planet in that system is designated as a dump." The corners of his mouth dropped into a frown. "Are you sure this isn't a wild chinto chase like the tunnels beneath the mall?"

Harold straightened his spine and nodded sharply. "As sure as I've ever been of anything, Reggie."

"I've heard that before."

Harold's expression hardened. "The Lost Weapons of Koroth are in the Grunge System, I promise you that."

Maddy narrowed her eyes. "How do you know the weapons are there and not just another clue?"

"Why, because of the good doctor's letter, of course," Harold replied as if it were obvious. "X marks the spot!"

Ed looked over his shoulder from the pilot's station and nodded. "Oh, sure. Of course, that definitely makes sense, Pops."

Reggie stared at him blankly. "I don't follow."

Harold tapped at his slate with a grin. "I've been marking the locations of the clues as we go. If you take into account stellar drift, relativity, gravitational flux—"

"Get to the point, Harry!" Maddy snapped with more than a touch of exasperation in her voice.

"I'll ask you to remember your manners, Madeline," Harold said primly and folded his paws over his slate.

Maddy wrinkled her muzzle and growled. Reggie quirked a brow at her, and the amusement in his eyes was enough for her to regain control of her temper.

Between clenched jaws she muttered, "Please get to the point, Harold."

"That wasn't so hard, was it?" Harold asked with a grandfatherly smile.

Behind his back, Reggie threw up a hand, his expression pleading. Maddy took a deep breath and didn't strangle Harold—but it was a close thing. Meanwhile, the old Joongee turned his slate so they could see the cross-section of their corner of the galaxy.

"With the help of the StarNav5500—"

"Thanks, Chad!" everyone shouted.

The Joongee all snickered, even Harold. After a brief chuckle, he cleared his throat and continued. "As I was saying, I was able to chart out our stops. If you replace our starting point at Galactic Solutions with Dr. Monschtackle's home world of Koroth, and add the Zoo, the Mall, and the Ahkal-Tiki system, what do you see?"

Maddy rolled her eyes. "A lopsided square?"

Harold turned the slate back to himself with a puzzled frown. His expression brightened, and he jabbed a finger at the center of the screen before turning it back to them. "*Now* what do you see?"

Reggie tilted his head at the slate and his brow furrowed. "An X?"

Maddy gave him a little side eye before tilting her head as well. "I mean… I guess it kind of looks like an X now."

Ed nodded his big head eagerly. "It totally looks like an X, Pops. Good job!"

Reggie rubbed at the spot between his eyes and sighed. "Good enough. Maddy, see if you can find anyone leaving for the Grunge System. If you can't find anyone leaving *right now*, we'll spend the credit on a solo gate transit."

Ed's ears flicked. "What's the rush? That's like, a lot of credit, Reg."

Maddy tensed, but Reggie just gave him an easy smile. "It's a race, remember, Ed? We've got to get to the treasure before anyone else figures it out."

Ed accepted the answer readily enough, but Harold frowned at Reggie and shot Maddy an outright suspicious glance. Maddy busied herself with trying to find transport. She hated the idea of spending all that credit simply because she'd messed up. A sigh of relief escaped her when she found a garbage scow heading out of the system for Grunge.

The Hariboon who answered her comm was a typical example of his race—red fur, black markings around the eyes and the tips of his rounded ears, and golden eyes. The adult male was roughly four times the size of Maddy, but his comfortably padded midsection made her think she could take him in a fight. The soft expression in his eyes and the genuine cheer he exuded made her think she'd never have to find out.

Behind the massive Hariboon, she could see a young Gurge. The brightly colored being was only as tall as Maddy, and his light blue skin was set off by the brilliant red, yellow, and orange markings on his face.

"Well, sure now, little Joongee. You can latch on for the gate transit, no problem. And don't worry about the fee. I got that covered." the Hariboon said in a jovial tone.

Maddy's jaw dropped. She'd managed to get them some good deals on this crazy adventure, but nobody offered gate transit for free. Not unless they wanted something other than credit.

"What's the catch?" she said suspiciously.

"No catch." He shrugged and added, "I'd be paying the same fee whether you tag along or not. Besides, it's a business expense." His eyes brightened and his lips curled up into a smile. "I can use it as a tax write-off."

Maddy grinned back. "Nice."

"Actually, Torque, there is a catch," the young Gurge piped up with a grin. He looked at Maddy through the screen. "You've got to *catch* us!"

The Hariboon winced and nodded as he checked his instruments. "Kit's got a point. We can't slow down to wait for you. If you can link up with us before our gate window, you're welcome to tag along."

Maddy's ears perked up, and she gave them a firm nod.

"We'll make it. Thanks!" She signed off with the Hariboon and passed the information to Reggie. "We can make it, right?"

She watched as he ran a quick course calculation with the navigation computer and held her breath.

Reggie gave her a fierce grin. "We can make it. Punch it, Ed."

Ed frowned back at him in confusion. "Why would I hit *HIADA*? She's a nice ship."

Maddy burst out laughing. Relief combined with genuine amusement to give her a solid case of the giggles, but she managed to explain before Reggie could. "He means max thrust, genius. We need to go as fast as this POS can fly to catch up with them in time."

Reggie tossed her a quick grin before he transferred their optimal course to Ed's flight console. "Think you can handle flying it?"

Ed smiled happily. "I've got this, Reg."

Ed pushed the throttles to their max, and all four Joongee grunted in discomfort as the sudden acceleration surpassed the capabilities of their G-force dampeners. It was a solid minute before the dampeners caught up, and the pressure eased off.

Reggie pinned his ears back. "Remind me to add upgraded dampeners to the list."

Maddy snorted. "I've seen your list. At the rate we're going, we might as well burn *HIADA* to the ground for insurance purposes and start over from scratch… we do have insurance, right, Harold?"

Harold rubbed the back of his neck. "Uh… sort of. Did I mention the lifetime coolant refills?"

"Yeah," Reggie said with a wry chuckle. "You might've mentioned it once or twice."

Maddy sighed. "I'll add dampeners to the list."

Reggie got up and stretched. Maddy averted her gaze. The last thing that would *ever* happen was getting caught drooling over *Reggie*. Even if his shirt had ridden up, because nope. So much nope.

The perfect distraction came to mind, and she grinned as she linked her latest playlist to the external speakers. "Well, if we're going to Grunge, we need the right soundtrack."

With a tap of her finger, she unleashed her new musical obsession onto the bridge.

Ed's ears perked up, and he bobbed his head along with the beat, but Harold pinned his ears flat and whimpered. "What is that *awful* noise?"

Reggie, though... he listened with his head tilted and a rapt look in his eyes. When he joined in on the second chorus, Maddy about fell out of her chair. Screw the pony song, she wanted to listen to him sing *this* on repeat.

"Good song," he said with a relaxed smile when it ended. He clapped Ed on the shoulder. "I'll take over when we get close. I want you to watch what I do to lock onto their ship so you can do it next time, okay?"

"You got it, Reg," Ed replied easily. "Hey, like, has anyone seen Boo? I hope that bit of acceleration didn't hurt her."

Maddy scowled on reflex. "I'm sure the furball's fine."

Reggie rolled his eyes at her. "You don't have to pretend you still hate her, you know. I've seen you sharing your coffee grounds. That practically makes you besties."

Maddy grimaced at the reminder of sharing her coffee with Aurelian. The last thing she wanted was a new best friend. She'd rather be besties with the furball than that pretty pink princess. Even if she hadn't been all bad. That remark about drowning those dare bear guys in sparkling coffee was hilarious... and surprisingly snarky.

"I'll go look for her." She stood with a grumble, but before she could take a single step, she spotted the golden-furred fluffball in the corridor outside the bridge. "See, Ed, I told you she was fine."

"That's a relief," Ed said with a wide smile. "Hey there, Boo-face. What've you got there?"

Boo *chirruped* as she walked backward onto the bridge dragging something large, golden, and sparkly in both paws. Harold and Ed tilted their heads in confusion and dawning horror.

Maddy waved her hands frantically. "I can explain!"

* * *

A few days later, they exited alter-reality into the Grunge System on the tail end of yet another grunge song. Maddy had apparently downloaded the whole collection, though there was one song she kept sneaking into the playlist. Reggie didn't mind. It was a really good song, and he loved the way her eyes lit up every time he sang it.

The Hariboon, who insisted they call him Trash Panda of all things, hauled them all the way to the fourth planet. According to the ruins on the planet, its actual name was Brekanstief. The Brekan were a long-extinct race who'd perished with their planet. As a species, they hadn't yet reached the stars. As far as evolution went, they were barely through their stone age, and had just begun to learn metal crafting when they died off.

The ruins themselves were chiseled into the sides of mountain ranges and went as deep as some three hundred feet. Aside from petroglyphs, stone carvings, and everyday handmade items, nothing of significance had ever been found by the many excavation teams.

"You guys sure this is where you wanna go?" Trash Panda asked doubtfully. "There ain't nothing there but dust, rock, and disappointment. You can ask the hundreds of excavation teams who've gone down already and left empty-handed."

"We're sure," Harold answered as Reggie unclamped *HIADA* from *Bertha*.

Trash Panda scratched behind an ear. "All right, then, if you say so. What are you huntin' for, anyway?"

"The Lost Weapons of Koroth," Reggie replied easily.

All the Joongee gave him an incredulous glare, while Trash Panda let out a belly laugh.

"What?" Reggie said with a dismissive shrug. "It's not like it's some big secret now. There's a whole contest full of hunters looking for them."

"He ain't wrong," Trash Panda said in amusement. "Lots of folks come through here on that wild scavenger hunt. Nobody ever finds them, though. Like I said, dust, rocks, and disappointment."

Reggie narrowed his eyes. "Define *lots*."

"Oh, tons!" Kit said excitedly. "Whole hordes of beings come here looking for the Lost Weapons of Koroth, ol' Pordobel's buried treasure, Asur outposts, you name it!"

"Yup, the kid's right," Trash Panda said with an indulgent chuckle. "Hell, they even come looking for some sword they call Excalibur. Apparently, some nut-job on Earth got it in his brain that the reason they never found it there was because aliens gave King Arthur the sword. Claims it was a conduit for some crazy powers. His theory is, the aliens came and took it back after he died and hid it in the cosmos somewhere. Some say they hid it in those very ruins down there."

There was a weight to the Hariboon's voice that gave them all chills. Reggie narrowed his eyes.

"That seems a bit outlandish," Reggie deadpanned, effectively breaking the spell.

"And the Lost Weapons of Koroth don't?" Maddy snapped back with a roll of her eyes.

"Like, she's got you there, Reg," Ed said with a grin. Boo bounced and chittered on his shoulder like she was agreeing with him.

"Fair enough."

Trash Panda chuckled, causing his belly to jiggle and his eyes to brighten. "Well, best of luck to you all. Me and Kit here gotta get this junk dumped and get back on our route." He tapped on his wrist slate. "Time is credit, and we got a schedule to keep."

Kit waved and smiled through the connection. "Hope you find your treasure!"

They all waved back. Maddy yelled, "Thanks for the ride!" and the call cut out.

Reggie, Ed, Boo, and Maddy all looked to Harold.

"Well, Mr. Historian, it's your time to shine and bring your life's work to a conclusion." Reggie pinned him with a challenging look. "Are you ready?"

Harold stood tall and smiled proudly. "I have never been more ready in my life. Let's go make history, pups!"

* * * * *

Chapter Twenty-Seven

"Harold," Reggie said with strained patience. "We've been orbiting this spectacular planet for a *week*. In a few more days, we'll have to leave for resupply."

In the last week, the four of them had searched every inch of the Brekan ruins, the area surrounding the ruins, and multiple possible locations not completely covered in trash on the planet. One particular cave seemed promising, but all they ended up finding were some old washing machines some enterprising being had tucked out of the weather with a faded sign stating his claim and that he'd be back to retrieve them. They'd even gone so far as to fly *HIADA* close to the ground and use the scanners to look for hidden caves or secret rooms. It was all for naught, as they came up with nothing but dust, rocks, and disappointment, exactly as Trash Panda predicted.

"No!"

Harold looked up from the mess he'd made of his station on the bridge. His appearance wasn't quite as bad as the last time he'd lost himself to the hunt. Maddy had been more herself this time around and had been quite vocal that he maintain proper hygiene and eating habits. Reggie had to admit, she was adorable when she was bullying the older Joongee into taking care of himself. Oh, she'd made it seem like it was all about sparing her poor nose, but he knew her well enough by now to catch the concerned gleam in those purple eyes.

"Not when we're so close," Harold added in a pleading voice.

Reggie sighed and scanned the gathered slates and references Harold had scattered over his workspace. "Come on, then. Let's get all this to the common area and have a clan meeting. We're stronger together, remember?"

Harold dragged his claws through his short mane. "Sorry, Reg. You're right, of course. I just... this is my life's work. I wanted to try to solve the final piece myself."

"That's the thing, *Harry*. You don't have to."

Reggie whipped his head around. Maddy leaned against the hatch to the bridge, arms crossed and a cocky grin on her face. Ed stood at her back, with Boo draped over his head like a weird, golden-furred hat. The little kinkakaijou chirped happily and waved a tiny paw.

A smile spread across Harold's face, and his ears perked up. "All right, then."

Reggie winked at Maddy and Ed and helped Harold gather up his things.

Once they were situated in the common area, Harold gestured to the various slates. "This is it. Everything I've gathered over a decade, every bit of evidence that launched us on this grand adventure. The Clue Song got us to the right system, but the final puzzle piece that'll lead us to the Lost Weapons wasn't in the song."

Ed tilted his head. "Then where is it, Pops?"

The old Joongee picked up a slate with trembling paws and took a deep breath. "It's in here. Somewhere."

Reggie placed a paw on his shoulder. "Then let's find it together."

Hours later, they'd gone through every document, every paper the doctor had ever published, every obscure bit of trivia Harold had managed to gather. They'd started with the children's books Monschtackle had published under a pen name—*The Adventures of the Red Herring Pirates*—as Harold believed they were the key, but despite reading the books in the original language of Koroth and the translated Earth Common, they hadn't found anything.

Ed had been particularly enamored with the stories and had drifted off, snuggled up with Boo in the corner of the room for most of the search. Reggie found the soft drone of his voice as he patiently read them aloud to the little kinkakaijou soothing.

Maddy looked up from her portion of the slates with a drawn-out groan. She was sprawled on her stomach on the couch, and her tail lashed in the air behind her. "I've got nothing."

"Same." Reggie leaned back in his chair and stretched his arms out over his head. He noted Maddy quickly ducked her head back down to her slate with mild confusion but dismissed it as unimportant. She probably just wanted to figure it out first. She was competitive like that.

Harold rubbed at his temples and remained hunched over his slates. "It's here. I know it's here. X marks the spot, remember? The Lost Weapons of Koroth are here, I can feel it in my bones!"

"Are you sure that's not just arthritis setting in?" Maddy muttered snidely.

Reggie bit back a snort of laughter before a frown crossed his face. Something was different. His ears flicked once, twice, before he realized a background noise had cut off abruptly.

Ed had stopped reading to Boo.

The big Joongee stood abruptly and hurried over to the table. He waved his slate in the air and was so excited he couldn't seem to get proper words out. "Guys! Slate… map… *argh*! Like, just look, guys!"

Harold finally tore his gaze off his own slate, and Reggie walked around to his side of the table so he could see. Even Maddy rolled off the couch and sauntered over to get a look.

At first, disappointment shot through Reggie. It was just the child's pirate treasure map from the first book. On the far left was a classic wooden pirate ship flying a black flag with a white rounded skull and crossed bones. In a dotted trail from the ship were islands of various sizes, some with palm trees, others with tentacled monsters, and even one with a jumble of… trash.

His head shot up, and he met Ed's eyes with a disbelieving stare. "The islands…"

Ed grinned back and brushed a finger over the trash island before pointing downward. "They're planets, Reg."

Harold instantly shook his head and spluttered. "No, that can't be right. A system map is much more complex, with planetary orbits, size and mass, distance from the sun. This is too, too—"

"Simple," Maddy breathed out and pointed to a small island off the coast of the large one with tentacles. "X marks the spot, Harry."

Reggie lunged for his slate and pulled up a basic overlay of the Grunge System. His eyes widened. "Harold, the pirate ship is the *sun*. Look!"

Harold muttered to himself as he looked between the two maps, comparing the planetary bodies to the cartoonish islands, before he shot out of his seat with a *yip* of excitement. "You're a *genius*, Ed!"

The layout of the islands on the pirate's treasure map was identical to the standard planetary layout for the Grunge System.

"I know," Ed replied with an easy smile. "Hey, where're you going, Pops?"

Harold dashed for the door with a wild cackle. "X marks the spot! We need to go to Naramethia's moon!"

Reggie grinned at Maddy and Ed. "You heard him, let's go! You want to fly, Ed?"

Ed grinned wide. "Like, for sure."

* * *

Zoritch, Naramethia's moon, orbited the gas giant at a slow pace, taking nearly five hundred days to make a full orbit. The moon was small, and therefore easy to search. Before long, they found a cave with *HIADAS'* scanners large enough for a being to actually enter.

"This seems to be the most logical location," Harold said as he studied the layout of the terrain. He scratched the gray fur on his chin. "Reggie, is the atmosphere breathable?"

Reggie ran an atmosphere test and frowned. "Barely. The level of carbon dioxide is higher than I'd like. I think we're going to have to suit up." He leaned back, spun his chair around to face them, and crossed his arms. "We could go without them, but it would be a risk. We could easily pass out or end up with CO2 poisoning. Especially Ed. He's bigger than all of us, requires more oxygen, and takes larger breaths. He'd probably be the first one to drop."

Ed became visibly uneasy at that and rubbed his neck. "Like, I think I'll be wearing my suit."

"We all should," Reggie said firmly as he stood from his chair. "Mads, Harold, you two suit up as well. Sorry, but that's an order. We're not risking anyone." He looked up at Boo, still perched on Ed. "Sorry, Tiny-bit, but you gotta stay on the ship again. It's not safe."

Boo let out some lower-than-normal pitched chittering and appeared to pout as she hugged her tentacles tight to her neck and crossed her little arms. Her tail twitched rigidly behind her.

Reggie gave her a sad smile. "Sorry, but it's for your own good."

"I don't take orders from you," Maddy said as she brushed past him, "but lucky for you, I don't want to die of CO_2 poisoning, either."

He smiled at her back as she sauntered to the bay, her tail swishing back and forth in silent defiance. "Lucky me."

* * *

Reggie craned his head back to stare up at Naramethia. The gas giant was so massive in comparison to Zoritch, it nearly covered the entire sky. *Huh, the rings around Naramethia do kinda look like giant tentacles.*

He closed the hatch and watched the ramp retract before joining the others, who waited patiently for him a dozen meters away.

"This place is seriously depressing," Maddy grumbled and crossed her arms. "It's all gray rock and dirt. Even the sky is dull and gray."

"That's because Naramethia blocks too much of the star's light and heat for anything to grow," Harold said in his patient teacher's voice as they reached the mouth of the cave. "It's unfortunate. The high levels of CO_2 might have made for some interesting plant life."

Reggie aimed his rifle and shined the flashlight down the tunnel. If there was anything in there, his light didn't reach it.

"I'll take point," he said grimly. "You guys stick behind me."

"Oh, my *hero*," Maddy snickered with a roll of her eyes. "I feel so much safer with the big, strong male leading me into an empty tunnel on a completely uninhabited moon with no sign of life anywhere."

Harold held up a finger. "I never said this moon was uninhabited, Maddy. It's entirely possible there are lifeforms here, either of a microscopic nature here on the surface, or perhaps larger lifeforms underground."

"*Great.*" Maddy pinned Harold with a glower. "So, you're saying we might run into some creepy cave monsters that want to suck out our insides for dessert."

"I love your optimism," Reggie said to her with a wink.

She snorted and flicked her gloved hands toward the dark tunnel. "Well, go on, fearless leader. Let's put those merc skills to use."

Reggie shook his head inside his helmet. "Everyone's a critic. Just stay behind me, Mads. I'd hate for you to accidently get shot in the ass."

Maddy stared at him. "Did... did you just threaten to shoot me in the ass?"

Reggie shrugged and bit back a smirk. "Squat happens."

"Like, I think Reggie's messing with you, Maddy," Ed said in his usual even tone, "but I think we should listen to him since he's—"

"Can we please just go into the cave?" Harold shouted.

Everyone turned to face him. His eyes were wide, and his breathing was heavy as he clenched and unclenched his paws.

"Easy, Harold," Reggie said soothingly. "We're going. No need for you to have that heart attack just yet."

"Yeah," Maddy added under her breath. "Maybe wait until *after* we find the treasure."

Reggie brought his rifle up into a ready position and swept the light back and forth as they eased into the opening. As they moved deeper, the ambient light dimmed, until his flashlight was the only light they had. They'd only gone twenty meters.

"Stop," Reggie ordered crisply. "Harold, clip our safety line to the loop on the back of my suit. Mads, you do the same to Harold, and Ed, you clip to Maddy."

He silently cursed himself for not having done that before they entered the cave. Once again, too many years behind a desk had caused him to make a tactically stupid mistake. Fortunately, this one was easily remedied. As soon as they were connected in a line, Reggie led them into the dark.

After about another thirty meters, something caught Reggie's eye. He told everyone to stop before he shut off his light. After a moment, his eyes adjusted to the dark, and he saw it again. Not too far ahead of them, a cluster of green lights hovered in the air. Reggie clicked his light on again and aimed it at the location of the green lights. They weren't hovering at all. It was a keypad embedded into the stone wall.

Reggie panned his light to the left and gasped. A massive set of steel doors was embedded into the end of the tunnel. Painted across them was a huge, red X.

X always marks the spot.

"It's a vault."

"No, my pup," Harold said with quiet awe in his voice. "It is *the* vault. It's Dr. Monschtackle's secret vault, where he hid the legendary Lost Weapons of Koroth."

Harold stepped up next to Reggie, pulling Maddy and Ed along with him, and stared up at the vault doors with wide, tear-filled eyes. Reggie held back a laugh as Harold attempted to wipe his nose on his sleeve, only to be stopped by his helmet.

* * *

Harold chuckled to himself as his hand bounced off his helmet. In his excitement and joy, he'd forgotten he was suited up.

He'd dreamed about this moment for over ten years. All his tireless research and hard work had paid off. He'd finally found it. With the help of his clan, of course, but he'd been right all along. And now before him stood the proof. None of them would call him crazy or tell him to stop chasing after a fantasy again. It was *real*.

He turned to his clan, his family, with a wide grin. "Let's get those doors open and claim our prize, shall we?"

* * * * *

Chapter Twenty-Eight

The vault doors were no less than fifteen feet tall and six feet wide, and they were constructed of solid steel. Reggie wasn't sure how thick they were, but he had a feeling they could withstand heavy firepower. His ears flickered uncertainly as he studied the ancient control panel with its raised individual buttons and strange symbols.

"Can you translate those, Harold?" he asked hopefully.

"Oh, easily," Harold said confidently. "Those are Korothian numbers. Starting with one down through nine on the first three rows, with a zero centered beneath them."

"So, it's a combination lock," Reggie said and tilted his head. "Do you know what the code could be?"

"Ah, well, uhm…"

"That's a no," Maddy said with a derisive sniff. "Great. That means there's only ten thousand possible combinations. And that's only if he used a standard four-digit code. Which I'm assuming he did, considering how frustratingly simple all his clues have been so far."

Everyone looked at her.

"What?" she said defensively. "Accountant, remember? Numbers are my jam."

"Oh, wow. Jam sounds amazing right now," Ed said, followed by a loud growl from his stomach. "On some toast with a chin to tail."

"You should weigh four hundred pounds, Ed," Reggie said with a chuckle, "but I agree. Not the chinto tail part, but the whole idea of lunch sounds amazing. Why don't we go back to the ship, grab lunch, and then we can get all the excavation gear down here. We can set up lights down the tunnel and bring down the cutting torches. If we can't figure out the code, we can just cut our way in."

"But—" Harold started to protest.

Reggie stalled him with a raised hand. "Patience, Harold. Nobody besides us has ever found this place. I don't think they're suddenly going to now. Relax. We can't work on empty stomachs, and we don't have enough oxygen left to get much done, anyway. We need to be properly prepared before we start. Agreed?"

Harold furrowed his brow and crossed his arms like a pup who didn't get his way. A low growl rumbled in his chest, but it wasn't until there was a second growl from his belly that he relented with a low chuckle. "Agreed."

Reggie smiled. "Good."

Four hours later, Reggie tossed their best plasma cutter to the cave floor. "Damn it!"

The torch *clanged* as it bounced off the pile of bent pry bars and various other cutting tools that had failed to get them through the doors. Maddy and Harold frantically punched in code after code at the panel. Rather than try to randomly guess the code, Maddy had compiled a list of all possible four-digit access codes on her slate. They were going through them one at a time. It was a painstakingly slow process.

"No luck?" Ed asked from behind him.

Reggie glared down at the scorched steel of the vault doors. All he'd managed to do was turn the area black with soot and scratch it with the pry bars. "Whatever kind of steel this is, it's too strong for the cutter we have, and the pry bars are less than useless."

"We're going as fast as we can over here," Maddy said, irritation thick in her voice and her purple eyes a little bloodshot.

"We'll come across the right code eventually," Harold added with a grin. Somehow, the older Joongee was still all bright confidence and bushytailed enthusiasm. Actually finding the vault had revitalized him to the point he seemed to have more energy than the other three combined.

Reggie sighed as his shoulder slumped with fatigue. "Unless the code is five digits, or six, or nine, or three. We might never figure it out."

Ed clapped a large paw on his shoulder. "Don't think like that, Reg. You gotta stay positive."

"Thanks, Ed," Reggie said as he sank to the ground and leaned against the vault doors. He checked his oxygen levels and sighed again. "Check your tanks. I need to swap out again. I'm sure you guys need to also."

Everyone but Maddy changed out their tanks. Reggie narrowed his eyes and double-checked her readout.

She batted his hand away with a snarl. "Do you really think I can't read an oxygen gauge? It's fine, Reg."

"Do I think you're capable? Yes." Reggie leaned down so he could look her in the eye. "Do I think our gear is crap and could potentially give you a false readout? Also, yes. I know you're smaller, and the gauge could be accurate, but I don't give a squat. Change your tank out anyway."

When Maddy looked like she was going to argue, he softened his tone and added, "Please, Mads. I don't want anything to happen to you."

Her ears angled back, but she gave him a slow nod and did as he asked.

"We should invest in suits with oxygen scrubbers," Ed said earnestly as his oxygen began to flow.

"If we ever get these doors open, we'll be able to afford the best suits on the market," Maddy said absently as she finished changing her tank out and went back to entering codes. She paused mid-code and looked over at them. "Not that I'll need them on my tropical island. I won't even need a diving suit. My tail will be parked on that beach with an umbrella over my head and an umbrella in my drink."

A few hours later, everyone's tail was parked on the cave floor. They weren't even a quarter of the way through Maddy's code list, and even Harold was ready to call it a day.

Reggie rolled his shoulders to release some tension and glowered up at that big red X on the doors. A simple bit of engineering was all that stood between his clan and the fortune and glory they deserved. The answer to all their problems, locked away behind a stupid door with an archaic lock. Opening it should be easy. Simple. Instead, here they were, a whole day wasted without anything to show for it.

Reggie froze. *Simple. Simple engineering. Simple clues. Simple. None of these clues have been difficult, yet they were all at the same time due to their simplicity. The puzzle seemed difficult, but a little bit of patience and a keen eye was all it took to put the pieces in the right spot. Same with the song. The lyrics told us what to do. Monschtackle literally gave us the answers every step of the way. You just had see it. So, what's the clue here?*

The X loomed over him as he thought furiously. He blinked and really looked at the mark. *Could it be* that *simple?*

"X always marks the spot," he murmured. His eyes drifted over to the keypad, then back to the X. Reggie stood and walked over to the keypad as if in a daze.

"Give it a rest, Reg," Maddy said around a massive yawn. "There's no way we're going to find the right code today."

"Yeah," Ed agreed. "Let's get back to the ship and get some sleep. Plus, I'm hungry again."

"You're always hungry, Ed," Reggie said as he studied the keypad.

X always marks the spot.

Without further thought, Reggie punched in six digits and held his breath. The sound of metallic locks releasing and the hiss of an airlock opening filled the cavern. The green glow of the panel turned blue, and the vault doors swung inward on hydraulic arms.

"Hell yeah!" Reggie roared with a fist pump as the others leapt to their feet.

"Reg!" Maddy shrieked as she jumped to her feet. "How the hell did you figure it out?"

Harold rushed over to him and stared up at the now blue panel. "What combination did you punch in, pup?"

"X always marks the spot," Reggie replied easily and grinned at them all.

"I don't understand," Harold said with a frown. "There are no letters on the pad."

"Yeah, I don't get it either," Maddy said as she crowded close to his shoulder.

"Nope," Ed added with a shake of his big head. "Like, I'm totally lost."

"He gave us the answer in his letter," Reggie said proudly as he pointed at the control panel. "X always marks the spot. Don't you see it?"

"Not... really." Harold said as his frown deepened.

Reggie grinned and traced a finger diagonally across the numbers and then again from the other angle. "I punched the numbers in to make an X. I'm right paw dominant, as are most beings in the galaxy, so I started with three, five, seven, and then did one, five, nine to make the X and it worked! X marks the spot! It wasn't a code at all!"

Maddy grinned up at him, her purple eyes sparkling. "Genius, Reg."

Ed clapped him on the shoulder and laughed, but Harold sighed and kicked at the ground.

"He made it all so simple," the old Joongee said plaintively as he shook his head. "Unless someone like me made it too difficult by overthinking it."

"Which explains why nobody else has ever found this place," Ed said.

"I don't know if he made everything all that simple," Reggie said and placed a paw on Harold's shoulder. "You're the only one to figure out how to piece that letter together. That was difficult. Maybe he thought that if a being could figure all that out, the rest would be easy."

Harold nodded. "It was rather difficult and time consuming, and—"

"And nobody but you could have figured it out, Pops," Ed finished for him.

"Yeah," Maddy said with a small grin. "Not too bad for an old geezer. Now why don't we break up this lovefest and get in that vault to see what we found?"

"Agreed," Harold replied and hurried over to the vault's threshold with the others at his heels. They all paused and peered inside.

Beyond the threshold was a well-lit corridor with long, plastic flaps hanging from the ceiling at the end. Even though the material was clear, the flaps distorted the view into the room just enough that they couldn't make out what kind of weapons of mass destruction lay beyond them. Everyone looked at Harold and waited, but the old Joongee seemed overwhelmed.

"After you, Harold," Reggie said gently. "This was your idea, and you did all the hard work to get us going. You should be the first to enter the vault."

Harold shook his head after a moment. "As honored as I am by your gesture, we did this as a clan." He leaned out and looked down the line at all of them. "We will end this as a clan. We step together, as one."

Reggie grinned as Harold lifted a foot and held it over the threshold.

"Ready?"

They all lifted their own feet.

"Go."

As one, they stepped into the corridor, grins on all their faces. Each step toward the draped plastic was faster and faster until they were running. In a flurry, they slapped the draped plastic strips aside and dashed into the main chamber of the vault.

"Wow." Maddy said as they drifted to a stop in the center of the room. "This is… underwhelming."

Reggie had to admit, she was right.

On the far wall of the main chamber was a large screen set above a medium-sized control panel. A large green button on the console had a single Korothian word printed on it. Reggie walked over and looked at it.

"Can you read this?" he asked Harold.

Harold trotted over and smiled. "It says, 'Push me.'"

"Hey, quick question," Maddy said brightly as she took a step back toward the entrance, "Should we be pressing random buttons in a secret vault supposedly housing weapons of mass destruction?"

"Should be fine," Ed replied sagely. "It's the big red buttons you have to watch out for."

"He's not wrong," Reggie said with a snort. Full of curiosity, he hovered a finger over the button. "We didn't come this far not to push the button, guys."

He glanced back at Maddy and arched a brow in challenge. It only took her a split second to flash him a savage grin and nod her agreement.

Reggie pressed the button and jumped back, tensed to flee like a host of space pirates and rabid ponies were hot on his tail. Everyone else tensed, too. Only, nothing bad happened. Instead, the screen above the console came to life, and a video of Dr. Bergan Monschtackle began to play. He was arguably much older than his picture on the kinkakaijou exhibit and wore a white lab coat.

"Hello there, brave adventurers. If you're watching this, you've managed to solve my trail of clues." The elderly Monschtackle took a ragged breath and ran a hand through what was left of his white hair. *"I only pray you haven't sought out my invention for the purpose of war. I never intended for it to become a means of death. I wanted to help my people and the rest of the galaxy, not destroy it."*

He shook his head as grief and guilt twisted his expression. It made him seem even older than before.

"But my government only saw a way to destroy their enemies, not a way to help their fellow beings and make our world a better place. So, as my letter stated, I gathered up every last piece of my deadly technology and fled my home."

He waved a hand around the room behind him. Reggie tore his eyes from the screen long enough to confirm the doctor was in the very vault they now stood in.

"I buried them here, in the shadow of a gray gas giant, beneath tons of gray rocks and steel, where only those smart enough, brave enough, could find them."

He leaned closer with pleading eyes.

"Please, please, don't corrupt my work. Not again. Use it for good. Use it to advance the medical world, use it to save lives, use it for anything other than to take lives. It's that potential for good that stayed my hand when I thought to destroy it all, that drove me to hide it instead. Unfortunately, by the time anyone discovers this location, I will be long gone and unable to guide you. The responsibility to use the power wisely rests on your shoulders, and your shoulders alone."

He looked off-screen for a moment, and then back again with a sad smile.

"You may be wondering where the Weapons of Koroth are as you stand in the middle of my vault. Fear not—the room isn't as bare as it may first appear. There is an orange button beneath the console. Simply press it, and all will be revealed. Additionally, the chamber will seal and fill with an adequate amount of oxygen so you may breathe freely without a suit. This moon has a harsh environment that played a major role in why I chose this location."

Monschtackle's expression hardened.

"There is also a second button under the panel. A red one. This button is linked to a series of explosives positioned to destroy and bury the weapons forever. Do not press this button light-heartedly. You will only have thirty seconds to reach safety before the first detonation is triggered."

"Heh, told ya," Ed said with a grin.

"Shh!" Maddy hissed.

"*The choice is yours. Take them and use them, or destroy them forever. I leave the final decision to you. Perhaps you can make better choices than I did, or maybe the governments of the future focus more on peace than they do on conflict. I certainly hope so. In any case, I've done all I can to ensure these weapons only fall into capable hands.*"

He smiled and straightened up in his chair.

"*This is Dr. Bergan Monschtackle, signing off for the last time. May the gods be with you and have mercy on your souls.*"

"Well... at least that wasn't ominous," Maddy muttered uneasily.

The screen went blank. Before any of them could move, the vault doors sealed shut, and the wall to their right rose up into the stone, exposing another brightly lit corridor. Green arrows flashed along the floor, indicating they should follow. The hissing sound of atmosphere filled the room as a mixture of gases was pumped in.

Reggie checked his suit-slate and found the gas mixture in the chamber was now safe to breathe. Cautiously, he removed his helmet and took a deep breath. When he didn't choke to death on poisonous gas, he looked at his clan and shrugged. The others removed their helmets and looked to him for guidance.

"Follow the green arrow road, I guess."

Together, they followed the arrows into the next chamber.

The new room was circular and rose six levels, with fifty caged lockers on each level. In the center of the room was a dust covered steel table with a square object directly in the middle. Surrounding the table were various operation centers and strange equipment. Reggie gazed around through wary eyes, but he didn't recognize anything and had no clue what any of it did.

Ed ambled over to the table and blew a layer of dust off the square object. "I think it's an old slate. Like, look how thick it is. They must not have had much battery life back then."

He swiped a finger across the object, leaving a clean trail in the remaining dust. Nothing happened. Reggie did the same and got the exact same result—nothing. Harold and Maddy crowded around the table, and all four Joongee gazed down at the object with various expressions of dismay.

"Maybe it's dead?" Ed guessed.

Maddy titled her head with a scowl. "Can we even find a replacement battery for something that old?"

Harold leaned closer to the object. His muzzle wrinkled up as he sniffed, and he laughed.

"My dear pups, it isn't dead," Harold said with a delighted smile. "It's not an electronic device at all. This is a *book*. A real book, made out of actual *paper*, not a replicated copy."

"Like, one of those ancient things made from trees?" Ed asked, wide eyed.

"Precisely," Harold said smugly.

Reggie gawked at the book. "Wow. Actual paper. Have you ever seen paper before?"

"Never," Harold whispered as he reached out and gingerly opened the book to the cover page. "It says, *Koroth Disintegrator Instruction Manual. Property of the Foundation of Koroth Defense.*"

"Disintegrator?" Maddy gasped as her eyes widened with savage delight. "Now that sounds awesome."

She turned away from the table and dashed over to one of the lockers with a wild cackle. Reggie's eyes widened, and he sprinted after her.

"Hold on, Mads!" he snapped as he ran. "Let me check to see if the doors are rigged to explode first!"

Before he could catch up with her, she shot him an exasperated glare and flung the door open. Alarm shot through him, and he tackled Maddy to the floor. He managed to cushion her head as they fell, and he braced himself for an explosion.

Nothing happened.

Nothing except for an irritated growl from the small female pinned beneath him.

"Do you really think he would go through the trouble of rigging up the red button, telling us about it, and giving us the choice, only to blow it all up anyway?" she demanded with a roll of her eyes. "Use your head, Reg."

Reggie started to reply, then closed his mouth with a *snap*. The words he wanted to use weren't appropriate for polite company.

He sucked in a deep breath and gritted out, "A little caution wouldn't have killed us, but *you* might have. Use *your* head, Mads."

Maddy grinned up at him, challenge bright in her eyes. "We didn't come all this way *not* to open the locker. Right, Mister Button-pusher?"

Reggie honestly couldn't argue with that logic, and he slowly grinned back at her. "Fair enough."

"Uh, if you two are done rolling around on the floor, you might want to look at this," Ed said with a snicker.

Reggie's eyes widened. He scrambled off Maddy with a muttered apology and extended a hand to help her to her feet. Maddy's expression turned flustered, and she wouldn't meet his eyes, but she placed her hand in his and allowed him to pull her to her feet.

"Thanks," she said and turned toward the open locker quickly.

Hanging on a hook was a suit woven from a thick, black material that seemed to be overly sturdy. The suit sealed in the front and had attached boots and gloves. On the shoulders was a guarded neck piece connected to a battle helmet and face shield. The entire ensemble was a single piece.

On a separate hook was a large device with a long cord that ran down into what looked like a rifle. The device had robust straps like a backpack and a center strap with a steel buckle. There were stickers and steel plates all over the device of different colors with writing on them.

"What do those say, Pops?" Ed asked as he pointed out a rather aggressive red sticker.

Harold leaned in and squinted as he translated, "Warning. Do not operate without wearing protective radiation suit. Faulty disintegrators may leak lethal amounts of radiation that could result in extreme sickness or death."

Reggie's eyes went wide, and he dragged Maddy and Ed a few steps back. "*Radiation*? You mean these things are nuclear?"

Harold shook his head. "It's a rough interpretation. It translates as radiation in our language, but it could be something else. I'm no expert, but these packs certainly don't look nuclear to me."

"Uh, like, maybe we should read further in the manual before we mess with this thing," Ed suggested, his ears pinned back in unease.

"Good idea," Reggie said and gently closed the locker door.

Harold rushed back to the table and turned the page.

"What's it say?" Maddy asked, impatience evident in her voice as she sauntered over to him.

Harold flipped through several pages, all the while being careful not to tear the paper. After about a dozen page flips he stopped on a large diagram of the suit and pack that covered both sides of the book.

Reggie tilted his head as he studied the diagram. He might not be able to read the language, but in this case, it didn't matter. As a merc, he'd undergone training on all sorts of weapons. He knew what he was looking at.

"It's a laser weapon."

"That is exactly what it is," Harold replied with a sharp nod. "They refer to it as a *light weapon*, but it is, without a doubt, a laser."

"Seriously?" Maddy deadpanned. "We just risked life and limb to find some old-ass laser weapons? Please tell me they're super powerful at least."

Ed nodded his head in agreement and gestured over his shoulder at the lockers. "Yeah, I mean, look at the suits they had to wear. They gotta be able to slice tanks in half or something."

Harold scanned over the section of the diagram with the pack. His finger stopped over some symbols that Reggie recognized from the entry panel.

"Well?" he asked when Harold went rigid. "What's it say?"

Harold cleared his throat nervously and said, "Four kilowatts."

Reggie couldn't believe his ears. "Did you mean *forty*? Maybe four hundred? There's no way you meant to say four."

"Afraid not, pup," Harold replied as his shoulders slumped.

"You're telling me the Lost Weapons of Koroth are four-kilowatt laser rifles." Reggie rubbed the spot between his eyes and counted to ten. Then he counted to ten again. "I thought they were supposed to be some sort of end-all doomsday weapons? I have a laser pen in my pocket that has more juice than that!"

"Yeah, no squat," Maddy chimed in with a low growl. Her ears were flat against her skull, and her muzzle wrinkled up in disgust. "This whole trip has been an absolute waste."

Ed patted her shoulder and smiled gently. "It wasn't a total waste, Maddy. Think of all the fun we've had."

Maddy stared at him and clenched her jaw. "Ed. We quit our jobs. We went hundreds of thousands of credit into debt. All for something I can buy in a pawn shop!"

Harold raised his palms in the air before the bickering could get out of hand. "Now, hold on pups. You have to remember how long ago these were created! Back then, this *was* an end-all weapon. As a matter of fact, it did end all. Their planet still hasn't recovered from the devastation wreaked upon it. The rumors of these weapons have been circling the galaxy for millennia for good reason."

Reggie's ears angled backward. "That devastation was caused by poor weapon design, not deliberate skill."

Harold sighed heavily, closed the book, and ran his paw over the cover. "Don't you see? The value here is the history, not the destructive capabilities."

"Yeah, well, historic value doesn't pay the bills, Harry," Maddy snarled and waved her paws around the room. "What the hell are we supposed to do with all this? The whole point was to sell it, get out from under our debt, and live the lives we always wanted… but no military is going to buy this crap from us. I want my beach, Harry! I want my umbrella drink!"

"I thought the whole point was to go on an adventure as a clan and have fun," Ed interjected. He lumbered into the center of the group and looked at each of them as he spoke, his expression oddly serious for him. "This treasure hunt has honestly been, like, the best thing I've ever done in my life."

Ed looked around at the lockers and equipment and shrugged. "So what if it's outdated tech? We still found it. We're the only ones to find it. Think about that. We're the only beings to stand in this room for thousands of years. How many have tried and failed where we prevailed?" He smiled and shook his head. "Like, tons of beings. We beat them all."

He pinned Maddy with a pointed look. "And we did it together as a clan. Like a family. We had each other's backs every step of the way. You said we'd be able to live the lives we always wanted to live? Like, I've been doing that since we left Galactic Solutions."

Maddy tilted her head, and her expression sobered.

"This trip was never about getting rich for me, it was about us. You wanna know what the real treasure is?" Ed looked at each one of them. "It's the connection we have with one another. It's the love and friendship we share. This trip, this treasure hunt, deepened that connection and made us a true clan. And I'd rather have that than all the credit in the Bith bank any day."

Reggie's jaw dropped as he stared at the larger Joongee. Shame flooded over him as he realized he'd overlooked everything Ed was talking about. He'd been so concerned with finding the weapons, scoring that credit, that he'd missed out on the bigger picture.

"You're right," he whispered.

For the first time in years, he felt like himself again. He'd stuffed himself into a box to fit into Galactic Solutions, but it had grated on him, and over time, he'd built up calluses until he could no longer feel the walls he'd trapped himself inside. This adventure had set him free. He'd grown closer to his clan, to the point he'd dropped his emotional barriers and allowed them to see the real him—the wild, fierce fighter who'd fought with a mercenary company. Not the browbeaten customer service rep they'd known for years.

"I'm sorry, Ed. You're absolutely right, and I'm an idiot. We all are."

He exchanged a wry smile with Harold before his gaze drifted to Maddy. She'd changed, too. When they first met, she'd been bitter, sarcastic, angry... and while she was still a little sarcastic ball of rage, she wasn't bitter anymore. She'd dropped her barriers, too, and become someone he genuinely liked and respected, with a fierce nature that was more than a match for his own.

All the times she'd followed his lead, the perfect gifts she'd bought them in the mall, sharing her precious coffee with Boo and Aurelian, and... and that night they'd spent in the gym after the Bruce incident. Her trust in him meant more than all the credit in the galaxy.

"I was so hung up on getting rich that I lost sight of what was most important to me," he said softly, his gaze still locked on those captivating purple eyes. "*You* are the most important thing to me."

Maddy's breath hitched in shock, and Reggie reluctantly tore his eyes from hers to include the rest of the clan in his next words.

"All of you," he said in a slightly louder voice. "We're clan, and no credit could ever buy the adventure we just shared to get here. It's something I'll cherish for the rest of my life."

Ed wrapped him in a huge hug and lifted him right off his feet in his enthusiasm. "Thanks, Reg."

Just when Reggie thought he might suffocate, Ed set him back down. He gratefully sucked in a breath of the extremely old, stale air and said, "Don't mention it."

He looked up in time to see Maddy quickly avert her gaze and look at Ed. Her ears flickered with uncertainty a few times before she perked them forward.

"Me too, Ed. What Reg said." She held up a hand when Ed took a step toward her and laughed. "I'll skip the hug, though. I like my ribs where they are."

"Well said, pup. Well, said." Harold patted Ed on the arm. "However, I'll also skip the hug. My old ribs aren't what they used to be."

"Thanks, Pops," Ed replied with a smile, "and you don't look a day over twenty-nine."

Reggie picked up the ancient book with careful paws and held it out to Harold. "All that aside, we still have bills to pay. You said the value is in the historical significance of the weapons. Do you think the Galactic Historical Society would be interested in buying this stuff?"

"Possibly." Harold rubbed his chin as he paced back and forth. "Then again, they may not pay anything at all. They've been known to tell beings they'll accept historical donations, but that they wouldn't buy the item. Dealing with them is always a gamble."

"What about an auction?" Maddy tilted her head thoughtfully, her expression distant, like when she ran numbers in her head. "I see that sort of thing on the net all the time."

"Yeah," Reggie said as his ears angled back, "but what they don't tell you is the auction house charges you a fee of 35 percent of the sale price. Plus, we might not earn enough at the auction to pay our bills off. We've got the Bith Bank loan and *HIADA* to pay for. I don't know if an auction is the right choice."

"What about Dezmire Assadh?" Ed asked suddenly. "He's got that contest going on. We could call and try to sell it to him."

Harold's eyes widened with excitement. "That's true, Ed. He would certainly want to purchase the weapons, or the location, at least. Obviously, we can't load all this onto our ship, but we could take a single suit, the manual, and the location to him. I'm sure he'd buy."

Reggie frowned and crossed his arms. "I don't know. Do you know anything about him? Is he good for it?"

"That's not the right question, Reg," Maddy said, with that distant expression still on her face. "This is a numbers thing. If he's willing to pay the winner of a publicized contest half a million credit, how much are these weapons actually worth?"

"That all depends on who wants it, and how bad," Harold answered before Reggie could. "Historical items are only worth as much as someone is willing to pay. Much like the auction, it is a gamble, no matter how you look at it."

"I don't think an auction is the way to go. They want too much," Reggie said. Everyone nodded in agreement. "So that leaves the Galactic Historical Society or Assadh."

"The Galactic Historical Society is not a great fan of me or my theories, and they may lowball us out of spite alone." Harold flicked his ears dismissively. "I think Assadh may be our best option."

"We could contact him and ask for a higher price than what he's offering. Not having to obey whatever contest rules he set up gives us a bit of leverage in the negotiating department." Maddy hesitated and waggled one hand in the air. "On the other paw, the society might be a little more above-board, since they're an official organization rather than a private party."

Harold narrowed his eyes. "My vote is for Assadh."

Maddy glared back, her hackles rising at his attitude. "Society."

Ed just shrugged and abstained from the argument.

Reggie could see the benefit to both options, but something about dealing with Assadh didn't sit right. What kind of being held an annual contest to find treasure that had been lost for millennia? It was strange, and he didn't trust strange. Still, this wasn't a military organization, and he wasn't the commanding officer. They were a clan, and they all got an equal say in the decision. Too bad they were at an impasse.

An idea struck him, and his eyes lit up. He reached inside his suit and into the side pocket of his overalls.

Maddy snorted a laugh. "Uh, whatcha doing over there, Reg?"

He rolled his eyes at her and pulled out a round metal object. On one side was the emblem of Charlie's Commandos. On the other was the company motto. *De Oppresso Liber*.

"What's that?" Maddy asked as he brushed a finger over the motto.

"An RMO," Reggie replied.

"Looks like a coin to me," Ed said innocently.

Reggie shot him a crooked grin. "You owe us all a drink, Ed. It's a party foul to call them the four-letter C-word. Each violation is punishable by a round of drinks. It's called an RMO."

Ed smiled easily. "Got it, Reg. RMO. And I got the first round next time we hit a bar, no problem."

Maddy held out her hand expectantly, and Reggie dropped it into her palm. She flipped it over and studied the crossed knife and rifle emblem before she passed it back to him. "So what's the coi—er, I mean the RMO for?"

"You get one after completing your first mission with the company," Reggie answered as he ran a finger around the ribbed edge. "I barely got mine. Nearly bought it in the first five minutes of battle…"

His vision began to blur, and he shook his head to clear the memory from his mind. It was too late, though. They were all looking at him expectantly.

"Not today, guys, okay? I'll tell you some other time." Nobody spoke, but they all nodded. He appreciated them not pushing the issue. "Anyway, the reason I pulled it out is so we can choose which way to go."

Harold furrowed his brow. "Meaning?"

"Meaning the moto side is for the society, and the emblem is for Assadh. Whichever side it lands on is what we go with."

"You seriously want to leave it up to fate?" Maddy snorted in disbelief. "Are you insane?"

"It's a gamble either way we go, right?" he said with a shrug and held the RMO up for all to see. "What do you guys say?"

Maddy groaned. "Sure, why not leave it up to a coi—RMO toss."

"I like it," Ed said. "It's fun."

Harold sighed and shrugged. "That's as good a plan as any."

Reggie smiled. "Here we go, then."

With a flick of his thumb, Reggie sent the RMO flipping straight up in the air. All four of them watched as it came down, bounced off the floor, and flipped several more times before it rattled to a stop with the crossed knife and rifle side face up.

Reggie smiled. "Assadh it is, then. To be honest with you, I was hoping it would land on that."

Harold pinned him with a confused expression. "Why is that?"

Reggie rubbed the back of his neck and chuckled. "It dawned on me as soon as I flipped that we don't have to choose one or the other if we go to him first. We can talk to him and see what he's willing to offer. If we don't like it, we can call the Galactic Historical Society, and if that's a no go, we go to the auction as a last resort. It's a solid plan. Harold, you'll be the judge on what Assadh offers, since you're the expert here."

Maddy narrowed her eyes at him. "So you just put us through all that suspense for no reason at all…"

"Pretty much," he said with a sheepish grin. "I'm tired. Cut me some slack here."

"I'm going punch you in the face one day."

* * * * *

Chapter Twenty-Nine

Reggie leaned back in the captain's seat on the bridge of *HLADA* and stretched. It was good to be out of the environmental suit. It had taken longer than any of them wanted to relocate one of the antiquated laser rifles with its battery pack and protective gear, but they'd managed to store it safely in the cargo bay, along with the book and a few other odds and ends Harold swore would add legitimacy to their claim.

He'd sent the rest of his clan to the common area to get dinner ready while he prepped the ship for takeoff. The last of the preflight checks flew by and were green across the board. Now, if only he knew where they need to go.

Reggie trotted off the bridge to the common area, where Harold was setting the table for dinner. The plan was to get a good meal and a good night's sleep before contacting Assadh in the morning. A direct gate call was expensive, but they'd decided it was worth it in this case.

"Smells good," he said as he took his seat.

"Chinto steaks and Earth potatoes," Ed said happily as he carried in plates loaded down with food. Maddy followed behind him with the drinks. "Best dinner ever."

As they ate, they talked about all the experiences they'd had up until that point. Hours flew past, full of laughter and good-natured teasing.

"We should probably get some rest," Reggie said as he leaned back in his chair, his belly and heart equally full.

"Spoilsport," Maddy snorted and flicked a potato at his face.

Reggie ducked, and it hit Harold square in the nose. His expression was less than amused, but the other three cracked up all over again.

"Madeline," Harold grumbled, "please keep the food where it belongs—on your plate or in your mouth."

"Sorry, Harry." Maddy yawned mid-laugh. "Okay, fine. Maybe Reggie's right."

Reggie leaned closer to her and cupped a hand behind his ear. "I'm sorry, could you repeat that?"

"So sorry," she replied playfully. "I'm too tired to repeat myself."

She tipped her mug back and drained the last of her coffee. Harold shook his head at her, but Ed laughed.

"How you manage to sleep when all you drink is coffee is a mystery I will never solve," Ed said between chuckles.

Maddy smirked at him. "It's my superpower. That and kicking the squat out of Joongee twice my size for talking crap about my coffee habits."

Ed stuck his tongue out at her, and she rolled her eyes.

"All right, pups," Harold said jovially with a brisk clap of his hands. "Time for bed. We have a big day tomorrow."

* * *

The morning came all too quickly as they took their places on the bridge. None of them were used to staying up that late anymore, and Harold in particular was looking rough. Maddy offered him coffee with a snicker, and for once, the older Joongee accepted.

Reggie piloted *HIADA* to orbit the fourth planet with the ruins. He didn't want anyone to trace their call back to the moon and discover the location of the hidden weapons. Let anyone who tried think they'd found the weapons on Brekanstief. The thought of them wasting time and effort digging in the trash brought a smile to his face.

"All right, Harold, it's all you," Reggie said once they were in a stable orbit. He held a finger up. "Remember, don't tell him we actually found it. Just that we have some new, vital information regarding the Lost Weapons of Koroth. We don't want to show our hand just yet. Let's see if he bites first."

Harold nodded. "I've got this, Reggie."

"I know you do, Harold," Reggie said with a warm smile.

Harold made the call, and after a moment, a female Prithmar appeared on the screen. "Mr. Asssadh'sss office, how may I help you?"

"Ah, yes, uhm, good morning," Harold said and cleared his throat nervously. "My name is Harold, and I was wondering if I might be able to speak with Mr. Assadh."

The Prithmar leveled him with an unimpressed stare. "Do you have an appointment?"

"Well, no, I'm afraid I don't."

"Mr. Asssadh isss a very busssy being, Mr. Harold. I'm afraid you'll have to make an appointment and call back then." She looked at her other screen for a moment then back to Harold. "I can ssschedule you in on the third Thursssday afternoon of next month."

"Next month?" Harold gasped. "I'm afraid that just won't do, madam."

The Prithmar looked at him with dead eyes. "Then I'm afraid there'sss nothing I can do for you. That'sss what'sss available."

"Don't let her push you around, Harry," Maddy hissed under her breath.

Harold visibly steeled himself and steadied his voice. "Please inform Mr. Assadh that if he can't spare five minutes to speak with me right now, I'll have to take the new information I've recently acquired about the location of the Lost Weapons of Koroth to someone who can. I'm sorry we couldn't do business together."

Harold reached over to end the call, but the Prithmar jumped and spoke before he could.

"Wait!" She smiled at him and gave a fake little laugh. "Don't be so hasssty, Mr. Harold. He may have a few ssspare minutesss before his next appointment beginsss. Let me check with him. It will take jussst one moment."

He gave her a curt nod. "Very well."

She placed him on hold, and the screen changed to a solid blue.

"Damn, Harold!" Maddy exclaimed and slapped him on the back. "Look at you, playing hardball! Good job."

Before he could respond, the screen jumped back to the Prithmar.

"Mr. Assadh jussst so happensss to have a spare moment or two to speak with you. I'll transsssfer you over to his office."

"Thank you, ma'am."

The screen flickered, and the image of Dezmire Assadh filled the screen. The Krugeri regarded Harold from under heavy-lidded, brilliant green eyes. Barely visible faint red stripes cut through the golden fur of his face. His jet-black mane was perfectly styled and draped down over his shoulders. Perfectly white fangs gleamed in the light as his upper lip slid back in a smile.

"Good morning, Mr. Harold," Assadh said in an all-too-smooth voice. "I feel I must apologize for the confusion with my assistant.

However, I'm afraid I really am short on time. She mentioned you might have some new information regarding the location of the Lost Weapons of Koroth?"

Harold swallowed hard under that predatory stare and cleared his throat. "That is correct, Mr. Assadh. I've come across some new information I would be willing to part with... for the right price."

"I see." Assadh narrowed his eyes and folded his paws over his desk, flexing his black claws as he did so. "Mr. Harold, I'm afraid I don't have time for games. Dozens of beings contact me every week claiming to have found some new clue or the location of the weapons."

The Krugeri's face melted into a blank expression that sent chills down Reggie's spine. All of a sudden, he wasn't so happy with the RMO toss.

"None of them ever turn out to be anything remotely reliable," Assadh said coldly with a deep rumble undercutting his voice. "If you're looking to scam me out of a few quick credits, you've wasted both our time."

"N-no, not at all," Harold stammered. "I've been chasing the Lost Weapons of Koroth for over a decade now. I really do have some useful information to sell you."

Assadh cocked his head to the side. "And why not use this information yourself and find them on your own? You must realize I hold a contest every year to find them, and the winner receives half a million in credit."

Harold gave him a sheepish shrug. "To be honest, I ran out of traveling credit and can't afford to go any further. I do know about your contest. That's why I called you to see if you were interested. I figured anyone else would be a waste of time."

"Hmm." Assadh tapped a claw on his desk thoughtfully. "And you really do have something to sell? This isn't some sort of scam? If it is, I can assure you there will be dreadful consequences."

Harold shook his head. "Oh, no. Not at all. I swear to you, this is the real deal. You won't regret it."

Assadh gave a single nod. "Very well. Where are you now?"

"In the Grunge System."

"Drat," he replied sourly as his rounded ears flicked backward. "That's a week's worth of gate travel from here. I don't have the time. I'm committed to another engagement in five days."

"What if we met somewhere halfway?" Harold asked pleadingly. "I have enough credit to make one more trip. If you buy my information, I'll be able to get home. Does that sound fair?"

Assadh continued to tap his claw on his desk. The rhythmic sound began to grate on Reggie's nerves, and his hackles rose involuntarily. He watched as the Krugeri picked up a slate and entered a few commands. "It appears Salvage System would be the halfway point. It says here they have two space stations. Why don't we meet there on Merc's Hub? It will make it that much easier to have you arrested if your intentions are... less than pure, shall we say?"

"Sounds good to me, Mr. Assadh," Harold replied with a sigh of relief. "I'm not selling bad information, and this isn't a scam, so I have nothing to worry about."

"Very well." Assadh sniffed. "I'll see you in Salvage in three days, Mr. Harold. Safe travels."

He cut the call before Harold could respond.

"Way to go, Pops!" Ed shouted.

"Yeah, Harold, that was impressive," Maddy said before she narrowed her eyes. "Kinda makes me wonder how you got us screwed so hard on this hunk of junk ship."

"She makes a good point," Reggie piled on with a grin. "But if we can get a good payday out of this, it won't matter, and we can stop picking at you about it."

"That would be nice," Harold grumbled, but managed to keep smiling. "Maybe after that you could tell me what *HIADA* means, Maddy."

"Maybe," Maddy said with a smirk.

Reggie shot her a narrow-eyed glance. He had his suspicions of what *HIADA* meant. Looking at his RMO had reminded him of another military tradition involving acronyms. He'd have to ask her about it later.

"So, I suppose it's off to Salvage System," Harold said eagerly. "I've read amazing things about it on the net."

"I never heard of it until you mentioned it the other day with the puzzle," Reggie said with a shrug. He turned to Ed. "Wanna fly us through the gate?"

Ed's eyes went wide. "Really? Yes!"

* * *

Three days later, the four Joongee waited with varying degrees of nervousness in a private meeting room for the arrival of Mr. Assadh. Upon entering Salvage System, they'd immediately been hailed by quartet of Nazrooth destroyers commanded by a Captain Urlak. Embarrassingly enough, he'd only hailed them because he thought their ship was broken down and they needed assistance. Once they assured him they were mechanically fine and declared their intentions, they'd continued on to the Merc's Hub space station.

A voice message from the Prithmar secretary had been waiting for them when they transitioned back to normal space. They listened to it on the flight in from the gate.

"Mr. Asssadh sendsss his regardsss. He has ressserved a private room on Merc's Hub so you may conduct your busssiness in peace and quiet. Please await his arrival and be ready to presssent your findings to him promptly."

There was a short pause, and she dropped her voice lower as if afraid of being overheard.

"For your sssake, I hope your information isss genuine."

The message ended. Maddy shook her mane out and tried to relax her tense shoulders. "I'm glad that wasn't ominous or anything. Reg, are you sure about this?"

Reggie had seemed uneasy ever since their call with Assadh. He tried to hide it, but it was obvious in the set of his ears and the wary look in his eyes. Something about the Krugeri had him spooked.

"I'm sure, Maddy." He shrugged, but his hands flexed repeatedly as if he were gearing up for a fight. "It'll be fine. Besides, we'll be on a public space station frequented by reputable mercs and Salvage personnel."

Ed glanced over his shoulder from the pilot console and grinned. "Yeah, relax, Maddy. It's not like we're meeting this guy in a creepy supervillain lair or anything."

"Relax, right," Maddy muttered.

Harold seemed perfectly relaxed and happy with their decision, despite having to take the lead in the upcoming negotiations. His content expression made her want to punch something. Unfortunately, all her research on Assadh during their gate transit had turned up nothing sinister. He seemed like just another overly successful entrepreneur who'd struck it rich on one of his many ventures and had continued in that vein ever since.

She'd asked Reggie what was wrong, but he couldn't put a claw on it. He'd just said something about rusty instincts and asked her to keep her eyes open. She snorted. *As if I wouldn't do that anyway.*

Reggie had patiently gone through the docking procedures with Ed and allowed him to dock the *HLADA* in their assigned berthing dock. From there, it was a quick lift ride to a higher level on the station and a short walk to the private meeting room.

Harold paced nervously, all trace of his former calm gone. "What if I mess it up, Reggie?"

"You're going to do great, Pops," Ed said easily.

A faint *chirp* of agreement came from the bag slung over his shoulder. After a brief argument, they'd all agreed that Boo could come with them, as long as she stayed out of sight. The sight of the little furball bouncing in happiness had almost been enough to make Maddy smile. Almost.

"Stick to the plan, Harold, and we'll be fine," Reggie said for the dozenth time since they'd arrived.

"Hmm, yes. And what plan would that be?" a smooth voice asked as the door slid open.

Maddy's ears flattened, and she sat up straight in her chair in the corner of the room. Assadh prowled inside, two female Krugeri in black suits and green ties at his heels. Maddy caught a glimpse of two more females taking up a guard position in the corridor before the door slid closed again.

Assadh flicked the top button of his navy-blue business suit loose as he slid into the chair at the head of the oval-shaped table. The female with a flowing brown mane stayed by the door, while the one with a spiky red mane stood at his shoulder with her arms resting behind her back in a casual parade rest. Maddy made a mental note to ask what mane products she used if she got the chance, because her hairstyle was on point. She also noticed the females didn't have the same horizontal stripes as Assadh did. *Must be a gender trait.*

"Well?" Assadh asked pointedly, his sharp green gaze shifting between Reggie and Harold. "What is this plan? I don't have all day."

"Uh… um, you see, that is," Harold said and wrung his paws together.

"You have information, yes?" Assadh prompted, the tips of his fangs peeking out. He tapped a single claw on the table, and the redhead placed a slate next to his hand. "Was this a waste of my time, or not, Mr. Harold?"

"We're not here to waste anyone's time, Mr. Assadh." Reggie crossed his arms, the muscles in his biceps flexing smoothly beneath the sleeves of his black shirt. "We have valuable intel on the Lost Weapons of Koroth. Right, Harold?"

Harold straightened his back and nodded. "Quite right, Reginald. We have information I guarantee will lead you directly to their hiding place. The question remains, how much is that information worth?"

The Krugeri regarded them through a predator's gaze. "That depends entirely on the accuracy of your information and whether or not it leads to the weapons, as you claim."

"Our information is accurate," Harold said stoutly.

"Prove it," Assadh replied with a lazy flick of his ears.

That single claw steadily tapped on the table again, and Maddy bit back a sigh. This back and forth was getting them nowhere, and they were losing his interest. This was a numbers game, and they had to play it that way.

She crossed her arms. "We found them."

Assadh raised an elegant brow and looked at the three Joongee males. "You allow your female to speak for you?"

"Maddy is an equal member in our clan and can speak as she wishes," Reggie snapped back without hesitation.

Maddy appreciated his support, especially considering she'd just upended his careful plan.

"Excellent," Assadh replied smoothly. "I detest backward species that treat their females as lesser beings."

To Maddy's surprise, he seemed sincere. The redhead behind him winked at her and grinned. She grinned back.

"Now that we've cleared that up," Maddy said with a roll of her eyes, "can we do business, or not? You want the weapons. We *have* the weapons. What's that worth to you?"

Assadh placed his elbows on the table and leaned forward with interest gleaming in his jade-green eyes. "If you know I run a contest, you already know the answer to that."

"Half a million credit for the suckers who agree to play by your rules." Maddy snorted. "We both know you can do better than that."

"I'm still waiting on proof," Assadh said with a faint smile.

Maddy studied his expression and flicked her ears. She'd seen that look countless times when bargaining for discounts. He wouldn't budge.

"Show him, Harold," Maddy said with an impatient snap of her fingers. When the older Joongee clutched his slate to his chest and frowned at her, she sighed and forced her tone to shift to something a shade nicer. "We're at an impasse. This is where we show him *what* we found. Not where."

Harold glanced at Reggie, who nodded his support. Maddy flashed him a grin. He trusted her judgement. That meant… a lot.

With a reluctant grumble, Harold released his slate to her. She pulled up the video they'd taken inside the vault. They'd recorded the lockers full of the archaic laser weapons, the operating stations and strange equipment, the actual paper book, and the clip of Monschtackle giving his long-winded monologue.

Assadh watched it all silently, his expression impassive. He looked back up with a slight twitch of his brow. "Is this everything?"

Reggie stepped forward. "We brought one of the weapons back, along with the book and a few odds and ends. Enough to prove we found the Lost Weapons of Koroth."

"Indeed," Assadh replied as he rubbed his chin in thought. "Well, as I said, you already know what I believe the weapons are worth. Half a million credit."

Maddy tilted her head and narrowed her eyes. "One million credit."

The Krugeri slid Harold's slate back across the table with a flick of his claws. "You've misunderstood. I'm not negotiating. I'm making an offer. Take it or leave it."

Reggie placed a hand on Maddy's shoulder before she could say anything else. "We understand. I'm sorry, but that's not what we were looking for. We'll leave it."

"Regrettable, but I'm not in a position to offer more at this time," he said with a sad rumble undercutting his words. "You have my contact information, should you reconsider."

The Joongee stood and nearly made it to the door before he spoke again.

"If you don't mind, where else were you going to try to sell the weapons?" he asked with a wistful note in his voice. "They've been an interest of mine for quite some time, obviously, and if it's to a museum or a similar public institute, perhaps I could see them some day."

Harold gave him a commiserating smile. "I quite understand. The Lost Weapons of Koroth are my life's work. If someone else found them, I'd want to see them as well. We'll see if the Galactic Historical Society has any interest, or perhaps a reputable auction house. I understand a number of museums and universities frequent those for items such as these."

Assadh stood and regally bowed his head in thanks. "You have my gratitude. As I said, please keep me in mind should you not find your other options… amenable."

The brown-maned Krugeri opened the door for them with a quiet smile. The males trudged into the corridor, but Maddy paused in the doorframe and glanced back at the redhead.

"By the way, I *love* your mane. What products do you use?"

She grinned broadly. "And I love the white spiky situation you've got going on. I'll get your contact info from our secretary and send you what I use."

"Thanks," Maddy said with a wave.

Before the door slid shut, she saw Assadh retake his seat, fingers dancing over his slate, and a frown of concentration on his face. She shuddered and trotted down the corridor after her clan. She was really glad she wasn't an entrepreneur like the Krugeri. That seemed way too much like real work. *Screw that. I'd rather be a pirate.*

She grinned and whistled an old sea shanty. Grunge was getting a little old. Maybe she should look up pirate music.

* * *

Dezmire tapped a claw on the conference table as the call connected to the gate. A moment later it was answered, and the Human face of Morwin Trecknall filled his screen.

"Morwin, my old friend," Dezmire crooned. "How are you?"

Morwin smiled and leaned back in his leather office chair.

"Hello, Dezmire. I'm doing just fine." He reached over, pressed an intercom button, and said in an aside, "Julie, could you hold all calls and appointments until I say otherwise, please? Thanks." His attention returned to the call. "I wasn't expecting to hear from you today. Have you made some new, amazing discovery?"

Dezmire steepled his fingers at his chest and rested his chin on the tips of his retracted claws. "Mmm… something like that. Tell me, how are things going at the society? Are you enjoying your role as the executive curator? We haven't spoken in quite some time."

A large smile split the Human's face. "Oh, it's amazing. The opportunity to study artifacts and lost cultures alone makes the stress of the business and political side more than bearable." He waggled his head side to side as his smile turned smug. "And to be honest, the company cruiser, credit card, and covered travel expenses are pretty nice, too."

"Excellent," Dezmire said with a sly smile. "This pleases me. However, I did not call you simply to see how you were doing."

"I figured as much." Morwin glanced over at the screen off to the side. "Is there something you need me to do?"

Dezmire's heavy-lidded eyes narrowed. "Are you familiar with an older Joongee by the name of Harold?"

Morwin's brow furrowed in thought before he nodded. "Yes, I believe so. He applied for an official membership several times and has always been denied. He claimed to have found some new clue regarding the Lost Weapons of Koroth, but it sounded like gibberish and was all over the place. Poor old fool." He arched a brow in surprise. "Why? He's not trying to sell you that useless information, is he?"

"That *poor old fool* was no fool at all, you imbecile," Dezmire replied coolly. "Not only did he find a new clue, he found the weapons themselves."

Morwin's jaw dropped. "You're kidding!"

"I never kid, Morwin," he replied with a low rumble threading through his cool tone. "Now, here is what is going to happen. You are going to be receiving a call from him very soon. He will offer you the opportunity to purchase the artifacts he has in his possession, as well as the location of the vault. You will inform him that the society is not currently purchasing any new artifacts, but will gladly accept any historically significant donations he might have available."

Morwin's jaw dropped lower, and his eyes bulged. For a long moment it seemed the Human had lost his ability to speak.

"You want me to deny the Lost Weapons of Koroth? Dezmire." He ran a shaking hand over his balding head. "I don't think I can do that. We've been searching for them for as long as the society has existed. Even longer than you have."

Dezmire's expression returned to that of a hunter, but his tone remained even. "Do you recall the last favor I did for you, Morwin?"

The man's eyes dropped the floor, and he swallowed hard. "Y-yes. I do."

"Then if you wish to remain the executive curator of one of the most powerful and influential societies in the galaxy, I suggest you do as I have asked." Dezmire extended a claw and pointed it at the screen. "I can remove you from that comfortable office as easily as I helped to put you there. It would be a shame if someone leaked even a small portion of those secret videos of yours to the media. Material such as that could ruin a being for life. Don't you agree?"

Morwin's shoulders slumped in defeat, and he gave a single nod. "I understand, Dezmire. I'll do as you've asked."

"Wonderful," Dezmire said with a thin smile that exposed his fangs. He decided to throw the Human a bone, as it were. "And don't worry, old friend—the society will still get their hands on the weapons."

A confused expression overtook Morwin's face. "I don't understand. You just said not to buy them."

A devious light brightened Dezmire's eyes, and his heavy lids rose a fraction. "I said not to purchase them from him. I never said anything about from me."

Morwin's posture straightened as the realization hit him, and his expression turned cheerful. "Well, then. I suppose I had better clear the lines and get ready for that call. Is there anything else I can do for you?"

Dezmire's expression smoothed out, and he dipped his chin. "No. Not at the moment. I'll call you when I have what I need in my possession."

"How do you know they'll sell it to you?"

"Because once you deny them, the only option they'll have is an auction house. I have enough clout to make that unfeasible. If they have any sense in their feeble little minds, they'll realize their only choice is to come back to me." Dezmire frowned and tapped a single claw on the table in a measured beat. "Regardless, those weapons will soon be in my possession."

Morwin smiled and nodded. "Ah, I see. I'll send you a text message through the gate as soon as I've spoken to him."

"See that you do. *Immediately*."

Dezmire cut the call before Morwin could lengthen the conversation further. He leaned back in the office chair and tapped his claw on the arm.

"Raiza, call the home office and have the cargo ship prepared. I want it ready in three days. Also, I want the yacht ready for my arrival in the same timeframe."

"Yes, sir," Raiza said from his side. "Would you like any companionship for this journey?"

"No," he replied with a slight shake of his head. "Unfortunately, this trip will be all business. Pleasure will have to wait." A wide smile split his maw as he glanced up at the redheaded Right Claw of his organization. "But there will be plenty to celebrate afterward."

Raiza winked at him, and gave Sariene, patiently waiting by the door, a brisk nod. Immediately the other female pulled out a slate and began entering commands.

"Do we wait and see if they come back, or head to your ship now?" she asked with a raised brow.

"Let's give them an hour," he replied as he rested his chin on his claws again. "That should be long enough to crush their hopes and dreams and bring them crawling back where they belong. Right here."

* * * * *

Chapter Thirty

"*Are you freaking kidding me?*" All three males flattened their ears at Maddy's outraged shriek. "What do you mean, they won't buy it?"

Ed pressed his hands over Boo's ears and frowned at her. "You know, Maddy, for such a little thing, you sure are loud."

Maddy rumbled a growl, but somehow managed to look pleased at the same time. Reggie shook his head and bit back a smile. His little Spitfire was such a fierce bundle of contradictions. He blinked. Not his. She wasn't his.

He shook his head sharply and focused as Harold cautiously lifted his ears and said, "I told you I was persona non grata with the Galactic Historical Society."

"Yeah, which is why Reggie made the call," Maddy pointed out with narrowed eyes.

Harold shrugged, but his narrow shoulders were slumped in defeat. "It would be a simple matter for them to connect the two of us. Regardless, Morwin Trecknall was quite firm. While the society will accept any and all donations, they're not interested in buying the weapons at this time."

Maddy groaned and slid down in her chair until Reggie could barely see her purple eyes over the console. They'd retreated to the bridge of the *HIADA* to make some calls, but he was starting to wonder if they should've retreated to a bar instead.

"So we move on to plan C," Reggie said as he lifted his slate to pull up data on auction houses.

Maddy snorted. "Way ahead of you, slick. I already contacted the top four auction houses that deal in relics and antiques. Their fees have recently gone up to fifty percent, and they're only willing to start the bidding at a thousand credit."

Reggie's ears flattened in dismay. "That's crazy. All four of them?"

"Yup," she replied, popping the 'p' with barely controlled aggression.

"So we go back to Mr. Assadh," Ed said as he scratched Boo beneath her tentacles. The tiny kinkakaijou purred happily and rubbed her head against his hand with an adoring expression. "It's better than nothing, and he looked so sad when we didn't take his offer. This way, everyone wins."

Harold flicked his ears nervously and shrugged. "I only ever cared about getting credit for the discovery, not actual credit."

Reggie rubbed the back of his neck. "Five hundred thousand isn't enough to pay our loans off. If we sell to him, we'll have to come up with a backup plan for what we do next. We can't just float out here jobless forever."

Ed smiled. "We'll come up with something, Reg."

Everyone looked at Maddy and waited.

"But... Reggie," Maddy said pitifully. Her lip stuck out petulantly but amusement lurked deep within her eyes. "My umbrella!"

Reggie's lips twitched into a smile. "I'll get you an umbrella, Mads. One for over your head, and one for your drink. Promise."

Maddy heaved a sigh. "*Fine*. We go back to Assadh."

"I'll send him a message," Harold said. Not three minutes went past before his ears shot straight up. "Well, that's certainly good fortune. He's still in the private meeting room. Apparently, he had business to conduct and is willing to meet with us again."

Reggie stood up. "Let's get this done."

When they approached the meeting room, the pair of Krugeri females standing guard smiled in welcome. The black-maned female, who looked so much like Assadh she must be a blood relation, tapped on the control panel and waved them through the open door.

"He's expecting you," she said in a velvety-smooth voice.

Assadh glanced up from his slate as they trooped into the room, a faint, hopeful smile on his face. "So, you've reconsidered my offer?"

"We have," Reggie replied slowly. It took an effort to keep his hackles flat. There'd been a flash of something predatorial in that stare that set off every instinct he had. In the next instant, it was gone, and he shook his head. *Rusty, so damn rusty.*

"Excellent," Assadh replied crisply as he set his slate down and gave them his full attention. "As I said, I can offer five hundred thousand credit for the weapons, all of the associated equipment and artifacts, as well as the location of the vault."

The Krugeri laced his claws together and regarded them from under heavy-lidded eyes. Reggie subtly shifted his stance so his weight was evenly balanced. The narrow-eyed glance from the red-maned Krugeri female standing at Assadh's shoulder told him the movement hadn't gone unnoticed, but he couldn't seem to help himself. His instincts were screaming danger, and he hadn't survived his stint as a merc to ignore them now, even if they were rusty as chinto-squat.

"I am known as a fierce entrepreneur," Assadh said smoothly, "however, I am not without sympathy. Forgive me the intrusion, but I ran a quick credit check on your clan while you were gone. I understand now why you held out for a better offer, and I managed to free up additional funds. I am prepared to offer you six hundred thousand credit."

"What's the catch?" Maddy said with a suspicious glare.

Assadh leaned forward and pinned that jade-green stare on Harold. "I want your research. Every note, every clue, everything that led you to the discovery of our lifetime! Since I couldn't be part of the discovery myself, having your research is the next best thing. It will allow me to truly appreciate Dr. Bergan Monschtackle's brilliance."

Reggie's ears angled back. They needed the credit, but something was off.

Harold lifted his muzzle defiantly. "The Galactic Historical Society thinks I'm nothing but a fool. So long as I get recognition for the discovery, I'm happy to share my research with you. It would feel good to prove them all wrong, especially after they treated me like an insane idiot for so many years."

"I assure you, I will give credit where credit is due," Assadh said earnestly with his paw on his chest and a slight bow of his head. "Do you accept my offer?"

Everyone looked to Reggie, and he looked at his clan. Harold nodded his agreement. Ed shrugged, unconcerned either way. Maddy had that distant expression that meant she was running numbers in her head again. When her eyes cleared, she silently mouthed the word *umbrella* with a sad expression but nodded anyway. Reggie hesitated.

The redhead behind Assadh cleared her throat discretely. "Your meeting with the Bohoca Group is in ten minutes, sir."

"Thank you, Raiza," Assadh replied smoothly. His expression filled with regret, and he met Reggie's gaze without an ounce of deceit in his eyes. "I'm afraid the additional credit is a limited-time offer. I was able to move that engagement I mentioned on our initial call to today, as this was a closer meeting location for the other party. That credit is earmarked for the Bohoca project, and how I handle my next meeting is entirely dependent upon your response."

Reggie drew in a deep breath. "We accept."

* * *

If ever there was a bar or restaurant a being could blend into and disappear, it was Space Brakes. The place was packed with all manner of beings. Mercs, blue collar, white collar, it didn't matter. They were all there and conversing back and forth with one another. It was awesome, to say the least.

Reggie walked back to their table with four bottles in his hands. The lovely, raven-haired Human woman at the bar with the nametag Ginger hadn't questioned his need to leave them sealed. She'd just given him an understanding nod and passed him a bottle opener along with the drinks.

He cracked open Harold and Ed's bottles of honey mead and slid them across the table to them. He passed Maddy her mudslide along with the bottle opener without comment. Her hands clenched around the bottle with a white-knuckled grasp, and she paused for a long moment. When she finally looked up at him, it was with such a grateful expression in her eyes that he had to look down at the table before he broke out into the idiotic grin that was trying to take over his face. Instead, he focused on popping the top of his own bottle with his thumb.

Reggie gave her a small smile and a little salute with his beer.

Maddy grinned at him and guzzled down her drink in one long pull. All three males stopped and stared in amazement. She slammed the empty bottle on the table, burped the cutest little burp Reggie had ever heard, and sighed happily.

"Chocolate, caffeine, and alcohol all in one amazing drink. I'm gonna need another one of those."

Reggie shook his head and laughed. "I'll get it."

When he came back the second time, she had her nose buried in her slate with her ears pinned back. He set the sealed bottle next to her, sat back with his beer, and waited. Her eyes flicked from one part of the screen to another, and her muzzle wrinkled.

Ed watched her various expressions as she worked with a grin. "It's fun watching Maddy do math. She hates it so much, but she's so good at it!"

"I can still hear you, you know," she grumbled as she swiped a finger across the screen.

Harold belched and patted his belly with a pleased expression. "At least the credit transfer went smoothly."

Reggie nodded and took a pull of his beer. "And handing over the weapon, gear, and artifacts was easy enough. Once he confirms the location we gave him, we're free and clear."

Maddy let her slate drop to the table with a thud. "Free and clear. Right."

Harold scowled at her. "Can't you ever just be happy?"

"I *am* happy," she snarled back. Everyone looked at her, and she shrugged and popped open her second mudslide. "I just show my happiness in... different ways."

Reggie snickered. "Okay, Mads, what's up?"

"I ran the numbers." Maddy tapped a clawed finger on her slate. "When you account for our loans, various interest rates, gate fees and travel expenses, blah blah blah... we mostly broke even."

Harold shook his head. "No, that can't be right."

Maddy snorted. "That lovely loan you got us on HIADA had an early termination fee clause buried in the fine print. So did the loan from the Bith. After we pay everything off, we've got just enough funds for a single gate trip and enough supplies for two weeks."

"You've got to be kidding me," Reggie muttered. He took a long drink and sighed. "Screwed over at every turn."

Maddy saluted him with her bottle. "Nope. And yup. Drink up, fellas, 'cause we're broke."

Harold shoved away from the table. "I'm going to need another round. Anyone else?"

Everyone chorused yes, and he ambled up to the bar and struck up what looked like a pleasant conversation with Ginger. He came back with yet another mudslide for Maddy, two honey meads, and a new, darker beer for Reggie.

Harold smiled at Reggie. "The nice Human at the bar said you could try this one, um… how did she phrase it? On the house."

Reggie eyed the label. "A Prithmar beer, huh? Never tried one of those."

He shrugged and tipped the bottle up. Fire bloomed across his tongue, traveled down his throat, and made a nice bonfire blaze in his belly. Tears poured down his cheeks, and he hacked up half a lung as he desperately tried to clear his throat.

Harold frowned at him in worry. "Pup… are you all right?"

"Reggie?" Ed asked with concern in his eyes.

Maddy bit her lip and then gave up. Her peals of laughter filled the bar. "What's the matter, Reg? A little too spicy for you?"

"Burns," he said hoarsely and panted, "and it's like drinking straight alcohol."

He gave serious consideration to scraping off his tongue while he was at it but settled for stealing Maddy's mudslide and using that to douse the flames.

"Hey!" she squawked.

Reggie ignored her protest as he swished the chocolatey drink around in his mouth. There must've been real milk in there, because it eased the pain. It was like the Prithmar took pure alcohol and fused it with the hottest pepper they could find. Or maybe the drink was so strong it *felt* like eating a pepper. Either way, it was way too spicey for him.

A large shadow fell over the table. Reggie looked up, and up, and up. His eyes met a sinister pair of blazing topaz balls of fire sunk into a winged black mass of nightmares, terror, and sheer ferocity. It was another Sheingal, only this one was bigger, and pure black. Reggie couldn't help but notice the sword on his hip. Eyes wide, he swallowed the mudslide still in his mouth and wiped his muzzle with his forearm.

"Uh… can I help you?"

The Sheingal smiled down at him, exposing a mouth full of black, razor-sharp teeth. "I noticed you didn't care for the Prithmar beer as I was walking by. If you don't want the rest of it, I would be happy to purchase it from you."

"Dude!" a Human male whisper-shouted as he stepped up next the Sheingal.

Reggie's brow furrowed. The human was also wearing a sword. It was an odd looking one, too. The sheath was very narrow and curved. One being wearing a sword was weird. Two was just wild.

"You better not let Ginger see you doing that," the Human hissed in exasperation. "You know damned well you're only allowed to have three. Last time she blamed me, and I caught all the crap for it!"

"Relax, Ryan." The Sheingal groaned and rolled his eyes. "What she doesn't know won't hurt her." He winked at Reggie. "So, what do you say? Can I buy it off you?"

"Nice, real nice," Ryan said and crossed his arms. "Don't say I didn't warn you, 'cause I'll rat you out this time. I'll roll on you like a roly-poly going downhill. I swear it on my honor."

Reggie was about to gladly give the massive brute the beer at no charge, but a tiny paw shot across the table before he could.

Maddy snagged the beer from Reggie and pinned her ears at the massive black-scaled Sheingal. "Get your own!"

She knocked back the beer like she was born drinking molten lava, wiped her muzzle clean, and winked at the dumbfounded males.

"Lightweight," she said with a teasing smile for Reggie.

The Sheingal's smiled turned into a bone-chilling grin.

"Well done!" He crossed his arms over his massive chest and gave her an approving nod. "You would fit in with the Joongee on our crew. I'm impressed."

Ryan sighed in relief. "Thank the gods. Now I don't have to worry about the wrath of Ginger." He shoved the scaled monster, not that he budged even an inch. "C'mon, Fafnir. We gotta get back to Sheinrah. We told your mom we'd be back in three days. It's been four."

The Sheingal groaned and gave them all a wave. "Thanks anyway. Perhaps we'll see each other again sometime."

As the duo walked away, Reggie heard the Sheingal grumble at Ryan. "What good is being emperor if I still have to come home when my mother says to?"

Reggie turned back to his clan and laughed. "What in the hell just happened?" They just shook their heads and laughed with him. He looked to Maddy with a smile. "You're full of surprises, you know that?"

Harold sniffed. "I could've told you she occasionally goes on a Prithmar beer bender, usually after one of her secret romance novels sells well."

"Shut *up*, Harry," Maddy growled. Her comm chirped, and she glanced down at it with a surprised frown before she declined the call. "Too drunk for that…"

"So," Ed said with a grin. "What're we gonna to do now?"

Reggie shrugged and pushed up from table to get himself a *normal*, non-fiery beer. "We'll come up with something."

* * * * *

Chapter Thirty-One

Maddy sat on the couch in the common area, her elbows on her knees and a boring white coffee mug clutched in her paws. "I can't believe the best plan we could come up with was to go back to work for Galactic Solutions."

Ed looked up from the coffee table where he was putting the Impossible Puzzle together again from the beginning. "Hey, at least they gave us our old jobs back. Like, it could always be worse, Maddy."

"Ed," she said flatly, "we can't even afford our own apartments. We'll have to live on this POS for at *least* six months."

Ed just smiled at her and passed the next piece for Boo to put into place. "More time together is a good thing, Maddy, you'll see."

Maddy growled several very not nice things under her breath and took a bracing sip of coffee.

"Must you be disagreeable about everything, Madeline?" Harold asked sourly as he walked in from the galley. "None of us wanted to go back to Galactic Solutions, but your attitude certainly isn't helping matters. You've complained about literally every single facet of our situation over the past few days. What is your problem this time?"

"My problem?" Maddy glowered at Harold over the rim of her mug. "My only problem is your judgy face."

"Hmm," Harold said and glanced at his slate.

Maddy narrowed her eyes to slits. "What do you mean, *hmm*?"

"Nothing. Just noting the date," Harold said with a pleased smile as if he'd solved some great mystery. "You're extra mean today."

It took her a moment to understand what he meant. Her eyes widened, and she shrieked in pure feminine outrage. "I am *not* mean!"

She hurled her half-full coffee mug at his stupid, judgy face. Harold's smile vanished, and the old Joongee ducked much faster than he would've been able to before the start of their adventure. The mug shattered against the wall, and he yelped as hot coffee splashed down onto his fur.

"Sorry, sorry! Forget I said anything," he said hurriedly as he exited the room at top speed.

Ed and Boo watched with near identical expressions of shock, and the metallic clanging from the engine room suddenly stopped. Reggie had grown tired of their bickering hours ago and muttered something about adjusting the G-force dampeners. He'd been hiding in the engine room ever since. Which was just fine by Maddy. His calm attitude about returning to Galactic Solutions was driving her crazy.

"What?" she snapped at Ed, who was looking between her and the shattered mug.

Ed chuckled. "Well, I was just thinking it's a good thing that wasn't your favorite mug. Then I remembered you left it behind at Galactic Solutions... so really, it's a good thing we're going back!"

An incoherent growl of pure rage tore out of her chest, and she bared her fangs at the much larger male. She wanted to punch something so badly, but she'd managed to break the punching bag yesterday, and they didn't have the funds to buy a new one. She'd have to fix it before she could beat the crap out of it again.

Her fists balled up, and she stood there shaking.

Ed cleared his throat and loudly whispered to Boo. "We should probably give her some space."

Boo chittered and leaped from the table to the pipes crisscrossing the ceiling. She swung out of the room like her tail was on fire, Ed hot on her heels.

"Cowards!" Maddy glared after them for a moment before she was distracted by a shrill *beep* from her comm. She jerked her head down to stare at the number and hesitated. Her ears flattened and she shook her head. "So not in the mood right now to deal with that."

She declined the call and stomped over to the galley to grab what she needed to clean up her mess.

* * *

It was hot down in the engine room. Working on the dampeners made it even hotter. Reggie didn't know what genius engineer decided they should be in the engine room of this particular ship model, but they deserved to be buried up to their necks beneath the Mall of Malls in the tunnel with all those nasty creepy crawlers. He shuddered as the memory of them crawling all over him returned. *Nasty little things.*

After the dampeners were readjusted, he set to work on the bent pry bars. He could have simply run them through the new replicator Maddy had found, but that wouldn't do him any good. He was angry and needed to let off some steam. With the punching bag out of commission, thanks to Maddy, this would have to do.

He set up a torch and turned it up on full blast. Slowly, he slid and rolled the warped pry bar through the blaze until it was red hot. He picked up his three-pound hammer, laid the glowing bar across his anvil, locked in place with the vice, and set to work beating it back into shape. Every strike released a small amount of frustration.

I've got to voluntarily put myself back in that tiny box at Galactic Solutions. Wham!

Despite everything we've overcome, we're right back where we started. Wham! *Thank you for calling Galactic Solutions, how can I be of service?* Wham! *No more adventures.* Wham!

No more being myself. I have to be a drone and cage my real emotions again. Wham!

The worst part of going back was they would still have to miss out on the Tunagra celebration back on their home planet. They couldn't afford the extra gate fee, nor did they have the supplies to last them that long. Choosing Galactic Solutions over Tunagra had really left a bitter taste in his mouth. Especially as the final call had come down to him as the clan leader. The company forcing them to miss Tunagra had been the main reason they'd quit in the first place.

Wham! WHAM!

Flashbacks of Glorp talking down to him and telling him all the reasons he was a subpar employee zipped through his mind. Chad's pompous voice bragging about his newest yacht and how his latest bonus was more than Reggie's annual salary echoed along with images of that smug look on his face in his fancy suits and perfectly knotted ties. *I hate ties!*

Wham! Wham! Wham!

I'd like to smash both their faces in and toss them down the dumpster chute. Wham!

He paused mid-strike and stared at the fading glow of the steel bar.

But I can't. No more fighting. No more letting my beast out of the cage. I have to box it away again, too. All of it. I have to stay in complete and total control.

My very livelihood will depend on it. I don't have a cushion of merc pay to fall back on this time.

That realization caused his anger and frustration to rise, and he felt himself begin to slip.

No. The control starts again now. I can't let it control me. Never again.

It wasn't that he'd released all his control while out in the galaxy with his clan, but he had loosened the restraints. It had felt amazing to let loose on those pirates and open the cage a bit. The bar fight had been equally as freeing. Maddy's experience at the bar ran through his mind, and Bruce's face flashed by.

I should've killed that bastard!

Wham! Wham! Wham!

Reggie stood there, chest heaving, hammer clutched in his gloved hand, and teeth bared. He closed his eyes, rubbed the spot between them with his free hand, and counted to ten. Then he counted to ten again and opened them.

"Damn it," he grumbled to himself.

In his anger, he'd hit the pry bar too hard too many times. It was now bent in the opposite direction than it had been before. He loosened the vice, spun the bar, and locked it down again. With a sigh, he grabbed the torch and set to re-heating the steel.

It was a while before he had all the pry bars straight again. His arms and hands were aching, but it had at least been a great upper body workout. He'd also managed to work out some of his mental issues. Things were what they were, and he'd just have to accept and roll with it. Even if it infuriated him. Even if it left him feeling a little sick inside.

He just couldn't let the rest of the galaxy see it.

A muffled shriek reached him all the way in the engine room, and he sighed. It sounded like his clan was having yet another petty argument. Now that he had his head on straight again, he could deal with playing peacemaker once more.

He ambled into the common area with his head down, studying a particularly nasty blister on his palm. *This one might need a bandage...*

"You know," he said in as upbeat a tone as he could manage, "it's actually a good thing we're going back this soon. If we'd been gone another week or two, we'd have lost all our time-in-service and had to work up to vacation time and our old salaries. Now we just step right back into where we were."

Only silence answered him, and he looked up to find Maddy was the only one in the common room. She was sitting at the table with her arms crossed and a scowl on her face as she glared at him. A cleaning rag sat in front of her, stained brown from what was most likely coffee.

He frowned. It wasn't like Maddy to spill even a single drop of her precious brew. "You okay, Mads?"

"Oh, just wonderful." She sniffed.

"All right, then."

Reggie shuffled past her to enter the galley but stopped when his boot crunched down on something. He looked down to see white shards from a shattered coffee mug in a relatively neat pile on the floor. Coffee was smeared all over the wall, as if Maddy had begun to clean up her mess and had given up partway through.

His brow furrowed, and his mouth dove into a deep frown as he spun back to Maddy. "Have you ever, even once, tried to control yourself? Or is that notion just foreign to you?"

"Oh, that's rich, coming from the likes of *you*." She snorted and pinned her ears at him. "Oh, wait, no it's not. None of us are rich, because we ended this whole stupid trip right back where we started!"

Reggie cocked his head and narrowed his eyes. "Exactly what do you mean by *the likes of me*?"

She pinned him with an incredulous stare. "Exactly what I said, Reg. The likes of you. An emotionless drone who never gets mad or cares about anything that goes wrong. You're always just so calm and collected, Mister... Mister..."

Reggie arched a brow. "I'm waiting for your devasting insult. Come on, hit me with it."

Maddy let out a little cackle and threw her hands in the air. "I can't even think of the right word. You drive me so freaking insane, I can't even *word* right now, Reggie!"

Reggie clenched his jaw. "The word you're looking for is self-control. I have it. You clearly don't."

"Don't you care? Doesn't it bother you in the least that we're going back to that hell of an existence?" Maddy shot up from her seat and rounded the table toward him, her eyes a mirror for every emotion he'd just spent hours suppressing. "I *saw* you, Reg. You were happy to leave that place. Every bit as happy as I was. And now that we're going back, you don't give a damn? You're *happy* we didn't wait any longer? What the hell is wrong with you?"

He'd heard enough. Reggie stalked closer, one slow step at a time. Maddy backed away until her back bumped against the table. He leaned down and braced his hands on the table on either side of her. His ears flickered back and forth, because he could've sworn her breath caught. She had to know he would never hurt her, though, no matter how angry he was.

He ducked his head until he could look her in the eye and said, "Look into my eyes, Mads. Tell me what you see."

Maddy seemed distracted for some reason. She slowly dragged her gaze up to his and blinked a few times. She tilted her head, and her expression brightened and softened all at the same time.

"That's... interesting. You're actually pissed off. In fact... I'd say you're just as angry as I am." She smiled slowly. "Holding all that inside isn't good for you, Reg. One of these days, you're going to blow like a volcano. I hope I'm there to see it."

She shoved past him and sauntered into the kitchen, then a second later reappeared with a full mug of steaming coffee in one paw and headed for her room. Reggie stared after her, sighed, and cleaned up her forgotten mess.

The rest of their trip through alter-reality was thankfully uneventful. Everyone was in a funk and not really in the mood to do much. Even Boo seemed to be a little depressed. When the time came to exit the gate and enter the system, they gathered on the bridge as usual.

Reggie let out a heavy sigh as the clock counted down. "Everyone ready for this?"

"No," Maddy groaned.

"Ready and slightly unwilling," Harold answered in a droll tone.

Ed just shrugged. "Like, I guess as long as I don't break any mop handles, it'll be all right."

HIADA exited alter-reality, and everyone groaned at the disorientation as they entered normal space again.

* * * * *

Chapter Thirty-Two

Two miserable weeks later, Reggie leaned back in his chair until his vertebrae popped all the way down his spine. The previous customer call had been a real doozie. Some beings were just too dumb to realize how dumb they actually were. As he stared up at the target on the ceiling tile, he took aim and flicked his stylus into the air. It rotated three times and stuck firmly in the red.

"The sad thing is, that's the biggest accomplishment you've made since we got back," Maddy's bitter voice grumbled from behind him.

He didn't bother to turn around. As they were all still living on *HLADA*, he'd see plenty of her angry face when they got home. Since they couldn't afford to pay any sort of long-term docking fees, they parked the ship at a Galactic Solutions employee docking ring during business hours. As long as one of them was on the clock, they could stay there. Ed had volunteered to take some night shifts in order to keep them docked for more than a day at a time instead of orbiting out in the black. Everyone was grateful for his sacrifice.

"Gotta have something to take pride in, I guess," he quipped as if he hadn't a care in the world.

He felt Maddy's eyes burning a hole in the back of his head, and his throat suddenly became very dry. Slowly, he leaned back up to a normal sitting position and transferred his computer screen to his wrist slate. Doing so allowed him to take calls while he was away from his desk. It was a little trick he'd discovered a couple years ago. Glorp hadn't caught onto it yet. Even if he did, there was no policy against it. Reggie had triple checked.

With a groan, he stood and ambled over to the office water cooler. One decent thing about Galactic Solutions was they paid the extra credit to have a decent water cooler that kept the water ice cold. He filled a cup, drank it down, then filled it again. Curious what was going on in the news, he side-stepped and peered into the break room and up at the tri-v. His jaw dropped.

"Maddy! Harold! Ed! Get in here!" he roared, not giving a squat about company policy regarding proper workplace etiquette in that moment.

Ed had come up to bring them all lunch and was down at Harold's cubicle. The two males ran over to see what was the matter while Maddy sauntered at her usual pace.

"What's the matter, Reg?" she asked sarcastically. "Did you see a pretty tie on a commercial you want for Christmas?"

He ignored her dig about his thinly veiled hatred for ties and jabbed a finger at the screen. "Look!"

Everyone followed his pointed claw and gasped.

On the screen was a live feed of the cave on Zoritch as teams in environmental suits carried large crates out of the tunnel and loaded them into shuttles. The video was being filmed from within a ship through a clear-steel portal. The reporter, a Pikith female in a snazzy business suit, was talking excitedly into the camera. The tri-v was on mute, and they couldn't hear what she was saying.

Harold rushed in, grabbed the remote, and unmuted it.

"*And now, we'll hear from Dezmire Assadh, the being who brought the great mystery of the Lost Weapons of Koroth to an end and shared it with the entire galaxy.*"

Assadh stepped into view with a big smile on his face. He wore a stylish black business suit that perfectly matched his dark mane. The Krugeri was much larger than any of them had realized, as he towered over the Pikith. His shoulders weren't overly broad, but his fitted suit didn't hide all the lean muscle beneath it.

"*Mrs. Logan, it is an absolute pleasure to be here with you. I cannot tell you how excited I am to finally have an answer to the question so many of us have been asking for millennia. Where did Dr. Monschtackle hide the Lost Weapons of Koroth, and exactly what are they capable of? Well, today, we answer those very questions!*"

Mrs. Logan smiled her brilliant smile up at him. "*I've been fortunate enough to be let in on the secret since arriving but tell all the fine beings at home exactly what you've discovered, Mr. Assadh.*"

Assadh beamed with pride as he folded his arms behind his back and leaned down toward the reporter.

"*Well, it's quite amazing, actually. As it turns out, Monschtackle's weapons are actually the earliest generation of laser rifles ever discovered in the known galaxy. When compared to modern day weapons, they are quite primitive, and admittedly highly unstable. It's no wonder the planet of Koroth still hasn't recovered to this very day.*"

Assadh shook his head sadly, and the Pikith reporter did an excellent job of showing the viewers a somber mien, but it was obvious this was a rehearsed segment. The Krugeri's expression shifted to earnest enthusiasm as he continued.

"*But you see, it isn't their militaristic uses, or the lack thereof, that make them such an amazing find. It's their historical significance. It's the lore and legend they bring with them. It's the understanding of what nearly brought an end to an entire race of beings, and actually did bring about the extinction of countless plants and animals forever.*"

The reporter took a deep breath and smiled at the camera, somehow making it seem as if she were smiling directly at the viewer. Reggie reluctantly admitted to himself she was quite good at her job, and exactly the kind of reporter to have in your corner.

"It is quite the discovery, indeed. Now, everyone knows you hold an annual search for the weapons of Koroth with a grand prize of half a million credit. Was it one of your contestants who finally unlocked the secret?"

Assadh ran a hand through his thick mane and turned to look into the camera with those green eyes of his.

"As you know, Mrs. Logan, I always give credit where it is due."

Ed patted Harold on the shoulder as the old Joongee inched closer to the tri-v. "Pops, Pops! He's gonna say your name!"

"And so, I take great pride in telling you…"

They all held their breath.

"I found the Lost Weapons of Koroth."

"What?" all four of them shouted at once.

Assadh stared into the camera without a trace of deceit in his gaze and seemed to answer the Joongee directly.

"That's right, it was me. All my years of hard work, dedication, and tireless research finally paid off. You see, I discovered, through no small feat, mind you, that Monschtackle actually published quite a large collection of children's books under a pen name. It was in these stories I found many, many small clues that added up to one large clue. The missing link, if you will. From there, the rest was quite elementary, actually. X always marks the spot, as they say."

"Incredible, simply incredible!" the reporter remarked enthusiastically. That excitement appeared to get the better of her professional bearing, and she practically vibrated with anticipation as she asked her next question. "Rumor also has it that the Galactic Historical Society has offered to purchase this amazing find from you for a whopping sum of one billion *in credit*. *Is there any truth to that rumor?*"

Assadh appeared to act embarrassed by the question but didn't succeed very well.

"*Let me be perfectly clear, Mrs. Logan. This was never about financial gain. It was about history and discovery. That is the real treasure here. One that I can share with the entire galaxy. Professor Morwin Trecknall, the executive curator, has been a close, personal friend of mine for decades. Oh, how I wish you could've seen the look on his face and heard the joy in his voice when I gave him the good news. It was nearly as wonderful as when I first laid my eyes on the weapons themselves. I would like to add that anyone else who wishes to be a part of this truly once in a lifetime find can absolutely do so by attending the exhibit unveiling at the Museum of Galactic History in three months' time. Please remember that any and all donations, no matter how big or small, will go toward preserving our galaxy's history. As far as what the society has offered me, all I can say is that I am a very fortunate individual who just got lucky.*"

He gave the reporter a devilish smile, and she immediately blushed and giggled. She turned back to the camera.

"*Well, there you have it, folks. The legendary Lost Weapons of Koroth are legend no more. They are real history and will soon be on display for all of you wonderful beings. Be sure to get your tickets to the unveiling, and I'll see you there!*"

"He... he played us." Harold dropped the remote with his jaw agape. "He played us like fools. It was all a setup. All of it. The society denied us for him. I bet he had something to do with the auction houses, too! I trusted him... I felt *bad* for him. I'm such an idiot!"

"You say that like it's a new thing," Maddy said with a roll of her eyes. She turned to Harold with a grim little smile. "You want to know what *HIADA* means, *Harry*? H-I-A-D-A. Harold... Is... A... Dumb... Ass!"

A snort of laughter escaped Ed, but Harold's jaw hit the floor, and his paw shot to his chest like he was finally going to have that heart attack. When he swayed dramatically, Ed reached out and steadied the old Joongee, his own expression a mix of dumbfounded and amusement.

"Calm down, Pops," Ed said gently. "And never mind Maddy. It'll be okay. I mean, we still got to have an amazing adventure, right?"

Harold just made choking noises and clenched his paws like he wanted to strangle someone. Whether that was Maddy or Assadh was unclear.

"Ed's right. We did have an amazing adventure," Maddy replied with sudden calm as she sipped at her coffee.

Harold tilted his head and narrowed his eyes at her. Ed's ears flickered in shock as the tiny female set her nearly full mug down on a breakroom table and crossed her arms with a positively evil grin.

"You know what's also amazing? Revenge." Her grin died, and rage flashed in her eyes as she whispered, "Payback's a real witch sometimes, and I just got a new broom."

Reggie's teeth were clenched so tight, his jaw popped. The plastic cup in his hand abruptly crumpled into a mess of plastic. Ice-cold water ran down his arm and dripped from his elbow and onto his shoes. He couldn't care less.

All the anger, the rage, the disappointment, the betrayal, and the failures hit him all at once. It was too much. His control snapped, and he slammed the crumpled cup to the office floor.

"*Son of a—*"

# # # # #

Authors' Note

Yes, that's really the end. We're not sorry and we regret nothing. Space Hyenas will return soon for a little revenge in Pirates and Payback.

If you'd like to connect (or yell, cuss, and berate) with the authors, you can find us on our new Discord channel https://discord.gg/Y9xpPzs5.

* * * * *

About Nick Steverson

Nick Steverson is your everyday, blue-collar liquor vendor. Using his Class-A CDL, he delivers wine and liquor from Pensacola to Tallahassee. When not on the road, he takes as many opportunities as possible to write down the chaotic musings of the deranged voices in his head. Since he was young, he has always wanted to write a book, but never took the time to actually sit down and do it. His wife and children were, and remain, his first priority, leaving little time for much else. Inspiration to make the time came from his father one night after sending a text about an idea for a race of characters in his father's books. The last answer he expected to get was, "*You* write it," but that's exactly what he got. So, he did. Sometimes, all it takes is a little nudge in the right direction, and the story writes itself. He now has multiple publications in the Salvage Title Universe including a wide variety of novels and several short stories. Additionally, he has short stories in the Four Horsemen Universe, Starflight Universe, and This Fallen World. He's not done yet, though. There are many more stories to come.

* * * * *

About Melissa Olthoff

Melissa Olthoff is a military science fiction and urban fantasy author who delights in sneaking in romance wherever she can. She is a lifelong geek of all things scifi and fantasy, as well as a veteran of the United States Air Force, both of which are incredibly useful when writing. Her degrees in meteorology and accounting are slightly less applicable to writing, but absolutely useful when it comes to supporting her family. She is published by Chris Kennedy Publishing, and is best known for her Salvage Title Universe novels, Hit World Valkyries, and numerous short stories. She can be found at her website melissaolthoff.net, Facebook, Twitter, and on her Amazon Author Page.

* * * * *

Get the **free** Four Horsemen prelude story **"Shattered Crucible"**

and discover other titles by Theogony Books at:

http://chriskennedypublishing.com/

* * * * *

Meet the author and other CKP authors on the Factory Floor:

https://www.facebook.com/groups/461794864654198

* * * * *

Did you like this book?
Please write a review!

* * * * *

The following is an
Excerpt from Book One of the The Seventh Shaman:

Running from the Gods

———————————

D.T. Read

Available from Theogony Books

eBook and Paperback

Excerpt from "Running from the Gods:"

On approaching our training sector, an empty patch of space marked only by the coordinates in our astrogation computers, I called, "Sector Control, this is Searcher Element entering sector Nevus-Indigo, proceeding to point oh-niner-two."

Sector Control acknowledged, and Kota made a half-roll so his ship flew inverted at my wing. In low planetary orbit, where "right side up" and "upside down" were irrelevant, flying inverted to one another provided near-complete visibility of our surrounding space.

At an altitude of four hundred ranges, Solienne's sun sparkled on the North Strelna Sea and cast the mountains into relief, shadowing their western slopes in blue. Clouds blurred the ragged cliffs of the coastline, as if a clumsy finger had smeared wet paint.

From the edge of space, I scrutinized clouds of stars. I had learned Solienne's constellations, of both northern and southern hemispheres, during Astrogation. The Sitting Dog, the Giant King, the Two Ships. Supremacy fighters could appear anywhere among them, in attack formation or as lone reconnaissance probes.

We searched the dark, constantly shifting our heads inside our helmets. Our faceplates' metallic coatings sharpened images and reduced the glare of reflected light.

We spoke little, except to answer Sector Control's requests for position checks. Minimal cockpit chatter broke the distant buzz in our earphones.

As we completed the third lap of our patrol track and began the fourth, my alert level ratcheted up. *Any minute. They'll expect us to be relaxed by now. They'll try to catch us when they think we've given up paying attention.*

"Lead," Kota said, *"I've got something, two-point-three-four and two-seven-six, distance six-two-niner ranges."*

"Right on time," I said under my breath when the blip appeared in my threat scope, too. "He's all yours. I'm on your wing as Two."

That was the rule. Whoever spotted the enemy got the first shot. I dropped back, maintaining cover from the inverted wing position, and let Kota take Lead.

"Targeting active," I ordered my computer, and tracked the incoming bogey's trajectory, a bright line of blips in my threat scope. "Check energy cannon charge."

We peeled out of our patrol loop and Kota said, *"Two, I'm vectoring for lead pursuit, activating energy cannon for warning burst."*

"Copy, Lead," I answered. I glanced at my weapons display. All lights glowed solid green.

I expected the single blip to split into two, maybe four, or even six as we closed to five hundred ranges. It didn't. It simply swelled on my scope, driving fast as if late for an appointment.

Kota opened the universal radio channel. *"Incoming ship,"* he said, *"identify yourself. I repeat, incoming ship, identify yourself."* I heard tension in his clipped words.

Coarse static answered, through which I made out a faint voice. The words consisted of harsh consonants and a guttural growl, but nothing I could understand.

Now they're even simulating lump head radio chatter. Anything to make War Phase more authentic. I chuckled.

As we completed our arc to intercept the bogey and began to close on him, red pulses like the heartbeat of a machine became visible against the dark. Wingtip running lights.

"Got a visual," I told Kota. "Forty degrees and low."

"Got it, too," Kota said. He switched again to the universal frequency. *"Incoming ship, identify yourself and withdraw from Soliennese space."*

Static-garbled words rattled in my earphones. I detected a defiant tone, the only thing I could understand.

"Split now,*"* Kota ordered, and I rolled clear.

He passed above the bogey, and I shot beneath it. As I did, I got a brief but clear view of it.

For training, veteran pilots experienced with Supremacy tactics acted as hostiles. They flew old Rohr-39 Spikes painted with the Velika crest and carried orange sim-missiles in their wing racks.

This ship resembled a thick carpentry screw, minus the threads. Its blunt nose, covered with sensor pods like blisters from a burn, contrasted with its three pointed canards. Too small to be real wings, they were mounted around the exhaust nozzle like an arrow's feathers.

My breath caught. On the spacecraft recognition chart in the intel shop, it was labeled as a Kn-T18 Asp, the Supremacy's one-man reconnaissance ship. Asps were lightly armed, with a single energy cannon in the nose, but they could inflict lethal damage.

My pulse jumped. My palms dampened in my suit's leather-lined gloves. Our only weapons were electronic simulators to light up the aggressor's damage display.

As required by regulations under the circumstances, I reclaimed my role as Lead. "Two, form it up." I gulped it as adrenaline quickened my breaths.

Kota had recognized the Asp, too. He locked in at my wing with a stiff, *"Yes, sir."* He sounded as if he'd gone pale.

"Sector Control," I called, "this is Searcher Lead. We have a real-world incursion in sector Nevus-Indigo. I repeat, real-world incursion."

*****

Get "Running from the Gods" here: https://www.amazon.com/dp/B0BHCMKH2L.

Find out more about D.T. Read at: https://chriskennedypublishing.com.

*****

The following is an
Excerpt from Book One of the Lunar Free State:

The Moon and Beyond

John E. Siers

Available from Theogony Books

eBook, Audio, and Paperback

Excerpt from "The Moon and Beyond:"

"So, what have we got?" The chief had no patience for interagency squabbles.

The FBI man turned to him with a scowl. "We've got some abandoned buildings, a lot of abandoned stuff—none of which has anything to do with spaceships—and about a hundred and sixty scientists, maintenance people, and dependents left behind, all of whom claim they knew nothing at all about what was really going on until today. Oh, yeah, and we have some stripped computer hardware with all memory and processor sections removed. I mean physically taken out, not a chip left, nothing for the techies to work with. And not a scrap of paper around that will give us any more information...at least, not that we've found so far. My people are still looking."

"What about that underground complex on the other side of the hill?"

"That place is wiped out. It looks like somebody set off a *nuke* in there. The concrete walls are partly fused! The floor is still too hot to walk on. Our people say they aren't sure how you could even *do* something like that. They're working on it, but I doubt they're going to find anything."

"What about our man inside, the guy who set up the computer tap?"

"Not a trace, chief," one of the NSA men said. "Either he managed to keep his cover and stayed with them, or they're holding him prisoner, or else..." The agent shrugged.

"You think they terminated him?" The chief lifted an eyebrow. "A bunch of rocket scientists?"

"Wouldn't put it past them. Look at what Homeland Security ran into. Those motion-sensing chain guns are *nasty*, and the area between the inner and outer perimeter fence is mined! Of course, they posted warning signs, even marked the fire zones for the guns. Nobody would have gotten hurt if the troops had taken the signs seriously."

The Homeland Security colonel favored the NSA man with an icy look. "That's bullshit. How did we know they weren't bluffing? You'd feel pretty stupid if we'd played it safe and then found out there were no defenses, just a bunch of signs!"

"Forget it!" snarled the chief. "Their whole purpose was to delay us, and it worked. What about the Air Force?"

"It might as well have been a UFO sighting as far as they're concerned. Two of their F-25s went after that spaceship, or whatever it was we saw leaving. The damned thing went straight up, over eighty thousand meters per minute, they say. That's nearly Mach Two, in a *vertical climb*. No aircraft in *anybody's* arsenal can sustain a climb like that. Thirty seconds after they picked it up, it was well above their service ceiling and still accelerating. Ordinary ground radar couldn't find it, but NORAD *thinks* they might have caught a short glimpse with one of their satellite-watch systems, a hundred miles up and still going."

"So where did they go?"

"Well, chief, if we believe what those leftover scientists are telling us, I guess they went to the Moon."

* * * * *

Get "The Moon and Beyond" here: https://www.amazon.com/dp/B097QMN7PJ.

Find out more about John E. Siers at: https://chriskennedypublishing.com.

* * * * *

Made in the USA
Middletown, DE
09 June 2023

31957552R00235